firefly

LIFE SIGNS

LIFE SIGNS

firefly

BY JAMES LOVEGROVE

TITAN BOOKS

Firefly: Life Signs
Hardback edition ISBN: 9781789092271
E-book edition ISBN: 9781789092288

Published by Titan Books
A division of Titan Publishing Group Ltd
144 Southwark Street, London, SE1 0UP.

First hardback edition: March 2021
1 3 5 7 9 10 8 6 4 2

This is a work of fiction. Names, characters, places, and incidents either are the product of the author's imagination or are used fictitiously, and any resemblance to actual persons,living or dead, business establishments, events, or locales is entirely coincidental. The publisher does not have any control over and does not assume any responsibility for author or third-party websites or their content.

A CIP catalogue record for this title is available from the British Library.

Printed and bound in the United States.

Did you enjoy this book?
We love to hear from our readers. Please email us at readerfeedback@titanemail.com or write to us at Reader Feedback at the above address.

To receive advance information, news, competitions, and exclusive offers online, please sign up for the Titan newsletter on our website

TITANBOOKS.COM

DEDICATED TO

Cat Camacho

for keeping us flyin'

I have clinched and closed with the naked North,
I have learned to defy and defend;
Shoulder to shoulder we have fought it out—
yet the Wild must win in the end.

Robert W. Service,
"The Heart of the Sourdough"

"When a battle seems unwinnable,
a soldier has two choices: to fight on,
or to accept the inevitable.
Often the two are hard to tell apart."

Browncoat General William Hubert Cole,
discussing the Battle of Serenity Valley

AUTHOR'S NOTE

The events in this novel take place between the
Firefly TV series and the movie *Serenity*.

1

"You know you got one of them upside-down faces?"

"Huh?"

"An upside-down face. You know what I mean."

"Don't reckon as I do."

"Bald on top, neck-beard below. You stand on your head, it'd look like your face was the right way up."

"You tryin' to be funny?"

"Merely tenderin' an observation. 'Course, from my current perspective, your face *is* the right way up."

"You're about to die. I really don't think this is the time to be making wisecracks."

"Personally can't think of a better time to be making wisecracks than when you're about to die."

The two men speaking were Malcolm Reynolds—Firefly captain, former Browncoat, buccaneering rogue—and one Desmond Rouleau, killer for hire.

The former was bound hand and foot and hanging by his ankles from a bough of a tall mesquite. The latter was standing in front of him, brandishing a hunting knife with a twelve-inch blade. It was night. Cicadas were singing. A trio of moons illuminated the scene, as did the headlights of a two-seater hover-gig parked nearby.

A couple of hours earlier, the pair had had an arranged meet in a cabin in the woods a mile outside a town called Lonesome Rock. This was on Odessa, a Rim world that lay a hop, skip and a jump from the Uroborus asteroid belt. There'd been the prospect of a job. Some cargo to transport. Paid work, something which had been pretty thin on the ground lately for Mal and his crew.

A condition for the rendezvous had been that Mal came alone. No sidekick, no backup. Rouleau didn't want a fuss. He was a low-key kinda guy, he'd said. They would talk man-to-man. "Get a person on their ownsome, look 'em in the eye, take the measure of 'em—that's how Desmond Rouleau operates."

Shots of bourbon were downed. A deal was sealed with a handshake. All at once Mal felt woozy, like he was descending a hundred floors in an express elevator. He got up from the table, fumbling for his gun…

And keeled over flat on his face, unconscious.

When his senses returned, he found he had been strung up from the mesquite and was dangling there like a human piñata. That was bad. Worse, perhaps, was the fact that his eyes were more or less level with Desmond Rouleau's crotch. There were pale, crusty stains on the front of the man's pants, and Mal didn't much care to know where they'd come from. Food grease, he hoped.

"Now then, Mr. Reynolds," said Desmond Rouleau, "I bet you're wonderin' why you're here, all trussed up and no place to go."

"Thought had crossed my mind." The blood was pooling in Mal's head. His face felt puffy, swollen. His temples throbbed and his sinuses ached. "I'm guessing you didn't slip a sedative into my drink and drag me all the way out into the boondocks and drape me from a tree just to discuss, I don't know, philosophy. 'Less you have, in which case I apologize for misreadin' the situation. It's just, you don't look the philosophy type."

"You're here," Rouleau said, in the tone of someone whose patience was being sorely tested, "to die. Can't put it any plainer'n that."

"Would've been my second guess. Not discussing philosophy? Then dyin'. It's normally one or the other."

"Want to know *why* you're going to die?"

"Be strange if I weren't a teeny bit curious."

Rouleau squatted down so that they were nose to nose. This was better than being nose to crotch, in visual terms at least. Unfortunately, Rouleau had terrible teeth and halitosis to match.

"'Cause you pissed off a rich, powerful man," he said, "and he wants some payback."

"Huh."

"That's all you got to say? 'Huh'?"

"Well, thing is, I've pissed off a fair few people in my time, rich folks among 'em."

Rouleau nodded sagely. "Even though I ain't but known you an hour or so, I can see how that might be possible."

"So you're gonna have to narrow it down for me," Mal said. "Who?"

"Name Durran Haymer mean anythin'?"

Durran Haymer. Sometime bio-weapons expert. Wealthier than God. Avid collector of Earth-That-Was artifacts. Had been the owner of a rare antique laser pistol, the Lassiter, until said weapon found its way into Mal's hands through a complex chain of circumstances which began with an encounter with an old Browncoat friend called Monty and ended with Mal marooned in the desert, bare-ass naked.

"Never heard of him," Mal said.

"Funny, 'cause he definitely knows you," said Rouleau. "Says you took something from him. Something he prized greatly."

"Oh, *that* Durran Haymer. Yeah, come to think about it, I did maybe help relieve him of a certain gun."

"Gun?" Rouleau chuckled mirthlessly. "Nobody's mentioned any gun. No, what you took from Mr. Haymer was way more valuable to him. A woman. His wife, to be precise. The love of his life."

That would be the lady known variously as Yolanda, Saffron and Bridget, although she had doubtless gone by many other aliases over the years. A thief, a grifter, possibly a Companion at one time in her life. Mal admired her and hated her in equal measure. He also found her damnably attractive.

"The so-called 'love of his life,'" Mal said, "who lit out on him and only went back, six years later, so's she could steal from him. Even if I'd had anything to do with deprivin' Haymer of her—which I did not—by any objective measure I did him a favor. And while we're on the subject of favors…"

"What?"

"Mind lettin' me down from this tree? Only, my head feels like a balloon about to pop."

Rouleau appeared to consider it, then grinned and shook his head. His knees cracked as he straightened up.

"Nossir. Mr. Haymer, see, he's payin' me good money to do away with you. 'I want it to happen somewhere remote,' he told me, 'and I want it to happen slow. Real slow.' And that's how it's gonna be. Ain't a soul around for miles. Nobody's gonna hear you scream—and you *will* scream, Reynolds, make no mistake. I got this here knife and I'm gonna take my time. Gonna cut you up bit by bit. Gonna carve slices off of you like some kinda… some kinda…" He frowned, trying to think of a simile.

"Christmas turkey?" Mal offered.

"Exactly! Like some kinda Christmas turkey. And I'm gonna enjoy it, too."

"That's mighty nice to hear. Can't fault a man who loves his work."

"Oh, I do, Reynolds," said Rouleau. "Very much."

"There's just one thing."

"What's that?"

"I have friends."

"How nice for you. I imagine they'll be right sad when they learn what's become of you." Rouleau held the knife to Mal's stomach, cutting edge upward. "Reckon here's as good a place to start as any." With a flick of the hand, he severed three shirt buttons. The shirt fell open, exposing skin. "This blade is finest Regina steel. I hone it daily."

"Still, you're forgettin'. I have friends."

"So you've said. Don't see none around, though." Rouleau made a show of looking in every direction.

"The kind of friends who wouldn't leave a fella hangin'. The kind that'd come to his rescue. I mean, come to his rescue soon. I mean, *soon* soon. As in, right now. Please?"

"Aww, ain't that sweet?" said Rouleau. "Begging for help, even though there's no chance any's comin'."

A shot rang out.

Rouleau doubled over, clutching his ear and hissing with pain. He drew his hand away and looked at it. The palm was covered in blood. He probed his ear gingerly with one finger. Most of its top section was missing.

Then he peered at Mal. "Now just what the—?"

A second shot rang out.

Rouleau's hand flew to his other ear. It, too, was now minus its top section.

"Gorramn it!" he yelled, peering around. "Whoever the hell you are, stop doing that! Hurts like a mother-rutter!"

"Drop the knife," a gruff male voice barked from the shadows beyond the hover-gig's headlights. "I done the right ear, I done the left. Next shot goes in the middle."

"Okay, okay." Rouleau let go of the knife. It thudded point-first into the ground. "You got the drop on me, whoever you are. I ain't gonna resist."

"Mal?" said the voice. "You found out what you need to know from this guy?"

"Yep."

"Then I guess there's no reason for him to stay breathin'."

"Wait. Wait!" said Rouleau. Blood was streaming down both sides of his neck, glistening in his beard. "What do you want? You want money? I'll give you money. The fee from this job, plus ten per cent extra as a goodwill gesture. How's that sound? And in return, you let me walk away. No questions asked. You won't never see me again."

The unseen sniper went quiet, as though giving the matter thought. Then he said, "Mal? We want this guy's platinum?"

"Sure could do with it," Mal said.

"It's yours, I promise," said Rouleau, with every appearance of sincerity.

"On the other hand," Mal said to Rouleau, "you did go on at some length 'bout how you were going to kill me slow."

"That was just talk." The killer for hire was sounding blustery and panicked again. "I'd've made it quick, honest I would."

"Decent of you. I just don't happen to believe you."

"Swear to God."

"Way I heard it, you were gonna get your sick, sadistic jollies torturin' me."

"Sometimes a fella says these things for effect." As he spoke, Rouleau was surreptitiously slipping a blood-smeared hand behind his back. "You know how it is. Gotta sound tough and menacin'. Gotta—"

Instead of finishing the sentence, Rouleau whipped out a six-shooter that had been lodged in the waistband of his pants, nestling against the base of his spine. He leveled the barrel with Mal's face, cocking the hammer at the same time.

Blam!

Rouleau keeled over backwards. The third shot fired at him had, as promised, been aimed between his ears. Now Rouleau lay on his back in the dust with a hole where his nose used to be and another, larger cavity where the back of his skull used to be.

And that was the end of Desmond Rouleau, killer for hire.

2

Serenity took off from the surface of Odessa at full burn, achieving escape velocity in under a minute.

On board, Mal was having a debrief with Zoë and Jayne in the cargo bay. River sat on the catwalk nearby, legs dangling over the edge. She appeared not to be paying the conversation below much attention. Instead she stared into the middle distance, humming to herself and twirling a lock of her hair around a finger.

"Haymer, huh?" said Zoë. "Should've known that sooner or later there'd be blowback from that whole business."

"Yeah," said Mal, "who'd've thought he'd mind losing one of his most precious possessions so much?"

"You talking about his Lassiter or YoSaffBridge?"

"You know how attached men get to their guns. Don't they, Jayne?"

Jayne was cradling his favorite rifle, the Callahan full-bore auto-lock he called Vera. "Ain't nothin' shameful about that," he said.

"But in this case," Mal went on, returning his gaze to Zoë, "I mean YoSaffBridge. Guess he shoulda found someone a bit smarter to do his dirty work, though. Rouleau's trap wasn't any too subtle. 'Let's meet at a remote cabin, just you and me, nobody else.' We knew the thing was a setup. Couldn't have been more obvious. Just needed to know who was doin' the setting up and why."

"But you surely could have come up with a better way of finding out, sir," said Zoë. "'Less, that is, you like getting tied up and having a knife held to you."

"I was hopin' to persuade Rouleau to spill the beans through the time-honored method of pulling a gun and threatening him with it. That was the plan, remember? Would have, too, if I'd gotten the chance. How was I to know the *gè zhēn de hún dàn* would spike my drink?" Mal was still feeling the lingering after-effects—fuzzy head, furry tongue—from whatever drug the would-be assassin had used to knock him out. "Or that he'd then hogtie me and drive several miles out into the wilderness to kill me? Good thing I had a guardian angel. That was some nice shootin', by the way, Jayne."

"You're welcome," said Jayne.

"Just curious, though. From the start, you were in position near the cabin. You could have taken Rouleau out as he was carryin' me to his hover-gig. Why didn't you?"

"Didn't have a clear shot. He had you slung over his shoulder. Couldn't guarantee I wouldn't hit you. I also didn't know if he'd gone and spilled the beans yet or not. I assumed not, so my only option was to follow you on the Mule bike at a safe distance. By the time I caught up, Rouleau'd already hung you up and started waving his knife around."

"And I was busy stalling him by keeping him talking. If it weren't for that, you might've been too late."

"I got there before any real harm was done, didn't I?"

"True, aside from some missing buttons." Mal looked ruefully at the front of his shirt. "Guess I can't complain."

"Pity of it is, I just went and bought myself this." Jayne patted his latest customization for Vera, a brand new night scope. "Was hopin' I'd have the chance to test it out, but there was enough light to see by that I didn't need it."

"Maybe next time someone's holding a knife on me you'll get your wish."

"Yeah. Fingers crossed."

Mal side-eyed the big man. Either he was joshing or he was being crass. With Jayne Cobb, it wasn't always easy to tell.

"Question is," said Zoë, "what are we going to do now? Haymer sent one paid killer after you. Chances are, when he finds out this one's failed, he'll send another."

"Chances are he won't." Mal gestured towards an aluminum-sided crate. "Not once we've dropped *that* off on his front doorstep."

The crate, which had more or less the dimensions of a coffin, held the mortal remains of Desmond Rouleau.

"Haymer's a Bellerophon blueblood," he went on. "Doesn't have the sand to pull a trigger himself, but he's happy to pay someone else to do it on his behalf. Man like that needs to be shown the consequences of his actions, needs to know what killin' really looks like—and opening up that crate and gettin' an eyeful of Rouleau's perforated carcass will surely do the trick."

"And if it don't?"

"Then the same thing'll happen with every other hired gun he sends, over and over. He'll get the message in the end."

"Works for me," Jayne opined.

"Kind of a risk," said Zoë.

"A calculated one."

"Still a risk."

Mal sighed. "That's our lives now, Zoë. Ain't nothin' *but* risk, calculated or otherwise."

Simon appeared on the catwalk, in time to catch Mal's last remark. "What's this about risk?" he asked River.

River craned her neck to look up at her older brother. "Mal was just saying he doesn't mind if people try to kill him." She *had* been listening in after all, in her own distracted fashion.

"Ain't what I said at all, River," Mal corrected. "Somebody pulls a gun on me, a knife, any kinda weapon, with a view to doin' me a mischief, I very much mind. Seems that's becomin' a more and more common occurrence these days, and I mightn't like it but it's something I just have to accept."

"So where are we headed now?" Simon asked him.

"Bellerophon," said River. "Mal has a present for Durran Haymer. One corpse, fresh off the production line."

"Corpse?"

"In that box."

"Seriously?"

"A point needs to be made," Mal said.

"He was a hero, you know," River said.

"Flatterin' of you to say so, River," said Mal. "I wouldn't exactly describe what I did as heroic, my own self. Brave, maybe, but not heroic."

"Bellerophon," said River. "Demigod from Greek myth. Son of Poseidon. Rode the winged horse Pegasus. Slew the Chimera, a fire-breathing monster with the head of a lion, the body of a goat and the tail of a serpent."

"Oh. That guy."

"You've heard of him?"

"No, but he sounds like a hero all right. Slayin' monsters and such."

"Bellerophon went too far, though. Heroes often do," said River. "He became arrogant. Because he killed the Chimera, he thought he deserved a place on Mount Olympus with the gods."

Jayne shook his head despairingly. "What is this, some kinda ancient fairytales lecture?"

Ignoring him, River continued. "Zeus sent a gadfly to sting Pegasus mid-flight. Pegasus threw Bellerophon off, and he fell to Earth, landed in a thorn bush and was blinded. He spent the rest of his days alone, humbled and miserable. It's called hubris. When mortals set themselves up as the gods' equals, the gods don't like it. They make them suffer for it."

"Your point being…?" said Mal.

She blinked at him. "Does there need to be a point?"

"You seem to be suggestin' I'm guilty of this hubris thing."

"No. Not a bit. But when we arrive on Bellerophon, I think you need to be prepared to fall to Earth with a bump."

"What?"

River gazed down at Mal from the catwalk, and looking into those big, soulful eyes of hers he had the sense that she knew something the rest of them didn't. The feeling was familiar to him from past experience, but no less eerie for that. Alliance scientists had meddled with River Tam's brain, gifting her with abilities some might call superhuman. These abilities—telepathy, precognition, extraordinary combat prowess—were gradually making themselves known, and it was unclear what their full extent might be. They came at a price, however. River was now damaged goods, mentally unsound. Sometimes that amazing mind of hers could resolve seemingly intractable problems; just as often, it caused them.

"What?" she repeated back.

"No, I said 'What?' first," Mal said. "You don't get to say it after I do. You get to answer me. How am I gonna fall to Earth with a bump?"

"Did I say that?"

"Here we go," Jayne groused. "Little Miss Creepybritches confounds us all. Again." He strode out of the cargo bay with Vera, muttering to himself.

"River," said Simon gently, "if you know about something that's going to happen, you'd best tell us."

His sister gave a puzzled frown. "*Do* I know what's going to happen?"

"On Bellerophon."

"Bellerophon. Demigod from Greek myth. Son of Poseidon.

Rode the winged horse Pegasus. Slew the Chimera…"

"You've told us that already. Is there something else we should know?"

River seemed genuinely nonplussed. "I don't think so, Simon."

"You sure?"

"Positive." It was as if she had no memory of the comment she'd made just half a minute ago. Indeed, she probably didn't. Abruptly she sprang to her feet. Tapping Simon on the arm, she cried, "Tag! You're it!" and ran out of the cargo bay.

Simon, with a shrug, set off after her. "I'll get you, River."

"No, you won't," came the singsong, laughing reply. "You never do."

Mal and Zoë exchanged looks.

"What do you reckon, Zoë?" Mal said. "Our own private crystal ball has given us a warning."

"I reckon we should be ready for trouble on Bellerophon, sir. Just in case River's on the money."

"I reckon that too. Mind you, it'd be worth taking precautions anyway, even if we didn't have Madam Nostradamus on board."

"Why's that?" said Zoë.

"'Cause, the way our luck runs, there's *always* gorramn trouble."

3

In the event, somehow they bucked the odds and there wasn't trouble.
Durran Haymer owned one of the floating estates that hovered
in clusters over the sea on Bellerophon, each kept aloft by an array of
conical antigrav generators projecting downward. Disc-shaped and
pretty much identical to one another, the estates resembled giant lily
pads suspended in midair at varying altitudes.

Mal and Zoë touched down on the landing platform at Haymer's
in one of *Serenity*'s two shuttles and hurriedly offloaded the crate,
which Mal had labeled "Special Delivery for Mr. Haymer—To Be
Opened By Him Only." They were airborne again within moments.
There was no point in hanging around. If they dallied, there was a
chance someone might call the authorities on them.

Looking out from the cockpit window, Mal saw a man emerge
from the main house. The guy shaded his eyes against the sun as
he watched the shuttle depart. It wasn't Haymer but some flunky
dressed in a servant's uniform, with a tailcoat and fancy vest. He
peered down at the crate, read the label on the lid, and went back into
the house, presumably to summon his master.

Mal half smiled. Durran Haymer was in for a hell of a shock
when he opened the crate. He'd have no trouble figuring out who

it was from and what it meant, and hopefully he would learn his lesson. He was basically a law-abiding-citizen type, after all. Out of frustration, or perhaps desperation, he had dipped a toe in unfamiliar water—the water Mal swam in on a daily basis. Mal was showing him how deadly dangerous that water could be.

They were halfway back to the rendezvous point with *Serenity* when Wash got in touch over the comms.

"Mal?" said *Serenity*'s pilot. "Incoming wave for you. One Stanislaw L'Amour. Want me to patch it through?"

"Sure. Go ahead."

A moment later, a screen on the shuttle's control console lit up. The exceptionally handsome face of Stanislaw L'Amour flickered into view.

"Captain Reynolds. Miz Alleyne Washburne."

"Mr. L'Amour," said Mal.

"Hi," said Zoë.

"Been a while," said Mal.

Their sole previous encounter with L'Amour had taken place several months ago on a remote, arid world called Thetis. He had helped the crew out of a jam, summoning a private army of security contractors who'd ridden to the rescue like the proverbial cavalry. He had done this to discharge a debt to Inara Serra, with whom he was old friends. L'Amour was that rare thing, an enormously wealthy businessman with honor and scruples.

"It has indeed been a while," said L'Amour. "You look well, Captain."

"You too."

This was not entirely true. Even though Mal could not claim close acquaintance with L'Amour, there was something *off* about him now. He recalled the genial, urbane fellow he had met on Thetis, someone who seemed to find life infinitely enjoyable. *This* Stanislaw L'Amour was a markedly different proposition. He looked and sounded somber.

"What can I do for you?" Mal said. "If you're after Inara, you obviously ain't heard that she's not with us anymore. She's left and gone back to House Madrassa."

There was a tiny hitch in his voice as he said these words. Inara had quit *Serenity* not long after the events on Thetis, for reasons which were still not quite clear to Mal but which, he thought, had a lot to do with him and his stubborn, damn-fool insistence that there was nothing going on between the two of them. Just at the point where he'd been about to admit he had feelings for her, Inara had told him she was leaving. Talk about bad timing—or rather, talk about putting things off until it was too late.

"Or could it be you've got a business proposal for us?" he added hopefully.

"No, this is about Inara, as you first surmised," L'Amour said, "but not in the way you think. Captain Reynolds…"

"You can call me Mal."

"Mal, then. Tell me, what do you know about Inara's condition?"

Mal felt a stirring of unease in his belly. "I'm sorry, condition?"

"Ah." The grave look on L'Amour's face deepened. "You had no idea."

"No, I had no idea about any condition, and I'd be more'n grateful if you could enlighten me."

"Mal, I must apologize. I assumed she had told you."

"Told. Me. What." Mal fired the words at the screen like bullets.

L'Amour hesitated, evidently plucking up courage.

"Inara is dying, Mal," he said. "Cancer. The doctors say she has, at most, a month to live."

4

Stanislaw L'Amour had homes all across the 'verse, including one on Bellerophon—and that was where, as chance would have it, he happened to be staying right now. The property lay in the north-eastern region of the largest of the planet's three main continents: an imposing two-story country mansion set in grounds which ran to fifty acres and which were landscaped to perfection.

Wash set *Serenity* down on a landing pad a half-mile from the house. An automated maglev transfer pod was waiting, and no sooner had Mal climbed in than it set off on its track, whirring along a series of sinuous curves through thickly wooded terrain.

On any other occasion he might have enjoyed the ride. The trees were in their autumnal prime, their foliage all russet, tawny and gold, the leaves clinging on, still glossy, not yet ready to drop. A gentle zephyr made the branches stir languorously. Of all the seasons, Mal loved fall the best. He loved the colors and the way it made him feel pleasantly wistful.

Not today, however. Today, all he saw around him was slow, inexorable decline.

Shortly the transfer pod pulled up outside the mansion's front door. A solemn majordomo ushered Mal through into an enormous vestibule, where L'Amour was waiting for him.

"Mal." L'Amour extended a hand. "Good to see you again in person. I wish it were under better circumstances."

Mal did not take the proffered hand. "Where is she?"

L'Amour nodded understandingly. "Upstairs in the guest quarters. She's being well looked after. I have oncologists on call, the best that money can afford, and there's nursing care round the clock. Everything is being done to make her as comfortable as possible during her final—"

"Take me to her."

"Of course, of course. This way."

Up a sweeping staircase, along a galleried landing, to a suite of rooms more spacious than most city apartments. The décor in the suite was sumptuous, from the swagged drapes to the flock wallpaper to the parquet tiles, which made the newtech medical bed in the center of the main room all the more incongruous-looking.

The bed, which floated a couple of feet above the floor, bristled with monitoring equipment and readouts. Intravenous drip bags containing various clear fluids hung from stands attached to the frame. It was angled to face a large picture window which looked over a lawn, a lake and a knot garden filled with topiary and statuary. Its contoured mattress was adjusted to prop up the occupant so that she could take in the view.

A nurse was bent over the bed, tending to the patient. She straightened up and stepped discreetly aside as Mal and L'Amour entered.

Mal walked to the bed, not hurrying now. He wanted to look at Inara. He didn't want to look at Inara.

She was dressed in a silk kimono with a hand-painted cherry blossom motif. Her face was gaunt and sallow-skinned, and her lips were dry and cracked. Her cheekbones stood out, skeletal, while her hair had lost its luster and was now as dull and brittle as tumbleweed.

But still beautiful. She was still beautiful.

She rolled her head on the pillow, turning to look at him, and it seemed an effort for her to focus her gaze.

"Mal?" A reedy croak, scarcely more than a whisper.

Mal couldn't speak.

"You came," she said. She braved a smile.

Mal continued to have trouble finding his voice. There was a lump stopping up his throat.

"It's good to see you," Inara said.

Finally the power of speech returned to him.

"Why didn't you tell me?" He meant it to sound plaintive. Somehow it came out accusatory.

"I tried to. Several times. Just couldn't quite bring myself to."

"But you knew. Right from the start, when you first joined *Serenity*. You knew even then. L'Amour told me."

He glanced round, looking for L'Amour, but both the billionaire and the nurse had withdrawn from the room to give them privacy.

"And Simon says you hinted to him about it," Mal went on. "That time when *Serenity*'s compression coil blew out and we were adrift and runnin' out of air. He said something about not wanting to 'die on this ship' and you said something about not wanting to die at all. He didn't think much about it at the time. Could've been you were just commenting in general on how death ain't such a fun idea. But he says you sounded kinda sad when you said it, and now that he knows you were sick, in hindsight…"

"In hindsight, he realizes I was subtly referring to the fact that I'd contracted a terminal disease."

"Yeah. But that was the only time you ever even came close to talking about it to anyone."

"How is Simon, by the way?" Inara asked. "Have he and Kaylee finally managed to, you know…?"

"Get together? Nope."

She rolled her eyes. "*Tiān xiǎo de!* Those two. Can't see what's staring them in the face. How about the others? How are they? Zoë, Wash, River… I've missed them. Even Jayne."

"I ain't here to talk about them." Everything Mal said was sounding angrier than he intended. Maybe he *was* angry. "You want to know how they're doing, ask 'em yourself. Only, you ain't going to. You've refused to let them come here. Said you'd only see me."

"Mal." Inara laid a hand on his. It felt as light as a sparrow. "Take a breath. Please. I didn't want the others to come because I don't want them seeing me like this. I want their last memories of me to be the person I was when I was fit and healthy. I didn't especially want *you* seeing me like this either, but Stanislaw convinced me I should. The way you're acting, I'm beginning to wonder if he was right."

"Okay. Okay." Mal tried to calm himself. Whatever emotions he was feeling, this meeting wasn't about him. It was about Inara. "I just… If I'd known, it might've changed things."

"How?" she said.

"I'd've asked you to stay on *Serenity*, for starters. Insisted on it."

"Which is just why I didn't say anything. You would have been doing it for all the wrong reasons."

"We'd have looked after you. We'd have done everything we could for you. Those are the wrong reasons?"

"Sure, you'd have shown me compassion. You'd also have shown me pity, and pity's something I can't abide. Not from anyone, most of all not from you."

"So instead you lied and said you were going back to Sihnon and House Madrassa. You had us all thinking we weren't good enough for you; you were ashamed of us."

"You mean 'me,' not 'us,' don't you?" Inara said. "Because I'm fairly certain none of the others would have felt that way. And besides, it wasn't a lie. I did go back to House Madrassa, for a while. Thing is, the type of cancer I have—Kiehl's myeloma—the symptoms can be held in check, at least to begin with. There's medication, a cocktail of proteasome inhibitors and immune response adjustors that can retard the progression of the disease. So while I was on *Serenity* I was injecting myself with it on a regular basis, and for a time it worked."

"I never saw you doing that."

"Why would you think I'd let you? I kept the syringe hidden away and made sure there was no one around whenever I used it. But I knew it wasn't going to last forever. The drugs were becoming increasingly ineffective. I was getting headaches, dizzy spells, weird blurry patches in my vision. They came and went, but they were getting more frequent. Next, I knew, I would start fainting. That's the usual pathology of Kiehl's. My kidneys would begin to pack up, I'd fall prey to infections… In short, I wouldn't be able to keep hiding it anymore. People would notice. Simon especially. He was the one I was most worried about—him and his doctor's eye. There was that one occasion I almost blurted out the truth to him, and countless others where I bit my tongue in time. It might have been good just to tell *someone* on the ship, and I knew I could compel Simon to physician–patient privilege so it wouldn't go any further."

"Or there was me," said Mal. "You could've trusted me. I'd've kept it a secret."

"If you'd known, Mal, everyone would have known."

"I wouldn't have told a soul," he protested.

"You wouldn't have had to. Your behavior would have done it for you. You'd have been different around me. You'd have been solicitous, sulky, mournful, overprotective—and the others would have noticed. I don't mean that as an insult. You just wouldn't have been able to help yourself."

Mal thought she was correct about that. Didn't make her *right*, though.

"I had to go," Inara said. "That's all there is to it. I couldn't stay on *Serenity*. I'd have been a burden to the rest of you, and a liability. I only wish you and I had parted on better terms. That was my greatest regret about leaving the way I did. I wish I'd been honest with you. But I couldn't. I did what I thought was best, and if that hurt you, I'm deeply sorry."

"You reckon—you reckon quittin' the ship without explaining fully why was the way to go about it? Letting me think it was 'cause of something I'd done, or hadn't done? That was best?"

All at once, Inara let out a hiss of pain. A spasm passed through her, making her arch her back and writhe beneath the covers. Several of the machines integrated into the medical bed start making soft pings and bleeps.

"Inara? Inara!"

"It's… It's okay," she replied through clenched teeth. "Just give it… a moment. The bed's… responding. There." Her body relaxed. She sagged back onto the mattress. "That's better." She raised an arm, showing him the tube that was feeding through a cannula into a vein. "Analgesic's kicking in. *Rén cí de fó zǔ*, what a relief. Normally it's okay, the pain isn't too bad, but once in a while I get these acute attacks."

"Inara…"

"Mal, please. Those big, sad eyes. I'm fine, really."

"You ain't fine. You're dying!" The anger was back, fiercer than before, unstemmable. He was furious. Not with Inara. With himself. With fate. With this godawful disease that was eating away at Inara, killing her by inches.

"And that's all right," she said. "Everyone dies. It's my time, is all."

"No. No, I'm not takin' any of this Buddhist *lè sè*."

Her eyes blazed. A flash of the old Inara. "Don't you call my religion 'garbage,' Mal. Don't you dare."

He bowed his head, contrite. "Yeah. Sorry," he mumbled.

Her voice softened. "Sometimes you just have to accept there's nothing you can do. Things are what they are. Raging at them, fighting them—it's pointless."

"Raging and fighting's what I do. What I've always done."

"I know, and I'm asking you to be different now, Mal. For my sake, and for yours."

5

They talked for another five minutes or so. Mal updated her on the crew's latest exploits.

"Platinum's hard to come by," he said. "So are jobs."

"No change there, then."

Inara was clearly getting tired, however. Speaking was becoming more of a strain for her.

"Mal…" she said eventually. "I've done bad things."

"No, Inara. No, you ain't."

"Why I left House Madrassa. Fiddler's Green. That client of mine letting slip about the offensive the Independents were planning at their base at Fiddler's Green. I thought it was right I should let the authorities know. Thought it'd prevent a massacre."

"Yeah. You've told me this."

"Didn't mean for it turn out how it did. The Alliance bombardment. The entire base destroyed. All those people. Those noncombatants. When I finally confessed to you about it, you were so mad."

"I know, but this ain't the time to start judgin' yourself."

"When death is hanging over you? If not then, when?"

"You need to think of the good you've done," Mal said, "not the mistakes you've made. You need to think of what you've meant to people, how you've changed 'em for the better."

"That include you?"

"Me most of all. Not that I'd admit that to anyone."

"Don't worry, your secret is safe with me. I'll take it to the grave."

In the end, she could barely keep her eyes open.

"Regrets, Mal."

"It's all right," he said. "You just sleep."

"You and I… We could have…"

"I know, Inara. I know."

She said a few more words, but they were so slurred he couldn't make them out. Then her eyelids fluttered shut and she sank into slumber.

He stayed at her bedside for another half-hour, watching her sleep. Then he stood and strode out of the room. He wanted to hit something. Didn't much mind what. There was a sculpture on a pedestal in the corridor outside, a three-dimensional patchwork of what appeared to be pieces of recycled metal. He wasn't sure what it was supposed to look like. A cat on stilts? A drunk giraffe? Regardless, he was sorely tempted to pick it up and throw it onto the floor. Stamp on it. Turn it back into scrap.

"Please don't," said Stanislaw L'Amour, walking up behind him.

"Huh?" said Mal.

"That's an original Oscar Navarre. Verrry expensive. You were thinking of doing something bad to it."

"Was not."

"You wouldn't be the first. Navarre's a controversial artist. Some reckon his work is genius, others reckon…"

"They could have knocked up something like it in their own toolshed in an afternoon."

"Exactly. Doesn't stop his sculptures fetching exorbitant prices at auction. This one's called *Old Paint*. Kind of a visual pun. It's a horse, you see, made out of paint cans."

"Ohhh. A horse. Yeah, I can sorta see that, now you say so."

L'Amour fixed him with a sympathetic look. "I get it, Mal. About Inara. I feel the same as you. We both love her. We hate what's happening to her. Makes you want to lash out at the world. But what good will it do? Come and have a drink instead. I have a bottle of Jīnsè De Mèngxiǎng downstairs. Best single malt you'll ever taste."

"Don't much fancy drinkin'."

Six generous measures of whisky later, Mal found that his anger had transmuted into dejection. That magic of booze. The alchemy of alcohol.

"You're sure there ain't nothin' can be done for her?" he said to L'Amour. They were sitting in a belvedere—"summerhouse" wasn't nearly grand enough a word for it—atop a rise some five hundred yards from the house. Nearby, the lake shimmered in the low afternoon sunshine. Now and then a golden-orange fish rose to the surface, creating small rings of ripples.

"Trust me, I've had just about every specialist in the 'verse take a look at her," L'Amour replied. "They all say the same. Kiehl's myeloma is, not to put too fine a point on it, a death sentence. It affects the production of plasma cells in the bone marrow, turning them against the body. Basically, it poisons you slowly from the inside out with your own blood. Most myelomas are curable these days—the wonders of modern medicine—but Kiehl's is one of the exceptions. It's a pernicious little bugger."

"I just wish Inara'd try and fight it. It's like she's simply layin' back and letting it run its course."

The billionaire arched an eyebrow. "You honestly think that's the case? Mal, listen. Inara has been battling the disease every step of the way since she got here. I've never seen a woman more determined to live. It's only recently that she's resigned herself to the inevitable."

"Why'd she come to you in the first place?"

31

"Yes, what have I got going for me, other than my immense charm and vast wealth?"

"Didn't mean no offence."

"None taken, Mal. I'm just teasing. You're asking why, of all people, did Inara choose Stanislaw L'Amour to help look after her and be with her in her final days. Why not someone else? You, even?"

Mal shrugged his shoulders. "Not necessarily me. Ain't as if a Firefly captain can compete with, you know, this." He swept an arm to indicate their surroundings. "But House Madrassa took her back in, even after everything that had happened—Fiddler's Green, her breaching the Companion confidentiality vows, all of that. Surprising, but they did. She could have stayed there, couldn't she?"

"There was still a residue of resentment among her fellow Companions," L'Amour said. "It wasn't comfortable for her at all. Inara needed to be somewhere where there'd be no unspoken criticism, no atmosphere of self-righteousness. She knew she could get that from me. As soon as she waved me, I dropped everything and went to fetch her."

"And I'm grateful, don't get me wrong. But…"

"Mal." L'Amour patted his arm. "I know what you mean to her, and she to you. Inara's told me more than once. Who knows how it would have gone if things were different. The main thing is, you've visited her now. You've had a chance to say your goodbyes. What I hope is that the two of you have reconciled. That you've both gotten some kind of closure."

In the transfer pod on the way back to *Serenity*, Mal broke down and sobbed. He howled. He hammered his fists against his thighs, hard enough to leave bruises.

By the time the pod reached the landing pad he had dried his eyes and regained his composure. He stepped out, game face back on, seemingly ready to cope with whatever life threw at him. Captain Malcolm Reynolds. The man who didn't back down. The man whom nothing could break.

He was braced for a barrage of questions from the crew. He was expecting them to ask how Inara was. Did she have any messages for them? Might they be able to see her at a later date? Was there really no chance of her getting better?

What he wasn't expecting...

Was a faint, flickering ray of hope.

6

While Mal was over at Stanislaw L'Amour's house, Zoë waved *Serenity*'s other erstwhile crewmember, Shepherd Derrial Book, to deliver the news about Inara.

Nowadays Book lived on Haven, one of Deadwood's moons, bringing the Word of God to a small colony there. He'd said that his experiences while consorting with *Serenity*'s crew were beginning to erode his faith. He'd also said that he feared his somewhat dubious past might catch up with him, putting them all in undue danger. On Haven he could keep a low profile, far from the strife and violence that seemed to dog the ship whenever she went, and see if he could start to hear once more the still, small voice of the Lord within him.

"That is just awful," Book said to Zoë. "Poor Inara. I shall pray for her."

"Can't hurt," Zoë said. *Although if God's listening and in a mood to dole out miracles, He'd better damn well hurry*, she thought of adding, but didn't.

"I shall pray for all of us, too. Often it's harder to be the friend of someone dying than the actual person who's dying. You have to carry the weight of knowing you're not going to see them again after they're gone."

"But you also have the consolation of knowing they'll be looking down on you from heaven, of course. Don't you?"

"That's the general idea. Not without reason, however, is death known as 'the great mystery.'"

"Sounds almost like doubting, Shepherd."

Book sighed. "Questioning one's beliefs, Zoë, isn't the same as undermining them. It's more like putting them to the test, to see how they hold up. More than ever that's the case when somebody one has grown to love and admire is in the last stages of life—and long before their time, what's more. Inara has cancer, did you say?"

"Yeah. The nasty kind."

"I'm not so sure there's a *good* kind of cancer."

"You know what I mean. Kiehl's myeloma, it's called. I looked it up on the Cortex. It's completely incurable."

"Hmmm." A faraway look came over Book's wise, distinguished features.

"What's that face for?" Zoë said.

"Completely incurable, you say?"

"According to all the sources I've found. According to Simon, too. He says Kiehl's is, and I quote, 'one of the most insidious and aggressive cancers around.' You can treat it but you can't beat it."

"That may not necessarily be the case," said Book carefully.

Zoë felt something stir in her heart, as delicate and tremulous as a butterfly. "Shepherd, please, *please* do not go claiming this thing is fixable if it isn't. That wouldn't be fair."

"Zoë, I am loath to give you false hope. However…"

"However…?"

Book paused, then said, "There is someone. A doctor. An oncologist. I recall reading about him not so long ago. He's considered something of a maverick in his field. He has conducted research into the more virulent forms of cancer, and supposedly he has had some success. It's even been asserted that he has developed a universal therapy for the cancers which have so far defeated medical science."

"Kiehl's myeloma included?"

"That I don't know, but if 'universal therapy' lives up to its billing, then one would assume so."

"Who is he, this doctor?"

"His name is… Oh, what is it again?" Book frowned, clearly racking his brains. "Age. My memory isn't what it was. Esau Weng! That's it. Dr. Esau Weng."

"And where can we find this Dr. Esau Weng?"

"That's the trouble. Dr. Weng hasn't been seen in a while. There are rumors about him. It's said he's been carrying out trials of his cure illegally, contravening Alliance Medical Association rules. In fact, I heard he'd been jailed for it."

"Jailed?"

"I don't know the details. I believe there are strict protocols about when you can and can't test a vaccine, antidote or suchlike on living humans. It sounds like Dr. Weng flouted them and has paid the penalty."

"How long a sentence would he be serving for that?"

"Hard to say. I guess it'd depend on whether the people involved were willing to be experimented on or not. If they *were* willing, and all he did was commit a breach of medical etiquette, then not that long."

"So he may even be out by now," said Zoë.

"Who knows?" said Book. "It's also perfectly possible that Dr. Weng is just some charlatan who has no idea what he's doing and he posed a serious risk to the health of his test subjects."

"But you reckon he's worth checking out?"

"I reckon you can do worse than to inquire into him, at least."

Zoë smiled. The butterfly in her heart, though still a tiny, fragile creature, was dancing around. Book hadn't brought her a miracle, but he'd provided something that was close.

"Shepherd, thank you. Sincerely."

"You're welcome, Zoë. Give my fondest regards to your

husband and the rest of the crew, and let me know how it goes with Weng. And when you're next in the Blue Sun system, if you're ever close to Haven…"

"We'll be sure to drop by."

"I would like that—provided, of course, that it's a social call and not some dire emergency."

"Dire emergency? Us?"

They both chuckled, and Zoë cut the connection.

Straight away she got on the Cortex to look up Dr. Esau Weng. The information she initially uncovered served to confirm the facts about him that Book had already supplied. Oncologist. Researching seemingly incurable cancers at a private laboratory, funded by grants from various charitable institutions. Regarded by the medical establishment as a fringe practitioner, his methods unorthodox, borderline irresponsible.

Then, yes, a prosecution and a jail term.

Life sentence, without parole.

Reading this, Zoë's eyebrows rose almost to her hairline. If they could have gone any higher, they would have when she found out *where* Weng was doing time.

7

"Say that again," said Mal.

Zoë had intercepted him just as he reached *Serenity*, in order to tell him about her conversation with Shepherd Book and the data she had gleaned on Dr. Weng from the Cortex.

"Atata," she said.

"Atata, as in the prison planet Atata?"

"Is there another one?"

"No, I just… Atata?"

"You can keep asking me, won't change the answer," said Zoë. "All the sources say that's where Weng is. Atata."

"*Dà xiàng bào zhà shì de lā dù zi,*" breathed Mal. "Ice world hellhole like that ain't hardly the sort of place you'd expect a doctor to fetch up. Hardened criminals, yeah, but not a nerdy lab-coat type. Not unless he's some kinda sick, depraved monster. Is that it? Was he, I don't know, carvin' up babies or something?"

"No mention anywhere of anything heinous like that. Only the charge of unlawful experimentation."

"That could be carvin' up babies."

"Book said he was carrying out human trials without permission."

"Could still be carvin' up babies."

"But it could also be that Weng just tested his universal therapy on people – people who'd agreed to be tested on – without filling out the proper forms first. From the looks of it, he's a wild card, so it's the sort of thing he might've done."

"If that was all it was, though, a paperwork oversight, then what the gorramn hell is he doing on Atata?"

"I looked into it. I ran a search for court records of his trial, but they've been redacted. The case was heard in a closed session."

"Now this is starting to seem a mite fishy," Mal said. "If the Alliance are prosecuting a fella and not doing it in public, then you might be forgiven for gettin' the impression it's a kangaroo court and he's being railroaded."

"You might well."

"In other words, Dr. Weng musta pissed off some grand high mucky-muck and it was decided to make an example of him."

Zoë rolled her eyes. "So cynical, sir."

"It's a cynical 'verse we live in, Zoë," Mal said with an exaggerated sigh. "You reckon Weng might be the answer to our prayers?"

"Doubt the Shepherd would have mentioned him if he didn't think it was worth a shot."

"But how're we gonna get to him? Supposin' that's what we choose to do."

"Well, that's the honking great question, isn't it?" said Zoë. "Never mind extracting the man off Atata. It's a tall order us simply landing there safely, undetected and in one piece. Fed ships are in constant orbit around the planet. Nothing arrives or leaves without their say-so, and if you don't have the appropriate authorization, they're apt to blast you to pieces."

"Yeah, yeah, tell me something I don't know."

"I'm just saying, I appreciate you like a challenge and all, Mal, but there's challenging and then there's crazy."

"Might be helpful if we knew a bit more about Weng," Mal said. "Like, is he deluded or is he the real deal?"

"Maybe the Doc'd be some use with that."

They found Simon in the ship's dining area. He and River were preparing dinner, a vegetable soup using the last few precious items of fresh produce on the ship before they turned bad. Simon was stirring the soup while River was chopping the vegetables to add to it. She wielded the kitchen knife with startling speed and accuracy. A carrot was reduced to disk-shaped chunks in just a couple of seconds, each slice precisely the same width as the others, to the millimeter.

"Esau Weng?" Simon said, in answer to Mal's query. "Name rings a bell. I think I remember reading about him in the *Hippocratic Chronicle* a couple of years back. He was working on something to do with the promotion of cellular regrowth and endogenous repair using targeted artificial immunomodulatory microorganisms."

Zoë shook her head bemusedly at all the jargon. Mal just looked blank.

"Robot viruses that can mend anything in the body," River explained to him, as if speaking to a ten-year-old.

"Oh," Mal said.

"Cutting-edge stuff," Simon said. "It could revolutionize modern medicine—if it's at all feasible."

"You don't think it is?"

"I don't know enough about it to say. The problem is, Weng has never published anything on the topic—not even an abstract—and he's never allowed his research to be peer-reviewed. That's made the medical world regard him with suspicion, and rightly so. Anyone can claim they're on the verge of a huge breakthrough, but if no one else can check what you're doing, you may as well be making mud pies in your backyard. Come to think of it, wasn't there a scandal involving Weng not so long ago? A court case or some such? I have a feeling there was."

"Trumped-up charges," said Zoë. "Leastways, that's how it looks, reading between the lines."

"What sort of charges?"

"Unlawful experimentation. Contravention of Alliance Medical Association rules. So Book says. The Cortex doesn't specify any further."

"Shepherd Book?"

"I waved him."

"Gray hair, no longer here," River murmured, quartering a potato in two deft strikes.

"Then," said Simon, "I suppose what I should be asking is: why's there this sudden interest in Esau Weng, of all people?"

"Because of Inara, silly," River said.

"Inara?" Simon said, putting it together. He looked at Mal. "You think Dr. Weng could cure her Kiehl's?"

"You think he can't?" Mal said.

"I have no idea. On the one hand, he sounds like a crank, and a shady one at that. On the other hand, if he really has developed artificial immunomodulatory microorganisms—"

"Heal-all robo-viruses," River chipped in, for Mal's benefit.

"It's okay, River," Mal said. "I got it the first time."

"Then," Simon continued, "technically there's no reason to think they wouldn't work on Kiehl's myeloma. But I've got to say, this is clutching at straws. I mean, I want Inara not to die as much as the next person, but if we're pinning our hopes on some untested, unproven form of therapy, one that may not even exist, then…" The sentence trailed off into a shrug.

"Doc," said Mal, "you have a better idea, I'd like to hear it."

"I wish it were otherwise, believe me—but no, I don't."

"Thought not. Me? I can't lay claim to any fancy medical

background, but I do know that if there's even the slightest chance this Dr. Weng has invented bitty little viruses that can reverse Inara's cancer, then we oughta try to find him and convince him give her some of 'em."

"That's all very laudable, but—"

"Whoa." Mal held up a hand. "Let me stop you right there, Simon. This ain't about what's laudable—if I even know what that means. This is about bringing Inara back from death's door. I'm prepared to do whatever it takes, even if it involves traveling to the ass-end of the 'verse. I'd like to think you would be too."

"I never said I wasn't willing to help," Simon replied defensively. "But what's this about 'the ass-end of the 'verse'? As far as I recall, Dr. Weng has been conducting his researches at a private laboratory somewhere in the Red Sun system."

"Not anymore," said Zoë. "He *did* have a lab. It was on Greenleaf. And it burned to the ground. Suspected arson. Happened shortly before Weng got arrested. Word is, he torched the place himself."

"Why?"

"Don't know."

"Then if he's not on Greenleaf, where is he now?"

"Well, that court case you were talkin' about," said Mal, "it didn't go too well for him."

"He wound up on Atata," said Zoë.

"Atata," Simon echoed, with a note of incredulity. "But only the absolute dregs get sent there. Worst of the worst. They're dropped off and left to fend for themselves. No wardens, no oversight, just survival of the fittest."

"It's an ice world, what's more."

"Yes, the terraforming didn't 'take.' Winter all year around except at the equator, and even there the temperature never rises much above zero."

"Named after one of the Eight Cold Hells in Buddhism," River offered. "The word echoes the sound of teeth chattering. The other seven Cold Hells are Arbuda, where the skin gets stripped off you by a freezing wind; Nirarbuda, where the same happens but you can't get out; Hahava, where—"

"Atata ain't a beach club resort, that's for damn sure," Mal said, butting in before she could go through the entire list. "But," he added, with finality, "it's where we're going."

8

"That's it?" said Simon, arching an eyebrow at Mal. "You've decided."

"Sure have, just now," Mal said. "We land on Atata, find Weng, grab him, get the hell out."

"Don't the rest of us get to have any say in the matter?"

"Nope. My ship, my rules. That don't sit well with you, you're welcome to step off."

"But that'd… You know River and I can't simply…" Simon collected himself. "It just needs to be said, Mal, that this isn't the greatest idea you've ever come up with. The cons far outweigh the pros."

"Cons," River commented. "Prison planet. Clever."

"I didn't intend it as a joke."

"Clever, all the same."

"Complain all you like," Mal said, "my mind's made up."

"I'm not complaining. I'm simply making the point that what you're suggesting carries a very high chance of failure. In fact, it's probably futile. But if you insist, then…" Simon sighed manfully. "I'm in."

"Glad you see it my way." Mal had known Simon would back down. It wasn't even a case of calling his bluff. The Tam siblings were wanted by the Feds, and their best—perhaps only—option for keeping out of the Alliance's clutches was to stay with *Serenity*. The ship was constantly on the move, making it hard to track their whereabouts. The downside of that, as far as Simon and River were concerned, was that whatever Mal proposed the crew do, they had no real alternative but to go along with it.

"I'm in too," said River. She twirled the kitchen knife on her fingertip, tossed it in the air, caught it and—*thunk!*—halved a zucchini longitudinally with a single blow. "Not that you asked."

"What about the others?" Simon inquired, with the air of a man trying to salvage some dignity. "Have they agreed to this?"

"Let's put it to 'em, see what they say." Mal reached for the intercom and summoned Jayne, Kaylee and Wash to the dining area. When they were all assembled, he swiftly brought them up to speed on the situation.

"This is Dr. Weng," he said, showing them a picture he had pulled up from the Cortex. It was of a middle-aged man with haywire jet-black hair and eyes set deep in pouchy folds of skin, like he was perpetually tired. There was an air of obvious intelligence about him, but also the slightly lost look of someone who found it hard to connect with everyday life.

"I ain't askin' for anyone's permission to go after him," he went on. "Just for consent."

"Zoë?" said Wash. "I'm guessing you're going along with this."

"I am," said Zoë. "Way I see it, there's two choices here. We can sit on our behinds and let Inara die, or we can—as Simon has put it—clutch at straws. I'd rather do something, even if it turns out to be a waste of time, effort and resources, than nothing."

"Then count me in," Wash said to Mal. "Whatever Zoë wants, I want."

"My man." Zoë slipped an arm around her husband's waist and kissed him. "That's why I love you."

"It's also why you haven't killed me all this time we've been married."

"Smart of you to realize."

Mal turned to Kaylee. "How about you?"

Kaylee looked pale and wrung out. Ever since hearing about Inara's cancer she had been near inconsolable, so much so that she had scarcely left the engine room. Tinkering with *Serenity*'s workings invariably brought her a measure of comfort.

Now, her face showed nothing but utter, rigid determination. "How soon do we leave?"

"Attagirl," said Mal. "Jayne?"

"Ask me, there's a thin line between doable and insane," Jayne said, "and breakin' somebody out of Atata crosses it."

"That a no?"

"Not necessarily. I take it you have a plan."

"Not yet. Not as such. The makings of one."

"It involve violence, threat and danger?"

"I'm hoping not," Mal said, "but you know how plans go."

"*Your* plans more'n most."

"Never known a little violence, threat and danger worry you, Jayne."

The big mercenary drew himself up to his full height. "Never has, never will. Inara's not done aught but right by me."

"High praise indeed," Wash muttered to Zoë.

"Figure the whore deserves a fightin' chance," Jayne said.

"Companion," Kaylee corrected him.

"Tomato, potato," said Jayne with a shrug. "I say we give it a shot. See where the line between doable and insane actually lies."

"Then it's unanimous," Mal said. "Unless, that is, you're still quibblin', Doc."

"I told you, I'm in," said Simon. "Let me just get this straight, though. What you're proposing is some kind of jailbreak."

"Yep."

"From a prison planet which, if I recall rightly, is patrolled by a number of Alliance ships."

"Yep."

"And there's no guarantee Dr. Weng is still alive. He's a medical researcher. He spends his life staring down microscopes and fiddling with centrifuges. Look at him in that picture. I can't imagine someone like that is equipped, mentally or physically, for life among vicious convicts. One of them's probably picked on him by now because he's easy prey. Taken one of those makeshift prison knives to him, what it's called?"

"A shiv," River offered helpfully.

"And stabbed him with it."

"Shanked him."

"You're up on your prison slang, River," Zoë observed.

"Never know when it might come in handy."

"Odds are Weng is dead," Simon concluded, "which makes the whole thing even more of a wild goose chase. Why aren't we considering going to Greenleaf and looking for his research data instead?"

"His lab burned down, remember?"

"But maybe he kept a copy of his notes somewhere else. At home, for example. Greenleaf's a great deal more civilized than Atata, and visiting there would get around the whole, you know, prison planet aspect of the other place."

"It did occur to me," Mal said, "and yeah, that would be a helluva lot more straightforward. But even if we did have Weng's research data, how easy do you think it'd be for us to figure it all out and cook up some of those viruses our own selves? And by 'us' I mean you, Simon."

"I *could* do it, I suppose," Simon said. "It would depend on how detailed the notes were. I'd also need all the right equipment."

"And even if you had everything necessary, how long do reckon it'd take you? Days? Weeks?"

Simon shook his head ruefully. "Months, more like."

"Inara ain't got that long. Not nearly."

Kaylee choked back a sob.

"No, Doc, time is of the essence," Mal said. "Like it or not, Atata is our best and only chance. 'Course, it's plain we can't just waltz on over there and touch down and grab the first passer-by and ask 'em where Dr. Weng is and then just whisk him away. This is one of those operations that's goin' to require a little finesse. It's also goin' to require your direct personal involvement, Doc."

"Me?" said Simon, pointing to himself.

"You."

"As in I go down onto Atata and participate?"

"As in exactly that."

"But why?"

"'Cause Weng's a doctor and so are you."

"How is that relevant?"

"It'll help when it comes to finding him."

"Do you think we in the medical profession can sense one another somehow? We have some kind of 'doctor radar' that bleeps when we're in close proximity?"

"No," said Mal, "but let's assume the worst and Esau Weng is dead. Maybe he'll have brought something with him to Atata, something that'll give us a clue to what he was working on, maybe even some of the actual viruses. You have the knowhow to be able to identify it. You're our ace in the hole."

Simon looked round at the others. Kaylee's was the last face his gaze fell on.

She fixed him with an imploring smile. "Please, Simon. The Captain's right. You're gonna have to go."

That seemed to clinch it.

"Very well," Simon said with a sigh.

Kaylee went up on tiptoe, pecked him on the cheek. "Thank you."

The blush remained on Simon's face for several minutes.

9

Commander Victoria Levine of IAV *Constant Vigilance* was a by-the-book kind of woman. She ran a tight ship and was a stickler for neatness and efficiency. Her uniform was always immaculate, not a loose thread or a button out of place, and she observed the timetable of shipboard life to the second. She had the same high expectations of her crew as she had of herself. Just because they were posted way out on the fringes of the 'verse, guarding a prison planet, there was no excuse for slovenliness.

Constant Vigilance was one of four Alliance corvettes that patrolled around Atata. Each of these large Hornet-class ships followed a set flightpath that crisscrossed its quadrant of near-world space—the same exact route, day in, day out.

It was undemanding work, no question—boring, even—and Commander Levine knew that some of the other crews regarded the posting as a bit of a joke. They lounged around, collars undone, feet up on the consoles, playing endless games of Tall Card while their ships cruised on autopilot. The crew of *Freedom to Choose* were the worst. Rumor had it they even drank while on duty.

But not Levine and her subordinates. Oh no. They had a job to do, and by heaven, they were going to do it well. If she had anything to say about it, that was; and she did.

So when a midbulk transport ship appeared on *Constant Vigilance*'s scanners, coming in on a direct heading towards Atata, Levine ran through the contact protocols exactly as she was trained to. She told her communications officer to hail the interloper on the common channel, and she addressed the ship in her most brisk, authoritative tone of voice.

"This is Commander Victoria Levine, speaking from the bridge of IAV *Constant Vigilance*. I'm talking to the Firefly-class vessel approaching on bearing two-niner-six. Please identify yourself."

The Firefly was still too far out to be distinguishable with the naked eye, a dot among the stars. *Constant Vigilance*'s external cameras zeroed in and increased magnification, bringing an image of it onto Levine's viewscreen, shaky and blurry at first, then fixed and focused.

She tutted. Shabby-looking hunk of junk. Streaks of rust and dents all over the hull. Barely seemed spaceworthy.

"I repeat, Firefly-class vessel, please identify yourself."

Still nothing. Commander Levine scowled. Lost its way? Or was there something else going on here? Whatever the Firefly's reason for straying into Atata's proximity, she could not afford to give it the benefit of the doubt. This wasn't some agrarian commune she was watching over. The planet was home to thirty-five thousand deviants, degenerates and desperados. Keeping them there, and protecting the rest of the 'verse from them, was her sworn duty.

"One last time, Firefly-class vessel. Identify yourself, or I shall be obliged to open fire."

"Uh, yeah, hi there," came the reply over the speakers. "This is Captain... Malcolm. Captain Ray Malcolm."

"Please switch to visual communication." Levine liked to see whom she was talking with. Liked to look in a person's eyes and get the measure of them that way.

A moment later, a face appeared on his videoscreen. Handsome fellow, floppy fringe, glint in his eye. Looked cocksure.

Levine did not like cocksure.

"Captain Malcolm."

"Howdy, Commander… Levine, was it? How's life in the Alliance navy treatin' you?"

Levine had no patience with small talk. "I have asked for identification. Kindly oblige."

"Sure thing," said Malcolm. "My ship is *Tranquility*. We're on a resupply run, bound for Correctional Unit #23."

Quickly Levine pulled up the schedule for deliveries. She ran an eye down the list.

"Captain Malcolm, I don't have any record of you and your vessel in my database."

She motioned to her weapons officer subtly, in a way that could not be seen on-camera. The weapons officer immediately engaged *Constant Vigilance*'s underslung cannons, training all four of them on the ever-looming Firefly.

"For that reason," she continued, "I am inviting you to turn about. This is a one-time-only request. If you do not comply, I am obliged by Alliance statutes to deploy lethal force."

"You want to try refreshing that database and checking again?" Captain Malcolm offered a slightly exasperated smile, as if to say that technology was not infallible and neither were people. "Can't believe we're not on it."

Commander Levine did not think she had made a mistake. That was not like her. Nonetheless, with a grimace of displeasure, she consulted the schedule again.

There it was. How could she have missed it the first time? *Tranquility*. Captain: one Raymond Malcolm. Due to arrive today, almost to the hour.

"Very well, Captain," she said, without a note of apology.

Commander Victoria Levine did not know the meaning of the word *sorry*. "We have you down, after all. Transmit your authorization codes."

"Transmitting."

A bright, loud *ping* from Levine's console indicated that the codes had been acknowledged by her own ship's computer and, moreover, were valid.

She punched keys to open the file containing *Tranquility*'s manifest. The ship was carrying protein bars, cleaning products, kitchenware and blankets. Sure enough, these were destined for Correctional Unit #23.

An annotation at the top of the manifest caught her eye. "You're a L'Amour Lines vessel," she said.

"That's us," Captain Malcolm said. "Flying the L'Amour flag with pride."

"I don't mean any disrespect, but usually L'Amour ships are a little..."

"Cleaner? Smarter? Slicker?"

"Well, yes."

"We get that a lot. Stanislaw L'Amour's been buying up a load of subsidiaries lately, bringing them in under the L'Amour Lines umbrella. We're independent contractors who've suddenly found ourselves working for the big boys. It's a hell of a step up, and we're doing our best not to disappoint. Speakin' of which, if you wouldn't mind, we'd be grateful if you gave us the go-ahead so's we can be on our way and get these goods on-planet. Time is money, and all that."

Levine hesitated. Everything about *Tranquility* checked out, and L'Amour Lines was one of the transportation firms the Alliance regularly employed. The company's name commanded respect.

All the same, something—some inner voice, some instinct— was telling her to beware. The situation was not quite kosher. This Captain Malcolm seemed wily.

Finally she said, "Your paperwork seems to be in order. You are cleared to proceed."

"That's mighty kind of you, Commander Levine."

"I'm beaming over your landing co-ordinates."

· Malcolm glanced down at something on his own console. "Received."

"I'll institute a remote lockdown at Correctional Unit #23, effective immediately. None of the inmates will be able to leave the main building for the next sixty minutes. The supply depot is always locked but will be opened immediately when the sixty minutes is up so that the inmates can gain access. That's your window to land, offload and take off again. I advise you not to exceed it. Correctional Unit #23 is home to some five hundred high-risk criminals, and the safety of you and your ship cannot be guaranteed if you linger."

"Understood."

"Take care down there," Levine said, "and don't catch frostbite."

It was her traditional little quip to all delivery crews. Inevitably they gave a polite chuckle in response, and the captain of *Tranquility* was no exception.

"Noted, Commander," Malcolm said, and fired her a jaunty salute. "You have a nice day." His face vanished from the videoscreen, to be replaced by an image of the AngloSino flag.

The sight of the flag's stars and bars rarely failed to instill a tingle of pride in Commander Levine. The good old red, gold and blue.

Not this time, however. This time, she was too preoccupied. As the Firefly angled itself for planetary entry, its rear-mounted engine nacelle pulsing brightly, she sat back in her chair pensively.

"Weps, stand down cannons," she said.

"Aye-aye, sir," acknowledged the weapons officer.

"XO?"

"Sir?" said the lieutenant commander who was Levine's executive officer.

"I want a dedicated surveillance lock on that Firefly. Full visual observation all the way."

"Aye-aye, sir."

Levine steepled her fingers and pressed their tips to her upper lip.

Yes. There was definitely something off-base here.

10

As *Tranquility*—a.k.a. *Serenity*—completed her entry burn and the glow from her superheated ablative hull plates faded, the landscape of Atata came into view from the bridge's forward ports.

Everything was white, interspersed here and there with smatterings of black and dark green—rocks and forest.

Wash guided the ship down through the planet's stratosphere, battling the powerful high-altitude air currents that buffeted her. Zoë was by his side, one hand on his shoulder. Mal stood next to her, leaning on the control console. At the rear of the bridge, Jayne, Simon and River clustered together. Each was grabbing onto a bulkhead or a wall fixture for support as *Serenity* slewed and yawed. Kaylee was the only crewmember absent. She remained in the engine room, making sure the ship's temperamental, sometimes downright cranky trace compression block engine behaved itself.

"Whoa mama!" Wash cried as a particularly heavy gust caught *Serenity* sidelong, sending her veering violently to starboard. "By which I mean," he added, trying to sound calmer, "that was a totally expected and in no way alarming incident of turbulence, which I handled in my usual cool, unflustered manner."

"Yeah, you did, honey," Zoë said, ruffling his hair. "I don't think anyone even noticed."

Another air current swept *Serenity* upward, then dropped her down abruptly with gut-churning speed.

Jayne's jaw was clenched, and the knuckles of the hand he was gripping the bulkhead with were white. When he caught River looking at him inquisitively, however, he put on a show of nonchalance. He even feigned a huge yawn, as if he'd never known anything as dull as this flight. River nodded and playfully pretended to yawn too. Jayne's subsequent scowl spoke volumes: he didn't understand how this strange girl's mind worked, and he didn't think he ever would.

"Should be smoothing out soon," Wash said, with an eye on the altimeter reading. "It's always better down in the troposphere, and where we're headed there's an area of prevailing high pressure. Clear skies and windless." *Serenity* jerked, juddered. "Just a couple more minutes of this, and it'll be plain sailing."

His prediction was borne out. All at once the descent became a silky glide. Wash's hands slackened their tight hold on the steering yoke. Everyone in the bridge visibly relaxed.

"Nice work," Mal said to his pilot. "Wasn't worried for a moment."

"Me either," said Wash, almost convincingly. "Just like I wasn't worried that corvette was going to blow a hole in us."

"Gotta admit, I was a mite anxious myself," Zoë said. "L'Amour told us delivery records can take a while to filter through the system, and '*Tranquility*' was very much a last-minute addition to Commander Levine's database."

"Yes," said Simon, "and if it had been too last-minute, we wouldn't be around to have this conversation."

"But we are," said Mal, "and that's that. Wash, how long till we reach our landing point?"

"Should be another ten minutes. How's it going to work when we get there?"

"Accordin' to L'Amour, every correctional unit has a dedicated supply depot located within half a mile of the main building. Cargo gets dropped there while the main building is in lockdown. Then, after the resupply ship has taken off, the inmates can go and bring the stuff in."

"There really are no wardens?" Simon said. "The prisoners run things themselves?"

"That's the system," Mal said. "Atata's privately owned. Company in charge is—surprise, surprise—the Blue Sun Corporation. They've figured they can save money on employees by, well, not employin' any. All's they have to do is the bare minimum: keep the convicts fed, warm and alive. Everything else is up to the convicts themselves."

"Isn't that a little inhumane?"

"It ain't kindly and compassionate, Doc, that's for sure. And it don't make for too happy an experience for most of those who get interned here."

"I'll bet it doesn't," Zoë said. "Your ordinary prison's bad enough, but one where the inmates make the rules?" She mimed a shudder. *Partly* mimed it, in point of fact.

"The life expectancy for the average Atata inmate isn't high," Mal said. "All manner of ways in which you can come to a sticky end. Don't get your fair share of the food and slowly starve. Cross one of the other inmates who's bigger and meaner then you and maybe has a taste for murderin'. Die of hypothermia, because the heating in the correctional units is only adequate at best."

"So it's a death sentence, getting sent to Atata," Simon said.

"Quite often, yeah."

"Seems like it'd be more merciful just to execute people."

"Price of a bullet, it'd be cheaper to as well," Jayne said.

"Hey, the Alliance doesn't want anybody to think it's completely gorramn heartless," Mal said with a wry twist of his mouth. "This here's compassion in action." He gestured at the wintry terrain below, which was growing ever closer. "And, as a bonus, they've put to use a planet no one's going to live on otherwise. Waste not, want not."

"Is everyone on Atata a lifer?" Wash asked.

"Not all," said Zoë. "When your time's up, you get returned to your homeworld. L'Amour told us that the correctional unit is put in lockdown, just like during a supply drop-off, with only sentence-served inmates allowed out. One of the Alliance corvettes swoops in. You and the other released prisoners assemble in the supply depot, and once you've passed the ID checks, you're lifted off-planet and transferred to a transport vessel in space."

"This is assuming you're still alive by that point."

"That's the deal. Make it to the end of your prison term, and you get to re-join society."

"I never realized the judicial system could be so brutal," Simon said.

"Why would you, growing up all lah-di-dah on Osiris?" said Jayne. "I'm amazed you've even heard of Atata. Guy like you, your background, if you ever got put in jail it'd be one of those cushy places, like a country club with a fence around it. And that'd be even if you'd beaten your own mother to death with a meat tenderizer. Atata's for the folk most folk would like to forget about."

"Still can't get my head around the idea of this Dr. Weng fella doing time here," said Wash. "Jayne's right. Weng doesn't seem the sort who'd rightfully belong on Atata. If his only crime was not following certain medical guidelines, why isn't he in a regular penitentiary? There's something hinky going on, if you ask me."

"I agree," said Mal, "but that's not our primary concern. The objective is retrieving Weng." He glanced outside. Jagged, snow-shrouded mountains paraded along the horizon. Directly ahead of *Serenity* was an expanse of dense coniferous forest. Everything else was sparkling white tundra. "How much further, Wash?"

Wash checked co-ordinates and airspeed and made a swift mental calculation. "Another fifty klicks. Five minutes, give or take."

"Then it's time our landing party got ready."

11

The depot was an enclosed compound, high walls crowned with razor wire surrounding a square some hundred yards across. *Serenity* descended, the downdraft from her thrusters sending snow flurrying up around her in thin, spiraling clouds that floated back to earth even as she settled on her landing gear. The depot's dimensions did not leave a great deal of wiggle room for a ship that was 269 feet long from bow to stern and had a 170-foot beam, but Wash slotted her in as neatly as a teacup into a saucer.

Serenity's engine powered down, and shortly after that her cargo ramp opened. The ramp formed a horizontal bridge to a loading dock that was sheltered by an angled awning, its floor virtually snow-free.

Wash, River and Kaylee began hauling out several dozen crates from the ship's interior, using the ship's newish Mule bike, a replacement for the one that got turned into a torpedo-on-wheels a few months back. They were able to lug the lighter crates off the Mule bike's trailer themselves. For the heavier ones, which numbered four, they took advantage of an electric chain hoist that stood on the loading dock.

The three crewmembers worked fast, exchanging few words and trying to get the job done as quickly as possible. They were clad in thermal gear—fleece-lined parkas with fur-trimmed hoods, matching pants, mittens—but still the air was viciously cold. Even through the fabric masks that covered the lower half of their faces, each intake of breath burned in their nostrils. Frost gathered on their eyebrows, making them look like old men, and the small strip of their foreheads that was exposed to the elements went numb.

With the last of the cargo deposited on the dock, Wash parked the Mule bike back aboard *Serenity*. He joined River and Kaylee at the cargo bay entrance, and together they looked out at the carefully stacked crates. The four large crates were separate from the rest, each sitting on its own.

"Don't seem right, just leavin' 'em there," Kaylee said.

"It's the plan," said Wash. "Mal knows what he's doing."

"Said no one about Malcolm Reynolds ever. They're walking into a prison! There's who knows how many crazies in that place. What if they don't make it back out?"

"They will. They have to."

"And it may all be for nothing, unless they find this Dr. Weng."

"Kaylee, it'll be okay."

"You know that for sure, Wash? 'Cause I gorramn well don't. If all this wasn't for Inara's sake…" Her lip quivered. "I can't believe she's dying. It ain't right."

River took her hand. "Don't cry."

"Too late." Tears spilled from Kaylee's eyes, freezing almost instantly to form tiny pearls on her lashes.

River stroked the back of Kaylee's neck while she sobbed silently, her chest shuddering. "I hate it when people cry," River murmured. "It's like they're bleeding see-through blood."

A siren sounded—a series of short, sharp blasts.

Then an automated announcement echoed forth from a loudspeaker mounted on the depot wall.

"ALERT. THREE MINUTES UNTIL END OF LOCKDOWN. ALERT. THREE MINUTES UNTIL END OF LOCKDOWN."

"That's our cue to go, ladies," Wash said. "Don't want to be around when the inmates turn up to collect their goodies."

He hit the switch to close the cargo ramp.

Within a minute, *Serenity*'s engine was running through its startup cycle. Within two, the ship was aloft, kicking up more snow flurries as she arose.

"ALERT. SIXTY SECONDS UNTIL END OF LOCKDOWN. ALERT. SIXTY SECONDS UNTIL END OF LOCKDOWN."

Up into the bright blue firmament *Serenity* roared.

"ALERT. LOCKDOWN ENDING IN TEN SECONDS. FIVE. FOUR. THREE. TWO. ONE."

There was an enormous *clank* as the bolts securing the depot's entrance retracted.

"LOCKDOWN TERMINATED."

12

The rumble of *Serenity*'s engine faded and silence settled over the supply depot. Minutes passed, and then one of the four heavy crates on the loading dock opened a crack. A pair of eyes peeked out.

Warily, Mal looked around the depot. The coast seemed clear.

Still, this was the dicey part. Mal was gambling on IAV *Constant Vigilance* being less attentive than its name implied. If he was wrong about that… Well, he probably wouldn't even hear the missiles that would come rocketing down from space, not until the very last second. There'd be a brief, shrill howl, an impact like God stamping His foot, and after that, oblivion.

Mal clambered out of the crate and stood stiffly upright, easing out cramped limbs and a kinked spine. He went to the nearest of the other large crates and rapped on the lid. Out came Zoë. Jayne and Simon followed in swift succession. Each of them, like Mal, was dressed in multiple layers of clothing, everything patched, ragged and torn. Scraps of cloth were wrapped around their heads to serve as scarves and mufflers; likewise around their hands to serve as gloves. This was more or less standard inmate wear on Atata, where prison jumpsuits were considered yet another expense that Blue Sun could do without.

They rearranged the contents of the crates they had lain in—

shrinkwrapped multipacks of protein bars—until it did not look as though there had been enough extra space to accommodate a person. Then they closed the lids.

"Can't hang around any longer," Zoë said. "Gotta move."

They ducked out from under the awning, making for the door. Mal yanked on the handle and rolled it open on its sliding track just far enough for them to slip through one at a time. He went last, pulling the door shut behind him.

He glanced towards the big, low cinderblock building that hulked half a mile away: Correctional Unit #23. The unit that Dr. Weng had been assigned to, according to Alliance records. A path marked with bright orange flags arrowed across the flat expanse of plain between here and there. The flags were in case of poor visibility, if fog set in, say, or a snowstorm.

As far as Mal could tell, no one had come out yet to make the journey from the depot. But that didn't mean he and the others shouldn't hurry. They had to find somewhere to hide.

So far, things had gone according to plan. It was safe—and wise—to assume that *Serenity* had been monitored every step of the way by *Constant Vigilance*, from atmo entry to landing at the depot and her subsequent departure. Their L'Amour Lines affiliation story had held up to scrutiny, but Commander Victoria Levine had sounded like the wary sort, and she'd be a fool not to keep the ship under observation.

Nothing *Serenity* had done at the depot should have aroused suspicion. Her crew had offloaded the cargo, stashing it beneath the loading dock's awning. This was where the crates were supposed to go. More importantly, it was where they could not be seen from space, the awning shielding them from an Alliance corvette's long-range, high-resolution cameras.

Constant Vigilance would now no longer be surveying the depot or its surrounding area. That was the ideal scenario.

But then a truly ideal scenario would be one in which *Serenity* hadn't encountered *Constant Vigilance* in the first place. Mal had made allowances for the eventuality of running into one of the corvettes, but it had definitely complicated matters.

He spied a stand of pines a couple of hundred yards away. Not perfect cover but good enough. He indicated to the others, and, crouching low, the foursome ran.

Reaching the pines, they settled down beneath the trees' snow-swathed branches and waited.

And waited.

And waited.

"Remind me again why this is a good idea," Jayne groused.

"It's called infiltration, Jayne," said Mal, his gaze fixed on Correctional Unit #23.

"I call it freezin' our peckers off."

"Speak for yourself," said Zoë.

"We ain't even got any guns," Jayne went on.

"You know why that is."

"'Cause we're tryin' to pass as prisoners, and prisoners don't carry guns."

"See? You *were* paying attention when I outlined the plan. Don't let anybody tell you you're no good at retaining information."

"But nothin'? Not even a knife?"

"Look, you gonna keep whining like a baby the whole time?" Mal said. "I might expect it from the Doc, but not from you. No offence, Doc."

"Some taken," said Simon. "Truth is, I'd probably be whining myself, if moving my lips weren't such an effort."

They waited some more, shivering in their makeshift cold-weather gear. Every now and then a trickle of snow sifted down from a pine bough. The sun was sinking.

"Is anyone even comin' out?" Jayne wanted to know.

"Give 'em a chance," Mal said. "They'll be mustering, gettin' themselves organized."

"We always knew we'd have to hunker down like this awhile, Jayne," said Zoë. "Ain't as if it's a surprise to you. So suck it up."

"Nobody said how long for, though," Jayne said.

"As long as it takes," said Mal. "Now please, *tiān ya*, will you shut your yap!"

More waiting, and the shivering was becoming uncontrollable. At one point, a small, white-furred mammal—something like an opossum, but with unusually enormous ears—ventured out from under a nearby rock outcrop. It sat up on its haunches, sniffing the air tentatively, those ears rotating in different directions like twin radar dishes.

"Just what in heck is *that*?" Jayne wanted to know, peering at the creature. At the sound of his voice, the animal peered back, its ears now fixed, pointing forwards. "Ain't never seen nothin' like it."

"Terrafreak," Simon said. "Must be."

"Terra-what now?"

"Genetically anomalous species that arises when the terraforming process doesn't work properly."

"Yeah, I've heard about those," said Zoë. "Weird hybrids and such."

"Ain't natural," said Jayne.

"And terraforming is?" said Simon.

The terrafreak opossum studied them with its round black eyes as though unsure what to make of them. Then, all at once, it scuttled back under the rocks for cover.

What had startled it was activity over at Correctional Unit #23. A door had opened at the building's base, and now a handful of figures emerged, nine in all. Each was huddled within bulky thermal outerwear, which made their movements somewhat clumsy, as though they were deep underwater.

"We got company," Mal said.

"'Bout gorramn time," said Jayne.

There was the faint sound of a motor starting up, and out through the doorway came a narrow, low-slung, open-topped vehicle, driven by a tenth person. It was a Slugger. Supposedly an all-purpose workhorse, the slow-moving, caterpillar-tracked Slugger was known for two things: being difficult to drive, and breaking down. Mechanics called it the masochist's machine, but some ranchers and loggers loved it. For those of a certain persuasion, its cantankerousness and unreliability were all part of its charm.

This one had a ski-mounted trailer hitched behind it. The other inmates clambered aboard the trailer, and off the Slugger went, crawling along the demarcated path towards the depot.

"Okay," Mal said. "Moment of truth."

13

Mal stood up. The other three followed suit.

To look at them, you would not necessarily think these four had arrived on Atata by ship less than an hour ago. Blue lips, frosted eyebrows and chattering teeth reinforced this impression.

Nerving himself, Mal stepped out from the trees and started waving his arms at the people on the approaching Slugger.

"Hey! Hey!" he called out.

The Slugger driver, spotting him, decelerated. The people in the trailer turned to look.

Mal waded towards them through the shin-deep snow, with Zoë, Jayne and Simon traipsing after him. They reached the Slugger just as it came to a complete halt.

"Who, in name of all that's holy, are you?" demanded the driver. He was a large man and was wearing a set of green-tinted goggles.

"Name's Mal. These here are my buddies."

"An' where in hell have you come from?" said one of the inmates on the trailer, a woman with a pinched, scarred face.

"Correctional Unit #22," Mal replied.

"You gotta be kidding," said the Slugger driver.

"Wish I were."

"That's a good two hundred fifty miles over yonder," said another inmate, a man with a chin speckled with gray stubble. "Ain't no way you've walked from there, not in these conditions. Could just about believe it if it were during the thaw season, but that ain't for another couple months."

"Nor did we," said Mal. "Had ourselves a Slugger just like yours." He gestured at the vehicle. "Got most of the way on that, 'til it up and died on us. Walked the rest. Musta traveled a good ten, twelve miles on foot, and as you can see, it's left us sore, weary and chilled to the bone. Frankly, we weren't sure we were even gonna make it."

The driver eyed them up and down. "CU #22, you say?"

"I do. Popularly known as the Big Cube."

"I heard things ain't too peachy there right now."

"You heard correctly. Part of the roof got blown off in a storm last month, and Blue Sun ain't sent nobody to fix it yet." This much was true, at least according to research River had done. She'd found a reference to the storm damage at CU #22 buried deep in a Blue Sun communiqué file, along with a note from someone high up in the corporation saying that effecting repairs was not considered a priority.

"Don't suppose they ever will," said the woman with the scarred face.

"Without a roof, the Big Cube became more like the Ice Cube. We were freezin' half to death, and us four, we decided enough was enough. Commandeered the Slugger and skedaddled for our nearest neighbors. Which is you. Wish we could've picked up some thermal gear like you have on, but we left in kind of a hurry."

"There's some mighty rough terrain between here and #22," said the Slugger driver. "It's a miracle your Slugger got you as far as it did."

"Our angels were watching over us, no doubt about it," Mal said. He held out his rag-swaddled hands importunately. "What we're hoping—praying for, even—is that you people will be angels yourselves and take us in."

The inmates looked at one another.

"Well now," said the driver, "it's not up to us. Ain't as if you're part of any official new intake, bussed in by Blue Sun. Then we'd have no choice about it. As things stand, this is a decision for Mr. O'Bannon to make."

"Mr. O'Bannon?"

"Guess you could call him our boss," said the stubble-chinned man. "Runs CU #23. Nothing happens on our block without his say-so."

"And how do we meet him?" Mal asked.

The Slugger driver cocked his head. "Tell you what. We just had some supplies delivered."

"I know. See those foot tracks there in the snow? Those are ours. Saw a Firefly come down at the depot and we were thinkin' we might try and sneak aboard. Maybe stow away, or maybe threaten the crew, persuade them it'd be in their best interests to fly us off this godforsaken snowball. Only, that didn't work on account of the depot door was locked, so we went away again and hung out among those trees."

This wasn't the story their tracks actually told, but the four sets of footprints were so muddled and messy that Mal reckoned nobody would notice they went in only one direction, away from the depot.

"Knew people'd come out of your unit eventually to pick up what the Firefly dropped off," he went on. "Thought we'd stick with Plan A and throw ourselves on your mercy."

The driver mulled things over, then said, "Well, what I'm thinking is, those supplies need to get onto this here trailer. The more hands doing the work, the quicker it'll take. Help us out, and it'll be a point in your favor. Meantime, I'll send someone back over to the block to tell Mr. O'Bannon about you. He says you can stay, then you can stay."

14

As they were transferring the crates from the depot loading dock to the Slugger trailer, Zoë briefly caught Mal's eye. Her look said what he was thinking. *We've made good progress so far, but the hard part's still to be done.*

Mal himself was wondering what sort of person this Mr. O'Bannon was and how best to deal with him. Assuming, that was, that Mr. O'Bannon gave permission for Mal and the others to enter Correctional Unit #23 at all. Otherwise their job had just become about ten times more difficult. Maybe, if necessary, they could plead their case to him and he would see reason. Then again, maybe not. Mr. O'Bannon was, after all, someone who held sway over a building filled with hardcore criminals. He was unlikely to have a caring, sensitive disposition.

At least the physical exertion of shifting crates around helped warm the four crewmembers up after that period of lying inert in the snow.

The work was nearly done when the person who had been sent over to consult Mr. O'Bannon returned. The Slugger driver relayed the verdict.

"Good news. Mr. O'Bannon says it's okay. You can stay. How

long for will depend on a lot of things, mostly how you behave. Don't rock the boat, and you should be fine."

Mal thanked him.

"Hey, don't thank me. Thank Mr. O'Bannon, when you get the chance to meet him."

A hurdle had been cleared, and Mal felt relief. He resumed hefting crates around.

Finally, with its trailer loaded, the Slugger rumbled off, retracing its journey to Correctional Unit #23. There was now no room on the trailer for people, so everyone except the Slugger driver had to follow on foot. The vehicle soon built up a lead, the gap between it and the people behind gradually widening.

As they trudged along in the grooves left in the snow by the Slugger, Mal noticed a young woman moving in close to Simon, who was walking a few paces ahead of him. Earlier, while everyone was busy with the crates, he had seen this same young woman shoot searching glances at all four crewmembers one after another, as if sizing up these strangers. She had subjected Simon to longer scrutiny than she had Mal, Zoë or Jayne, and now she was clearly making an approach.

"Hi," Mal heard her say to Simon. Her face was mostly covered up but her eyes were visible—large, long-lashed, baby blue—and Mal recognized the look in them. It was appreciative. Acquisitive, even. Just the look a young woman might direct at a handsome young man she'd taken a shine to.

"Uh, hi," Simon said.

"I'm Meadowlark. Meadowlark Deane."

"Hi, Meadowlark Deane. Meadowlark. That's a lovely name."

There was a pause, then Meadowlark said, "Ain't you going to tell me yours?"

"Yes. Of course. Sorry. It's Simon."

"Simon. I like the name Simon. Sounds dignified. Nice to meet you, Simon."

Meadowlark Deane held out a hand sheathed in a mitten, and Simon shook it.

"So," she said, "CU #22, huh?"

"That's right."

"Did you like it there?"

"Uh, no. Not really. It's jail. What's to like?"

This was far from being the wittiest thing anyone had ever said. Still, Meadowlark laughed as though it was utterly hilarious.

"You're funny, Simon."

"I am?"

"Yeah. I like a boy who can make me laugh."

"Oh," said Simon, sounding mystified. "Well, I'm glad I did."

Only a blockhead would fail to realize that Meadowlark was flirting. It seemed, however, that Simon was that blockhead. Not for the first time, Mal was amazed at how someone with so much smarts and book-learning could be so hopeless when it came to human behavior. Simon knew everything about how a person's body worked but next to nothing about how *people* worked.

"If you don't mind my asking, why're you on Atata?" Meadowlark said. "Only, by the looks of you, you aren't the average inmate."

Here we go, thought Mal. *First test of your cover story, Simon. Don't blow it.*

"I'm here for the food and the fine wine," Simon said.

Good boy. Just like we practiced. Deflect first.

"Gotcha," said Meadowlark. "'Shut up, Meadowlark. Don't be so nosy.'" She did not shut up, though. "I'm betting it's something financial. I'm good at reading people, and you don't strike me as someone who's ever, for instance, killed somebody. Not like your pal over there, the big guy." She nodded towards Jayne. "Him I can see getting hauled up on a murder rap, but not you."

"Well, I don't really like to discuss it, Meadowlark."

"But it *was* financial? I'm right?"

Simon, with a show of reluctance, nodded. "Embezzlement. I was convicted of misappropriating funds from the investment strategy firm I worked for."

"How much? Or is it impolite to ask that in embezzler circles?"

"Let's just call it 'a lot' and leave it at that," Simon said. "Thing is, I didn't actually do it."

Mal had decided that no one would buy Simon Tam as a crook, even a white-collar one. He was just too straightforward and clean-cut. Therefore he had to be the victim of a miscarriage of justice.

"It was my department manager," Simon went continued. "He was squirreling all this money away. He'd been doing it for months. I spotted some irregularities in the accounts and I realized what was going on. I confronted him, and he tried to buy me off. I said no, and that was my big mistake. The department manager went to the board of directors before I could. He made it look as though I was the one who'd been embezzling. Left a trail that led right to me. Set me up good and proper. And of course the board of directors believed him over me. He'd been with the company for years, and I was just a lowly junior."

"Don't tell me," said Meadowlark. "They ganged up on you. Really went to town."

"They said they were going to make an example of me, so that no one else would dare try to do what I did. They hired lawyers, I hired lawyers, but their lawyers were way bigger and more expensive than my lawyers. I didn't stand a chance."

"Oh, Simon." She touched his arm. Her hand lingered a fraction too long for it to be considered just a friendly gesture. "You poor thing."

Simon looked brave and resigned. He was doing a good job, Mal thought.

Better than I'd hoped. Lying doesn't come naturally to the Doc. It must be the months he's spent on Serenity. *All those scrapes we've gotten into. All those brushes with the law. It's taught him a thing or two.*

"What about you?" Simon asked Meadowlark.

"What's a nice girl like me doing in a place like this? Good question." Meadowlark tilted her chin up and to the side, as if making a show of considering. The mannerism reminded Mal of River. "Reason I ended up here is much the same as you: I pissed off the powers-that-be. I had this graffiti protest campaign going for a while, you see, on Aberdeen. 'Fed up with the Feds.' 'Screw the Al-LIE-ance,' with the emphasis on the 'lie.' Spray-painted slogans like that on walls everywhere: Alliance offices, police stations, municipal buildings, monuments. I thought it was kinda harmless, you know? Like a joke, more than anything. But the Feds didn't see it that way."

"They've never been famous for their sense of humor."

"Ha ha! Another joke, Simon. You keep making me laugh like this, I might get to thinking you like me. Anyhow, one day I was caught in the act. Charged with defacing public property. That's just a misdemeanor, and I'd've got off with a fine, maybe probation and community service. But I was also charged with 'promoting seditious anti-Alliance sentiment,' and that sank me. The state's attorney came down on me hard. It didn't help that I was disrespectful to him at the arraignment. Suggested his mother mightn't've known who his father was and that he enjoyed close relations with goats. I've always had a problem with authority figures, ever since I was a kid, 'cause I never met one who wasn't abusing their position of power or on the take or something. They threw the book at me. I couldn't believe it when the judge said 'Atata—five years.' Thought she must be kidding."

"Same at my trial," said Simon. "I assumed I'd misheard. I had to ask the judge to repeat himself. 'Atata, Your Honor?' I said. 'Are you sure?' Turns out he was. Very sure."

"Gotta say, my first few days here, it felt like a nightmare," said Meadowlark. "But you know what? It ain't so bad, once you get used to it. It's a lottery, which correctional unit you get sent to, but I was lucky. We all are at #23. Some of the units, it's a living hell, or so they say. No rules, no organization, just pure anarchy. We've got Mr. O'Bannon, though, and he's tough but fair. So long as you don't cross him, you should be okay."

Mal mentally filed this nugget of information.

Meadowlark leaned a little closer to Simon. "Stick with me, Simon, and you'll be even okayer. I mean it. I can show you around, give you some idea how things work, teach you the ropes. How's that sound?"

She fired a quick, eager wink at him, then moved away.

Simon turned to look at Mal, his eyebrows raised interrogatively.

Mal gave him a discreet nod. *You did fine.*

Simon canted his head in Meadowlark's direction.

Mal responded with another nod. *Do as she says: stick with her. She could come in useful.*

The Slugger had reached Correctional Unit #23 and disappeared inside. The procession of people behind it covered the remaining couple of hundred yards, their breath vapor wreathing around their heads in gauzy wisps.

Mal felt encouraged by Meadowlark's description of Mr. O'Bannon as "tough but fair." He thought of himself in much the same terms. Perhaps the man might be easier to handle than expected.

The building loomed over him, low but casting a lengthening shadow. Small, slot-like windows peered from its outer walls like narrowed eyes. Its concrete was dark gray and weathered, with snow and ice packing every crack and crevice. Overall, the structure radiated a sense of hostility and despair, as its architects had no doubt intended. Like a hut or a cave, it promised the bare minimum: shelter from the elements, perhaps not even that.

Above the main entrance, its official name was spelled out in whitewashed letters a foot high:

CORRECTIONAL UNIT #23

Just below, someone had added a single word. It was jaggedly etched, probably with the edge of a rock:

HELLFREEZE

Every correctional unit on Atata had a nickname. Here was #23's.

Not exactly "Shady Pines" or "Green Acres," Mal thought.

In twos and threes the group passed through the entrance. Simon, Jayne and Zoë went in ahead of Mal.

At the threshold, he paused. This was it. No going back now.

For Inara, he told himself.

With a grim set of the jaw, he followed his crewmembers inside.

A heavy door slammed shut behind them.

For Inara.

15

Back in the Black, *Serenity* clawed her way free of Atata's gravitational pull. As the planet receded behind her, its snow-covered landmasses and frozen oceans merged together, becoming indistinguishable from each other, a seamless white whole. Night was encroaching, the terminator between light and dark creeping westward.

In the ship's belly, River and Kaylee were having a heart-to-heart.

"What I don't get," Kaylee said, "is why you ain't down there with the others. You can fight. You're good in a pinch."

"Put me in, coach," River said.

"Yeah! That's it. Mal keeps you on the bench all the time, and it just seems odd."

"Secrets." River pointed to her own head.

"I know. They did stuff to your brain that no one can explain."

River frowned at her. "No. I'm not good at holding secrets inside. Secrets are like soda when you shake the bottle. They keep fizzing out. That's not helpful when you're trying to keep things back from other people."

Kaylee nodded in comprehension. "Okay. I get that. Mal and the rest want to pass themselves off as convicts. You went with them, you might say or do the wrong thing and land 'em in trouble. Makes sense. Maybe, though, if you'd gone, you could've kept an eye on Simon. Mal, Jayne, Zoë—this is their kinda gig. If it gets rough, they can handle themselves. But Simon…"

"A doctor."

"Exactly. A doctor. He fixes people, not breaks them."

"What if Mal or Jayne or Zoë needs fixing?" River said.

"There is that, I guess."

"Don't be scared for him." River reached out a hand to her.

"Ain't you?"

"My big, bad brother? Never!" River said brightly. "Simon got me out of the Academy. He was brave and he saved me. A brave saver, bravely saving."

"I worry about him still."

"That's because you love him."

Kaylee eyed her keenly. "Is it that obvious?"

"Duh!" River jeered. "I'm the one with the wibbly-wobbly brain, and *I* can see it. And he feels the same way about you, only he's too Simon to realize."

"Too Simon." Kaylee chuckled. "Yeah, that about sums it up."

"Maybe you should tell him."

"Tell him what? That this lowly ship's engineer has the hots for the fancy-pants doctor?"

"That the really pretty and really smart girl deserves a boy who's clever and kind and who'll treat her right."

"Plus good-looking. You forgot to mention how good-looking he is."

"Ewww." River wrinkled her nose. "He's my brother."

Kaylee smiled, but the smile quickly faded. "I just want 'em to come back from Atata safe and sound, River. All of them, but Simon especially. I also want 'em to get ahold of Dr. Weng and take him to Inara so's he can save her. Is that too much to ask?"

At that moment, *Serenity* began to slow. In the vacuum of

space, the ship's artificial gravity insulated those aboard her from the effects of inertia and momentum. Acceleration and deceleration could not be felt. They could be *heard*, however, through an increase or decrease in the throbbing pulse from the engine. Both Kaylee and River detected the sudden lessening in the engine's power output.

"Why're we braking?" Kaylee wondered. "I thought the idea was we were going to retreat beyond range of the Alliance ships' scanners, hold position there till we get word from Mal to return and collect him and the others. We ain't nearly far enough from Atata yet. Come on. Let's go see what Wash is playin' at."

She hurried off to the bridge, River in tow.

"Wash, what's going on?" Kaylee asked as the two of them stepped through the doorway.

"Nothing much," came the reply. "Just that."

Wash motioned across the control console towards the forward ports.

Hovering dead ahead of *Serenity* was an Alliance corvette. The silvery Hornet-class ship, with its hulking stern section and low-hung front end, had much of the intimidating sinisterness of the insect it was named after.

"It's *Constant Vigilance* again," Wash said.

"*Tā mā de*," Kaylee groaned. "What in heck do *they* want?"

"I imagine they're about to tell us. But just for your information, they have a target lock on us." He pointed to a warning light blinking on his console. "All weapons."

"Not shiny," said River, in a pitch-perfect imitation of Kaylee's voice.

16

Commander Levine looked at the Firefly that had now come to a complete stop, half a klick off *Constant Vigilance*'s bows.

She cherished moments like this. She had the full weight of the Alliance behind her. Her power was absolute.

"*Tranquility*," she said over the common channels. "Thank you for saving me the bother of telling you to halt. Might we have this conversation in visual mode?"

She was good at feigning politeness, making an order sound like a request.

"Sure," said a voice from *Tranquility*, and a moment later a face appeared on Levine's videoscreen. It wasn't Captain Ray Malcolm. It was a sandy-haired man wearing a lurid Hawaiian shirt. He looked unassuming, a bit naïve maybe. The type Levine felt she could easily intimidate.

"Hi there," said the man with an obliging but slightly nervous grin. "How can I help you, ma'am?"

"You aren't Captain Malcolm," Levine said.

"That I'm not. Name's Race. Jed Race. That's my name. Good name for a pilot. Which is what I am. Pilot of *Ser—Tranquility*."

"Where is Captain Malcolm?"

"The Captain is… indisposed right now, sir. I'm authorized to speak on his behalf."

"That's as may be," said Levine. "However, I don't wish to deal with the monkey. I wish to deal with the organ grinder. Would you do me the honor of fetching him? Right now?"

Jed Race's eyes shot furtively to one side. It was a tiny, unconscious gesture but it was a dead giveaway.

"Captain's, ah, he's having some shuteye," he said. "You really want me to wake him up? He gets all kinds of grumpy if you wake him up."

"I want you to do precisely that, and I want you to do it this instant."

"I'm just saying, he's going to take it out on someone, and that someone is going to be me. He doesn't get his full forty winks, he can be the proverbial bear with a sore head."

Commander Levine balled her hand into a fist and then, with some effort, relaxed it.

"I am surprised," she said, "that your captain has been able to retire to his sleeping quarters and nod off so soon after your ship made landfall and offloaded its cargo. That seems remarkably fast."

"Well, when you've gotta nap, you've gotta nap."

"You may not be aware, Mr. Race, but after our previous encounter I placed *Constant Vigilance* in geostationary orbit directly above Correctional Unit #23. We have been watching your ship the whole time, from descent to touchdown all the way through to liftoff and atmo exit. At the depot we saw three people offloading crates. Not one of them was Captain Malcolm."

"That's our captain. He's a talker, not a doer."

"We did not even see him supervising."

"That'll be because we're a good crew and he trusts us to get the job done without him breathing down our necks the whole time."

"I am still very keen to speak with Malcolm directly, and now," Levine said. The pilot's blithe obstinacy was starting to grate on her. She felt she had been right to accost *Tranquility* a second time. Increasingly her suspicions about the ship were, it seemed, being borne out. Its crew was up to something, although what that something might be, she had no idea.

"How's about I get him to call you later, when he's up and around again?"

"How's about this?" Levine retorted. "By the authority vested in me by the Union of Allied Planets, I hereby demand that you allow me to board your vessel with immediate effect. Failure to comply straight away with this demand will be regarded as a seditious act, punishable by the instant and fully justified use of lethal force. Hold position while we move to docking distance."

"Okay," said Jed Race hesitantly. "Just give me a second…"

17

Two minutes earlier

"Tranquility," came the voice of the commander of the IAV *Constant Vigilance*. "Thank you for saving me the bother of telling you to halt. Might we have this conversation in visual mode?"

Wash took a deep breath. "Sure," he said, and punched the button for video communication.

There, on his screen, was Commander Levine, looking if anything sterner and more purse-lipped than last time. Her military-grade buzzcut seemed to have been inflicted on her by someone who hated hair and wanted to punish it. Her eyes were as hard and gray as flint.

"Hi there," Wash said. "How can I help you, ma'am?"

"You aren't Captain Malcolm," Levine said.

Score one for eagle-eyed Commander Levine, Wash thought. *Nothing gets past her.*

"That I'm not," he said. "Name's Race. Jed Race."

Well, if Mal could have a pseudonym on this mission, so could he.

"That's my name," he added. "Good name for a pilot. Which is what I am. Pilot of *Ser*—" He caught himself. "*Tranquility*."

Damn it.

Levine didn't appear to have noticed the slip-up. Or at least, if she had, she gave no sign.

"Where is Captain Malcolm?" she asked.

"The Captain is… indisposed right now, sir. I'm authorized to speak on his behalf."

"That's as may be. However, I don't wish to deal with the monkey. I wish to deal with the organ grinder."

Hurtful, Wash thought.

So far the conversation had not gone well, and he had a hunch it wouldn't get any better.

He had best put in place a contingency plan. Just in case.

"Would you do me the honor of fetching him?" Levine said. "Right now?"

Wash fired a sidelong glance at Kaylee. Both she and River were out of shot. Levine could not see either of them.

Kaylee canted her head inquisitively.

"Captain's, ah, he's having some shuteye," Wash said, keeping his gaze steady on Levine. At the same time, he motioned with his hand, out of sight of the camera. He jerked a thumb towards *Serenity*'s aft. The engine room. Then he opened his fingers out four times in swift succession.

"You really want me to wake him up?" he went on. "He gets all kinds of grumpy if you wake him up."

At the periphery of his vision he saw Kaylee nod in understanding. She tapped River's arm, and together the two of them snuck out of the bridge.

"I want you to do precisely that," Levine replied, "and I want you to do it this instant."

"I'm just saying, he's going to take it out on someone, and that someone is going to be me. He doesn't get his full forty winks, he can be the proverbial bear with a sore head."

A flicker of irritation passed across Commander Levine's features. The woman was losing the composure she strove so hard to maintain.

"I am surprised," she said, "that your captain has been able to retire to his sleeping quarters and nod off so soon after your ship made landfall and offloaded its cargo. That seems remarkably fast."

"Well, when you've gotta nap, you've gotta nap," Wash said, keeping a smile on his face and his tone of voice upbeat. It was fun, sometimes, to irk people by being resolutely chipper. Not least when you were dealing with someone who took herself as seriously as Commander Victoria Levine did. The thicker a person's skin was, the more amusing it was to get under it.

"You may not be aware, Mr. Race," Levine said, "but after our previous encounter I placed *Constant Vigilance* in geostationary orbit directly above Correctional Unit #23. We have been watching your ship the whole time, from descent to touchdown all the way through to liftoff and atmo exit. At the depot we saw three people offloading crates. Not one of them was Captain Malcolm."

"That's our captain. He's a talker, not a doer."

"We did not even see him supervising."

"That'll be because we're a good crew and he trusts us to get the job done without him breathing down our necks the whole time."

A green light on Wash's console winked into life. This was the sign from Kaylee that she had reached the engine room and was ready.

"I am still very keen to speak with Malcolm directly, and now," Levine said.

"How's about I get him to call you later, when he's up and around again?"

"How's about this?" Levine said. "By the authority vested in me by the Union of Allied Planets, I hereby demand that you allow me to board your vessel with immediate effect. Failure to comply straight away with this demand will be regarded as a seditious act, punishable by the instant and fully justified use of lethal force. Hold position while we move to docking distance."

"Okay," Wash said. "Just give me a second…"

18

Instead of staying put, Wash stepped on the gas.

He pushed a lever on his control console all the way to its stop. He slapped a sequence of switches. He hauled back on the steering yoke.

Down in the engine room, Kaylee felt *Serenity* lurch, and immediately she yanked on a couple of handles hard.

River, taking her cue, turned a crank mounted on the engine itself, in accordance with the instructions Kaylee had given her on their way there.

Together, these operations dumped every erg of power in *Serenity* to the engine. Lights dimmed throughout the ship as the engine roared into life, going from stationary to flat-out in a split second.

This was the significance of Wash's hand signal, which Kaylee had correctly interpreted. *Serenity*'s burn rate was graded in quarter increments. By moving his fingers in an explosive pattern four times, Wash had been indicating "four quarters output" or, to put it another way, full burn. Both he and Kaylee knew the only way to achieve that from a standing start was complete power redistribution from all the ship's systems, and the only way to do *that* was by overriding the engine inputs and rerouting the flow manually.

The intense power surge put an enormous strain not just on the engine but also on the ship herself. *Serenity*'s frame shuddered horrendously, as though she was suffering convulsions. It was possible—not likely but possible—that she might even shake herself apart. At the very least the sheer amount of torque being exerted on the engine could tear the trace compression block free from its mountings, with devastating consequences.

None of the three crewmembers was ignorant of the risk they were taking. Wash and Kaylee knew *Serenity* inside out and had a clear understanding of what she was and was not capable of. River, in turn, was attuned to their thoughts; in a way, she knew the two of *them* inside out.

They just couldn't afford to be waylaid by the Feds, however. Commander Victoria Levine seemed fairly certain their captain was no longer aboard, and if she didn't know for sure, she would once she had had her junior officers search the ship from stem to stern. Whether or not she understood why "Captain Malcolm" had elected to remain on Atata, she would arrest the three crewmembers. She would also impound *Serenity*, or else just destroy her.

It was one of those fight-or-flight situations, and seeing as *Serenity* lacked ordnance of any kind, the fight option was out and all that remained was flight.

Wash felt *Serenity* buck and heave beneath him. The steering yoke juddered in his grasp. It was all he could do to keep ahold of it. *Serenity* was responding, however. Grudgingly, perhaps, and with plenty of groaning and bellyaching, but nevertheless this beautiful, battered, brave old ship was giving her all, accelerating to flank speed in a fraction of the time it ought to take. She was going to get them out of there, too fast for IAV *Constant Vigilance* to follow.

Or so Wash hoped.

First, though, he had to outmaneuver the corvette.

Instead of doing a one-eighty and turning tail, Wash flew straight at *Constant Vigilance*. At the very last instant, mere meters from impact, he heeled *Serenity* over on her longitudinal axis. She careered past the Alliance vessel, so close her underside practically brushed the corvette's starboard thruster array.

. It was the last thing Commander Levine would have been expecting, and Wash was counting on her being too startled to react right away. That crucial few seconds of delay might be enough to buy them their freedom. *Constant Vigilance* could give chase, but by the time it had come about and attained maximum speed, *Serenity* would have opened up too large a lead to be caught.

Still shuddering, still straining, her tail end blazing like a comet, *Serenity* rapidly put distance between herself and *Constant Vigilance*. Wash allowed himself a small whoop of triumph. They were going to make it. In just a few more seconds they were going to be out of range of the corvette's weapons.

There was going to be hell to pay for this little stunt, he knew. Several of *Serenity*'s parts were likely going to get burned out by the power surge, and Kaylee would be repairing the damage for hours if not days afterwards.

But as long as they got away and were able to return later to collect the landing party, he would count it as a win.

"Eat my dust, Feds!" he chortled.

Then a large red light on his console started flashing. It was accompanied by, of all things, the sound of a duck quacking.

"Oh no," Wash breathed. "Oh, no, no, no, no, no. *Wǒ de mā hé tā de fēng kuáng de wài shēng*, please tell me this isn't happening."

The red light was a fitted-as-standard console fixture. The duck quacking was a recent customization Wash had made himself. He'd thought it amusing at the time, a zany sound effect to lighten a tense moment. Now that that moment had arrived, however, the quacking just seemed ridiculous and inappropriate.

What these two indicators—visual and aural—signified was

that *Constant Vigilance*'s weapons lock on *Serenity* had gone from passive to active.

The Alliance vessel had opened fire.

Wash checked the rear proximity sensor readout.

Missiles.

Three of them.

Closing in fast, in tight formation.

Wash was not very religious. He prayed sometimes, not often, and usually only in situations like this, when his ass was on the line.

He prayed now, harder than he had ever prayed before. He prayed that *Constant Vigilance*'s targeting solution was incorrect. That one or more of the missiles might be a dud. That all of them would run out of fuel before they reached *Serenity*.

But prayer did not always solve everything. Sometimes you had to take matters into your own hands.

Wash threw *Serenity* into a series of tight barrel rolls. She spun, leaving a corkscrewing trail of phosphorescence in her wake.

As the missiles homed in, their onboard computers strove to adapt to their target's abnormal behavior. The software made countless minute course corrections. The missiles' flightpaths shifted and shifted again, until all at once, perhaps inevitably, the tailfin of one touched the tailfin of another.

Instantaneously the two projectiles whirled out of control, colliding with each other. A huge, silent burst of fire, and they were gone.

That left the third missile, still relentlessly pursuing *Serenity*.

The rear proximity sensor readout informed Wash that two of the missiles were down. It also registered that the third was gaining ground with each passing second. Barrel-rolling wasn't going to help any, not now. A lone missile couldn't exactly collide with itself, could it?

He leveled *Serenity* out. There was one other trick he could try. He just had to get the timing exactly right.

Not yet.

Not yet.

Now!

Hauling back on the yoke, Wash put the ship into an Immelmann turn. *Serenity* veered up and round until she was heading back the way she had come, inverted. Wash flipped her over. Now she was making straight for *Constant Vigilance*.

The tenacious missile followed the same trajectory. It was a couple of hundred yards from *Serenity*'s aft, dangerously close, but also just where Wash wanted it.

Serenity and *Constant Vigilance* zoomed towards each other at a combined speed of 2,000 miles per hour, give or take a hundred. The gap between them narrowed precipitously. Within a matter of seconds, one ship would be almost on top of the other.

Wash knew Commander Levine had no choice. It was too late for evasive maneuvers. *Serenity* had brought with her the missile like a dog on a leash, and it was about to hit. At this rate, the missile would blow up *Serenity* when she was directly adjacent to *Constant Vigilance*. The corvette would get caught in the blast, and the collateral damage would be extensive, potentially catastrophic. Levine had to abort the missile.

Essentially, Wash was wagering his, Kaylee's and River's lives against Levine's sense of self-preservation.

"Do it," he said through gritted teeth, as if addressing Levine. "Do it."

In the event, Commander Levine did something else.

19

Twenty seconds earlier

"Sir," said *Constant Vigilance*'s lieutenant commander, "that *qīng wā cāo de liú máng* has about-turned and is coming straight at us."

"I can see that, XO," replied Commander Levine, "and there's no call for profanity. I will not abide foul language on my ship."

"Yes, sir. Sorry, sir."

"Sir, what should we do?" asked the weapons officer.

There was precious little time to decide. Levine understood fully what Jed Race was attempting. It was sheer lunacy. It was bold as hell. *Tranquility*'s pilot was clearly gutsier than he looked, not to mention trickier.

"Should we abort missile, sir?" the weapons officer prompted.

"No," said Levine. "Detonate prematurely."

The weapons officer, knowing better than to question orders, entered the detonation command on his console.

The missile exploded a dozen yards behind the Firefly, while the Firefly itself was virtually the same distance from *Constant Vigilance*.

The blast wave propelled the Firefly forward. She hurtled round and round, careering into *Constant Vigilance* belly-first and rebounding.

The impact boomed through the Alliance ship like some sort of apocalyptic gong. Everyone aboard was hurled sideways.

As Levine picked herself up off the floor of the bridge, she demanded a status report. Alarms were wailing. Every console screen she could see was flashing a warning or caution of some kind.

"No hull breach, sir."

"Thrusters one and two have taken a pounding, sir. Both are down."

"Engine room reports fuel core leak, sir."

The viewing ports showed that, outside, space was spinning. *Constant Vigilance* had been sent into a spiral by the collision.

"Do we have power to correct our rotation?" Levine asked.

"Afraid not, sir. Controls are temporarily offline. System is rebooting."

"As soon as they're back up, straighten us out."

"Aye-aye, sir."

Levine had known it would be a close call, detonating the missile when the Firefly was so near *Constant Vigilance*. She had been hoping at least to cripple the other ship. In the event, through what she considered to be sheer bad luck, the Firefly had crippled hers, albeit temporarily.

It had undoubtedly paid a price for that, however. *Tranquility* could not have emerged from the clash of the two ships unscathed. It was the smaller of the two vessels, and the less well-armored.

In fact—a consoling thought for Levine—although things might be bad for *Constant Vigilance*, they were surely much, much worse for the people aboard *Tranquility*.

20

The thing about *Serenity* was, she was old, yes. She was beaten-up, yes. And yes, she had about eighty million space miles on the clock, well above average for a ship of her class.

But she was also built to last.

She skimmed *Constant Vigilance* more than struck, taking the brunt of the blow on her underside, her best-reinforced section. She now had several fresh dents and scrapes to add to her collection, but remained fundamentally intact.

She bounced away from the collision, cartwheeling end over end.

Inside, the artificial gravity held, but still everything was chaos. As Kaylee and River staggered to their feet in the engine room, circuits around them were blowing, showers of sparks were flying, and the engine itself was making some very unhappy grinding and shrieking noises.

"*Tì wǒ de pi gǔ,*" Kaylee gasped. "What the heck just happened? Did something just hit us?"

"*We* just hit *something,*" said River.

Dazedly, Kaylee took stock of the state of the engine room. A number of small fires had started. They were the most urgent problem, and she grabbed the fire extinguisher off the wall and attended to them.

Out of the corner of her eye she noticed River heading for the door.

"River, a little help here! I need you to disengage the transmission vector connection and harness the ancillary drive. I'll talk you through it."

"Can't," River said. "Wash."

"What about Wash?"

"He's hurt."

Kaylee didn't ask how River knew. She just said, "Okay. Go see to him," and carried on directing a stream of carbon dioxide from the fire extinguisher's nozzle at the various blazes, which were proliferating. Once they were out, she could turn her attention to the engine. It was in serious danger of overheating, and by disengaging the transmission vector connection and harnessing the ancillary drive she could give it a chance to cool down and recover.

Wash was hurt.

She hoped with all her heart that it wasn't too serious. As well as being an incomparable pilot, Wash was the kindest, gentlest person on the ship. If he was badly injured…

Or worse…

Kaylee bit her lip and focused on the matter at hand.

21

River hurried through the ship, skipping over dislodged items on the floor—crates, bits of furniture, tools—and ducking under lengths of duct and cable that had broken loose from their mountings.

In the bridge, Wash sat slumped in the pilot's chair, arms dangling. Blood poured from a gash in his forehead, covering half his face. Next to him lay a section of cladding, one edge of it also bloodied. The piece of heavy steel had clearly fallen from the ceiling, straight onto him.

River checked his carotid and found a pulse. It was thready and irregular, but it was there. Wash was alive but unconscious, out for the count.

And *Serenity* needed someone to fly her.

River could see IAV *Constant Vigilance* out there. As *Serenity* twirled through space, the Alliance vessel appeared in the forward viewing ports at regular intervals, sweeping into and out of sight. It was in a spin too, and was getting further and further away. River noted damage to a couple of its thrusters and also the little expulsions of glowing plasma from its emergency vents that spoke of a fuel leak. For now, *Constant Vigilance* was dead in the water. But for how long?

Hornet-class corvette. Standard engine reboot cycle under ideal conditions: two minutes. Add another eight or so for isolating the leaking fuel cell and diverting power away from the damaged thrusters.

That meant *Serenity* had a window of ten minutes in which to make a clean getaway, moving beyond *Constant Vigilance*'s scanner range.

Taking hold of Wash by the shoulders, River hauled him out of the chair. She might be slight of stature but she was strong and she knew how to use her muscles in order to distribute a load evenly and efficiently across her entire body. *Recruit the abdominals. Lift with the legs.* She lowered the dead weight of him to the floor, then knelt and tore a strip of fabric off his shirt. She wrapped this tightly around his head, creating a pineapple-patterned bandage. It wouldn't stop the bleeding—*blood flows freely from head wounds*—but it would slow it down.

Then, hopping into the pilot's chair, River performed a swift analysis of the controls.

To look at her, you might have thought she resembled a bird, the way her head darted this way and that, her eyes alighting on the screens, buttons and switches one after another. Nothing on any of the consoles was strange to her. She had watched Wash fly the ship countless times, taking in everything he did and storing it in her memory. Now, she was simply refamiliarizing herself. River's brain was like an infinite warehouse. It could hold pretty much everything that was put into it, and she could retrieve the information at will. There were some things in there she couldn't even remember learning. There were also some things that, try as she might, she couldn't forget.

For the time being, *Serenity* still had enough juice left to get them clear of the area. Ignoring the warning messages that glared on every screen in front of her, River goosed both of the main thrusters. By angling them and calibrating their output carefully, she managed to retard the ship's spin. *Serenity* stabilized, her long series of somersaults at an end.

River hit the intercom switch. "This is Pilot River at the helm," she said, affecting an authoritative baritone drawl like that of a spaceliner captain. "I have the ship and I'm getting us the heck out of Dodge. Copy."

A moment later, Kaylee's voice came from the speaker. "River, we can't fly yet. We need to shut down the engine awhile first."

"That's a big negative, Engineer Kaylee. We have one shot at escaping and we've got to take it. Can you maintain power while we do? Copy."

"I can," came the hesitant reply. "*Serenity* won't like it, but I can."

"Then kindly oblige."

"Okay. River, what's happened to Wash? How is he?"

"Pilot Wash is temporarily out of action."

"But he's gonna be all right?"

"That's an affirmative."

"Thank God. And—hate to ask—but are you sure you can fly the ship?"

"Sure as shootin', li'l lady."

River broke the intercom connection and closed her fingers around the steering yoke's twin handles.

"You and me again, *Serenity*," she said, resuming her usual voice. Her tone was soft, almost loving. "I'm not on you. I am in you. I *am* you. River's gone."

She tapped the throttle.

"Let's fly."

22

All things considered, it could have been worse.
      A lot worse.

You couldn't forget that Correctional Unit #23 was a prison block. There were rows of cells, each with bars and a sliding door. They occupied two balconied tiers that surrounded a central hall and were connected to one another by skeletal metal stairs and walkways. All this was unquestionably prison-like, as was the fact that every item of furniture, from bunks to tables, was bolted down. The lighting was harsh, too, most of it shed by recessed fluorescents which seemed designed to leave no corner in shadow, although some additional, gentler illumination came from a large pyramidal skylight through which the last fading glow of the day filtered down.

In short, you would never mistake the place for a health spa, say, or a five-star hotel.

It was warm inside, however. Relatively, at least. Outdoors it must have been ten degrees below. In here, it was perhaps a smidgeon above zero. Positively tropical.

It was quite peaceful, too. There was the background clatter and clamor of five hundred people going about their business in an enclosed space, the occasional shout, the odd guffaw, the shuffle of footfalls; but nobody was arguing and nobody was berating or threatening anybody. The aggression levels were low to nonexistent. In fact, the atmosphere in CU #23 seemed subdued overall, as if people were nervous about stepping out of line even though there were no guards around to keep an eye on them and punish rule-breakers.

Mal had never done jail time. This was not for want of trying. He had just never got caught. He had served a spell or two in police custody, however, not least during his hellion days on Shadow. As a tearaway youth he'd had numerous run-ins with his nemesis Sheriff Bundy, who was what passed for a lawman in Seven Pines Pass, Mal's hometown.

Nonetheless he had a fairly good idea of what a prison was usually like, thanks to first-hand accounts he'd picked up from ex-cons he had met over the years. A prison was noise and rage, twenty-four seven. It was jeers and catcalls, and the stench of sweaty bodies and bad food. It was the ever-present possibility of violence, like a stew of pent-up aggression ready to boil over at any moment. It was constantly watching your back and doing your best not to provoke any of your fellow inmates. It was a minefield, a cat's cradle of tripwires, where any misstep could be your last.

Here, in the building its inhabitants had dubbed Hellfreeze, there was none of that. There was a sense of, if not calm, then docility. Mal had observed this as soon as he entered the premises, from the way that people had gathered around the Slugger trailer and begun removing the crates in an orderly fashion, opening them up and carting the contents off to various destinations elsewhere in the building. Everyone seemed to know what was expected of them, and did it diligently. And as he and the other three crewmembers proceeded through the correctional unit, led by the stubble-chinned man and the woman with the scarred face, nothing he saw contradicted his initial impression.

Whoever this Mr. O'Bannon was, he'd got people here firmly under his thumb. Mal wondered whether the man was loved or feared as a leader. Most likely it was a combination of the two, that special, heady cocktail of adoration and obeisance which dictators had relied on down through the centuries.

The two inmates showed the newcomers to a pair of adjacent, empty cells, each with a steel-framed double bunk bed, a sink and a lidless porcelain commode.

"Make yourselves at home," said the stubble-chinned man. "We'll see about gettin' you some bedding."

"Dinner's at eight sharp," the woman with the scarred face added. She pointed towards an exit leading off from the central hall. "Refectory's through there. Just follow the crowd."

"And Mr. O'Bannon himself?" Mal asked. "I'm curious to meet the boss. That gonna happen any time?"

Mal wasn't actually that keen on making Mr. O'Bannon's acquaintance, but it might be advisable to introduce himself to the guy and maybe cozy up to him. In fact, it might arouse suspicion if the four of them, as guests in this little penal kingdom, *didn't* seek an audience with its king.

"You'll meet him when he's good and ready to meet you."

"And when might that be?"

"Ain't for us to decide," said the stubble-chinned man. "Mr. O'Bannon does things in his own way and in his own time."

"You'll tell him we'd like to make his acquaintance, though? To say thanks, if nothin' else."

"For sure," the woman with the scarred face said. She and her companion turned to leave.

Mal motioned to Simon. *Go ahead. Now's your chance.*

Simon cleared his throat. "Excuse me."

"Yeah?" said the stubble-chinned man.

"As I recall, there's a friend of mine who's… resident here."

"That so?"

"Yes. I mean, I could be wrong, but I'm fairly certain he ended up in #23. It's one of the reasons we decided to come to this unit rather than any other. Familiar face and all that."

"What's the fella's name?"

"Weng," Simon said. "Esau Weng."

At that, the stubble-chinned man and the woman with the scarred face seemed to flinch. Each darted a worried look at the other, before the stubble-chinned man turned back to Simon. Leaning in close, he hissed, "Listen to me, pal, and listen good. I'm going to pretend I never heard you say what you just did, and if you're wise *you'll* pretend you don't know that person whose name you mentioned. You don't speak about him to anybody. You don't refer to him ever again. This is the one and only time I'm gonna tell you this. Okay?"

The change that had come over the two inmates was startling. In a flash they had gone from comparatively hospitable to downright frosty. And not just that. Mal thought they looked scared. It was as though the words "Esau Weng" were a curse or something.

"Okayyy," Simon said.

Without another word, or even a backward glance, the stubble-chinned man and the woman with the scarred face strode away.

23

"Can someone explain to me what all that was about?" said a perplexed Jayne. "Those two just ran off like a coupla scalded cats, and all 'cause the Doc asked 'em about Weng. That ain't natural behavior."

"You'd think Weng had murdered their first-born or something," Zoë chimed in.

"It's as if his name's taboo," Simon observed.

"Don't look at me," Mal said, as their gazes turned on him. "I thought if Simon was the one inquiring about Weng—guy acting and sounding the way Simon does—it'd be plausible. They'd just go, 'Esau Weng? Oh yeah, you *would* know him. Head down that corridor, take the first right, fourth cell along, can't miss him.' There's somethin' funny going on here, that's for damn sure."

"They *had* heard of him, though," Zoë pointed out. "So at least we're on the right track."

"What's the play now, Mal?" Jayne asked. "If we're not supposed to mention Weng's name to anyone, how're we gonna find him?"

"We know what he looks like. That's a start."

"There's a good five hundred folks to choose from."

"Around a third of whom are female," Zoë pointed out, "so we can count *them* out."

"I guess our best bet is to mooch around looking for him," Mal said. "What we don't want to do is make it *look* like we're looking. Don't know if you've noticed, but our welcome here wasn't super enthusiastic and we're on kinda shaky ground. We act like we're anything other than we say we are, it's liable to get us thrown out on our asses, or worse. So we have to be discreet."

"Discreet," said Jayne. "I can do that."

Mal tried to keep the skepticism from showing in his face. "Whyn't we do this in pairs? You and Zoë, Jayne. Me and the Doc."

"Seems reasonable," said Jayne. "I'm just glad to be gettin' on with this. I don't know about you all, but I'm eager not to hang around a moment longer'n I have to. There's somethin' about jail that don't sit well with me. Maybe on account of it's, y'know, jail, which is somewhere I've always been at pains to avoid endin' up."

They split up, Zoë and Jayne heading one way, Mal and Simon the other.

"Try not to rubberneck, Doc," Mal said in a low voice as they walked along the row of cells. "Remember, you've already been doing a stretch at Correctional Unit #22. None of this is new to you."

"Got it."

Nonetheless Mal himself found it difficult not to stare. Some of the cells they passed were bare and unadorned, but in others the occupants had attempted to make them look a little more homely. Sheets had been hung up as screens. Pictures had been sketched on walls in charcoal, some crudely rendered but others showing considerable artistic merit. In one cell they spied one man adorning another with a tattoo, using a paperclip and ink that was most likely made from soot mixed with shampoo. In another, a mother was nursing an infant.

Down in the central hall there was a workout area where some very large individuals were lifting dumbbells made out of rocks and rebar. Their grunts of effort were punctuated by the thud of the makeshift weights being returned to their rests. There were also several games of checkers going on, with homemade boards and slivers of bottle cork standing in for pieces.

Now and then an inquisitive look came Mal and Simon's way. It was clear word of the refugees from #22 had already got around, so their presence was not challenged. Still, their faces were unfamiliar, worth a second glance.

Nowhere did Mal spy the mild, unworldly features of Dr. Esau Weng.

Then someone came sidling up to them.

"Hey, Simon."

It was the girl from before, Meadowlark Deane. Now that she was no longer wrapped up against the cold outdoors, her face bare, Mal could see that she was very pretty indeed. She had a pert little snub nose to go with those big, blue eyes, and her smile was broad and guileless. Of course, she wasn't showing any interest in *him*. Her attention was on Simon exclusively.

"Meadowlark," Simon said.

"How are you finding it?"

"It's not like #22, that's for certain."

"I know, right? We have it good here. Some of the other correctional units, they're, like, *zoos*. In particular, if you're a woman in one of those, you've got to be prepared to fight tooth and nail to protect yourself, or you're going to get crushed. Here, Mr. O'Bannon won't tolerate aggression of any kind. He says we're all equals, and anyone who abuses or molests anyone else is going to regret it."

"He sounds like a terrific fellow."

"You won't get any disagreement from me," said Meadowlark. "Say, do you want me give you the guided tour?"

"Uh…"

"Come on!" Meadowlark linked her arm with his. "It'll be fun."

Simon looked at Mal.

"You go right ahead," Mal said. It was evident that Meadowlark's invitation did not include him. "I don't mind."

"But shouldn't we arrange to meet up again somewhere?" Simon said to Mal. Meadowlark was already dragging him away.

"Dinnertime. The refectory."

Mal offered Simon a discreet little nod. Looking over his shoulder, Simon returned it. He'd got the hint, Mal thought. Maybe Meadowlark Deane would be willing to reveal something about Dr. Weng when no one else would. Being as she was so obviously smitten with him, Simon had leverage over her, and he should use it.

24

Meadowlark Deane was certainly talkative.

As she escorted Simon around Correctional Unit #23's kitchen, its food store, its communal bathroom, its poorly stocked library, and the room that housed its geothermal power plant, she gabbled away, scarcely pausing for breath. She seemed on friendly terms with everyone they encountered, and introduced Simon at every opportunity. He got the sense that not only was she showing him around, she was showing him *off*.

This was, in its way, quite flattering. There was no denying Meadowlark was attractive. But it was also problematic. Simon had done nothing to encourage her interest, and he definitely didn't want any romantic entanglement while he and the crew were on a mission. Especially not this mission, with Inara's life at stake.

Then there was the small matter of Kaylee Frye. She and he weren't lovers, that was for sure, but there was *something* going on between them. Simon couldn't put his finger on what it was exactly, but it existed and it was undeniable. Kaylee was unlike any of the women he had gone out with back on Osiris. His dates, from his college years onward, had been educated, professional types, respectable, cultured. He had never been in a relationship with a woman he felt his parents might disapprove of. Kaylee was different. He could imagine how Gabriel and Regan Tam would respond if he ever had the opportunity to bring her home to meet them. They would be incredibly polite, they would feign interest as Kaylee explained what her job as a ship's engineer involved, they would pretend to be enchanted by her lack of sophistication—and then afterwards they would make it plain to Simon that they had no interest in seeing her again and neither should he. The Tams employed people like Kaylee; they did not socialize with them.

Not that that meeting was likely to happen. Simon had burned all bridges with his past, including with his family. He had thrown away his career as a trauma surgeon, his entire future, all for River's sake, and now he was a… He wasn't even sure what he was. Part of a band of outcasts and reprobates who roved the 'verse, scrabbling to make a living and getting embroiled in various harebrained escapades. Like this one.

The one redeeming feature of the whole situation Simon found himself in, aside from the fact that it protected River from the authorities, was Kaylee. She was beautiful, lively, intelligent, and so cheery in her outlook that at times being with her was like basking in warm sunshine. Even when she was down—and Inara's plight had certainly brought her low—you had the sense that she was still striving to find the positive in it. So many times Simon wished he could just get over himself and tell her how he felt.

Meadowlark Deane definitely reminded him of Kaylee. The enthusiasm, the talking, the way her eyes lit up when she looked at him. But it wasn't as if anything was going to happen between the two of them. Simon anticipated being on Atata for a day at most. As soon as the crew found Dr. Weng, they'd be gone; and by the same token, if they couldn't locate Weng anywhere in Correctional Unit #23, or they discovered that he was dead, they would beat a hasty retreat. Mal would send an alert beacon to *Serenity* using the tiny mid-range transceiver he was carrying, and Wash would swoop in and scoop them up.

Meadowlark was just a distraction, that was all. A sidetrack.

An interesting one, though. Simon rather liked being the center of her attention. He wasn't a vain man, but it was nice when a woman took a fancy to you and made no secret of it.

The guided tour wound up at the laundry, where work had just finished for the day. The smells of steam and washing powder still hung in the air. Freshly pressed sheets were heaped in hampers, while folded clothing lay in neat stacks.

Meadowlark cast a glance around the room. "Okay, everyone's gone. Coast's clear. Can I show you something?"

"Uh, sure."

"But you gotta keep it a secret. Swear?"

"All right."

"Say 'I swear.'"

"I swear."

"Cross your heart."

"And hope to die," Simon said, making an X shape over his sternum.

"Wouldn't want *that*," Meadowlark said with a small smile.

She reached between the wall and the back of one of the dryers. There was a loose section of paneling which she worked free, revealing a hole. Squeezing herself behind the dryer, she slid into the hole, then beckoned to Simon.

"It's fine, honest," she said. "Come on. You'll like this."

A touch hesitantly, Simon followed her into the hole.

He found himself in a crawlspace roughly two feet wide, with sufficient headroom as long as he crouched. Large metal pipes ran above. There were blankets and pillows on the floor, piled up to form bedding like at the bottom of a hamster cage.

"What is this?" he said. "Some kind of burrow?"

"That's exactly what it is," said Meadowlark delightedly. She pulled the section of paneling back into position. A tiny bit of light crept in around its edges from outside, just enough to see by. "My private little burrow. Warm, isn't it?"

It was, if not balmy, then plenty warmer than anywhere else Simon had been in Correctional Unit #23.

"These pipes carry heated water straight from the geothermal plant," she said, sitting down cross-legged and inviting Simon to join her. "Smells a bit as well, I know. Like sweaty clothes? That's 'cause the drain outlets from the dryers run through here too, and one of 'em's got a leaky seal."

There was a distinctly musty odor, that was for sure, although it reminded Simon less of sweaty clothes and more of rancid food.

"You sleep here?" he asked.

"Sometimes. I've got a cell, of course, but my cellmate—well, she snores. I mean, *really* snores. Like a chainsaw. So most nights I sneak out and come here and get all cozy. Sleep like a baby."

"I didn't realize you can leave your cells at night."

"Can't you at #22?"

"No, uh, we get locked in. Curfew at nine sharp every evening."

"Well, not all correctional units are the same," said Meadowlark with a shrug. "Another reason to be grateful for Mr. O'Bannon. He trusts us to behave."

"Presumably there are consequences if you don't."

"Oh yeah. But seeing as everyone knows what they are, we don't care to invite them on ourselves."

"And what are they, these consequences?" Simon asked. "After all, if Mr. O'Bannon lets me and my friends stay, we ought to have some idea of the rules."

Meadowlark pondered her response. "Put it this way. Mr. O'Bannon has this bunch of goons. There's, like, six, seven of them. He calls 'em his Regulators, and they hang around with him all the time. You get out of line, and they'll come down on you hard."

"How hard?"

"It's on a sliding scale. The punishment suits the crime. Like, if two people get into a fight, the Regulators will break it up then beat up both of 'em. You attack somebody, they'll take you off somewhere and bust a bone, maybe a couple of bones. You kill somebody… Well, you get the picture. So if you're thinking of killing anybody, Simon, my advice to you is be very careful about it. I'm kidding, by the way. You aren't the killing type."

"No, I'm not."

Things were already quite snug in the crawlspace. Now Meadowlark butt-shuffled herself even closer to Simon, pressing herself against him.

"You are just so not like anyone else on Atata," she said. "It's refreshing. You're clearly smart, and you've got this—this *openness* about you. I feel I can talk to you about pretty much anything."

Simon chose his words carefully. "Is there really no one else like me in CU #23?"

"Really. You're special, and I'm the one you've singled out to get close with, and that makes me feel special too."

He could have debated her interpretation of events. Had *she* not singled *him* out? Instead he said, "It's just… I'm thinking about somebody I know. Somebody I'm convinced ended up in #23. A friend of mine."

"Another embezzler like yourself?"

"No. This guy is a doctor."

"We don't have any doctors at Hellfreeze, that I'm aware of. I mean, there was that one fella who got on the wrong side of Mr. O'Bannon. This was a few weeks back, not long after I got sent to Atata, and as I recall…" Meadowlark abruptly broke off, shaking her head.

"As you recall…?" Simon prompted.

"Nuh-uh. My mistake. Don't know what I was saying. Must've

been confused. There's never been any doctor at #23. Leastways not while I've been an inmate."

"But you just said…"

"I was talking about some guy who got on the wrong side of Mr. O'Bannon, yeah, but now that I think about it, he wasn't a doctor. He had 'Dr.' in front of his name, but he wasn't a *doctor* doctor. He was a dentist. That's what he was. A doctor of teeth."

"Are you quite sure about that?"

"Simon." A hardness had entered Meadowlark's voice. "If I tell you there's never been a doctor at Hellfreeze, there's never been a doctor at Hellfreeze. It's a fact, and you'd best remember it."

Simon wondered how far he could push this. If Meadowlark liked him as much as she appeared to, there was a good chance he could convince her to open up. He didn't credit her excuse about a dentist for one second. She had quite evidently been referring to Dr. Weng but had remembered that she was under constraint not to talk about him, just like the two inmates earlier.

It wouldn't hurt to show her a little affection, would it? Openly reciprocate the attraction she was showing towards him. Soften her up that way.

"Meadowlark." He spoke her name tenderly, with a smile. "I've got to say, meeting you… For the first time since they dumped me on Atata, I'm not feeling like I'm completely alone."

Her face brightened. "You mean it? Because I feel that way too."

He felt terrible doing this. Meadowlark was naïve, needy. He shouldn't be manipulating her like this. Yet he had to.

"I do mean it," he said. "There's something… The way you homed in on me when we were walking behind the Slugger. It's like we were drawn to each other."

"Oh my God. Yes, Simon. That's just how it was. Like we were made for each other."

"Yes." Guilt was welling up inside him, twisting his stomach in knots. He forced himself to think of Inara. This was all for her. Toying with Meadowlark's emotions was wrong, but if it helped with finding Dr. Weng, that made it justifiable. Just about. "Is it crazy to think that way?"

"Crazy, but who cares?" said Meadowlark. She was beaming from ear to ear now. "Maybe, together, we can make Atata make sense. You and me, Simon. The two of us can be like our own little boat and we'll weather any storm."

"I'd like to feel that we'd never have any secrets from each other."

Was that too much? Had he overplayed it?

Meadowlark was now pressed up against him so tightly that her breath caressed his face. "No," she said, the word as soft as a sigh. "No secrets. I'd love that. I'd know everything about you, and you'd know everything about me. Oh, Simon. You're such an open, trustworthy guy. I knew that, soon as I set eyes on you. Makes me mad how your company treated you. But then that's only to be expected. I told you I have a problem with authority figures, didn't I?"

"Uh, yes. You mentioned it."

"What it really is," she said, "is I have a problem with dishonesty."

"How does that relate to authority figures?"

"Oh come on, Simon! They're the most dishonest people of all. We're supposed to trust them, because they're in charge, they're theoretically the best of us—and yet they always lie. They always let us down."

"Well, I suppose quite a few of them do."

"Your department manager did. Your board of directors did."

"I guess so."

"And that's typical of authority figures. For instance, there was this Shepherd I knew in the town where I grew up, back on my homeworld Salisbury. Handsome fella, he was, and he preached righteousness and morality, and he did it with fire and fervor, and to look at him you'd think he was the noblest, holiest, most upstanding man you'd ever met. But you know what? All along he was carrying on with a local woman, a married one, behind her husband's back. It was like this open secret. Everybody in town knew—except maybe the husband himself, who'd always been kinda slow on the uptake—but nobody did a thing about it. Nobody called the Shepherd on it. He just went on doing it, betraying God's word, the same word he hammered on about from his pulpit every Sunday. Hypocrite in a back-to-front collar was what that man was."

She spoke with frank disgust.

"What happened to him?" Simon asked. "Did he get found out? Tarred and feathered? Run out of town on a rail?" On a backwater planet like Salisbury—famed for the export of a fertilizer product based on bat guano, and not much else—it wasn't impossible that residents of some small, remote community would dish out summary justice.

"Not really," said Meadowlark. "He did get what was coming to him, though, in a way. There was this bum who'd been hanging around town for weeks, causing trouble. Big, mean drunk. He broke into the chapel one night, hoping to steal the communion wine. The Shepherd caught him in the act, and the bum killed him. Cut his throat."

"Oh. Poor guy."

"What's that?"

"I said poor guy. The Shepherd. So, okay, he shouldn't maybe have committed adultery. But the way you put it, it's as though getting killed by a hobo was some kind of divine retribution. As though he got his just desserts. Whereas in fact it was senseless murder, nothing more, nothing less. What is it, Meadowlark? Why are you looking at me like that?"

Her face was creased up, her eyes narrowed. It took Simon a moment to realize that she was furious with him.

"Why would you say such a thing?" she snapped.

"Say…? I was only… I mean, I just think you're being a mite hard on the Shepherd, is all. He did something wrong, sure, but he's only human. Nobody's perfect."

"He should have gone on lying to us, is that it?" Meadowlark growled. Her anger was so intense, Simon felt himself shriveling before it like ice under a blowtorch. "Playing us for fools? Treating the scripture that he was supposed to live by like it didn't matter? Like it was a bunch of rules for everyone else but him?"

"No, that's not what I'm saying. I'm saying… I mean, dying in such a horrible manner, it's…" Simon was flailing. "Look, Meadowlark, I'm sorry, okay? I misspoke. I never meant to upset you. Can we agree to disagree?"

"Why don't you just go?" She shoved away the loose section of paneling. "Go on. Git."

Simon gave her a beseeching look. Meadowlark refused to meet his gaze.

With a hapless grimace, he crawled out of the hole. Meadowlark slid the section of paneling back into place behind him with unmistakable finality.

Simon stood in the laundry for several seconds, overcome with bewilderment. The change that had come over Meadowlark had been as stark as it had been sudden. He must have inadvertently touched a nerve, although he didn't know how.

All he knew was that he'd learned something about Dr. Weng from Meadowlark Deane, albeit not very much. He had also, through no fault of his own, lost any chance of eliciting any further information out of her.

Maybe that was no more than he deserved. Leading Meadowlark on like that—it was unfair on her. She was far more vulnerable than she appeared, her insecurities well concealed but near to the surface nonetheless. He had trampled all over her like some sort of devious, heartless cad. If Simon Tam had a motto, it might be, "Treat others as you yourself would like to be treated," and in this instance he had not lived up to it.

The sound of a gong reverberated through the building, ringing repeatedly.

Dinner, he guessed, was served.

He made his way towards the refectory, praying that the other three crewmembers had had better luck than him.

25

After parting ways with Simon, Mal roamed through the building but saw no sign of Dr. Esau Weng. Nor could he find anybody willing to be drawn into a discussion about the presence of a doctor at Correctional Unit #23.

He did discover a no-go area, however. One end of a row of cells was cordoned off from the rest by a partition made of drywall with a doorway carved into it. Standing guard outside this crude portal were two intimidating-looking individuals. One was a heavyset man-mountain, with a chest like an oil drum. He was missing an ear. The other was a sturdy woman, not tall but very broad, with a lopsided haircut, half close-cropped, half down to her chin. Each of them had a metal star attached to the front of their clothing, fashioned from what looked to be a piece of tin can, with a crude "R" stamped in the middle. The star reminded Mal of a sheriff's or deputy's badge of office, but what the "R" stood for, he had no idea.

As Mal wandered towards this pair, the one-eared man-mountain twirled his finger in the air in a "turn around" gesture, while the woman folded her arms across her chest and tilted her head to one side.

The message was clear but Mal chose to ignore it and kept walking.

"Where d'you think you're going, pal?" the man-mountain challenged.

"Mr. O'Bannon ain't seeing visitors right now," said the sturdy woman.

"Well, I may not have an appointment with Mr. O'Bannon," Mal said, thinking on his feet, "but I was wondering whether he—"

The man and the woman, in unison, moved in on him.

"You deaf or somethin'?" the man-mountain said, looming over Mal.

Mal could have said—but didn't—that if anyone here was deaf, it was likely to be the fella with only a single ear.

"You best go back the way you came, right this second," the man-mountain went on, "or you'll be picking up teeth from the floor."

"*Your* teeth," the sturdy woman added, somewhat superfluously.

"Yeah, I figured that about the teeth," Mal said. "Wouldn't make sense as a threat if they were someone else's. There any way Mr. O'Bannon would make an exception, just this once? Only, I'm new here, and I thought I should drop by, see the man in charge, say hello. Seems the polite thing to do."

"Yeah," said the woman, "we heard there'd been some people come over from #22, and I thought I didn't recognize you."

"Don't change a thing," said her male counterpart. "If and when Mr. O'Bannon wants you to see him, he'll arrange it. He will at some point, just to give you and your buddies from #22 the once-over, check you out. Till then, you all should keep your heads down, your noses clean, try to fit in, don't make waves."

"That's sound advice, Otis," the woman said.

"Why, thank you, Annie," man-mountain Otis replied. "I thought so too."

"Okay," Mal said, weighing up his options. He didn't much fancy the idea of mixing it up with these two. This was one of those occasions when discretion was the better part of not getting your face bashed in.

Offering Otis and Annie a pleasant salute, tip-of-the-hat style, he beat a retreat.

Shortly after that he met up with Zoë and Jayne, who had also drawn a blank in their search for Dr. Weng, and shortly after *that* the dinner gong sounded and they filed into the refectory along with the other inmates.

There, having collected tin trays of food from the serving hatch, they sat down at a table. Simon soon joined them.

Unlike the others, Simon at least had something to show for his investigations, albeit not much. He told them what Meadowlark Deane had said about the doctor who'd "got on the wrong side of Mr. O'Bannon" a few weeks ago.

"That it?" said Mal. The four of them were keeping their heads together, their voices confidentially low. "Got on the wrong side of?"

"That's all she said. She claimed straight afterward that she'd been talking about a dentist, but it was just a clumsy attempt to cover up a gaffe. I'm certain she was referring to the unmentionable Dr. Weng."

"You couldn't get more out of her than that?"

"I tried, but Meadowlark, it seems, is a little... delicate," Simon said.

"You mean flaky."

"You could say that. We ended up arguing. *She* was arguing with *me*, at any rate. I don't think she likes me very much anymore."

"Shame. You two lovebirds seemed to have a good thing going on."

"You know what I think this means?" said Jayne. "Means Weng's dead."

"Could mean that," said Zoë. "Could mean anything."

"But if he ain't around in this dump anymore," said Jayne, "odds are he's six feet under. Where else is he gonna be?"

"He could have left this place and moved to another Correctional Unit," Simon said.

"Ain't an easy thing to do, though," Jayne countered. "Those guys we met at the depot had a hard time believing we'd come all the way over from #22, and that's the nearest unit to this one. 'A few weeks ago' was back in the depths of winter, when it'd have been even worse for traveling."

"Also," said Zoë, "it seems unlikely Mr. O'Bannon would simply allow someone who'd crossed him to just up and leave. From what I've been hearing, he's not a man you can piss off and expect to come out of it unscathed."

"That's what I've been hearing too," said Simon. "Meadowlark told me about these enforcers Mr. O'Bannon has. Regulators, they're known as. It's how he maintains order. Do something wrong, and they'll step in and set you straight—with violence."

"I think I came across a couple of 'em just lately," Mal said. That explained the homemade metal stars with an "R" on them. The Regulators' badges of office. "Right friendly pair."

"What do you reckon, Mal?" Jayne said. "If Weng's quit, or dead, then we're on a hidin' to nothing here, right? May as well call Wash in to pick us up. 'Less you've taken a liking to prison life and want to stay on and keep eatin' this…" He paused to look down at his meal, his lip curling. "This whatever-it-is."

Their dinner consisted of a brown slop that was based around lumps of protein bar and seemed to think it was some kind of casserole. Accompanying it were mashed potatoes and creamed corn, although since both were made from powder it was hard to tell which was which, plus a limp, anemic-looking bread roll on the side.

"You talkin' about giving up, Jayne?" Mal said.

"I'm talking about cutting our losses. We've tried. We've looked for Dr. Weng. He ain't to be found. No point hangin' around any longer. Ping *Serenity* with that transceiver of yours, and we can be offworld in a couple hours."

"And then what? I go back to Bellerophon and walk into Inara's room and tell her sorry, we could've saved you but it was just too much effort?" Mal was keeping his voice even but there was passion in his eyes, and pain. "You didn't see her, Jayne. You have no idea what this sickness has done to her."

"She wouldn't *let* us see her," Jayne pointed out. "Only you."

"That's by the by. She was a ghost of herself. She was fading away right before my eyes. That *xī niú* cancer has eaten her up and left just a husk. But if there's still a chance we can bring her back, even if it's a chance in a million, then I ain't giving up. Not unless I know for damn sure that Weng's dead."

"There must be some way of establishing what's happened to him," Simon said.

"At least one person here knows the answer, and that's Mr. gorramn O'Bannon. We need to get ahold of that guy and have ourselves a serious chat with him."

"He doesn't sound to me like the sort of man you can schedule a meeting with," Zoë said.

"He ain't," said Mal, "but it seems, from what Simon's saying, that there's ways of catchin' his attention. Or at any rate the attention of those Regulators of his."

"How?"

"By doing what I do best: misbehave."

"You mean start a fight?" said Jayne.

"That's exactly what I mean, Jayne."

"But you'll run the risk of the Regulators hurting you," said Simon. "That's how they operate. You crack someone's head, they crack yours."

"Lucky thing I was born with a thick skull," Mal said.

He cast a look around the refectory. His gaze alighted on a large man seated at a table nearby. He sized the fellow up. The inmate was massively muscled, but it looked like gym bulk, there for show rather than power or efficiency. His shaved head was as round as a soccer ball and covered in tattoos. So many images crowded together on his scalp that they merged into a single indeterminate mass of blue, red and green.

Mal got to his feet, tray in hand, and strolled over to the large man.

Simon buried his face in his hands. He couldn't look.

Jayne, by contrast, *could* look, and was grinning in anticipation.

As for Zoë, she just shook her head resignedly. "That's right, Mal," she murmured. "Go for the biggest, meanest-looking person you can find. Because *that's* going to end well."

26

Picking the biggest, meanest-looking person he could find made sense to Mal. Taking on someone smaller than himself would look like bullying. Taking on someone his own size would be more sensible but still lack impact.

He needed to get noticed. He needed to create a ruckus. And big, massively muscled men with tattooed heads did not like strangers coming up to them and starting trouble.

Tattoo Head, he was sure, wouldn't submit meekly. He would kick up a fuss.

Mal was a couple of yards away from his intended opponent when he appeared to stumble. His tray went flying. He had left half his meal on it, and this now went splattering all over Tattoo Head. Globs of brown and yellow foodstuff showered his multicolored pate and oozed down his blue-gray jumpsuit. The tray itself slid off him and clattered to the floor.

"What the—?"

Tattoo Head leapt to his feet and pivoted around.

"Who the hell did that?" he barked. He jabbed a finger at Mal. "Was that you?"

All at once the entire refectory went quiet. Heads turned.

Eyes goggled.

"Yeah," Mal said with his most supercilious smile. "Oops. Butterfingers. You don't mind, do you? I just kinda tripped over my own feet. Look at it this way. You wanted second helpings? Now you've got it."

Tattoo Head seemed to swell up with rage. His eyes bulged. His cheeks reddened. A vein in one temple throbbed.

Here it comes, thought Mal. *He's going to take a swing at me.*

Mal planted his feet in readiness.

All at once, Tattoo Head deflated. The color faded from his cheeks. He wiped some of the so-called casserole off his brow. He put on a pained smile.

"Yeah, well, accidents happen," he said. "No harm done. I'll just go wash myself up, fetch a clean outfit from the laundry."

Mal blinked. "What?"

"You didn't do it on purpose." Tattoo Head could not have sounded more reasonable. "I'm kind of a klutz myself sometimes."

"Now hold on, wait a moment," Mal said, confused. "I just dumped a tray-load of crap all over you, and you're okay with it?"

"I'm…" Tattoo Head took a deep, self-steadying breath. "I'm absolutely fine with it. Let's put 'er there, friend, shall we?" He held out a hand. "No hard feelings."

Mal stared at the proffered hand in disbelief. "You ain't angry in the least? Like, so mad you feel like punching me?"

Tattoo Head's eyes said yes. "Nope. No, sir. Why would I wanna do that? You seem like a decent enough fella. You made a mistake. You've apologized for it."

"No, I haven't."

"As good as."

At last it dawned on Mal what was going on here.

Tattoo Head was desperate to fight but didn't dare. He knew there would be repercussions. He was more afraid of what Mr.

O'Bannon's Regulators might do to him than he was of failing to be seen to defend his honor.

This little enterprise was going to be a whole lot more complicated than Mal had thought.

Tattoo Head had to land the first blow. That was important. Mal could not look like a troublemaker; he had to look as though he was simply an innocent victim, fending off an aggressor. That way, the Regulators would go easy on him if they weighed in, and might even have some sympathy for him. So he hoped, at any rate.

Which meant he had to provoke Tattoo Head without *appearing* to provoke him.

"It's a funny thing," he said.

"What is?" said Tattoo Head.

"Well, normally when a guy like you gets made to look a fool— and believe me, with all that grub dripping down you, you do—he reacts by beating seven shades of *gŏu shĭ* outta the guy who humiliated him. It's only right and proper. Yet here you are, acting nice as pie. I'd like to congratulate you on that. See, there's some'd call it cowardice, but not me. To me it's self-restraint. Easily mistaken for cowardice, I know, but subtly different."

The big man was scowling hard. He had heard the word *cowardice* twice. He did not like it being tossed in his direction, not even once.

"Those are fine and noble sentiments," he said, "and to some extent I agree with them."

"I suspect you, sir, are quite unaccustomed to being called a big, fat yellowbelly."

"It ain't a name I'd take kindly to, if'n I were." The strain was really starting to show now. Tattoo Head's mouth was a rigid oval. His teeth were bared. Without seeming to realize it—a reflex action—he had clenched his fists.

"And I'm not gonna do so," Mal said, "even though when a

man backs down instead of standing up for himself, it's kind of the fitting description."

"I. Really. Think. You. Need. To. Stop. Talking."

Tattoo Head was at war with himself. Every tendon and sinew in his body was stretched taut. Mal could see that the impulse to lash out was becoming almost impossible for him to resist.

A tiny bit more goading should do it. One last prod.

"Spineless," he said. "It's not often you hear people say that anymore, is it? Lacking in backbone. Gutless—that's another one. Seems there's a whole heap of things you can call somebody who hasn't got the cods to retaliate when it's required. Luckily for you, they none of 'em apply in this situation, which, if I may say, you're handling very well. Ain't a lot of folk who'd stand there and just take it, the way you are. Most'd hate themselves if they—"

And now, at last, it came. Tattoo Head couldn't keep his rage in check any longer. He lunged at Mal, fists flying.

27

Just in time, Mal managed to raise a forearm to deflect the first punch. Tattoo Head followed it up with another, a straight shot to the jaw, and this one Mal failed to block. He reeled sideways, head ringing.

He came back, moving inside the other man's arm range to deliver some jabs to the torso which, though they were pretty decent, seemed to have little effect. Tattoo Head's muscle mass just absorbed them. Mal tried an uppercut to the chin, but his opponent shrugged it off and seized him in an almighty bear hug. He rammed Mal backwards against a wall and started squeezing. Mal linked his hands and pounded Tattoo Head's head and shoulders. All the while the big man was bellowing, insulting Mal in a combination of English and Mandarin.

As for the other inmates, they were on their feet and roaring their approval. A chant of "Fight! Fight! Fight!" echoed around the refectory, with fists pumping the air in time. This kind of brawl was a rare spectacle in Correctional Unit #23, and therefore all the more cherishable and thrilling when it happened. Finally, all that aggression these people were reining in, all that frustration they had to damp down, could be vented. It was like a dam bursting. They couldn't help themselves. The two combatants were gladiators whose antics provided an outlet for everyone else's repressed grievances and animosities. For a few precious minutes the other inmates could watch this pair tussle, clobber, pummel, wallop: basically do everything they themselves often wished to, but were too frightened.

Mal felt his ribs creak as Tattoo Head increased the pressure. It was getting hard to draw breath. He realized he had made a serious miscalculation. The man's muscles might be gym muscles but they were still strong and—when used to crush the life out of someone, as now—very effective.

Only one thing for it. Mal head-butted Tattoo Head on the bridge of his nose.

No dice. The guy didn't even flinch.

Mal then flattened out his hands and karate-chopped Tattoo Head on both sides of the head, just behind the ear. This succeeded in breaking his hold. The big man staggered away, stunned. Mal had struck a pair of vital nerve clusters, and the result was dizziness and disorientation.

Temporary dizziness and disorientation. Tattoo Head quickly recovered his equilibrium and lurched towards Mal again, head down like a bull's. Mal himself was bent over, busy catching his breath after being held for so long in that vice-like clinch. The best he could do was latch onto Tattoo Head as he charged and let himself be carried along. He slammed butt-first into a table—painfully—and the two of them tumbled to the floor, tangled together.

In seconds, Tattoo Head was on top, straddling Mal and bearing down on him with his full weight. This was not a position Mal much desired to be in. He could scarcely move. All the wriggling and writhing in the world wasn't going to extricate him. Tattoo Head had him at his mercy.

And Tattoo Head was not in a merciful mood. He started raining down punches. Mal parried, but it was a case of mitigating rather than negating the force of the attack. Blow after blow got past his guard and hit home.

Mal could take a licking, but this was worse than that, way worse. This was a downright *pasting*.

Faintly he hoped that someone would intervene. Maybe Jayne would see that he was losing—badly—and come to his aid.

As it happened, deliverance arrived from another source.

Suddenly the great mass of Tattoo Head was lifted from him. Mal glimpsed arms enfolding the big man, two formidable-looking figures grappling with him. They pinned him to the ground. Two of Mr. O'Bannon's Regulators, judging by the tin-can stars each wore.

Then a third, even more formidable-looking figure appeared. It was the heavyset man-mountain Mal had met not so long ago. Otis.

Otis was carrying a two-foot length of wood, formerly part of a broom handle. He used this as a baton, belaboring Tattoo Head viciously and relentlessly around the head with it. Blood flowed, adding dark crimson to the palette of food stains and ink. Tattoo Head screamed.

Mal was about to offer up thanks to his saviors when he felt himself being hauled roughly to his feet. Before he could regain his balance, a ferocious punch to the solar plexus knocked the wind out of him and doubled him over.

Wheezing, he looked up into the face of Otis the man-mountain's compadre, the sturdy woman called Annie.

"Wait," he gasped. "You got this all wrong. He started it. All's I was doing was lookin' out for myself."

Annie did not have the face of someone who cared. She rammed a fist into Mal's lower abdomen, powerfully enough to lift him off his feet. Then, as he staggered groggily away, groaning, she swept his feet from under him with a low-level roundhouse kick. Mal collapsed. Annie stepped behind him and slipped an arm around his neck, going for a chokehold.

Mal's response was to grab her wrist and twist her arm away. At the same time he lashed out backwards with his heel, catching her on the shin with a satisfyingly jarring impact. Annie hollered in pain and indignation. Mal reared up, ramming a shoulder into her ribcage and sending her flying.

He was lucky that any of these actions had worked. They were born of desperation and clumsily executed. Clouds were closing in around his eyesight, and his breath was ragged. Everything ached. He was on his last legs and he knew it.

He tottered round to face Annie, in time to see her pulling something from her back pocket.

A shiv.

He tried to raise his hands in order to put up a guard, but his arms now felt as heavy as lead. His legs were much the same, like his feet were glued to the floor.

Annie came for him, the shiv weaving in the air like a cobra about to strike. She knew how to use it, Mal could tell, and he wasn't sure he was going to be able to stop her.

At that moment, a familiar figure slipped between the two of them. Zoë.

"Allow me," she said.

Mal couldn't help but grin.

Now *this* was going to be interesting. Zoë had got involved. It was going to be her versus Annie. The Regulator might have a homemade knife, but Mal still didn't rate her chances too highly.

Zoë, however, did not even look at Annie. Instead, she closed in on Mal.

The punch was as swift as it was unexpected. Mal barely saw it coming. Fireworks rocketed across his field of vision. Zoë had a mean left hook. Mal had never been on the receiving end of it before, and now that he had, he very much regretted it.

"Zoë…?" he said, his tongue feeling so thick that the word came out sounding like *showy*.

"Damn you, Mal, you always mess things up for us!" Zoë said. She hit him again. "Our very first day, and already making enemies!" She hit him a third time. "Why can't you, for once in your gorramn life, just get along with people?" And a fourth. "Is that too gorramn much to ask?"

By now, Mal wasn't fully registering what she was saying. Unconsciousness was creeping in, a black fog encroaching on his brain.

In the very last second, before a fifth blow came and he was sent spiraling down into oblivion, he thought he saw Zoë wink at him.

Thought he did.

But he couldn't be sure.

28

Somewhere out in the Black—far from Atata but not so far as to be out of reach of the signal from a mid-range transceiver—lay a cluster of debris.

Once it had been a ship, a Leviathan-class freighter capable of hauling multiple-thousand-ton loads from one end of the 'verse to another. Then, a few years ago, there had been an accident: a meteor strike that had punctured the main body of the vessel all the way through, practically breaking it in half. Sudden explosive decompression. Instantaneous loss of all hands.

Recovery specialists had come and collected the bodies. The damage to the Leviathan was too great, however, for them to tow it away. The freighter was simply in too many fragments, and the job wasn't viable either practically or financially. So instead they had planted a buoy in the vicinity that emitted a radio beacon warning passing ships to steer clear.

The Leviathan's remains hung motionless—the sundered ship itself, along with bits of hull and framework, clumps of insulation, tangles of wiring, pieces of broken furniture, anything too busted-up or worthless to be of interest to salvagers and scavengers. All of these were suspended in a static, glinting cloud, preserved for all eternity by the vacuum of space, never to shift from this spot or alter their positions relative to their neighbors. It was like a frozen explosion, a perfectly poised snapshot of the disaster.

And now, right in its midst, hung *Serenity.*

River had maneuvered the ship into place with meticulous precision and slowness. She had been at pains not to disturb the debris, for fear that nudging one piece would send it bumping into another, which would in turn bump into another, and so on and so on, creating an escalating series of collisions that could disperse a large portion of the cluster and therefore render it less effective, if not entirely useless, as a hiding place.

Serenity was now occupying a hollow spot near the center of this constellation of space garbage. Nestling close to the Leviathan's shattered hulk like a baby whale beside its mother, she was practically undetectable. She was at a complete standstill, with her engine powered down and producing no heat traces, so that to the scanners of, say, an Alliance corvette she would not show up as anything but part of the wreckage; and anyone looking with the naked eye would need very keen vision indeed to spot her among so much chaff.

Those aboard her were safe from IAV *Constant Vigilance*.

For now.

As soon as River had brought the ship to a halt, she and Kaylee lugged the still-unconscious Wash between them from the bridge down to the infirmary. They laid him out on the med couch, and Kaylee left River to work on suturing the gash in his head.

River handled the needle and organopolymer thread with great dexterity. She had watched her brother tend to a considerable number of wounds during their time on *Serenity*, and thanks to her brain's enhanced eidetic capacity she was able to remember what he had done and emulate it almost perfectly. She tied off each of the dozen stitches with a basic square knot, and when the job was complete, she inspected her handiwork and was pleased. Simon himself might have achieved a neater result, but not by much.

Meanwhile, in the engine room, Kaylee got down to carrying out repairs of her own.

The two women's approaches to their respective tasks were somewhat different. Where River wore a surgical mask, Kaylee had a bandanna fastened around the lower half of her face to filter out the acrid fumes which hung in the engine room. Where River's movements had to be small and nimble, Kaylee's were large and mostly strenuous, involving the use of hammers, wrenches and screwdrivers in a sometimes very forthright manner. Where River's fingers became smeared with blood, Kaylee's gathered a patina of oil and carbon dust.

The engine itself was not in good shape. Kaylee almost lost count of the parts that had cracked, burned out or come loose—all three at once in the case of the axial variance-bearing shaft. It pained her to see all this damage, and she derived only a small consolation from the fact that it had been inflicted in a good cause: namely, getting them away from *Constant Vigilance*.

River joined her in the engine room.

"How's Wash doing?" Kaylee asked.

"Sleepy-head but no more bleedy-head."

"That's good. How long do you think he'll be out for?"

River hummed. "Can't say. Big bang to the cranium. It's shaken his brain like jelly, and we'll have to wait for it to stop quivering. You'd have to ask Simon."

"Simon ain't here," Kaylee said, sounding more than a little wistful. She mopped her brow with a rag. "Hopefully, Wash'll come round by the time Mal signals us and we need to go fetch them. Of course, I have to get *Serenity* shipshape and spaceworthy first, or we ain't going nowhere."

"You can do it," River said. "*Serenity* loves it when you tinker with her. Did you know that? It makes her toss her mane and whinny through her nose."

Kaylee considered this comment. From anyone else, to anyone else, it would have sounded nuts. From River Tam, whose mind was a vortex of strange imagery and odd ways of seeing, it wasn't unusual; and to Kaylee Frye, who had a strong affinity with all things mechanical and a particular love for *Serenity*, the idea that the ship responded to her touch like a contented mare was poetical and enchanting. Sometimes that was exactly how it felt: as though *Serenity* was a living creature that you needed to handle with respect and care, and once she'd grown to trust you, as she had with Kaylee, she would repay you by giving her all.

"Well," she said, "that's good, 'cause I'm going to be working on her awhiles."

"I can help. Tell me what to do."

"See those pipes?" Kaylee had detached the engine's six main backflow conduits and set them aside on the floor. "They need a good scrubbing out with that there wire brush. You're gonna get yourself all grubby doin' it. You mind?"

"Nuh-uh."

"Girl after my own heart," said Kaylee.

As River set about cleaning the conduits, she said, "They'll find us eventually."

"Who? The Feds?"

"Yes. They're looking for us already."

"You know that? Like, psychically?"

"Logic, dummy," River said with one of those loose, disarming smiles of hers. "You cause the Alliance trouble, they don't stop looking for you. They *never* stop looking."

"I suppose so. That Commander Levine don't strike me as someone who gives up easily. She must realize *Serenity*'s injured and can't have gone far. She's going to scour the area until she finds us, and there aren't that many places hereabouts to hide. She'll start poking around this Leviathan wreck soon enough. Question is, how soon?"

"Why ask me? Am I an oracle?"

Sometimes, thought Kaylee.

"Guess we should assume we don't have long," she said. "Better get a move on, then."

"Less mouthing, more mending," River agreed, and resumed work on the backflow conduits.

Kaylee tried not to think about *Constant Vigilance* hunting for them. She tried not to think about Wash lying comatose in the infirmary. She tried not to think about the four crewmembers down on Atata, Simon among them, in the midst of those frozen wastes with no one but criminals for company.

It was all going to be okay.

Dear Lord, please let it all be okay.

29

"Okay," said Zoë. "You can put the shiv away."

A hush had fallen in the refectory. Now that the Regulators had got involved and the fracas was over, the inmates resumed their previous meek, cautious state of being. They continued to look on avidly, but there was no more cheering or chanting; nothing that would be deemed unruly or disobedient.

"You can't make me," the Regulator replied, hefting the crude weapon in her hand. "I take orders from only one person, and, honey, he ain't you."

"I ain't ordering, just asking." Zoë gestured at the sprawled form of Mal, whom a few seconds ago she had punched into insensibility. "The man is subdued." She poked him hard in the ribs with her toecap. "See? No need to go waving that thing around anymore. What good's stabbing him going to do?"

"You're new here," said the woman, "so you might not be up on the ground rules yet. Me and these fellas with me, we're Regulators. That means we regulate. How we do that—the nature and extent of our regulatin'—is down to us to decide. Your friend—his name Mal? That what you called him? Your friend Mal just got into a fight, and at Hellfreeze that's a big no-no. Soon as we heard all the fuss, we came running. We took stock of what was going on and, as Mr. O'Bannon requires us to do in such situations, we dealt with it with a firm hand. What level of force we employ is very much at our own discretion, and that entitles me to use this here knife as I so please. Makes no nevermind whether the person I use it on is resisting at the time or not."

"I get that, but I've helped you deal with the problem. Mal's down and not getting up again any time soon. Same as that other guy." The man with the tattooed head was, in fact, in a far worse state than Mal. The huge Regulator with the broom-handle baton had battered him so severely Zoë wasn't sure he would recover. His head had actual dents in it. "It makes me uncomfortable that your knife is still out, is all."

The shiv had made Zoë uncomfortable from the moment she'd seen the Regulator draw it from her back pocket. Mal had clearly been in no fit state to defend himself against it, and Zoë had been sure he was about to get a rough-edged seven-inch blade embedded in his belly. But her stepping in would all be for nothing if the Regulator decided to stab him regardless, and the way the woman looked right now, all puffed up and hyper, she seemed set to do just that.

"Look," Zoë said, "I appreciate that you're the law here. I respect you for it."

"You can't do. Otherwise you wouldn't have gotten in my way."

"What you may not realize—you got a name?"

"Annie. Ornery Annie they sometimes call me."

"What you may not realize, Annie, is that Mal ain't my friend. Just because I came with him from CU #22, doesn't mean him and me are best pals. Far from it. Everything was turning to *gǒu shǐ* and I needed to get the hell out. Mal had a plan, and I went along with it, and so did they." She nodded at Jayne and Simon. "And then what does he do, pretty much as soon as we arrive? He manages to irk some great big tattooed lummox, and next thing you know, they're smacking each other around like a pair of angry walruses. Way to ingratiate ourselves with our new hosts, know what I'm saying?"

Zoë said all this with a weary, longsuffering air. She thought she detected, if not empathy in the other woman's eyes, then at least commiseration.

"I mean," she continued, "I wouldn't go so far as to call Mal a boneheaded, dick-swinging moron, but... Well, no. He *is* a boneheaded, dick-swinging moron."

Ornery Annie with the asymmetrical hair almost chuckled at that, and her knife hand dropped a fraction. Zoë felt that at last she was getting somewhere.

She darted a glance at Simon and Jayne. One of them seemed to understand what she was attempting to do. The other just sat there rubbing his goatee in a puzzled fashion, as if unable to fathom why Zoë was busy distancing them from Mal. Jayne was smart enough, however, to keep his mouth shut. He could at least tell she was working some kind of angle.

"As a matter of fact," Zoë said to Annie, reaching the point she had been building up to, "I'm wondering if you mightn't have a vacancy for another Regulator."

"You puttin' yourself forward?"

"I'm military. Least, I used to be."

"Thought that about you," Annie said. "The way you hold yourself. That take-no-crap attitude. Plus, that was some pretty neat punching you did, like someone who's been trained to hit properly. Alliance?"

"Nah. The other side."

"The losers."

"The ones who got screwed over, yes," Zoë said before she could stop herself.

Annie laughed mirthlessly. "Sore spot, huh?"

"Little bit."

"Still, military's military. So knocking your buddy Mal down, that was an audition for being a Regulator?"

"I reckon," said Zoë, "that a gal like you might want to have a gal like me keeping the peace alongside her."

Annie looked her up and down, then said, "Know what, lady? I'm thinkin' you might be right about that an' all." She pocketed the shiv, to Zoë's relief. "What do you call yourself?"

"Zoë."

"Come with me, Zoë. There's someone you should meet."

30

As Ornery Annie escorted Zoë out of the refectory and across the central hall, she said, "That 'losers' crack I made just now…"

"Yeah?"

"I was just yankin' your chain. I fought for the Independents too. Only, it doesn't always pay to admit it."

"Don't I know it," said Zoë. "Who were you with?"

"42nd Skylancers. You?"

"57th Overlanders."

"The Balls and Bayonets Brigade. Heard things about you people."

"Good things?"

"Mostly. You never backed down, that's what folk say."

"And folk'd be right."

"Even when it cost you dear."

"Can't put a price on a just cause."

"Amen to that."

"That's a nice shiv you've got, by the way," Zoë said. "How did you make it? Sharpened a piece of iron bedpost, would be my guess."

"Bingo. Chunk of wood for the haft, all bound together with a strip of cloth. No proper blades on Atata, not even kitchen knives. Meals are made out of stuff you pour out, add water to and stir. That and only that. Nothin' you have to chop or pare. So a girl's gotta get inventive."

"And nobody but a Regulator can carry a weapon in Hellfreeze?"

"Not unless that person wants it taken from them and used on them. It's all about keeping the peace."

"Through violence."

"The *threat* of violence," Annie clarified, "and the willingness to resort to violence if the threat is no longer enough. As a former Browncoat, Zoë, you ought to understand that. No point being all vocal about stuff if you ain't prepared to back it up with action."

Using forceful coercion as a means of maintaining control sounded much more like the *Alliance* way, as a matter of fact. But Zoë didn't argue the point.

"I suppose you'd like to know what I did to get shipped off to Atata," she said.

"Ain't polite to ask, usually," said Annie, "but since you raise the subject…"

"After the war, I had a hard time accepting the outcome."

"You ain't alone in that."

"So I kind of carried on regardless."

"Resisting?"

"Co-ordinated raids against Alliance property and shipping. Guerrilla attacks. Disruption."

Annie reflected on this. "Terrorism, in other words."

"I prefer 'radical insurgency' myself."

"You were one of them so-called Dust Devils?"

"I was."

"They were the bunch who set off that bomb at the second Unification Congress on Beylix. And hit the Blue Sun munitions plant on Lilac. And took out the Feds' refueling base on Bernadette."

"Among other things."

"Shoot. The Dust Devils were hardcore. You really ran with them?"

"God's honest truth."

And it was. Up to a point. Zoë had indeed been a member of the Dust Devils for a time, post-Unification. Like many Browncoats she had felt there was still a chance the outcome of the war could be changed. Or else maybe she'd simply been so angry how things had turned out that she'd wanted someone to lash out at, and the purple-bellies had been as good a target as any. Either way, belonging to the loose coalition of disaffected ex-Browncoats had fulfilled a need in her.

After a while, though, it had begun to seem futile. The Dust Devils hadn't been much more than a minor annoyance to the Alliance, certainly not a realistic challenge to the Feds' supremacy, and Zoë had grown increasingly uncomfortable about the number of noncombatants—innocents—who were dying as a result of their activities. She had quit, with regret but also relief, and gone looking for something else to channel her energies into. Soon she'd fallen in with Mal Reynolds, joined the crew of *Serenity* and, best of all, met her future husband, and the course of the rest of her life had been set. The Dust Devils themselves had dispersed eventually, much like the short-lived little whirlwinds they derived their name from, and were now history, largely forgotten.

"I thought I'd finished with the Dust Devils," she said to Ornery Annie, "but it seemed they hadn't finished with me. Or, to put it another way, that part of my past wasn't over."

"Caught up with you in the end, did it?"

"The Feds did, that's for sure. They had special-ops squads out looking for us. Undercover agents combing the Rim, chasing down former Dust Devils. Rooting out these 'terrorists,' as they called us. Making arrests. I was holed up on Three Crosses, keeping my head down, but they found me anyway. I came quietly."

"I'll bet you didn't."

"Ha! No, you've got it. It wasn't pretty. Took four of them to bring me in, and two of those four have got the scars to show for it. I wasn't allowed a defense attorney. The judge heard the evidence against me and delivered a sentence, all in the space of about five minutes. Maybe the quickest trial ever."

"Know what?" said Annie. "I believe you. Every word of it."

"Why wouldn't you?"

"I'll tell you why. 'Cause most inmates I've met will never be straight with you about what they got sent down for. To hear them talk, they're as pure as doves. It's always, 'Oh, I was framed,' or, 'My attorney was a useless lump of *gǒu shǐ* who didn't know one end of a law book from another,' or, 'The evidence was sketchy but they busted me anyway.' All the murderers here didn't mean to shoot the other guy, the gun just went off in their hand. All the rapists say they could've sworn it was consensual. All the thieves were just taking back something that belonged to them."

Her tone was deeply sardonic.

"So when someone like you comes along and says she was a victim of the Feds," she went on, "I have a right to be skeptical. We all want to think we're victims, not felons. Heroes, not villains. But if you actually were a Dust Devil—and I reckon you were—then there's no reason to doubt that you got hunted down and imprisoned for it, like you say. You're just lucky the special-ops team didn't execute you on the spot. They could have."

"Lucky? When the alternative is a life stretch on Atata?"

Annie laughed. "Got that right. Putting a bullet in you, they'd have been doing you a favor."

By now the two women were nearing the drywall partition Mal had mentioned earlier. There was a single Regulator guarding the doorway this time rather than two. Presumably this man was all they could spare while the other Regulators were over in the refectory quelling trouble.

"Whozzat?" he demanded of Annie, with a nod at Zoë. His top incisors were missing, replaced with homemade steel implants which were rough-hewn and, to Zoë, looked extraordinarily uncomfortable.

"This, Cleavon," replied Annie, "is the woman who's gonna take your job, you don't smarten up and grow a brain."

"You're mean, Annie," Cleavon said, his expression registering hurt. "You're a mean, nasty lady."

"And you're dumb, Cleavon, and that's just plain fact. Deal with it."

Even based on just a few seconds' acquaintance, Zoë found it very hard to dispute Annie's assessment of Cleavon. His slow and simple speech patterns suggested someone who was childishly dull-witted, an impression reinforced by the slight lisp his false teeth gave him. Added to that, his eyes were set too close together, and his forehead overhung them like an ape's brow. Guarding a door was probably the most you could ask of this man. Anything more complicated than that would be beyond him, except maybe hitting people.

"We're going in to see Mr. O'Bannon," Annie said to the adult-sized infant.

"'Kay, I guess."

"Wasn't asking your permission, just telling you how it is."

Again, Cleavon looked hurt. All his life, he would have been belittled and mistreated, and he had never got used to it. He still had feelings, but no one seemed to care. Doubtless somebody had pushed him too far one day, had assumed Cleavon possessed an endless capacity for taking abuse, and had paid the penalty for that assumption. Cleavon had retaliated with a toddler's ferocity and a fully grown man's strength, and now he was on Atata. That, Zoë reckoned anyway, was his story.

"Well," he said, stepping aside from the doorway, "s'pose you can go on through."

"Why, how gracious of you," Annie drawled. "Come on, Zoë."

As they passed him, Zoë shot Cleavon a look. It was mostly neutral but there was a hint—just a hint—of kindness in it. She added a brief smile.

Cleavon responded by furrowing his brow. It was as if he was struggling to remember the last time anyone had smiled at him. Smiled, that is, in a way that wasn't condescending or sneering. Then hesitantly, sheepishly, he returned the smile.

Zoë thought it wouldn't do any harm to get on Cleavon's good side. It might well come in handy.

Beyond the partition there were a handful of cells that were decked out in relative luxury. Extra pillows on the bunks, extra blankets. Convection heaters that kept the air markedly warmer than in the rest of the building. Sinks that were clean, not coated in oxidization stains. Each commode boasted plentiful amounts of toilet paper, rather than the single meager roll Zoë had seen elsewhere. Tinned food and protein bars lay all around in tidy stacks.

"Perks of the job," Annie remarked, seeing where Zoë's gaze was straying. She gestured towards jars containing a thick reddish-brown liquid. "Even got us some homebrewed liquor, although, word of warning, you ever get the chance to drink some, go easy. Looks harmless enough, but it's been known to make people go blind."

"I suppose Mr. O'Bannon gets first dibs on whatever the supply ships drop off."

"You could consider it fair recompense for the stability that he brings to Hellfreeze," said Annie, "and that us Regulators ensure. Now then, he's just down here."

She steered Zoë towards the last cell along, which was screened off with swags of material. This drapery, with its neat folds and variety of colors, was almost opulent, like the tent of some desert-dwelling potentate.

"I'll just go check how he's doing," Annie said. "Prepare the ground, as it were."

With that, she disappeared through a gap in the drapery, into the cell. Zoë heard a muffled conversation, and tried to paint a mental portrait of Mr. O'Bannon, based on what little she had learned about him. She thought of all the criminal types she knew. Did he have the wiry edginess of a small-time crook like Badger? The sinister avuncularity of a syndicate boss like Adelai Niska? The strutting aggression of a corrupt mercenary like Lieutenant Womack? To lord it over a prison full of lawbreaking delinquents, you surely had to have the qualities of all three of those men, and more besides.

Annie poked her head out through the gap in the drapery and beckoned to Zoë.

"Mr. O'Bannon has agreed to see you," she said.

Zoë straightened her spine and entered the cell, only to find that Mr. O'Bannon was nothing like she had imagined.

Nothing whatsoever.

31

Simon and Jayne carried Mal to one of the two cells that had been assigned them. Nobody offered to help. As far as the other inmates were concerned, the group from Correctional Unit #22 weren't outsiders anymore, they were outcasts. Associating with them could be risky, like they were carrying some sort of highly contagious disease. It was better to leave them be, at least until they had learned to assimilate better with the rest of Hellfreeze's population, if that ever happened.

They laid out the unconscious Mal on the lower of the two bunks, and Simon gave him a thorough examination. Between the inmate with the tattooed head, Ornery Annie and Zoë, he had received an almighty drubbing, but it looked worse than it actually was. Contusions were bulging all over his face, distending it to ugly proportions. One of his eyes was swollen almost completely shut. However, the bones beneath the skin—including the most fragile of them, the zygomatic bones and the two maxilla—remained intact. Mal's torso was likewise a mass of bruises but none of his ribs, again according to the evidence conveyed by Simon's practiced fingers, was broken.

"Zoë was *helping* Mal?" Jayne was still trying to fathom it out.

"Helping all of us, I think," Simon said. "And keep your voice down. Sound carries in a place like this."

"How was she helping all of us?" Jayne said, somewhat more quietly. "I don't get it."

"Not only did she save Mal from getting seriously hurt, possibly even killed, but she's gained the trust of one of the Regulators. That, in turn, has got her an entrée with Mr. O'Bannon."

The big mercenary scowled. "An entrée? Like a main course?"

"Like a way in. Access. Now all she has to do is gain his trust, get him to talk, and maybe we can learn what's become of you-know-who." Even when speaking softly, Simon thought it wise not to say Dr. Weng's name out loud.

"I'm beginnin' to think we're never gonna find the guy," Jayne opined. "Not alive, anyways. Maybe we should get us one of them weejee boards and contact him that way. Or maybe your nutso sister can speak with the dead. Ever think of that? Seems like alla the time she's hearing things none of the rest of us can hear. Why not ghosts?"

"River is not 'nutso,'" Simon said firmly. "If the Alliance had done to you half of what they did to her, you'd be pretty damn messed up, Jayne."

"Okay, okay." Jayne held his hands up in a warding-off gesture. "No need to get all hoity-toity about it. I wasn't being serious."

"What if I called your brother nutso? Or your mother? How would *you* feel?"

"Nobody insults Mama Cobb!" Jayne declared.

"Exactly."

At that moment, they heard a voice calling tentatively from nearby. "Hello? Simon? Where are you?"

"Oh dear," Simon murmured.

"Who is it?" hissed Jayne.

"Sounds like Meadowlark."

"Who? Oh yeah. The flaky girl. Great. Like we don't have enough of those in our lives."

Simon shot him a look. Then he turned round, in time to see

Meadowlark Deane appear in the doorway.

"There you are," she said. "They told me you'd been assigned a cell somewhere along here."

"Meadowlark. How are you doing?" Simon put on his brightest smile, but a worm of misgiving was squirming in his stomach. It wasn't as if he and she had parted on the best of terms.

Meadowlark's face, however, showed none of her previous vitriol. She looked concerned, more than anything.

"I'm okay," she said. "How about you? I heard there was a fight in the refectory and one of the people from #22 was involved. I was worried it might have been you."

"I'm fine. It wasn't me, it was Mal here."

"My God! Poor him. Looks bad."

"He'll be all right," Simon said. "I've given him a full trauma survey and the prognosis is good."

"Prognosis? You sound like a doctor, Simon."

"Do I?" Simon realized he had erred. He was supposed to be a financier, not a medic. "Yes, well, you see, I took a first-aid course once. It was a workplace requirement at the investment strategy company. The investment strategy company where I used to be an employee, until I did that thing. Stole all that money. Because I'm a convicted embezzler."

He caught a sidelong glance from Jayne that said *nice save* but without sincerity.

His clumsy effort to cover up his mistake seemed convincing to Meadowlark, at least. "Oh wow," she said. "You are a man of many talents."

"You say that, but there are lots of things I can't do. I can't sing very well, for instance."

"Modest, too. Listen, Simon. Can I have a word?"

"Um, sure."

"In private?" Meadowlark looked at Jayne.

Jayne got the hint. "Fine," he grumbled. "Don't mind me. I'll just go and… not be here." He exited the cell.

"Simon, about before…"

"It's all right, Meadowlark. I said the wrong thing."

"You didn't. I overreacted. It seemed, in the moment, like you were, I dunno, questioning my integrity or something. I felt like my values were under attack, and I didn't take it well, and… I guess I'm trying to say I'm sorry."

"Apology accepted. And I'm sorry too. I said it then, and I'm saying it again now."

"It's about standards, really," Meadowlark said. "I hold myself to a high standard. I hold other people to a high standard, too, but myself more than anyone. And if I feel somebody's doubting that, I get cranky. Real cranky. It's not your problem, Simon. It's mine. I just think integrity is really important, above everything else. The most precious thing in the 'verse. I look for it everywhere. I look for it like a prospector looking for gold, and when I find it, I treasure it."

"That seems like a noble goal."

"Oh, it is. It is. All's I'm hoping is we don't let what happened come between us. We're going to be here for a while, aren't we? And I'd like to think we're going to be good friends, and maybe more. I wouldn't want us to keep having to avoid each other the whole time. So, bygones?"

She held out a hand for him to shake.

Simon took it. "Bygones," he said.

Abruptly, Meadowlark leaned in and kissed him, full on the lips. The kiss did not last long and was not passionate, but it was heartfelt and seemed a promise of something greater.

For Simon's part, he was too startled to reciprocate, but neither did he back away. He let the kiss happen, and he even enjoyed it, brief as it was.

"That was nice," Meadowlark said, letting go of his hand. "*You're* nice."

"Thank you," he said. It was a weird response, almost a reflex. Simon had been brought up to be polite and show gratitude when someone paid him a compliment.

"I'll be seeing you around, then."

"Yes. Definitely. Around."

"Cool." Meadowlark skipped out of the cell on tiptoes, as though dancing.

A few moments later, Jayne reappeared. "Hey there, Romeo."

"Is she gone?" said Simon, poking his head out the door and checking both ways.

"Oh yeah. Way gone. Scooted off down that corridor like the sweet, honesty-loving girl she is."

"Ah. So you were listening in on our conversation."

"Every word. I was literally right outside. Congrats. I never thought of prison as a dating service before, but I guess you've proved it can be. You and she gonna, y'know, have a minglin' of nethers before the mission's over?"

Simon snorted. "Of course not."

"*She* certainly seems to think it's on the cards. Not that I'm criticizing, mind. Far as I can tell, you've been going through a pretty long dry spell, and since it ain't happenin' with Kaylee…"

"Jayne, would you kindly *guǎn nǐ zì de shi.*"

"Why shouldn't I make it my business, when it's so much gorramn fun watching a girl come on to you and you get all squirmy?"

"I'm pleased you find it amusing."

"You're damn right I do," said Jayne, grinning. "Precious few laughs about this situation, so I'll take 'em where I can get 'em."

"Well, if you don't mind, I've got other things to think about."

"Sure, Doc. Such as?"

"Mal, for one."

Simon turned and bent over Mal. He examined him again, although this time it was just for show. There wasn't a lot he could do for his patient except keep an eye on him and wait for him to wake up.

Jayne quickly grasped that he was being ignored, and he settled down in one corner of the cell and started gnawing on his fingernails.

Simon couldn't help reflecting on the feeling of Meadowlark's lips on his, the warm pressure, the taste of her. Loath though he was to admit it, Jayne was right. He *had* been going through a pretty long dry spell. All that time, he'd been preoccupied with River, of course, and the whole being-on-the-run-from-the-Alliance thing. He'd had a lot else on his mind, and finding love was far down on his list of priorities. But wasn't he due a little female attention? Overdue, as a matter of fact. And Meadowlark Deane was, if nothing else, bewitching. Those eyes.

He recalled her words: *I just think integrity is really important, above everything else.*

Simon had integrity. He believed that about himself, quite firmly. He was trustworthy, he was dependable, and he liked to think he would be able to prove that to Meadowlark, even if he wasn't going to be in her life for long.

Admittedly, he was here on Atata under false pretenses, playing the role of a convicted embezzler. Nevertheless, even if it involved a little deceit, maybe he could offer Meadowlark Deane some of that gold she was prospecting for.

32

The man in the cell was stretched out on the bunk, head propped up on pillows, blankets drawn up to his chin. He looked to be in his mid-forties, with a lean, sparse frame and a shock of raggedy salt-and-pepper hair. His skin bore a yellowish tinge, as did the whites of his eyes. His lips were pale and cracked, his cheekbones hollow.

It was clear to Zoë that he wasn't reclining languidly like some grandiose aristocrat. This impression was underlined by the faint sickly smell that hung in the air.

The man was enfeebled.

He was bedridden.

He was *ill*.

This? This was the fearsome Mr. O'Bannon? This was the figure who ruled Hellfreeze with a rod of iron?

Zoë managed, she thought, to keep the shock from showing on her face. She nodded a greeting to him, which was returned, although the simple action of tilting his head forward seemed to require great effort.

"Good evening, Zoë," he said. His voice like a breeze-blown sheet of paper rustling across pavement. "Bartholomew O'Bannon, but you can call me Mr. O'Bannon. Everybody does. Nice meeting you."

"You too, Mr. O'Bannon," Zoë replied guardedly.

"You're one of the folks from CU #22."

"That's right."

"I trust you're being well looked after."

"Can't complain. You and your people took us in. You could have left us to freeze to death out there."

"It would have been inhumane not to show hospitality, not to mention morally wrong," said Mr. O'Bannon. "What is it the Bible tells us? 'Be not forgetful to entertain strangers: for thereby some have entertained angels unawares.'"

"Maybe wouldn't go so far as to call us angels," Zoë said. "Especially since one of us started causing grief not long after we arrived."

"Yes, Annie told me everything. She also mentioned how you, Zoë, stepped up and helped resolve matters in the refectory. You impressed her, and it takes a lot to impress Ornery Annie."

"Sure does," Annie agreed.

"Just did what I thought had to be done," Zoë said.

"And now you reckon you're Regulator material?"

"Ain't up to me to decide if I am or not," said Zoë. "All I know is that a person has choices. You can be a cowherd or you can be one of the cows. Me, I like to think I'm of the cowherdly persuasion, and hence I could be useful to you."

"Annie says you were a Dust Devil once."

"Back when that sort of thing still mattered to me. Nowadays, I guess I'm resigned to the way the 'verse is."

"Didn't stop the Alliance from punishing you for your past misdeeds."

"Alliance ain't big on the old forgive-and-forget."

Mr. O'Bannon laughed—a weak, rattly sound, like a pebble falling down a drain. "I just don't know whether a self-professed rebel, someone who wouldn't give in even when she knew she ought to, would make for a good subordinate. You don't strike me as a team player."

"Depends on the team. And the captain. Right team, right captain, I'll be your MVP."

"Neat answer. You're feisty, Zoë. I like feisty."

Zoë, for her part, did not like the word *feisty* and liked being called it even less. Talk about patronizing. However, she simply shrugged and smiled, as though accepting an accolade. "Been told it's my outstanding quality."

"One thing that interests me."

"Yes? What's that?"

"You've seen me now," said Mr. O'Bannon. "Seen how I am. The state I'm in. You haven't once queried it or asked for an explanation."

"Is that wrong of me?"

"I'm assuming Annie warned you in advance."

"As it happens, she didn't."

"No, I didn't," Annie said. "You know how we don't like to talk about... your condition, Mr. O'Bannon."

"And nobody else did?" said Mr. O'Bannon.

"Not a soul," said Zoë. "Up until a couple of minutes ago, I figured you for this tough, uncompromising, untouchable boss. The aloof-leader type, cultivating a mystique by showing yourself as little as possible. Letting people's idea of you build you up in their imaginations."

"Time was, I wasn't like that at all. I was approachable. I was hands-on. I got personally involved in business. Nowadays, not so much. Nowadays, the less I'm seen, the easier it is for everyone. My fellow Hellfreezers know I'm unwell but don't like to be reminded of it, so I keep apart from them."

"Well, I still wasn't that far off the mark."

"And what do you make of me? Now that you've laid eyes on me."

"It's obvious you aren't well. Got some kind of chronic disease. I'm no doctor, but some kind of liver disease would be my guess. Jaundice?"

"Worse than that," said Mr. O'Bannon. He stirred in his bed, grimacing, as though gripped by sudden discomfort. "Way worse.

Jaundice I wouldn't mind. It'd be a picnic compared to what I've actually got."

"Which is?"

"Whole thing started out as a backache. That's all I thought it was. Then stomach pains, which I assumed was gallstones or something. Took a while, but eventually I got informed by a reliable source that I didn't have a bad back and I didn't have gallstones. By then I was losing weight fast and my skin was turning this lovely shade of yellow that you see, all down to waste materials not getting filtered out properly and building up in my bloodstream. Pancreatic cancer. That was the expert opinion, and I have no reason to doubt it."

"I… Well, I guess I'm sorry to hear that," said Zoë.

"Not as sorry as I was," said Mr. O'Bannon with a dry crackle of a laugh. "It would be treatable, naturally, if I were anywhere else but on Atata. Docs could do their medical voodoo and I'd stand a fair chance of recovering. Down here, though, we're sent basic drugs only. Antibiotics, painkillers, insulin if you're lucky. That's all our captors trust us with. Any other prison in the 'verse, you get visiting physicians, a hospital ward, a fighting chance if you're seriously sick. On Atata it's, 'Tough titty, you're on your own, we wash our hands of you.' You start dying of something, that's it, you're gonna die. Unless you manage to hold out until the end of your sentence and get back to civilization in time. But that option isn't open to me, on account of I'm here for keeps. I'm thinking it might be the same for you, Miz Former Dust Devil."

"Not far off. I'm due for release sometime around my eightieth birthday."

"By which time, assuming you even make it that far, you'll be too rickety and frail to raise hell anymore."

"I'm hoping not, but it ain't as if the Atata lifestyle is a recipe for good health."

"You can say that again," said Mr. O'Bannon. "Know what an oubliette is?"

"I'm not familiar with the term."

"It's a kind of dungeon, from Earth-That-Was times. The worst kind. Basically, a hole in the ground with a door on top, like the lid on a jar. Word comes from the French *oublier*, meaning 'to forget.' And that was the point of it. When the king or duke or whoever chucked you in an oubliette, it was as if you'd been forgotten about. You'd get left to rot down there in the cold and the damp and the dark, on a floor covered with your own filth. It's probably the most degrading kind of imprisonment there ever was. And that's what this place is. Atata. It's a gorramn oubliette. An oubliette the size of a planet."

For all the husky thinness of his voice, Mr. O'Bannon spoke with righteous indignation, and Zoë couldn't help but be swayed by it. He wasn't wrong. Atata was an unusually cruel form of jail. Even if you had earned your incarceration, nobody surely deserved incarceration like *this*.

"Anyways," he said, "listen to me, ranting on like a crazy old coot. I think I like you, Zoë. I like the cut of your jib, as they say. You go away and I'll have a ponder about you becoming a Regulator. I reckon you might be an asset. Doesn't hurt that you're easy on the eye, too."

Again, patronizing. Again, Zoë bit her tongue.

"Annie will show you the way out."

The interview was over. And an interview was what it had been, Zoë realized as she and Annie left the cell. She had been applying for a job, and Mr. O'Bannon, her potential employer, was going to consider her résumé and come to a decision about her suitability.

"You did well," Annie confided. "Mr. O'Bannon doesn't normally take to someone on first meeting."

"I wasn't in there long."

"You were, by his standards. Talking takes a lot out of him, see. He'd never show it, but the fact that he talked with you even for just five minutes—that's a good sign. You should be honored."

"Okay, then I am," Zoë said. "How long do you reckon it'll be before I know?"

"Whether he wants you as a Regulator? Hard to say. A day, maybe a couple of days."

It would have to do. The sooner Zoë joined the Regulators, the sooner she could start probing them about Dr. Weng. Already she was beginning to think that Dr. Weng and Mr. O'Bannon must have had some close interaction. This was based on the latter's references to "a reliable source" and "expert opinion" with regard to his cancer. Who better fit that description than an oncologist?

Zoë's eye fell on the jars of homebrewed liquor once more. This gave her an idea.

She nudged Annie's arm.

"I'm pretty parched after all that jawing," she said. "You don't suppose…"

Annie followed the direction of her gaze. "Want to try the local firewater, huh?"

"It allowed?"

"Only as long as I join you. It's not for non-Regulators. No alcohol for anyone but us folks with the stars 'n' Rs on our chests, in case it makes people get rowdy."

"Want to? Drink, I mean, not get rowdy."

Ornery Annie considered it a moment, then said, "Yeah. I could do with a drink. And you seem like good drinking company."

She snatched up a jar of the rust-colored liquor. "My cell's that one. Come on in. Let's you and me get ourselves a little pie-eyed, shall we?"

33

The liquor managed to taste both sweet and sour at the same time.

"What the hell is this made of?" Zoë asked, choking on her first sip. "Cough syrup laced with battery acid?"

"Not far off," said Ornery Annie. "Hard candy and sauerkraut are the main ingredients. We use breadcrumbs for the yeast. Wrap the mixture in a sock and leave it to ferment, then squeeze it out to strain it, and *wah-lah!* Chateau Prison Hooch."

"Delicious." Zoë took another sip, then handed the jar back to Annie. Her throat burned and her eyes were watering.

"Ah, you get used to it," the other woman said, knocking back a huge swig.

As the level of liquid in the jar went down, the two of them fell to reminiscing about the war. About fighting for, and failing to win, independence from the Alliance. They swapped tales of hardship and heroism. Camaraderie in the trenches. The brothers- and sisters-in-arms they had known; the ones who'd made it and the ones who hadn't.

Then Annie brought up the subject of her two kids. Stevie and Billie were their names. They would be nine and eleven years old by now. She missed them like mad. Didn't miss her ex-wife anywhere near as much. Bitch had taken the rugrats with her when she left.

Refused Annie visiting rights. Called her an unfit parent and had a restraining order put on her. Annie had broken the restraining order countless times, trying just to get a glimpse of her little ones. She was the one who'd carried them inside her, after all. She had a right to be with them, care for them, raise them. Just because she liked to party a bit, just because she had a wild streak, didn't mean she wasn't a good role model. Well, okay, maybe it did a bit. But she loved them still.

She'd never meant to hit Georgia, her ex. Never meant to beat her black and blue. Never meant for her to end up on a ventilator, barely alive. She'd just got so frustrated, is all. And now she wasn't ever going to see the children again, not until they were fully grown. Like, in their thirties. They would barely remember her. What would she be to them by then, after all? Practically a stranger, and also the person who'd damaged their other mother so badly she couldn't walk without a cane.

"It's all so unfair," Annie lamented. "So ruttin' unfair." By this stage the jar was half empty, and most of the booze was inside her. Zoë, by contrast, had kept her intake to a minimum, confining herself to small sips while still making it look as though she was not holding back. She wasn't sober by any stretch of the imagination. Her head felt lightly tethered to her body, bobbing around like a kite on a string, and there was a mistiness at the edges of her vision. But she was nowhere near as far gone as her companion.

"You got a partner, Zoë?" Annie asked.

"Yes. A husband."

"Miss him?"

"Every time we're apart, it's like I've lost a part of myself." Zoë wasn't pretending. This came from the heart. Being separated from Wash for even just a day or two always left her feeling disoriented and off-kilter. She would think about him constantly and fret because she wasn't there to protect him. "Him and me, together, we can handle anything."

"What's he gonna do, knowing he ain't gonna see you again for decades?"

Now Zoë had to pretend once more. She had to imagine, theoretically, how Wash would cope if she was sent to jail for most of the rest of her natural life. She was pretty sure she knew the answer.

"He'll have fallen to pieces. Thrown himself into his work just so's he doesn't have to think about it. He's a pilot, and he loves flying almost as much as he loves me. He'll just shoot around the Black, from one world to the next, racking up the space miles, and everywhere he goes he'll see something, something that reminds him of me, and he'll need to move on."

"You don't worry he'll find hisself another lady?"

"After this?" Zoë said, sounding mock-offended. She ran a hand up and down herself like a sales rep showing off the goods. "Who could compare?"

"You make a good point," said Annie. "I feel I should apologize for Mr. O'Bannon, by the way. That remark he made about you being easy on the eye. Not that you aren't. I mean, you're gorgeous. But it wasn't appropriate."

"Oh, it's nothing. I've had worse."

"It's just the way he is. He may be sick as all get-out, but he's still got an eye for a pretty face. You should have seen him in his prime, Zoë. Not much more'n half a year ago, he was handsome and strong. Everyone admired him. He'd walk around the place, and you'd see people just gravitate towards him. He had whatchemacall—charisma. Had it by the bucket-load. He *swaggered.* Us Regulators, we were there beside him all the time, just in case. Kinda like bodyguards. But we weren't really necessary. More a show of strength than anything. If there was a dispute between inmates, Mr. O'Bannon would arbitrate, and we'd make sure his decision was abided by. He still does this, as and when, and so do we. Folks come visit him in his cell to petition him. He hears them out, makes a judgment, and we see that they stick by it. Wisdom of Solomon, he has. But it's gettin' harder and harder for him, the more he sickens. He can't concentrate for nearly as long. He sleeps a lot. It's a regular tragedy, watching him fade away, day by day."

Zoë thought of Inara and nodded with genuine sympathy. "I know how you feel. I have a friend who's in much the same state. Cancer, too. Haven't seen her in awhile, but just knowing how she's suffering, how she's slowly sinking…"

Zoë was not one for crying, but she was close to it now. Fighting back the tears, she held out a hand for the liquor jar.

"I just wish there was something could be done for her," she said as she tipped a little more of the firewater down her throat. Maybe she *was* pretty drunk, because the taste of the stuff didn't seem nearly so bad anymore. "She's got all these specialists, they've been treating her, but none of 'em's been able to help. Doctors, huh? All that training, all that money they charge you, and at the end of it, when you really need them, you just get a shrug and a 'sorry.'"

"Yeah. Doctors," said Annie morosely.

"You had a bad experience with one? Sounds like it."

"Not me personally, but…"

Zoë handed back the jar, and Annie took a long pull, wiping her mouth on her shirtcuff. The Regulator had begun slurring her words and swaying a little, and her eyes were glassy and pink.

"Look," Annie said, "I shouldn't be telling you this…"

Half an hour later, Zoë traipsed through Correctional Unit #23, trying to locate the cells she was sharing with Mal, Simon and Jayne. It wasn't easy. The building was confusing: rows of cells, more rows of cells. She must have crossed the central hall a dozen times. The main lights had been switched off, too, to be replaced by dim red nightlights, and the inmates were settling down to sleep. Everything was crimson and empty and echoing.

It mightn't have been so bad if she'd been completely sober. She was just glad she hadn't swallowed as much Chateau Prison Hooch as Ornery Annie had. By the time Zoë left her, the Regulator had passed out, and she would doubtless be nursing a monster hangover when she woke up.

Eventually, more by luck than judgment, Zoë found her way to where she was going. Simon and Jayne were together in one of the two adjacent cells, sitting on the floor while Mal lay unconscious in the lower bunk.

"Hey, Zoë," said Jayne. "Been having fun with your new gal pal?"

"Not in the way you're thinking," Zoë said.

"How do you know how I was thinking?"

"Because I know you, Jayne, and I know how your sordid little mind works."

"Don't bother me none if that's what you're into. 'Sides, look at the Doc here. He's been busy hooking up. Why not you? When the cat's away, and all that."

"Please stop talking."

Zoë turned her attention to Mal. His face seemed to have been replaced with a heap of overripe plums. She had done that to him. She felt remorse, which her state of mild inebriation did nothing to dull.

"He gonna be okay?" she asked Simon.

"I reckon so," Simon said. "What with you and those two inmates, he took quite a beating."

"The man's strong. He can handle it. Main thing is, I think it's been worth it."

"How do you mean?"

"Well, while I was 'having fun with my new gal pal'"—Zoë fixed Jayne with a wry glance—"I was actually ferreting out information."

"And?" said Simon.

"And I think I know where he is."

She didn't say who "he" was. She didn't have to. Both Simon and Jayne knew who she meant.

34

Just then, someone in a nearby cell called out, "Hey! The new guys! Keep it down in there, will you? Some of us are trying to sleep."

"Sorry," Simon replied.

"Whatever you're talking about, it can wait till morning."

Zoë, Simon and Jayne continued their conversation with their voices lowered to just above a whisper.

"So you know where Weng is?" said Jayne.

"To be more accurate," Zoë said, "I know where he *isn't*."

"Which is?" Simon asked.

"He isn't in Hellfreeze. He's gone. Lit out a few weeks back."

"Why?"

"I'll get to that in a moment. Weng got sent to Atata about a year ago. Soon as he arrived in Correctional Unit #23 and they found out he was a doctor, Mr. O'Bannon took him under his wing. He knew how valuable Weng was: a doctor, to look after inmates who got sick. Precious as gold, and having a medical man in his pocket would further cement his authority. Is there some water, by the way? I could do with it."

Simon fetched a cup, filled it from the sink faucet, and handed it to her.

Zoë drank the lot in a single gulp, followed by a second cupful.

The first rule of boozing: rehydrate or suffer the consequences.

"Weng went along with it," she said. "Sounds like he's no fool. He knew he was better off inside Mr. O'Bannon's inner circle than outside it. People came to him with their ailments and he did what he could for them with the resources available. Bit like you and us on *Serenity*, Simon. Everything was fine and dandy, until the day Mr. O'Bannon himself got sick. Seriously sick."

"Who did you get all this from?" said Simon. "That Regulator, Annie?"

"None other. That's what the drinking was all about. She had way more than me, and it lowered her defenses."

"And Mr. O'Bannon's sick?"

"There's the irony of it all. He has cancer."

"Huh," said Jayne.

"What sort?" Simon inquired.

"Pancreatic."

Simon winced. "Well, that isn't necessarily terminal. Not like Kiehl's myeloma, say. Gene therapy can hold back metastasis and reverse tumor development."

"Nothing like that is available here on Atata," Zoë said. "But still, once Dr. Weng diagnosed what was wrong with Mr. O'Bannon, Mr. O'Bannon got it into his head that Dr. Weng could cure him. He became fixated on it. Dr. Weng was going to be his savior."

"Not a chance. Unless, that is, Weng's artificial immunomodulatory microorganisms could do the trick."

"The impression I get is that Weng never once mentioned his cancer-killing viruses. He was an oncologist, people knew that much, but not, it seems, that he was researching radical new treatments. He must've kept quiet about that."

"Even after Mr. O'Bannon got cancer?" said Jayne. "Ask me, that'd be just the right time to bring it up. 'Hey, guy who runs the joint and makes sure I have a cushy ride. You know you're dying?

So happens I got just the thing.'"

"Not much use if you don't have the equipment you need," Simon said. "If I understand it right, we're talking about an incredibly complex and delicate process which requires the very latest med tech. It'd be the same as if Weng had said, 'I'm going to give you a million credits, only first I have to get ahold of a printing press, paper, ink, and the engraving plates. Any idea where I can find all those?' No, all he could do would be to provide palliative care for Mr. O'Bannon, and under the circumstances it'd be extremely limited."

"The point is," Zoë said, "Mr. O'Bannon was desperate for Dr. Weng to fix his cancer, and Dr. Weng couldn't. He told him he couldn't, several times, but Mr. O'Bannon either wouldn't listen or refused to accept it. I guess, when you're staring death in the face, it's hard to stay reasonable. He started threatening Weng. Told him if he carried on being so obstinate, he was going to have his Regulators torture him. It'd start with beating the hell out of him, and graduate from there to cutting and lopping."

"To which notion Weng did not take a liking," said Jayne.

"Weng did not, and so Weng did the sensible thing and hightailed it."

"I don't blame him," Simon said. "He was in an impossible predicament."

"Way Annie tells it, Weng was here one evening, and not here the following morning. He snuck out of Hellfreeze during the night and headed for the hills. Literally. There's a mountain range to the north, maybe thirty, forty klicks. They're called the Great White Mountains. Weng made off towards them."

"He just walked out? You can do that?"

"CU #23 has locks on its external doors, but they only come into effect when the entire unit is put in lockdown remotely. Otherwise they're not needed. You've seen for yourself what it's like out there. That said, it has been known for people to leave. Annie told me there's been a couple of instances lately when somebody's disappeared, presumably to try their chances elsewhere. She's not sure why they would, given that Hellfreezers have it better than most on Atata, thanks to Mr. O'Bannon. She thinks maybe it's a suicide thing. They've had enough, they're know they're liable to die on this world anyway, so they just decide to bring the date forward. For most, though, the conditions out there are a good enough reason to stay put. That and the wildlife."

"Wildlife?" said Jayne. "You mean like that weird-ass opossum thing we saw this afternoon?"

"Worse."

"Worse?"

"You know how terraforming works, don't you?" Simon said.

"Sure I do," said Jayne. "But," he added brightly, "maybe you oughta explain it to me like I don't."

"Every world is seeded with the full suite of life form potential. If the terraforming doesn't go to plan, as here, the result can be an ecosystem—vegetation and weather and such—that's still viable, just not necessarily human-habitable. That includes all the relevant fauna, everything from insects to the higher-order mammals. They'll all be congruent with the climate, so in Atata's case that'll be Arctic-adapted animals."

"And of course," said Zoë, "there'll be apex predators among them. Wolves and grizzlies and such, or maybe terrafreak versions of those."

"Ugh," said Jayne. "Seriously?"

"Seriously."

"And Weng still decided he'd rather face those beasts, and all that snow, than Mr. O'Bannon."

"If the alternative was beatings and torture, wouldn't you?"

"But how do they know he was going towards these Great White Mountains?"

"Because Mr. O'Bannon sent out a couple of his Regulators after him," Zoë replied. "Weng had left a clear trail in the snow and they followed it. The Regulators would catch up to him and drag him back by the scruff of the neck, that was the general idea. He had a head start, but they had a Slugger. Trouble was, a snowstorm set in. Soon Weng's tracks were covered over and the Regulators had to give up. They almost didn't make it back to #23, the snowstorm was so bad. As it was, they came home empty-handed and Mr. O'Bannon wasn't best pleased about that. You know that Regulator who's missing an ear? The giant? He was one of them. He used to have the standard matching pair of ears. Punishment for failure."

"Nice," said Simon.

"The other Regulator had several of his fingers removed, but he ain't around anymore because the wound got infected and he died of sepsis."

"Nicer."

"So this is why nobody's allowed to talk about Dr. Weng now," said Jayne. "Mr. O'Bannon won't have him mentioned."

"According to Annie, it's not some order Mr. O'Bannon has given; it's a voluntary thing," said Zoë. "The inmates are doing it as a mark of respect. Everyone has decided collectively to forget Dr. Weng ever existed, and they get angry if they're ever reminded."

"They're acting like it's Weng who's responsible for Mr. O'Bannon dyin', not the cancer."

"I guess they need a scapegoat," Simon said. "Someone they can pin the blame on for something that's actually nobody's fault. It's strange, but they really seem to love Mr. O'Bannon, don't they?"

"He's like an abusive parent," said Zoë. "He's got them thinking, in a twisted-up way, that whenever he's cruel to them, he's justified. That it's worth it, because in the bigger picture it keeps the peace. It's for their own good."

"Maybe it is," Jayne said. "I mean, you got to hand it to the guy. His system works. Consider what this place might be like if he wasn't runnin' things: gorramn bedlam. Whereas, as it is, it ain't paradise, but it ain't terrible neither."

"So Weng's been in the wild for weeks now," said Simon. "Do you think he made it safely to one of the other correctional units?"

Zoë shook her head. "Annie doesn't reckon so. Weather was particularly nasty for several days after he left. Nature dumped about eight feet of snow in the course of twenty-four hours and then kept adding to it. Besides, if Weng continued going north to the Great White Mountains, he was traveling in the wrong direction. All the correctional units are due east or west of here, along roughly the same line of latitude. Annie said he probably wouldn't even have reached the mountains. He'd have frozen to death halfway."

"He might have diverted before he got there," said Jayne. "Turned west or east after all, and the whole 'north' thing was just a ruse."

"Could be," said Zoë, "but even in that case, it's two hundred and fifty miles to the nearest correctional unit, the one we're supposed to have come from, #22. Could he have managed that on foot, in atrocious conditions? I'm saying no."

"So he *is* dead." This had been Jayne's theory pretty much from the outset, and he was quite satisfied to think he had been proved correct.

"It's looking that way," Zoë admitted.

"Time for Mal to fetch that transceiver out of his pocket, then, and call in the cavalry."

"Time for Mal to do no such gorramn thing," said a croaky voice from the bunk.

35

Mal propped himself up in the bunk on one elbow.

"Mal," said Simon. "You're back with us."

"Yeah," Mal rasped, "and kinda wishin' I wasn't, given how everything's hurting so much. Wouldn't be so bad if someone hadn't gotten herself of a mind to use me as a punch bag."

"I was doing you a favor," Zoë said. "I hadn't butted in, Ornery Annie would have carved you a new smile with that shiv of hers."

"Yeah, I realize that."

"A thank-you would be nice."

"I'll say thank you once my face is no longer throbbing like a sonofabitch and I can open this eye of mine fully again." Mal tried to sit up, and let out a gasp of pain. "Yeowtch. *Tài kōng suǒ yǒu de xing qiú dōu sāi jìn wǒ de pì gǔ.*"

"Best if you try not to exert yourself," Simon advised.

"Yeah, I'm gettin' that impression, Doc." Mal lay back down. "Just so happens I've been awake awhile and I've been laying here listenin' to you all flapping your yaps."

"So you've heard about Dr. Weng then," said Zoë.

"Heard everyone thinks he's dead."

"You don't?"

"All there is, is assumptions. It's *assumed* Weng didn't get to another correctional unit. It's *assumed* he died out there in the snow. What if he didn't?"

"You think he could still be alive?"

"He's a doctor. He's a smart guy. He could've found shelter, a food source, figured out how to survive. Why are we writing him off just 'cause everybody else has?"

"Okay," said Jayne, "let's say he *is* still alive somewhere out there, which I don't believe for one moment, but whatever. It's a big damn planet. He could be anywhere. You're proposin' we head out and start searching an entire world? It'd be like looking for—for something tiny in somewhere large."

"Like a needle in a haystack, you mean, Jayne?" said Simon.

"Yeah, but I never understood that expression. Why would you even look for a needle in a haystack? If you want a needle, whyn't you just buy yourself one from, like, a needle shop or something?"

Simon said nothing.

Mal said, "It ain't necessarily that big of a task, Jayne. We know where Weng was aiming for. Those mountains. Could he have gotten over them, gone beyond? Maybe, but it's unlikely. You must've seen 'em on the way in. They're huge, jagged, probably impassable. More likely he stopped when he reached them. We go that-a-way, we stand a good chance of coming across him."

"Do we, Mal?" said Zoë. "Or is that just what you *want* to think?"

"You saying I'm kiddin' myself?"

"I'm saying your head isn't clear. Dr. Weng is Inara's last hope and you'll do anything to cling on to that. You'll have us hunt through a vast tract of wilderness in subzero temperatures for who knows how long—days, maybe weeks—when there's not even any guarantee that the person we're hunting for is still breathing."

"We even find him," Jayne added, "might be he's frozen solid, like a human popsicle. Or he's lining the floor of a grizzly bear's cave."

"It's just ridiculous." Zoë softened her tone a fraction. "Mal, can't you see that we've done all we can? We've given it our best shot. It's time we cut our losses. From what you told us about your visit with Inara, she's made her peace with her dying. Maybe you should too."

"No," Mal said, as loudly as he dared. "*No*, gorramn it! Inara is… Inara is our friend. She's one of us. I'd search a dozen worlds, a hundred, if there was even the remotest possibility Dr. Weng was on one of them. You think she wouldn't do the same, it was you had the terminal cancer? Or any of us? No, this is how it's gonna go, and I don't want to hear any arguments. We're gonna gather supplies and outerwear, we're gonna steal ourselves a Slugger, and we're gonna get us to those mountains. Once we're there, we're gonna look for Dr. Weng until we start running out of food. Need be, we'll call in *Serenity* and use her to widen the scope of the search. Her sensors might pick up a heat signature, if Weng's made himself a campfire or some such."

"But one of the Alliance corvettes might intercept her as she comes in."

"That's why it'll be a last resort. We know getting off Atata is going to be even trickier than getting on was. Feds might get suspicious, they spot *Serenity* making a second 'resupply run' so soon after the first. They'll definitely get suspicious if they track her and she doesn't land at any depot but instead starts nosing around a patch of uninhabited territory. That's why the original retrieval plan has her sneaking in at lightning speed, grabbing us and sneaking back out again, so fast she hopefully won't be detected."

"Huge risk for Wash if we ask him to join in the search," Zoë said. "The corvette gets wind of what he's doing, it could follow him down and start shooting."

"Wash is a heck of a pilot."

"He is, until the day he's persuaded to do something totally reckless and his luck runs out." Zoë paused, her expression grim, as if even the thought of losing Wash was too much to bear.

"Well, like I said, last resort," said Mal. "It may not come to that. First and foremost, we get out of Hellfreeze and look for Weng."

He fixed each of the others in turn with his one good eye. There was a determined glint in it, and something adamantly imperious in his expression overall. You could be forgiven for thinking that he was jettisoning common sense, that his desperation to save Inara had driven him over the edge.

In the event, Zoë, Simon and Jayne gave nods of reluctant assent, one after another. Each harbored doubts, and each was considering some way of talking Mal out of his plan. That, or going along with the plan for the time being but convincing him to pull the plug on it when its futility became obvious, which would surely not be long.

"Okay then," Mal said. "Let's everybody grab a couple hours' shuteye. Then we'll go rustle up those supplies and that Slugger. Yeah?"

The others mumbled in agreement. Jayne and Simon retired to the adjacent cell—Jayne had already called dibs on the upper bunk—while Zoë remained behind, since she was sharing with Mal.

As she clambered into the upper berth of their double bunk, Mal said, "And don't even think about it, Zoë."

"Think about what?"

"Tryin' to sneak the transceiver off of me at some point and using it to summon *Serenity* yourself."

"Never even crossed my mind."

"Sure it did. I've got the thing tucked inside my pants. You start rooting around in there, you can bet I'll feel it."

"I have no wish for my hand to go inside your pants, Mal. Not even if you were the last man in the 'verse."

"Just givin' you fair warning."

Silently, Zoë removed her boots and drew the covers over herself.

* * *

Mal lay awake, listening out. He and Zoë had bunked together many times during the war, and he knew she had the ability to nod off in a matter of moments, whatever the situation. Once, as he recalled, she had even catnapped in a dugout trench during an artillery bombardment.

Sure enough, in no time her breathing had slowed and deepened, and he knew she was fast asleep.

Only then did he relax.

Mal himself was in so much pain, he wasn't liable to sleep. Instead, he lay in the dark and counted the minutes until they could leave Hellfreeze and get outside to begin the next phase of the search for Dr. Esau Weng.

Weng was out there at the Great White Mountains. He *was*.

Mal could not contemplate the idea that he might not be.

36

Commander Levine had already had her crew run a top-to-bottom diagnostic on *Constant Vigilance* twice, and now she had them running it a third time, just to be sure. It was this kind of thoroughness that made her so good at her job and would soon, she was certain, earn her a promotion to captain. Dedication to duty was inevitably rewarded, was it not?

Not that climbing the ladder of rank was Levine's primary motivation. It was a privilege simply serving aboard an Interstellar Alliance Vessel, as far as she was concerned. But someone as efficient and hard-working as she was could be even more of an asset the higher she rose. And why stop at captain? Why limit her ambition? Why not, one day, Rear Admiral Levine? Or just plain Admiral?

"Engine at 95 percent of operational capacity, sir," said her engineer over the intercom. "We've stress-tested the seal on the fuel leak and it's still holding."

"Nav computer is online and fully functioning, as before," said her navigator from his console, just to her left.

"All ordnance is a-okay," said her weapons officer.

"Ship-wide systems are green across the board," said her XO. "Sir, we are good to go."

If there was an edge of testiness in the crewmembers' voices, a hint of their feeling that this third diagnostics check was redundant because the results were the same as in the first two, Commander Levine ignored it. She knew she was a harsh taskmaster, but there was a big difference between that and a martinet. The difference was a crew that respected you rather than one that resented you.

"Very well," she said. "Let's go looking for that—"

She was interrupted by an incoming call from *Freedom to Choose*, one of the three other ships patrolling Atata.

The face of Commander Marvin Ransome appeared onscreen, scruffy-haired and unshaven.

"Hey there, Vicky. How's it going?"

"It's 'Commander Levine,' Commander Ransome," said Levine drily.

"Oops. Yeah. My bad. Formality at all times." Ransome gave a salute that somehow managed to be both crisp and sarcastic. "Commander Levine, this is Commander Ransome of IAV *Freedom to Choose*, bidding you good morning from the day side."

"What do you want, Ransome? I'm busy."

"That's just it. *Are* you busy? Because I was consulting the patrol logs just now, as I do over my first cup o' joe every morning, and what do I see? *Constant Vigilance* has failed to meet its regulation patrol remit. Your ship has not moved position for several hours. That's kinda curious, and it got me to wondering. I said to myself, 'Marv,' I said, 'seems like there's something untoward going on with that there ship. I better get on the line to old Vicky Levine and see what the matter is.' Which is what I'm doing."

Levine stifled a grunt of exasperation. Trust Ransome to pick up on this. The man was forever trying to catch her out.

"We've had a slight mishap, that's all," she said. "There was an… incident."

"Incident?"

Briefly, and with a certain amount of chagrin, Levine outlined *Constant Vigilance*'s two encounters with the Firefly *Tranquility*.

Ransome could scarcely keep the glee from his face. "Let me get this straight. You tried to blow another ship out of the sky and ended up nearly blowing your own ship out of the sky? *You*, Commander Levine? The woman who never puts a foot wrong? And then the Firefly practically rammed you, and now *Constant Vigilance* is dead in the water? Boy, that's a hoot. Wait'll I tell Walton and Goldsmith. They'll fair bust their britches."

Commanders Walton and Goldsmith were in charge of the other two Atata patrol corvettes, *Madame Xiang's Dream* and *The Forge of Vulcan* respectively.

"Rest assured, Ransome, *Constant Vigilance* is back to full fighting fettle. We're about to go after the Firefly, and when we find it, this time there'll be no leniency and no comebacks. They're not getting away from us again."

"You even know those people were doing anything wrong? From what you've said, it strikes me they were just carrying out a standard resupply run until you spooked 'em."

"Their manner was evasive and they failed to comply when I ordered them to stand by and prepare to be boarded."

"Exactly. You spooked 'em."

"But why were they so easily spooked? They wouldn't have been if they weren't engaged in some form of illegitimate activity. My belief is that a number of their crew, including their captain, disembarked on Atata's surface. A search of the ship would have confirmed it."

"What in heck would anyone do that for? You'd have to be out of your mind to put yourself on Atata willingly."

"I don't know the whys and wherefores of it," said Levine, "nor do I care. Finding that Firefly is all that matters. Maybe, if we disable rather than destroy it, we can capture the crew and have some questions answered. But if things don't pan out that way and we're obliged to blow it to smithereens—well, I won't be losing any sleep over it. One way or another, the people on that ship are up to no good. I'd swear to it."

"You ain't gonna find it, though. By now it'll be thousands of miles away."

"Not necessarily. The Firefly was in poor shape after the collision. They can't have gotten far before they had to stop to make repairs."

"You don't know that."

"I'm counting on it. Hence I've felt confident about waiting until *Constant Vigilance* is at her very best again before starting to track them down."

"Counting on something ain't the same as it being true."

"It's close enough, in this instance. Now, is there anything else, Commander Ransome? Time's a-wasting, and I'd like to be under way."

Ransome paused, then said, "I think you could do with some help. An extra pair of eyes."

"You have a job to do. Your quadrant won't patrol itself."

"Neither will yours. But Walton and *Madame Xiang's Dream* can cover for me, and Goldsmith and *The Forge of Vulcan* can cover for you. That's why there's four ships orbiting Atata. Multiple redundancy. One ship can handle two quadrants almost as well as it can a single quadrant. Ain't as if traffic's heavy round these parts."

"We can manage on our own."

"Truth is, I ain't making you an offer, Levine. I'm telling you how it's going to be." Ransome was trying to act steely, but to Levine he just seemed peevish more than anything.

"We'll be fine," she insisted.

"Look, Commander, I'll level with you," said Ransome. "Nothing ever happens on this assignment. You know that. It's as dull as dry-humping a nun. Same thing every day: patrol, random checks on inbound vessels, patrol some more, maybe an inmate pickup once in a blue moon. Me and the guys on *Freedom*, we're so damn bored, we're climbing the walls. And now, finally, there's a break from the norm, a bit of action, and I want in on it, and you ain't gonna deny me that. I don't even need your permission. We're coming with you, and that's all there is to it."

Levine cursed her luck. Ransome was right, there wasn't much she could do to prevent *Freedom to Choose* tagging along. She couldn't order him to stay put—she and he were of equal rank—and she knew that no amount of protest or objection was going to deter him.

What made it all the more galling was the fact that the crew of *Freedom to Choose* was the least disciplined of all the corvette crews. Ransome and his lot were, not to put too fine a point on it, complete slackers. If she hadn't known this anyway, she only had to look at Ransome himself right now as he smirked out at her from the screen—haggard, unkempt, bloodshot-eyed from a late night or a revelrous evening or both—to confirm it. Having them join in the hunt for the Firefly was like bringing your drooling idiot cousin to a cotillion. The potential for disaster and disgrace was high.

Through gritted teeth, Levine said, "All right, Ransome. You can come."

"That is really most obliging of you, Commander."

"On two conditions."

"Okay," Ransome said amusedly.

"One: *Madame Xiang's Dream* and *The Forge of Vulcan* don't have to know about this."

"We're not telling 'em where we're going or why?"

"They'll know we've left orbit. They don't have to know the reason."

"The fewer people aware of your mistake, the better, huh?"

"It won't be a mistake once I've caught the Firefly."

"And you don't think it's sensible to have Walton and Goldsmith keep an eye on our quadrants in our absence?"

"There's every chance we're not going to be gone that long. Besides, you said it yourself: traffic isn't heavy round these parts."

"Fair enough," said Ransome. "And condition two?

"Two: I take the lead. We look for the Firefly together, but it's mine to deal with when it's found."

"Because this is personal? Because that ship didn't only put a dent in your ship but in your pride as well?"

"No. Not at all," Levine replied stiffly. "It's called responsibility. A word that you, Commander Ransome, may not be familiar with. The Firefly got away from us, and I aim to redress that state of affairs. What has happened is not ideal, and it's down to me to make it good again."

Ransome rewarded her with a crooked smile. "If you say so, Commander."

"I gorramn well do."

She cut the communication so that she didn't have to look at Ransome's smug, insinuating leer one second longer.

Of course it was personal. Ransome had hit that particular nail right on the head. The situation with the Firefly was an embarrassment. It spoke to ineptitude and poor decision-making on Levine's part. It was a blot on her otherwise unblemished record, and she was determined to erase it before it became an indelible stain.

Which was going to be somewhat harder with Ransome and *Freedom to Choose* in tow, but she would just have to cope.

"As I was saying," Levine resumed, addressing everyone on the bridge again, "let's go looking for that Firefly. Those good-for-nothings got lucky once. They won't a second time."

"Aye-aye, sir," chorused the crew.

Constant Vigilance thrummed into life.

The hunt was on.

37

Simon followed Mal, Zoë and Jayne as they padded through Correctional Unit #23, single file, amid crimson-hued gloom.

All around them, inmates snored, grunted, rolled over in their bunks, farted, sleep-babbled, moaned—the subdued cacophony of the night.

Zoë looked somewhat worse for wear. After only a couple of hours' sleep, the firewater hadn't yet worked its way out of her system. Her eyes were bloodshot, and from the grayness of her complexion Simon judged that she was feeling a tad queasy. She may not have drunk that much, but the booze was evidently pernicious stuff. He knew she would be okay, though. Zoë could handle anything, even a bellyful of gut rot.

Mal, he wasn't so sure about. The man was moving stiffly, hunched over, shuffling, as though he had aged about fifty years. His injured ribs in particular seemed to be giving him grief. In fact, when Mal had woken them up a short while earlier, Simon had taken one look at him and said, "You really need more rest. You're in no shape even to be standing up, let alone heading outdoors into wintry conditions."

To that, Mal had responded, "I'm always ready to follow your advice, Doc, but remind me how me sittin' on my ass is gonna help Inara."

The remark told Simon a great deal about Mal's state of mind, none of it good.

Eventually the foursome reached the garage where the Slugger was housed. Mal got to work gassing up the vehicle while Zoë began loading spare canisters of fuel onto the flatbed of the trailer. Meanwhile, Simon and Jayne were entrusted with going to the kitchen to fetch food.

In the kitchen, Jayne found a four-wheel pushcart dolly in a supply closet, and they began stacking cans and protein bars from a storeroom onto this. Soon the dolly was heaped high with provisions. Simon then rummaged around and rustled up a can opener—the basic butterfly type with two hinged arms and a key that turned a serrated wheel. Nothing worse than to have all these rations and not be able to use a significant proportion of them. He also grabbed an igniter wand to make starting campfires easier and a large saucepan so that they could melt snow for water. Preparation was key. If he'd learned anything from being a surgeon, it was that.

Jayne grasped the dolly's handle with both hands, bent forward from the waist and started rolling. It was heavy, and he grimaced with effort. The rubber wheels trundled more or less silently along the floor, although the axle of one squeaked ever so slightly.

They were in a broad corridor, halfway back to the Slugger garage, when a figure loomed ahead.

As one, Simon and Jayne froze.

The figure was in silhouette, a black outline amid the dim red illumination, but they could tell from the person's startled posture that he or she had spotted them. Simon and Jayne could not pretend that they were doing anything other than what they *were* doing, namely pilfering a whole heap of food from the kitchen.

Simon knew Jayne was thinking the same thing he was. Was this a Regulator? If not, the person might still raise the alarm; and if it was, they would definitely raise the alarm.

Only one thing for it. Whoever this was, he or she had to be subdued immediately.

Jayne stepped round the dolly and broke into a loping run. Simon, for his part, snatched up one of the larger, weightier cans—three dozen hotdogs in brine—and followed. Out of the two of them, Jayne was obviously better suited for bringing the person down, but if need be Simon could always deliver a decisive blow to the head with the can.

"Wait. Wait!" said the figure, palms held out defensively.

Simon recognized the voice. "Jayne!" he hissed. "Don't!"

Jayne, within springing distance of the person, paused. "What do you mean, don't?"

Simon overtook him, handing him the can. "Meadowlark?" he said.

"Simon?" said Meadowlark Deane. "Sheesh. You guys gave me a fright. What are you doing?"

"I could ask you the same."

"Can't sleep. My cellmate's snoring again. I'm going to my burrow. What's your excuse?" Her eye fell on the dolly. "Wait. Is that food? Why are you carting a whole bunch of food around in the middle of the night, Simon? Because that's in no way suspicious or anything."

"Want me to flatten her with this?" Jayne said, brandishing the can.

"No," Simon said.

"Then why'd you give it me?"

"To hang on to. For safekeeping. To show Meadowlark I'm not a threat."

"I know you're not a threat, Simon," said Meadowlark mildly.

"And neither is Jayne," Simon said. "You surprised us, is all. We didn't know it was you."

"I didn't know it was you either. And now I'm going to ask again, and I expect an answer. What are you doing with all that food?" Her tone of voice became shrewd. "Are you going somewhere? Are you sneaking out of Hellfreeze?"

Simon tried to think of alternative justifications for their nocturnal activity, and came up with none. None that would be convincing, anyway.

"And if we are?" he said.

"I knew it," said Meadowlark with a note of triumph. "I knew there was something funny going on with you people."

"Why are we standing around yakkin'?" said Jayne to Simon. "We gotta get going."

"Just a minute, Jayne. Meadowlark, listen. There isn't time to go into the ins and outs of it. All you need to know is that, yes, we are leaving Hellfreeze, and it'd be really great if you didn't tell anyone. Especially not Mr. O'Bannon. I'm not asking you to lie. I know how you feel about that. I'm just asking you to… keep quiet."

Meadowlark folded her arms. "No. Not good enough. Where in heck are you off to? Back to #22?" Comprehension dawned in her eyes. "Is that what this has been about? You came here to steal food off of us, because you haven't got enough of your own at #22 after the storm blew off your roof?"

Simon wished he had had the presence of mind to come up with this explanation himself. "Yes. That's precisely it. You've rumbled us."

"*That's* why you were hanging around the depot after the supply drop-off. You were planning to break in and grab the delivery, but we showed up before you were able to, so you had to think of another way of getting ahold of it."

"Rumbled us again," Simon said.

Meadowlark shook her head. "Nah. I don't buy it. You haven't got enough there to feed an entire correctional unit for even a day."

"There's only so much Jayne and I can carry at any one time. We'll be going back for further loads."

"Also, the other guy, your friend, the troublemaker—why'd he get mixed up in that fight in the refectory if you're here to steal stuff? It doesn't make sense. The last thing you want to do, surely, if you've got some ulterior motive, is make a nuisance of yourselves. You want to keep things on the down low."

"Um, it was a distraction tactic? Or maybe he—"

"Simon," Meadowlark said forthrightly, speaking over him, "I won't be treated like a fool. Honesty at all times, remember? Come clean with me."

"Doc, just let me clobber her," Jayne said, hefting the can. "One good knock to the noggin, and we can be on our way."

"'Doc.'" Meadowlark nodded to herself. "He called you 'Doc,' Simon. And the way you talked, back in your cell, about your friend when he got hurt... 'Full trauma survey.' 'Prognosis.' You're no embezzler. Who the hell *are* you?"

"Meadowlark..." Simon made a move towards her.

Meadowlark backed away a couple of steps, hands held out in a warding-off gesture.

"Don't," she said. "Don't you dare. Touch me, and I'll scream. I'll scream so loud, it'll wake everyone in the building. You'll have Regulators all over you in seconds."

"Meadowlark, please, I beg you. I realize there's a lot to take in here. Please just trust me. We're not bad people. Nor are we taking all of Hellfreeze's food. If you'd simply, you know, look the other way a moment, we'll be gone and there'll be an end of it."

"Gone where, though? Back to #22? I don't think you even are from #22."

"Just... gone."

Meadowlark's expression abruptly changed. The mix of confusion and indignation vanished, to be replaced by resolve.

"Take me with you," she said.

"What?"

"Wherever you're going, I want to come."

Simon was flustered. "But... No, Meadowlark. You can't. It isn't..."

"Isn't what? Safe?"

"Well, yes. That and we aren't going anywhere you think we might be."

"I don't care. I want out of here. If what I'm beginning to suspect about you people is right, then you aren't even inmates. You're something else. You've got some way to get off Atata. That's it, isn't it?"

"No…"

She was piecing it all together. Simon could see it in her eyes. "The fight. You being a doctor. Asking me those questions about Dr. Weng. It's him. It's all about Dr. Weng, isn't it? You've come to Atata to spring him. Yeah! And you've figured out that he isn't in Hellfreeze any longer. He left a while back, so you're going outside into the snow to look for him. Hence the food. I'm right. I know I'm right. I can see it in your faces. Yours especially, Simon. You really aren't that good of a liar."

Simon looked haplessly at Jayne. Jayne, in turn, looked at the can, then at Meadowlark.

Simon was starting to warm to the idea of Jayne hitting her with it. Meadowlark had seen right through him. Her threat about screaming the house down was sincere. What was he supposed to do about her now?

"Take me with you," Meadowlark said again, her eyebrows rising in the middle to form a plaintive, circumflex shape. "I promise I'll be no trouble. I can even help. You're going to take the Slugger, right? You'd be stupid not to. Well, I'll tell you, that machine is as cranky as all get-out. Ignition's faulty. Almost never starts from cold unless you know what you're doing. There's a trick to it, see, works every time, and I'll show you—but only on condition that I come with."

She spread out her hands.

"It's as simple as that, fellas. Either I'm in, or you don't get out."

38

"No," said Mal. "No way. Nuh-uh. Not happening. Not in a million years. How many other ways can I put it? Nada. Nope. A big, fat negatory."

"Mal," said Simon, "I don't think we have a choice."

"*I* have a choice, and I've made it."

"Meadowlark says she can help with the Slugger."

"I can drive a Slugger. Controls ain't so different from a Mule's."

"This one's temperamental, apparently. Needs finessing to get it going."

"Don't they all," Mal said. "Still, we can't afford an extra body. Bad enough you and Jayne had the misfortune to bump into her in the first place. Now she has to tag along?"

"It can't do any harm, can it?"

"Can't do any good, either."

"Come on, Mal. Have a heart."

"I refer you back to my previous negatives, Simon."

Jayne joined in. "I shoulda knocked her out when I had the chance. Still could, if you like."

"No one is knocking Meadowlark out, Jayne," said Simon. "And even if you do, she won't stay knocked out forever. Soon as she comes round, she goes to see Mr. O'Bannon, and then we'll have Regulators on our tail before we've hardly gone any distance."

"Tie her up, gag her. Or else," Jayne added, lowering his voice, "I can silence her more permanent-like."

"Or," said Simon long-sufferingly, "in the version of reality where we don't contemplate casual, cold-blooded murder, we let her come with us."

"Excuse me?" Meadowlark piped up. "I'm standing right here. Am I allowed to have my say?"

"Not really," said Mal.

"You need me."

"But just go on talking anyway," Mal muttered under his breath. "Don't mind me."

"You have to believe me about the Slugger," Meadowlark continued. "It's tricky as hell. Not only that, but you start it up in here, you'll wake up half the building. You're going to have to roll it out a ways, by hand. Get it to the forest, then the trees will muffle the engine noise."

"I'd already thought of that," Mal said, although it sounded like he hadn't.

"A fifth person pushing could make all the difference, and I'm stronger than I look."

"Mal," said Zoë, "every minute we stand around discussing this means one more minute someone might stumble across us. A Regulator, even."

"You're thinking we should take her?"

"I'm thinking it's not desirable but it's not the end of the world either."

"The girl's a total stranger," said Jayne. "We have no idea who she is. She could be a gorramn serial killer, all we know."

"Meadowlark was imprisoned for sedition," Simon said. "Daubing anti-Alliance slogans on public buildings. She hates the Feds almost as much as we do."

"*More* than you do," Meadowlark declared.

"That'd be hard," said Mal. "Look, Simon, I can see she's turned your head. She's got a fetchin' little face and she's into you. Congratulations. But she's also gonna be an extra mouth to feed, someone else we got to look out for…"

"I'll look out for her," Simon said. "Meadowlark will be my responsibility. For what it's worth, I don't reckon she belongs on Atata."

Mal's good eye widened in disbelief. "So now we're taking her off-planet with us, too?"

"All she did to earn her sentence was piss off the Alliance, and if that's a crime, well, Mal, hands up who here isn't guilty of it?"

"Ain't a crime if it's the right thing to do," Mal said.

"So, when the time comes, why not let Meadowlark leave Atata with us? We can drop her off at the first world we come to. That way, even if we don't locate Weng, at least we'll have done *some* good."

Mal threw his hands in the air. "This a doctor thing? You can't help yourself, you just got to save people the whole time?"

"It's a decent-human-being thing."

"Meaning I'm not a decent human being?"

"Are you?" said Simon.

Mal mulled it over.

"Mal?" said Zoë, expectantly.

"Mal?" said Jayne, grimly.

"Mal?" said Simon, hopefully.

Meadowlark looked at Mal, her eyes big, her hands clasped together beneath her chin. The pose was as appealing as a cartoon character's, and she seemed to know it.

Mal raised his shoulders to his ears, then dropped them in resignation, with a loud huff.

"Okay. She comes."

"Thank you!" said Meadowlark.

She launched herself at Mal, arms wide to hug him, but he fended her off. "No offense, girl, but if you think my face looks bad, my ribs feel ten times worse."

"Okay. Didn't know about that. Sorry."

Mal turned to Simon. "There's a 'but' here, though."

"Of course there is," Simon sighed.

"She drags us down, holds us up, makes a pesterance of herself in any way, it's on you. You'll have to deal with it."

"Understood."

"We clear about that?"

"Crystal."

"Good," said Mal. "Now come on. Zoë, grab an extra one of those thermal outfits hanging up over there. Jayne? Open the outer door. Slow and quiet as can be. Then everyone put a shoulder to the Slugger. This is gonna be hard work."

39

The door rolled open on its track with a muted rumble. Mal engaged neutral gear on the Slugger, then stepped off and joined the others in pushing.

The Slugger budged. Slowly, reluctantly, it allowed itself to be heaved out of the garage in reverse. The plates of the caterpillar tracks clacked on the concrete floor one after another, and then were silent, deadened by snow.

The faces of everyone pushing the vehicle were mostly hidden by mufflers, but their eyes showed the strain. In Mal's case, they showed pain as well.

They shoved the Slugger around on its own axis so that it was facing away from the building. Zoë and Jayne hauled out the trailer and hitched its towing arm to the hook at the Slugger's rear. Then Jayne closed the door behind them.

A bright full moon shone down, making the snowy landscape glow. Stars glittered icily. The world was bicolored, black and silvery-white, with every detail picked out clearly by the moonlight like the finest filigree.

The four crewmembers and Meadowlark rested a moment, gathering their strength before setting off.

Pushing the Slugger all the way to the forest, with its fuel- and food-laden trailer sliding behind, was not just hard work, as Mal had predicted. It was an ordeal, a Herculean labor.

Admittedly, it wasn't so bad to start with. At first they were following the grooves the Slugger had carved between the correctional unit and the depot. The packed snow was firm enough not to provide too much resistance.

Beyond, however, in the fluffier virgin snow, the machine kept getting bogged down, and when brute force wouldn't move it, the group had to dig its segmented treads free using the pair of short-handled shovels that were fastened to its bodywork by clips. Soon they were sweating profusely inside their thermal gear, and their breath was coming in short gasps, little plumes of vapor billowing out through the mufflers.

The forest lay a good half-mile distant and didn't seem to be getting closer in a hurry.

They toiled onward beneath the moon's pitiless gaze, shunting the Slugger along with their backs, their arms, their shoulders. They took short breaks to rest, which became more and more frequent, the intervals between briefer. All in all, it took them an hour and a half to get from CU #23 to the forest, a distance they could have covered in fifteen minutes at a brisk walking pace.

When they reached the treeline they were near collapse. They pushed the Slugger just inside the forest, then halted and, as one, sank to their knees.

"Five minutes," Mal panted. "Catch your breath. Grab a bite of a protein bar. Then we carry on."

Another hour of strenuous shoving, and the Slugger was deep in the woods. Deep enough, they hoped, that they could at last start the vehicle. Pines and spruces clustered around them, their boughs thickly furred with snow. They could no longer see Correctional Unit #23.

"All right, Meadowlark," Mal said. "Time to step up and prove yourself."

Meadowlark clambered into the driver's seat. She flicked a couple of heavy-duty toggle switches. "Battery on. Have to warm up the converter coil first, get it to exactly the right temperature. Too cold, no ignition. Too hot, it'll trip and disconnect. You can hear when it's ready. Makes a high-pitched whine, like a mosquito." She patted the dashboard with a gloved hand. "Come on, champ. You can do this."

Jayne nudged Simon. "Girl talking to a machine like it's alive?" he said in an undertone. "That put you in mind of anyone?"

"No," Simon said, guiltily.

"You sure? 'Cause to me, she's acting a hell of a lot like Kaylee. Looks a bit like her, too. Could be that's why you find her so beguilin'."

"I don't know what you mean."

Meadowlark, oblivious to this exchange, now depressed a rubber-sealed button with her forefinger. The Slugger coughed. Spluttered. Fumes blurted from its tailpipe. The engine churned into life.

Then rattled bronchitically and died.

"Usually takes a couple of goes," Meadowlark said.

Mal folded his arms, his expression skeptical.

Meadowlark went through the steps of the ignition process again, and this time, when the engine caught, it stayed running.

She looked pleased. And relieved.

"All yours," she said, giving up the driver's seat to Mal.

There was room on the trailer for two, and the engine cowl on the back of the Slugger could seat another two, albeit not in great comfort.

"Zoë, Meadowlark," Mal said, "trailer's yours. It's heavy enough as it is, what with all that food and fuel, but someone's got to go on it, and you two weigh less than Simon and Jayne. The lighter the load, the less likely it is the trailer's skis'll get bogged down."

Accordingly, the two women stepped aboard the trailer while Jayne and Simon climbed up on the Slugger itself, behind Mal.

Mal eased the dual throttle sticks forward. The Slugger dug its tracks into the snow and lumbered off.

He threaded a course between the tree trunks, gentling the vehicle along. The thing was as easy to drive as a cinderblock. Rather like steering a boat, you had to anticipate each turn well in advance. Mal figured this out after a couple of near-misses with trees.

There was, however, a compass inset into the dashboard, and thanks to this Mal was able to keep them on a roughly northward bearing.

The Slugger crawled through the forest at an average speed of six miles per hour, and miles ahead, unseen, the Great White Mountains loomed.

40

The white hare burrowed down through the snow and found what it was looking for: a patch of sorrel. It nibbled at the plant's tiny leaves, popping its head up every so often to keep a watch for predators. The sun was coming up, dawn light spreading across the landscape like honey. The trees around the forest clearing where the white hare sat were growing pale blue shadows.

Suddenly a sound caught its attention. The hare went up on its hindlegs, peering around, its black-tipped ears pricked. Its nose twitched inquisitively.

The sound grew in volume. It was unnatural, a low growl, monstrous and menacing, and it was accompanied by a vibration like an earth tremor. The louder the sound became, the harder the ground shook beneath the hare.

Though thoroughly unnerved, the hare stayed put. This was its habit when alarmed. Its dense white fur was perfect camouflage against a snowy background. If it kept stock still, whatever was making the noise might not see it. It might pass right by the hare, unaware.

Now the thing came into view, emerging into the clearing. It was an animal like none the hare had ever seen—huge and black as a bear, but much longer and broader, and jointed in the middle, as though it had a tail almost as large as its body. Its roar was constant and terrible. It stank of bitterness and smoke.

And it was coming straight for the hare.

The hare at last broke into a run, darting for the safety of the trees. Huddled behind a fallen branch, it peered out as the black beast battered its way back into the forest on the far side of the clearing. The hare spied other, smaller animals on its back. It wondered, in its little lagomorph brain, why the beast was doing this. Were they its young? Did beasts of this kind help their leverets get around by carrying them?

Then, promptly, the hare forgot about it. As the beast's roar faded, the hare's thoughts returned to the patch of sorrel. Keeping itself fed was all-important. Spring was on the way, the mating season. The hare needed to be at full strength for that, after which it could enjoy the few brief, glorious days of summer when the snows thawed and greenery was plentiful and its belly was always full. At present, there was precious little food available—moss and lichen, mostly—and the hare had to scrounge for every last scrap.

It lolloped back out into the clearing, when all at once there was a scuffling of paws to its right. The hare felt a sudden sharp pain in its haunch. There was the sensation of being lifted into the air, a crunch...

And then nothing.

The wolves divided the dead hare between them. The dominant male, who had made the kill, got the best bits—the hindlegs with their plump, juicy muscle—sharing them with his mate, the dominant female. These two were patriarch and matriarch of the pack. The rest, consisting of their half-dozen offspring, made do with the leftovers—bones, brains, innards, skin. The younger wolves snapped and snarled at one another, each vying with its siblings for a larger portion.

They were wolves, yes, but Atata's failed terraforming had lent them unusual size, so that even the smallest of them stood four feet high at the shoulder, while the largest was nearer five. They had the lean, arched hindquarters of a greyhound, too, and the speed to match, while their jaws were broad and powerfully chunky like a bulldog's. Their pelts were the gray-white of woodsmoke, and their eyes were so deep orange they were practically red.

When the meal was done—and a single hare was slim pickings for eight ordinary full-grown wolves, let alone eight as large as these—the pack settled down to lick the blood off their muzzles.

The patriarch was restless, however. The acrid, alien smell of the large creature that had crossed the clearing a few moments earlier still hung in the air. And there were other odors mixed in with that smell: the scent of living beings, things of flesh, blood and bone. The patriarch had seen the five creatures accompanying the beast. He knew they would be a good meal, if caught. Plenty of food for all.

With a couple of sharp yips, he brought the pack to their feet. One among them, the youngest of the litter, did not get up as quickly as his father would have liked, and received an incentivizing nip on the hindquarters.

The patriarch circled twice on the spot, in a show of urgency, then set off in the wake of the clanking, roaring beast. The matriarch was at his side. The other wolves fell in behind.

The pack loped along at a cautious, rhythmic pace. Long, lithe leaps propelled them gracefully through the underbelly-scraping snow. The beast's spoor was not in the least bit difficult to follow, nor its smell.

Soon it was in sight. The patriarch and matriarch slowed, and the other wolves, following their parents' lead as ever, did likewise.

Now they were matching the beast's speed but holding back just far enough so that it, and the lesser creatures on it, would not see them.

Like this, steadily and stealthily, the terrafreak wolves pursued their prey. They could maintain the pace for hour upon hour. It was nothing to them. The beast would surely tire before they did.

And then, when it did start to flag, the pack would seize their opportunity and pounce.

41

"B oss? Boss!"

Otis shook Mr. O'Bannon gently. The dying man's eyelids fluttered open.

"Hate to wake you up," Otis said. It was mid-morning, and Mr. O'Bannon often slept late. The rule was don't disturb him unless absolutely necessary.

"What is it, Otis?" said Mr. O'Bannon, thickly. "Whatever it is, it better be damn important. Otherwise I'll have someone remove that other ear of yours."

Otis touched his remaining ear, a reflex action, like someone checking their wallet was still in their pocket.

"It *is* important, Mr. O'Bannon," he said. "It's gone, you see."

"Gone? What's gone?"

"The Slugger. Somebody's taken it."

"Has a supply delivery just come in? Because if it has and this is a false alarm…"

"No, boss. And that's not all. The new guys, the ones from CU #22…"

"What about them?"

"They're gone too."

Had Mr. O'Bannon been any less sick, he would have sat bolt upright. As it was, he craned his head up off the pillow, his lips pulling back from his teeth in a rictus of effort.

"Say that again, Otis. The people from #22…?"

"All four of 'em. Ain't in their cells. Ain't nowhere to be seen. We've looked. Chances are it's them as took the Slugger."

"You reckon?" Mr. O'Bannon drawled. "Listen to me. Get everyone together. Cleavon, Annie, Pops, all the Regulators. Run a full search of the place, then report back here. Now."

The Regulators were assembled in his cell—the full complement, all seven of them—and Mr. O'Bannon had managed to maneuver himself into a sitting position. Holding himself up like this was clearly a strain. His chin kept lolling onto his breastbone, as though his head was too heavy for his neck muscles to support.

The Regulators shuffled their feet nervously. Whether or not it was their fault, something bad had occurred at Hellfreeze and Mr. O'Bannon was displeased. One or more of them might pay the penalty for that.

"Just so's we're clear," Mr. O'Bannon said, "the four who came to us yesterday from the Big Cube aren't here any longer. That's a fact, right?"

Answer: a few mumbled yeses.

"And they've made off with our gorramn Slugger."

Again, mumbled yeses.

"Slugger tracks lead off away from the building, towards the forest," said Pops. He was only in his forties, not nearly as old as his name might suggest, but with his prematurely craggy face and hoary white hair he looked like someone's grandfather. Not, however, the kind of grandfather whose lap a small grandchild might happily sit on. More the kind nobody in the family really wanted to visit. "Can't help but think they've jacked it, maybe to go back to #22."

"Some thermal outfits are missing," another of the Regulators chimed in. This was Michael Pale Horse, a man with a blunt nose, small dark eyes and long black hair that formed a sharp widow's peak at the front and was swept into a ponytail at the back, tied with a leather thong. "Five of them."

"How many did you say?" Mr. O'Bannon said.

"Five of the hooks where we hang the thermal outfits up are empty, boss."

"So somebody else has left with those four."

Pale Horse looked back at him placidly. His facial default setting was *deadpan*. "Seems so. Or they took a spare outfit, for some reason."

"It could be," Otis added slowly, "that they've helped themselves to some of our food as well. Kitchen guys reckon there's a bunch of stuff missing. Cans, protein bars."

Mr. O'Bannon digested this information. Then he turned his yellowed eyes on Ornery Annie.

"Annie, you brought that #22 woman to me last night. The one who used to be a Dust Devil. What was her name?"

"Zoë." Annie's voice sounded a little hoarse, and her eyes were bleary.

"That's her. You seemed quite taken with her. Thought she might make a good Regulator."

Unconsciously or not, all of the other Regulators edged a half step away from Annie, putting a slight distance between them and her.

"Mr. O'Bannon, I had no idea any of this was going to happen," Annie said. If she was quivering inside, her voice did not betray it. "You must believe me."

"Of course you didn't. You'd have come to me and said something if you had."

"I most assuredly would have."

"But tell me, is there anything Zoë said to you that might give us some indication why she and her pals have made off with our

Slugger? Or where they might have gone with it? Anything at all?"

Annie scratched the shaven side of her head. "I don't think so."

"Search your memory, Annie. Take your time."

"Well," Annie said eventually, "we did talk awhile, her and me, after she'd visited with you. Friendly-like. Getting to know each other better, type of thing. And…"

"And?" Mr. O'Bannon prompted.

"A name came up. A name we… we don't like to use anymore."

"Don't be squeamish, Annie. Even if it's the name I think it is, you can say it."

She hesitated. "Esau Weng."

Mr. O'Bannon was quiet for a moment. The Regulators tensed. It was as though Ornery Annie had blasphemed in church.

"I see," said Mr. O'Bannon. "Knows him, does she?"

Before Annie could reply, Otis cut in. "Kinda funny, 'cause a coupla people mentioned to me that the strangers were askin' 'em about doctors."

"One doctor specifically?" said Mr. O'Bannon.

"Not so far as I know, but…"

"I heard they did ask about *him*," said Pops. "About Weng."

"Huh," said Mr. O'Bannon. "Anybody here think any of this is a coincidence?"

Heads were shaken.

"That's good, because neither do I." Mr. O'Bannon looked thoughtful. "Those four ain't from the Big Cube, that's pretty much a given. Ask me, they're on Atata for one thing only, and that's Dr. Weng. They want him, and they've discovered he isn't in Hellfreeze so they've gone to look for him outside. Sound likely to you guys?"

Heads were nodded.

"They won't find him," said Pale Horse. "He's got to be dead."

"Sure," said Mr. O'Bannon with a ruminative air. "Sure, sure, sure. But… just suppose he isn't."

"Sir?" said Pops.

"Just suppose they know he's alive and they've got a lead on him. Or maybe they haven't but they're chasing after him anyway, hoping against hope. Seems to me if they're desperate enough to get ahold of him that they'd land on a prison planet, then they'd be desperate enough to go searching for him through an icy gorramn wilderness."

"So, uh, what do you want us to do about it, Mr. O'Bannon?" asked Otis.

"Otis, you and Beau went after Weng when *he* left. Didn't work out so well for either of you."

"I know. I'm sorry. I can't say it often enough, sir."

"Doesn't matter. It's in the past. I'm going to give you a chance to redeem yourself, though. I want you out there. You, Pops, Pale Horse, the whole damn lot of you. Even you, Cleavon."

Cleavon nodded, as if pleased to be included even though he wasn't clear why Mr. O'Bannon had singled him out for a special mention.

"All of us?" said Pops.

"Did I misspeak?" said Mr. O'Bannon.

"No, sir.

"Did I stutter?"

"No, sir."

"You got both your ears, unlike Otis?"

"No, sir. I mean, yes, sir."

"Then you heard me aright."

"It's just... who's gonna keep an eye out for you while we ain't here?"

"Rope in a few of the regular inmates," said Mr. O'Bannon. "There's plenty want to get in my good books. Tell 'em it's a dry run for becoming actual Regulators. That'll keep them keen, thinking they've got a shot at earning themselves a star."

"You don't think anyone'll try and, y'know, make a move on you?" said Annie. "Seeing as you won't have us to protect you?"

"It's good of you to show concern, Annie, and no, I don't. My body may be lettin' me down but I still rule the roost, and everybody knows that."

"Okay. If you say so."

"I gorramn do."

"So you want the Slugger back, boss," said Pale Horse. "What about the four ringers? You want them back too?"

"Them and whoever it is has had the cods to go with 'em."

"Alive?"

"Don't all have to be," said Mr. O'Bannon. "Annie?"

"Boss?"

"You're in charge of this here little expedition."

"Got it."

"Everyone else, what Annie says goes. You answer to her as though she's me. Are we clear on that?"

Nods all round.

"Then get to it."

As the Regulators filed out of the cell, Mr. O'Bannon said, "Annie, a word, if I may."

When the two of them were alone, he beckoned her close to his bedside.

"Is everything okay with you?"

"Sure, boss," Annie said. "What makes you think it wouldn't be?"

"Only, you seem a mite antsy. Have you done something wrong, Annie?"

"I haven't, sir."

"Sure about that?"

"Sure as I can be."

Mr. O'Bannon looked her up and down. "You're a good woman. You look out for me. You've got my best interests at heart."

"I definitely do."

"That's why I put you in charge of the search party. Because you're smart and you're sharp and I trust you."

"Thank you, Mr. O'Bannon."

"And also because I'm thinking that that Zoë woman may have played you in order to get to see me. She was trying to get the inside track, finagle her way into my confidence, learn about Weng. Didn't work, but it was a nice try all the same. And you were the patsy."

"I don't think that's what—"

"If she did, I ain't holding you accountable," Mr. O'Bannon said. "Don't fuss about that none. But it just might make you feel like you owe her something. A little payback, maybe. Might give you a personal stake in this."

Ornery Annie clenched her jaw. "You mightn't be wrong on that score, sir."

"What it also means is that I'm holding you responsible for how things turn out. Fully and solely. You do it right, it'll be no more than I expect from you. Do it wrong, and…"

He did not spell out the consequences. That was not Mr. O'Bannon's way.

"You think I'm crazy, don't you?" he said. "Sending you Regulators off to catch that Zoë woman and her friends. A dying man, clutching at straws."

"Ain't my place to make that judgment, sir. I think it's unwise leaving yourself unguarded, but you're right, you do still rule the roost here."

"Well, could be it *is* desperation on my part. Could be they haven't a hope in hell of finding Weng, even if he is still alive. But that ain't the only bronco in this rodeo."

"I don't follow."

"Those people came for Weng, to get him off-planet. That means a ship dropped 'em off and it's waiting somewhere to pick 'em back up. Yes? Make sense to you?"

"Now that you mention it," Annie said, "it does."

"So, maybe they find Weng, maybe they don't. Either way they're gonna call in that ship at some point and haul ass off of Atata."

Annie saw what he was driving at. "And you could be on that ship with them."

"If they were presented with the right incentive to take me aboard," said Mr. O'Bannon. "A little hostage-taking, perhaps. A threat or two. Making an example of one of them. That might just be the persuasion they need."

"And if you can get to another world, you could find treatment."

"Exactly, Annie. Exactly. On the outside, I can find a place to hole up and doctors to fix me. Everything could be jake."

"So that's why you want us to bring them back alive."

"Some of them. The rest you can do with as you please. We only need one or two of them to secure us passage aboard that ship."

"Us?" said Annie.

"You don't think I'd leave without my most trusted lieutenant?"

"Boss… I don't know what to say, boss." Annie was genuinely choked up.

"We find a way off this crap-hole of a planet, I'm taking you with me," Mr. O'Bannon said. "The other Regulators, them I don't care about so much. But I'd need someone I can trust by my side. Someone to watch over this enfeebled old body of mine, until I'm better again. A protector."

"That would be me, sir."

"Of course it would, Annie. Of course it would. And now…"

Mr. O'Bannon sagged back down to a supine position. Plainly, all this talking had left him exhausted. Pain was etched into his emaciated features, giving them a taut, almost mummified appearance.

"Now I gotta rest," he said in a dry-leaf whisper of a voice. "Go get 'em, Ornery Annie. Go get those bastards and drag them back. Weng too, if they happen to find him. For my sake. And," he added, "for yours."

42

It wasn't as if Mal Reynolds believed in God anymore.

He *had* been of a religious inclination in the past. More than once during the Unification War, in the thick of combat, he had drawn strength from the little gold crucifix that hung around his neck. Sometimes he had even kissed it for luck. He'd been convinced that the Good Lord was watching over him, keeping him safe. This sense of assurance had carried him through some dire predicaments, right up until the Battle of Serenity Valley.

That was when everything had changed. A just God would not have allowed the Alliance to triumph or the Independents to suffer such a decisive and humiliating defeat. God did not side with tyrants and oppressors, did He?

Evidently, however, He did. And if the Alliance's total victory was all part of the Lord's great plan for the 'verse, well, then it was a lousy plan, and He was a lousy deity.

In the aftermath of Serenity Valley, Mal's faith had swiftly eroded until now hardly a vestige remained. He and Shepherd Book had had many an argument about religion during Book's time aboard *Serenity*. Book would insist that God's will was unknowable and that we, his children, simply had to take it on trust that He wanted what was best for us. Nor, the Shepherd maintained, was God cruel or vindictive, whatever Mal might claim.

"The Lord," Book had said on one occasion, "sees to it that we are given no burden we cannot carry. It may be heavy but He has built us to bear it."

To which Mal had responded, "Sure would be nice, though, if He pitched in from time to time. Being as He's all-powerful and such, is it too much to ask Him to lend a divine hand?"

"What if He *is* doing so already?" Book had replied with a damnably enigmatic smile. "Ever think of that, Mal? What if the burden would crush you under it, if God weren't already taking much of the weight?"

Right now, as Mal drove the Slugger through the seemingly endless tract of forest, he wished God was taking some or even all of the weight of this quest they were on. Furthermore, he wished the Lord might give them a sign that they were on the right path, that they were definitely going to find Dr. Weng.

Mal knew that, in seeking Weng amid all this snow-blanketed emptiness, he was asking for a lot. In fact, he was asking for a miracle.

He knew, too, that he was dragging his three crewmembers along against their will and, indeed, their better judgment. He was forcing them to aid and abet him even though they all of them understood how pointless the whole exercise was.

Then again, how could God let a woman as noble and compassionate and all-round beautiful as Inara Serra die such a horrible, lingering death? Was that in any way right or fair?

Maybe God just wanted her for Himself; that was why He was busy gathering her up into heaven. Maybe He was greedy, as well as a ruthless bastard.

Mal wondered what Book would have made of him thinking of God in those terms. No doubt the Shepherd would have just shaken his head, sighed, and said something like, "I'm certain He's been called worse and shrugged it off. Might be He feels the same way about you, Mal, but forgives you all the same."

Mal was of the view that God, if He did exist, was less about the forgiving and more about the persecuting. Certainly He was that way when it came to one Malcolm Reynolds.

It was at that moment, while Mal was in the midst of these ruminations, that the Slugger's engine faltered. The vehicle slowed. Mal nudged the throttle sticks forward, thinking the caterpillar tracks had merely hit an unusually deep patch of snow and needed a little power boost.

The Slugger continued to slow, until it became positively sluggish.

Mal checked the fuel gauge. Still a quarter of a tank. He tapped the glass, in case the gauge was faulty. The needle pointed steadfastly at a quarter.

The Slugger ground to a halt, its engine stuttering into silence.

"What's going on, Mal?" said Jayne behind him. "Why're we stopping?"

"*God!*" Mal hissed.

Not an imprecation.

More an accusation.

43

Meadowlark made several attempts to restart the Slugger. Nothing doing.

Mal popped the engine cowl and had a look beneath the hood. He waggled a few leads, tugged at a few pipes, and asked Meadowlark to try again.

Still no use.

He pulled out the sparkplugs to examine them.

There was the problem. The sparkplugs were so old and corroded, Mal was astonished they'd kept working as long as they had. One of them even crumbled to bits in his hand.

He looked round at his companions.

"Hate to be the bearer of bad tidings, but unless one of you's got a spare set of sparkplugs on you, this rusty heap of junk ain't going any further."

Their reactions ranged from aggrieved to relieved. Mostly the latter.

"Well, that's that," said Jayne. "Game over. Let's call up Wash and get our asses off this gorramn snowball."

"Not so fast," Mal said. "By my estimation we've covered twenty-some miles. The ground's been on an upward gradient this past hour.

We've got to be in the foothills of the Great White Mountains, and if not, then gettin' near."

"Wait," said Simon. "You're proposing we walk from here on?"

"Put it this way. I'm proposin' we don't give up."

"Sir," said Zoë, "the Slugger is shot. Between us we can carry maybe four days' worth of food, max. We have no protection from the elements apart from our thermal gear. We don't even have tents to shelter in at night. Then there's the fact that Mr. O'Bannon is likely going to send a search party after us from Hellfreeze. He'll want his food and Slugger back. Now, we could've kept ahead of them if the Slugger hadn't've broken down. But since it has…"

"Your point being, Zoë?"

"It's madness to go on. Jayne's right, we should call Wash. There's got to be something else we can try, something other than this. What if we tracked down where Weng lived on Greenleaf, like we discussed before? Got ahold of his research notes, on the off chance he kept a copy at home. Might be Simon could rustle up some of those viruses quicker than he thought he could. Ain't that right, Simon?"

"Perhaps. Yes."

"No," said Mal, "you told us it'd take weeks, Doc. Months, even."

"I know, but—"

"Do I need to remind you all that Inara hasn't got weeks? She's hangin' on by a thread."

"Who is this Inara person?" Meadowlark asked.

"She's the reason we're here," Simon said. "The reason we need Dr. Weng."

"Okay. And am I right in thinking she's dying and Weng could save her, if you can find him?"

"Yes."

"Well, it's none of my business, but I'm with Mal."

"It *is* none of your business," Mal said, "but thank you."

"It's obvious Inara is someone you guys are close to," said Meadowlark. "Real close to. Else you wouldn't be doing all of this for her. It's rare to see people care about a person so much that they're willing to put their lives on the line to help them. It's a wonderful thing, and I say we should see it through as far as we can. Four days' worth of food you said, Zoë? Why don't we give it those four days?"

"Because it's got nothin' to do with you, girl," Jayne growled, "and it ain't gonna make a damn bit of difference anyway. Inara is going to die of cancer. Hate to be the one who has to lay it out like that, but it's the truth. It's inevitable. Just like it's inevitable we ain't gonna find Weng. We can tramp around this godforsaken nowheresville for four days or forty, and all we'll have to show for it is frostbite."

Mal strode up to Jayne, thrusting his face into the bigger man's. "It ain't inevitable Inara's going to die of cancer. *Nothing* is inevitable. There's no fate the 'verse lays out for us that we can't change. All's we have to do is try."

With that, Mal went to the trailer and started grabbing cans off it until he had an armful. Then he about-turned and made off with his load in a roughly northerly direction.

The others watched him walk away, exchanging looks, each expecting someone else to say something.

Eventually Zoë spoke up. "Mal. Mal! Wait up!"

Mal did not stop.

"Gorramn *bái chī*," Zoë muttered. "Mal, you're just going to head on out on your own?"

"Sure am," Mal replied over his shoulder.

"Carrying stuff?"

"Why not?"

"Won't your arms get tired?"

"Nope."

"Don't you need a can opener?" Simon said, holding up the one he'd acquired from the kitchen at Hellfreeze.

Mal halted. "Damn it." He turned round and trudged back sheepishly. "Give me that," he said to Simon.

That was when Zoë made her move.

44

Mal had his arms full. Zoë knew there wouldn't be a better moment to try to get the transceiver off him.

She lunged, tackling Mal from behind, knocking him to the ground. The cans flew from his grasp.

Mal was on his front, Zoë on top. She yanked one arm behind him, twisting it towards his spine. At the same time she dug a knee in between his shoulderblades, to pin him in place.

He bucked beneath her, trying to throw her off. Zoë twisted his arm further round, grinding his face deeper into the snow.

"Submit," she said, "or I'll dislocate your shoulder."

"Zoë? You gone nuts?" said Mal, craning his head back to look at her.

"I just want the transceiver, Mal. This has gone far enough. You know I'd follow you to the gates of Hell if I had to."

"Then why not now?"

"Because there ain't a good reason to. You're not thinking clearly anymore. You're letting your feelings about Inara cloud your judgment. Now, pull that transceiver out and give it to me."

"No."

Zoë wrenched.

Mal howled.

His shoulder was not dislocated, not quite. But the arm was in danger of coming free from its socket. Tendons were being stretched to their limit.

"Last time," Zoë said. "Please don't make me do this."

"All right, all right," Mal said. "'Uncle'. Let go, and you can have the gorramn transceiver."

Zoë eased up on his arm. She clambered off him.

"Don't do anything stupid," she warned.

Mal got to his knees. He worked his arm around in a slow circle, wincing. Then he unzipped his parka and delved inside the waistband of his thermal pants. After a brief rummage he produced the transceiver.

He held it out to Zoë. "Here."

As she reached for it, Mal dived away from her. In the same motion, he slammed the transceiver down onto one of the cans he had dropped.

The small device broke into pieces.

Zoë was aghast. "*Yē sū, tā mā de…*"

"Seriously, Mal?" said a no less appalled Jayne. "*Seriously?*"

Mal got shakily to his feet, brushing snow off himself. The swelling around his left eye was starting to go down, and between the puffed-up lids the eye itself glittered defiantly, as did its uninjured counterpart on the right.

"Seriously," he said.

Simon picked up a few of the pieces of transceiver, looked them over, then tossed them aside. The thing was a jumble of broken circuitry and casing, smashed beyond repair.

"That's just perfect," he said. "We're stranded."

"We're committed," Mal said.

"But how are we gonna contact *Serenity*?" Jayne wanted to know.

"They don't hear from us, they'll come lookin'."

"That's a mighty big assumption."

"Zoë? Think Wash'd just abandon us?"

A pause. Then, "No," said Zoë.

"What about River, Simon? Think she would leave you here without trying to find you? Or, for that matter, Kaylee?"

Simon shook his head.

"There you are. May take 'em a few days before they decide it's been too long and they return for us, but they *will* return. Meantime, what else have we got to do but keep on going?"

Mal grinned. It was not his charming grin. It was his *screw-you* grin. Zoë, Jayne and Simon had all seen it before, but aimed at other people, not at them. The usual context for it was when Mal was getting his own back on some business associate who'd stiffed him, or dealing with practically anyone in an Alliance uniform. It seemed all the more insulting when the recipients were his own crew.

"You know I'm right," he said.

"I know you're an asshole," said Jayne.

"An asshole who's right."

"Still an asshole."

Zoë let her shoulders slump. "Okay, well, we are where we are." Her tone was pragmatic. "There's no great advantage in staying put, so we might as well do as Mal says and move on. As far as carrying food's concerned, best thing for it is to make a travois. We can do that using branches lashed together with strips of bark."

She charged Jayne, Simon and Meadowlark with gathering those items. The branches, she told them, needed to be the straightest they could find.

As they set about their task, she leaned in close to Mal.

"Sir."

"This an apology?"

"What do you think?"

"From the looks of you, I'm figurin' not."

"My respect for you goes back a long ways, Mal. I've always

trusted in your leadership. But so help me, you ever pull a dick move like that again, you will regret it."

Mal touched his shoulder gingerly. "I already am. Please understand, Zoë. I only did what I had to."

"That's just it. What *you* had to, and to hell with the rest of us. Inara dying is bad enough, but if one of *us* dies here on Atata because Malcolm Reynolds is too stubborn to see reason…"

"Nobody's dying on Atata."

"Let's damn well hope not."

She turned to go and help the others. Mal caught her by the arm.

"Zoë, you remember what General Cole said about Serenity Valley?"

"I remember, when he was being tried for war crimes, he made out as though we'd have won if only we'd fought harder."

"Cole was one of the few Browncoat brass who didn't want to surrender."

"I'll give him that. Makes him one of the few who didn't deserve to face an Alliance firing squad."

"But what he said about Serenity Valley, it's stuck with me ever since. 'When a battle seems unwinnable, a soldier has two choices: to fight on, or to accept the inevitable. Often the two are hard to tell apart.' And it applies here."

"Does it, Mal?" said Zoë. "'Cause if you still can't tell the difference, maybe you need to take a long, hard look at yourself."

So saying, she strode off.

Mal watched her go, and only then, when no one was looking, did his face soften. Where his expression had been truculent before, now it was rueful. Zoë's words had hit home.

Unbeknownst to Mal, or to any of the others, they were being observed.

Eyes peered out at them from the depths of the forest.

Orange-red eyes set above pointed snouts.

Snouts belonging to large, lupine bodies with fur the color of woodsmoke.

The terrafreak wolves had caught up.

For several minutes, crouching low to the ground, their ears pricked, the wolves had watched the pack of humans. The giant animal the humans had been riding on had come to a halt and appeared dead. The wolves had seen tensions within this other pack of creatures boil over and a snarling, yapping fight ensue between two of them.

Now, as the humans went about their strange foraging activity, the wolves continued to watch.

Hungrily they licked their chops and bided their time.

The patriarch and matriarch would together choose the moment to attack.

And when it happened, the slaughter would be swift and merciless and glorious.

45

Ornery Annie exited Hellfreeze with a look on her face that could have soured milk.

She wasn't mad at Mr. O'Bannon.

She wasn't even mad at Zoë.

She was mad at herself.

Hungover, too. Excruciatingly so. Her head felt split open like someone had taken an ax to it.

But that just made her madder.

Zoë had played her, all right. Had acted like they were friends. Had said things like, "I reckon that a gal like you might want to have a gal like me keeping the peace alongside her." Had got Annie drunk. And Annie had gone and told her about Mr. O'Bannon and Dr. Weng. Blurted it all out.

Annie prided herself on being nobody's fool, but this time she had dropped her guard. She had let herself down. Worse, she had let Mr. O'Bannon down.

Annie loved Mr. O'Bannon. She loved him like a father. Her own father had been a loser and a deadbeat, with a mean streak a mile wide. She wouldn't have spit on him if he'd been on fire. Mr. O'Bannon, on the other hand, although he could be strict, was never unjust. Annie was happy to serve under him, and hated that he was dying.

Mr. O'Bannon didn't seem to know that it was Annie who'd spilled the beans about Dr. Weng to Zoë. It wasn't a betrayal, as such, but it was careless, unworthy of her, and she bitterly regretted it. The more so since he had selected her to accompany him off-planet as his personal guardian.

This spurred her. She was going to run down two-faced Zoë and her pals, and she was going to make certain they learned what it meant to abuse Mr. O'Bannon's hospitality and trust. Her boss may have specified that one or two of them had to be kept alive, but that still left some who *didn't* have to—and one of those could, and should, be Zoë. Mr. O'Bannon must never find out who had told them about Dr. Weng. Annie could not afford the truth getting back to him. Zoë had to die.

As she strode out through the snow, Annie cast a look back at her fellow Regulators. There were Michael Pale Horse and Otis, close behind her. Both of them were reliable, dependable. They would do as they were told.

Next came Cleavon. Poor addle-brained Cleavon, dumb as a box of rocks. But he, too, was a good follower of orders.

Pops was maybe not so easy to boss around. He was quick-witted and sly. Needed keeping an eye on.

And then there were the twins, Belinda and Matilda Hobhouse, who were taking up the rear of their little procession. They hardly spoke with anyone else, those two. Kept themselves to themselves, like they were living in their own shared world, a private place nobody else could enter. They had ferrety little faces, and their fingernails were filed to sharp points, like talons. They went around hunched over all the time, more like they were skulking than walking, and often they tittered to each other, for no apparent reason.

Annie had never been quite clear what Mr. O'Bannon saw in the Hobhouse twins, why he thought they deserved to be Regulators.

Other than, maybe, they were creepy as heck and you didn't want to have anything to do with them, so you kept your head down and minded your own business when they were around. They were on Atata because they'd murdered the extended family who lived next door. Using their bare hands, they had slaughtered them all, from the grandparents down to a couple of very young kids. They'd even killed the pet dog. All because the family had been having a big birthday get-together and had become rowdy, and this had annoyed them. And after the massacre Belinda and Matilda had danced barefoot in the blood that covered the floorboards, singing a made-up song of their own.

Which was all the more reason to toe the line in their presence. You didn't want it to be *your* blood they danced in next.

These six were Annie's to command now.

But it didn't hurt to reinforce the point from the outset.

"Pick it up, you two," she said to the twins straggling at the back. "This ain't a job for dawdlers."

Belinda and Matilda Hobhouse shared a glance, and Annie could easily imagine the unspoken message passing between them, something along the lines of *Shall we kill her or not?* Then they turned back to look at her and nodded in unison, before jogging to come alongside Pops. The way the pair of them mirrored each other's actions was downright unnerving, and Annie shivered a little inside her thermal gear.

At least the tracks left by the Slugger were clear. There was no doubting where the impostors had gone. The marks of the caterpillar treads were like two unending ladders in the snow, flanking the parallel grooves dug by the trailer's closer-spaced skis.

"We can't overtake a Slugger on foot," Otis observed. "Not unless we run, and nobody's able to run for long in snow this thick."

"They'll have to halt sometime to rest," Annie said. "Can't just keep driving and driving."

"Can if they take it in turns at the controls."

"Otis, 'less you've got something useful to say, don't say nothing."

"It's just… I don't want the same thing to happen this time as happened last time."

"Then you'd better keep walking, hadn't you?" Annie said curtly, and accelerated her own pace to a brisk semi-trot.

The others emulated her, and that was a good sign. She was leading by example and they were following.

The group entered the forest, and Annie drew some comfort from the fact that a Slugger's top speed would be significantly reduced when you had to steer a course around trees all the time. Despite the considerable lead already built up by Zoë and company, the Regulators only had to keep doggedly pursuing them and they would have them in sight soon enough.

Annie believed this.

She had to.

46

Wash's first word as he regained consciousness was "Ouch."
This was followed by a groan, another "Ouch," and a succession of oaths.

Dà xiàng bào zhà shì de lā dù zi! He had the mother of all migraines.

He pressed a hand to his head and snatched it away again because it made the pain sharper and fiercer. He had felt coarse-textured fabric beneath his palm. Bandages. So, not a migraine. Worse.

He searched his memory, piecing things together. He recalled the missile attack on *Serenity*. Playing a game of chicken with IAV *Constant Vigilance*. The explosion. He couldn't recall actually being injured but obviously that was what had happened. *Serenity* must have taken a hit, and her pilot had been collateral damage.

Wash blinked around. Everything was blurry and doubled. He could just about make out that he was in the infirmary, lying on the med couch. He tried to sit up. The effort sparked fresh pain, more intense than ever, like a lightning bolt zigzagging down through his brain into his spine. He collapsed back onto the couch, dizzy and nauseated. The pain gradually abated from magnesium-flare whiteness to mere lava-hot redness.

A little while later, a face appeared in his field of vision. It was a fuzzy pale blob but Wash could tell it belonged to River Tam. It bobbed around in front of him like a will-o'-the-wisp.

"Wash." River's voice was faint and echoey as though reaching him from the far end of a drainpipe. "You're back with us."

"River." Wash's own voice reverberated through his brain like a drill. "You okay? And Kaylee?"

"We're both fine."

"*Serenity*?"

"She's fine too. 'Least, she will be once Kaylee gets done fixing her."

"Where are we? Where's that Alliance corvette?"

"We're safe. And secret. For now."

"I feel like a steaming pile of *gǒu shǐ*. Did something hit me?"

"It rained indoors. Hard."

"Huh?"

River mimed an object dropping onto her head, knocking her unconscious. She did it a few times, ever more emphatically, until Wash latched on.

"A piece… of the bridge's ceiling… fell on me? Yeah?"

She put her finger on her nose and nodded. "Yeppity-yep."

"Makes sense," said Wash. "And I'm guessing we haven't heard from Mal and the others yet."

"Noppity-nope."

"Well, I'm ready to fly us down to grab them when we need to."

"I don't think so, Mr. Washburne," River said in a singsong tone. "How many fingers am I holding up?"

Wash peered up at her, squinting hard. However much he tried, he couldn't get his eyesight to settle down. Everything shimmered and swam, as though he was underwater.

"Uh, three?" he guessed.

"Wrong. None."

"That was going to be my next answer."

"No, it wasn't," River said with solemn certainty. "Looking at you right now, do you know what I see?"

"A monkey on a unicorn, waving a cavalry saber?" Wash thought this was a pretty safe guess, given who he was talking to.

"Not at this precise moment. And anyway it's a mermaid, not a monkey."

"What then? Tell me."

"I see someone not even fit to be in charge of a tricycle."

Wash couldn't deny the truth of this. He could barely see, let alone stand. "So who's going to go fetch the guys off Atata if they need us?"

River's hand shot up, like a schoolkid in class. "Ooh, I know the answer to that one."

"Yes, River? Who?"

"You. But only if you're well enough."

"Right. But what if I'm *not* well enough?"

River's hand shot up again.

"Yes, River?" said Wash.

"Me."

"You?"

"Yes. Me. I got us away from Atata, didn't I?"

"No way. You?"

"Who else do you think did it?"

Wash frowned. Even frowning hurt. "I guess… I'm not sure. It was really you?"

"It was," River said. "And I can get us back there, in case you can't. Promise I can."

It was difficult for Wash, with his reeling, aching brain, to process what River was saying. "You can…?"

"Just rest," River told him. "Relax."

Wash slumped back onto the med couch, too sick and in too much pain to keep talking.

Rest?

He could do that.

But relax?

He wasn't so sure.

Zoë was down on Atata, along with Mal, Jayne and Simon, and she was counting on him for evac. He'd had no idea that River could fly *Serenity* and it wasn't clear how skilled she was as a pilot. Returning to the planet would require dodging the IAV corvettes, and that was a feat Wash himself would find tricky to pull off, never mind an untested flyer like River. And then there was navigating, and landing…

He could only hope he recovered in time to do the job.

47

R iver quit the infirmary and headed aft to the engine room.

Kaylee had been up all night, toiling away. River had helped her out as best she could, while also checking on Wash intermittently and monitoring for Alliance ship proximity on the bridge. Kaylee, however, had done the bulk of the repair work, and she looked exhausted. The dark circles beneath her eyes merged with the grease smudges that covered the rest of her face.

"How soon?" River inquired.

"Till *Serenity*'s ready and raring to go again?" Kaylee glanced around. The floor was littered with engine parts. "Can't say. I've patched up what needs patching up. Now it's a case of putting it all back together. Maybe another four, five hours?"

"You should take a break."

"I am pretty bushed, but it ain't nothing strong coffee can't fix. How's Wash doing?"

"He's awake now, but his brain is all…" River rotated a forefinger in the air. "Spin cycle. And you." She lowered the finger and pointed it at Kaylee. "I poke you in the chest, you'd fall over. You need to take a time out. Grab some shuteye."

Kaylee turned her gaze towards her rainbow hammock. A

sudden, enormous yawn overcame her.

"Maybe a few minutes," she said. "No more'n half an hour. Wake me up after that, promise?"

"Promise," said River, crossing her heart.

Kaylee staggered over to the hammock, crawled into it and was asleep in seconds.

River went forward to the bridge. She stepped over the fallen section of steel cladding that had knocked out Wash and plumped herself down in the pilot's chair. The mid-range scanner showed that two of the four Alliance corvettes patrolling Atata had left their prescribed mission routes and were roving away from the prison planet. They were conducting a grid-pattern sweep of the immediate area, moving further and further out in a widening spiral. The search was methodical, thorough, painstaking. River thought of two lionesses prowling the veldt, hunting for zebra. It was only a matter of time before the corvettes caught the scent and homed in.

Serenity might be hard to distinguish amidst the wreck of the Leviathan-class freighter but she wasn't completely invisible. There was every chance one or other of the Alliance vessels might spot her if they came close enough. Then she would be a sitting duck.

Worried though she was for herself, River was even more worried for Simon. Simon looked after her, it was true, but equally she looked after Simon. More and more River was realizing that her big brother needed protecting as much as she herself did, and that she was capable of providing that protection. She wished she could be with him right now, down on Atata. She had a feeling—not quite an intuition, more like a nagging certainty—that he was in danger. Some kind of predator was close by him, dogging his footsteps, eager for his death. He wasn't defenseless, she knew. He was with Mal, Zoë and Jayne, all of them tough, resilient and resourceful individuals. None of them, though, would ever fight on his behalf as fiercely as she, River, would. None of them loved him so much they would be willing to die for him.

"Be safe, Simon," River whispered.

48

Simon was cold. Colder than cold. Despite the thermal outerwear, his limbs were growing numb and starting to seize up. He could scarcely feel his fingers anymore. His feet were like lumps of frozen concrete.

The thin shafts of sunlight that speared down between the trees brought some respite—moments of relative warmth—but they were few and far between. Mostly there was bluish dismal shade, and the constant trudge through shin-deep snow, not to mention hidden tree roots lurking within the snow, keen to trip you up.

To his rear, at a distance of some several yards, were Zoë and Jayne, a pair of sullen presences. Meadowlark Deane was next to him, while up ahead, Mal pulled the travois. The makeshift framework of branches and bark juddered behind him. With its strapped-in cargo of cans it must have weighed a couple of hundred pounds, and the effort of lugging it along was clearly immense. Then there was the stress it must be putting on Mal's traumatized ribs, an added impediment. Yet still Mal persevered. Hands clamped around the ends of the two main struts, he strained forward, back bent, head down, like some sort of human packhorse.

Simon didn't know whether to admire or pity him. Mal's refusal to abandon their quest was noble, but it was also pigheaded. He was driven by his love for Inara, and yet it was a love he could barely admit to himself, let alone to her. Beneath that roguish image he liked to project, there were dark currents—emotions so complex, swirling so hard, that even he himself could not always make sense of them. Mal seemed to bear a deep-seated and abiding grudge against the 'verse and defined himself as much by what he stood in opposition to as what he stood *for*. Perhaps he was desperate that Kiehl's myeloma would not claim Inara's life simply because, as in the Unification War, he was facing an enemy with overwhelming strength and all the advantages. He knew he could not win against the cancer, but the more futile a cause was, the more Malcolm Reynolds relished the battle.

"Sir?" Zoë called out to Mal.

Mal didn't stop, so she called out again.

When he still didn't stop, she jogged past Simon and Meadowlark and took Mal by the shoulder, bringing him to a halt.

"We've been going like this for three hours straight," she said. "Maybe we should rest up, grab a bite. Huh?"

"No," said Mal.

"Yes," said Zoë determinedly. "Even if you don't care about the rest of us, you can't keep driving yourself on like this. Look at you. You're about ready to collapse. Twenty minutes, that's all I'm asking. It can't hurt."

Everyone else was standing, looking at Mal. Mal studied their faces.

"Ten," he said finally.

"Fifteen," said Zoë.

"I ain't bargainin'."

"Neither am I."

With a huff of resignation, Mal set down the travois. "Okay. Fifteen. But not a minute more."

Zoë doled out protein bars, and the group started chowing down hungrily.

"Penny for 'em?" said Meadowlark to Simon. He was perched on a fallen log, and she had sat down beside him.

"My thoughts?" Simon said. "Not sure I have any apart from, 'Damn I'm freezing.'"

"Me too. Still, I don't mind. I'm with you. I like being with you."

"I like being with you too."

Meadowlark seemed extremely pleased to hear this. Her lips, pale from the cold, broke into a smile. "Sometimes good things come out of bad circumstances." Then the smile faded a fraction. "I have a couple of questions, though, Simon."

"Okay."

"And you're going to have to be honest with me. No more secrets. Yes?"

"Of course."

"First off, that whole embezzlement thing…"

"Just a sham," Simon said. "A cover story. I'm sorry, Meadowlark. It was a lie, yes, but it was a necessary one. You must understand that."

"All right," said Meadowlark. "Fine. Fine. I guess, as these things go, it isn't that big of a deal. I can overlook it."

Simon was relieved. "Is that all?" he said. "You did say questions plural."

"Yes," said Meadowlark. "Who's River? Mal talked about someone called River not so long ago. Said something about how she would never leave without you."

"River is my *mèi mèi*."

"Your little sister? Aw, that's sweet. I don't have a sister, or a brother. Always wished I did, but I was destined to be an only child. Only and lonely. What's she like?"

"She's… beautiful. She dances. She's super smart. She…" Simon didn't want to bring up the awful things the Academy had done to River. At that moment, he wanted to think about River as he liked to imagine her, rather than as she actually was. He was in low enough spirits already. No need to make it worse. "I couldn't ask for a better baby sister."

"I'd like to meet her sometime."

"You will, when we get off this miserable damn planet."

"I look forward to it. I'm sure she and I will get along. And Kaylee? That was another name Mal mentioned. Who's she? Another sister?"

Simon hesitated, only briefly, but the hesitation gave Meadowlark her answer.

"Is she your girl?" she said. All at once the temperature of her voice dropped a few degrees, becoming almost as icy as the air around them. "She is, isn't she?"

Simon struggled to respond. "Kaylee is the engineer on our ship. She's… I guess I'd call her a friend."

"No. She were just a friend, you'd have said so straight away."

"It's complicated."

"I don't think relationships should be complicated. You're either in one or you're not. It's that simple. So which is it, Simon? You and Kaylee, are you going steady or aren't you?"

"Going steady? Definitely not."

"But she means something to you."

"I suppose—"

"Don't be stringing me along, Simon," Meadowlark cut in. "If I'm just some convenient little side-bet while you make up your mind whether you're going to go all-in on this Kaylee girl or not, then you should take a long, hard think about what you're doing, mister. Nobody plays those kind of games with Meadowlark Deane."

Her face had lapsed into a pout, but there was a glint in her eyes that was more than petulant, that spoke of genuine, heartfelt recrimination.

Simon felt moved to give her reassurance, while at the same time knowing that he shouldn't have to justify himself. "I don't play games, Meadowlark. I'm not that guy. I could never two-time anyone. You only have to look at me to know it's true."

Meadowlark studied him gravely. Simon had the distinct impression that, as with Mal, here was someone not in full command of their emotions. But whereas Mal directed his seething inner uncertainty outwards, against the 'verse, Meadowlark directed hers inward, against herself. She was her own worst critic, and wherever she saw unfairness, she took it personally.

"I—I do want to believe you, Simon," she said, and she was about to say more, but then there was a cry of alarm from Jayne, and a sudden, ferocious growling, and all hell broke loose.

49

The terrafreak wolves came in from three sides at once.

One line of attack was from the rear. The patriarch led this assault himself, accompanied by three of his children.

The two remaining pairs of wolves zeroed in on the other humans from the left and right. One pair consisted of the matriarch and her eldest daughter. The other comprised two brothers.

Collectively the pack had spent several minutes sneaking up on their prey, getting into position. They had flitted from tree to tree, moving with all the low-slung cunning of their species, ears flattened and tails down. The forest was to them as the ocean was to a shark, a medium through which they could glide unseen, undetected, unsuspected, until the crucial moment.

Now, all at once, they had sprung into action.

Call it instinct. Call it luck. Call it some kind of sixth sense. Jayne Cobb just happened to turn round as, behind him, four wolves broke cover and made their attack run.

His eyes bulged in shock. Four ghost-pale shapes, sprinting towards him from the forest at top speed. Jaws agape, fangs bared.

All but silent, their paws kicking up small flurries of snow as they ran. And huge. Bigger than a wolf had any right to be.

The frontmost wolf sprang, its leap taking it on a perfect trajectory for Jayne's throat.

Jayne reflexively threw up an arm to shield himself. The wolf's teeth latched on to his forearm, just above the wrist. The momentum of its lunge sent Jayne crashing to the ground, the wolf falling with him. The animal landed off-balance but managed to maintain its grip on Jayne. Jayne wrenched his arm from side to side in an effort to shake it off, but the wolf simply bit harder. Fabric tore. Blood spurted. Jayne screamed.

Zoë, who was close by Jayne, was able to sidestep the first wolf that came at her. It shot past, then tried to perform an about-turn but skidded in the snow and fell onto its side.

A second wolf caught up with her, but thanks to her near-miss with the first wolf Zoë was ready for this one. With scarcely a pause for thought, she knocked its legs from under it with a sweeping kick. While the wolf lay on its side, struggling to rise, she grabbed it by the hindlegs. Before it could twist round to bite her, she planted her feet firmly in the snow, hoisted the wolf into the air and swung it round in an arc. Its head struck the first wolf just as it was recovering its footing. There was a meaty smack as their muzzles collided. Both wolves shrieked in surprise and pain.

Zoë swung the flailing wolf back in the opposite direction, catching the other wolf another hefty blow to the chops. The creature took a few steps backwards, shaking its head agitatedly.

Not daring to let go of the wolf she was holding, Zoë swung it once again, this time at a nearby tree, to devastating effect. The animal's skull crashed against the tree's trunk with a loud crunch of splintering bone. The wolf was half dead as Zoë tossed it aside. It lay in the snow, legs twitching spasmodically, while its nervous system shut down bit by bit until at last all life left it.

Mindful of the first wolf, which was dazed but not out of action, Zoë raced over to Jayne, snatching up a fallen pine limb as she ran. Jayne was still grappling with the wolf that was locked onto his arm. He pounded its head with his free hand, cussing and yelling at it all the while.

"Get offa me! Get the hell offa me!"

The wolf, however, heeded neither the shouts nor the punches. Instead it dug its paws into the ground and began twisting its head this way and that, tearing at Jayne's flesh. Jayne let out a guttural roar and hit the animal even harder.

Brandishing the sturdy pine branch double-handed like a baseball bat, Zoë whacked it against the wolf's ribs. There was a satisfying crackle of bones breaking, but the wolf, though hurt, was not giving in that easily. Zoë struck again, and a third time, before finally it had had enough punishment. Letting go of Jayne's arm, the wolf tottered away, then lay down panting and whimpering.

Zoë would have finished it off there and then, but she had still two wolves to contend with. One was a rangy-looking thing, probably the runt of the litter. It was holding back from the fray, wary. The other was the first wolf she had encountered, the one she had clubbed with its fellow wolf. This one looked older than the rest and, to Zoë's way of thinking, had unusually intelligent eyes. It was sizing her up, seemingly reevaluating the threat she posed.

"You thought I'd be easier meat than this, huh?" she said to it. "Well, guess again, buster."

Jayne, clutching his bleeding, injured arm to his chest, staggered to his feet. "Crack its brainpan open, Zoë," he urged, gritting his teeth against the pain from the wolf bite. "Show that lousy mutt who's boss."

Tightening her grip on the branch, Zoë braced herself for the next attack.

As a commotion erupted behind him, Mal whirled round. He took in the situation at a glance: Zoë and Jayne deep in battle with wolves, and more wolves making for Simon and Meadowlark, both of whom were rooted to the spot in panic. These other wolves, four of them in groups of two, were coming together from opposite directions in a pincer movement.

Mal's right hand flew to his hip, where his sidearm was holstered. His fingers closed around empty space.

Of course.

No Liberty Hammer. No kind of weapon at all, dammit.

Then again…

Mal dived for the travois and seized two of the largest food cans. Then, a can in each hand, he ran towards Simon and Meadowlark.

He reached them just in time to intercept the nearest of the four wolves. He swung the can in his right hand with all his might, hitting the animal hard enough to send it flying sideways. He swung the other can and struck a second wolf a similarly powerful blow. The rim of the can caught the animal's eye, tearing it free from its socket. The little ball of jelly splatted onto the snow. The wolf howled in agony and shied away, pawing at its wound.

Without hesitating—because if he had stopped to think about it, he probably wouldn't have done it—Mal spun round and charged at the other two wolves. He pounded one of them on the top of the head. The *crack* of metal on skull was loud and resonant. The wolf collapsed, stunned.

The remaining wolf halted. Its lips pulled back to reveal interlocked fangs, and a low, menacing snarl issued from its throat. It steadied itself, getting ready to spring.

Mal drew back his right arm and hurled a can at the animal.

Bullseye!

The can split open on impact, spraying chocolate pudding onto the snow.

The wolf yelped, then fixed Mal with a very surly stare.

"I got another one," Mal said to it, switching the can in his left hand to his right. "You want another processed-food fastball, straight to the kisser? Then come at me. I dare you."

The wolf appeared to be thinking about it.

Mal feinted a throw.

The wolf cringed. It had figured out that the human could hurt it from a distance. It didn't seem any too keen on getting hit again.

"Yeah. Thought not."

A cry from Simon: "Mal!"

Mal turned.

The first two wolves he had clouted, including the one he had rendered half blind, were back on their feet and menacing Simon and Meadowlark again. The pair of youngsters were kicking out and managing to fend off the creatures, but the wolves were getting bolder by the second.

"Little help here?" said Simon.

"Kinda busy," Mal said, looking back at the wolf he was already dealing with. It seemed heartened by the fact that he was distracted. It moved one pace forward, ears flattened, poised to launch itself.

Out of the corner of his eye, Mal spied Zoë and Jayne. They still had a couple of wolves of their own to contend with. Zoë was holding the animals at bay with a tree branch, swinging it at them whenever they crept close, but as with Simon and Meadowlark, there was no telling how long the stalemate would last. As for Jayne, he looked pretty badly injured. Blood soaked his sleeve and streaked the front of his parka. His breath came in short, hissing gasps and he seemed unsteady on his feet, on the verge of passing out.

"Mal, what's the plan here?" Simon said. He was trying to keep his voice calm. He was not succeeding. "What do we do?"

"Ain't sure there's much we *can* do," Mal replied.

"What if we try and make a run for it?"

"Outrun wolves? Don't think so. No, I reckon we've just got to stand our ground and be ready to go down fighting."

"This is your gorramn fault, Mal," Jayne called out. "So help me, we get outta this, I'm gonna kill you."

The wolves were confident of victory now. They had taken casualties, but that was perhaps to be expected. No hunt was without its risks, certainly not when the prey was large and fierce. They had drawn blood, though, proving that the humans were vulnerable. They also still had the advantage in numbers.

The patriarch eyed up the two humans in front of him, the injured one and the one who had proved a formidable opponent. The smell of spilled blood was thick in his nostrils, heady, delicious. He let out a growl.

The matriarch let out a similar growl in response. It was time for a decisive attack. The matter had to be settled, now or never.

She tensed. The patriarch tensed. Their four children who were still in the fight picked up on this. They knew that one last assault was expected of them. If they gave it everything they had, the pack would eat today. They would *feast*.

That was when the bear came.

50

With a tremendous, bellowing roar, the grizzly bear shambled out from the trees.

It reared up on its hindlegs and waved its massive, talon-tipped paws in the air.

All at once, the wolves cowered. The certainty and cohesion the pack had shown just moments ago dissipated. They began to pace from side to side fretfully, casting anxious looks at the bear. For all that they were predators themselves, they seemed well aware that they were in the presence of a superior predator.

The bear roared again, and the majority of the wolves broke rank and made for the sanctuary of the trees. A couple remained, the two largest and oldest-looking. The bear lumbered towards the bigger of the pair. The wolf refused to be intimidated. Standing its ground, it let out a warning growl.

Then the bear produced a smooth, straight tree branch whose tip had been whittled to a sharp point. It launched this homemade spear at the wolf. The weapon flew with more force than accuracy, catching the wolf a glancing blow on the flank and opening up a small gash.

The wolf yelped loudly, sounding more indignant than anything.

"Darn it! Missed!" said the bear.

That was when Zoë overcame her surprise and lunged at the same wolf with her own tree-branch weapon. She slammed it into the animal's flank, on the spot where it had just been injured.

The wolf retaliated with a swipe of its paw, which Zoë narrowly evaded. She lashed out again, and then Mal joined in with his food can. Between them, they drove the wolf backwards, pummeling it when they could and doing their best to stay clear of its snapping jaws and flashing claws.

Soon the wolf had plainly had enough. It was battered, bruised, altogether demoralized, and it seemed to at last conclude that these humans were in fact more trouble than they were worth. It turned tail and limped off into the forest, casting the odd aggrieved look over its shoulder. The other remaining wolf followed suit, melting in amongst the trees.

When all the still-living wolves were gone from sight, a few muted, desultory howls sounded in the distance, a chorus of dismay and resentment.

Now Mal, Zoë, Jayne, Simon and Meadowlark all turned their attention to the grizzly bear.

The grizzly bear who had spoken and thrown a spear.

They looked at it. The bear looked back at them with shriveled, empty eye sockets.

"What?" said the bear.

"Who in tarnation are you?" said Jayne. He still had a hand clamped over his forearm, to try to stem the blood flow from the savaging he had received. "You're no grizzly, that's for damn sure."

"Of course I'm not a grizzly," said the bear. "But as far as those wolves were concerned, I might as well have been. To them, I looked like a bear. More importantly, I smelled like a bear. Wolves are afraid of bears, you see, and the mere presence of one is enough to send them running. Most of them, at any rate. That big wolf, for instance, was made of sterner stuff. I'll wager anything it was the dominant male, the pack leader."

"No, wait, just hold on a second," said Zoë, with a touch of impatience. "I get that you're not a real bear. You're just some guy covered in a bearskin."

"Obviously."

"But who *are* you?"

"I could ask the five of you the same question," the bear retorted. "Escapees from Hellfreeze would be my guess. You aren't any of Mr. O'Bannon's Regulators that I recognize. I wouldn't have intervened if you were. You apparently have decided to try surviving outside the confines of Correctional Unit #23, and if that's case, then I applaud your choice, but I counsel caution. It's far from easy, living off the land—especially land as inhospitable and ungiving as this. I don't recommend it."

"You still haven't answered my question."

"And you still haven't thanked me for helping you out of the jam you were in just now."

"Thank you, sir," said Meadowlark brightly.

"You're welcome, young lady," said the bear, with a nod of its shaggy head.

"You can't be some native mountain man," Simon said. "Atata doesn't have any of those."

"How very astute of you."

"But what does that leave?"

Mal piped up. "Come on, people," he said. A slow, incredulous smile was spreading across his face. "Ain't you worked it out yet?"

"Huh?" said Jayne. "Worked out what?"

"There's only one person this can be."

"My God..." Zoë breathed, cottoning on.

Jayne still looked nonplussed.

"Think about it," Mal said. "He knows about the Regulators.

Means there's every chance he's from Hellfreeze himself. And *that* means…"

"It can't be," said Simon.

"It's gotta be," said Mal. "Ladies and gentlemen, I give you… Dr. Esau Weng."

51

The man drew back the scalp of the grizzly which shrouded his own head like a cowl.

Beneath were the features familiar to Mal from the picture of the oncologist that he had found on the Cortex. His hair was longer and even wilder now, and a thick, unkempt growth of beard covered his cheeks and chin. He looked a lot thinner, too. But here were the same deep-set eyes, the same intelligent but somewhat unworldly expression.

This was unquestionably him. Dr. Esau Weng, in the flesh.

"You have me at a disadvantage," Weng said. "You know me, but I have no idea who you are."

"We," said Mal, "are the folks who've risked their necks to find you."

"You were looking for me?" Dr. Weng adopted a defensive posture, as if getting ready to run. "So Mr. O'Bannon sent you. You *are* Regulators after all. Oh, Lord!"

"No," said Mal quickly. He held his hands out in a pacifying gesture. "I mean, yes, we've been looking for you, but no, we ain't Regulators. No stars with an 'R' on them under these thermal togs. Honest, we're friendlies, and we've come to take you off Atata."

Weng did a double-take. "Say that again?"

"Please believe me. We've traveled a long way and gone through a hell of a lot to get here. I'm having a hard time acceptin' that we've actually succeeded. I hoped we would. I prayed we would. It's just… Anyways, here you are. Holy crap! I am so pleased to see you, Doc, that I could just about kiss you."

"Take me off Atata?" said Weng. "Do you mean it?"

"Never meant anything so sincerely in all my born days."

A tentative smile appeared on Weng's face. Then a thought seemed to occur to him. He looked at Mal askance. "How do I know this isn't a trick? How do I know you're not lying and you're just going to lull me into a false sense of security, then grab me and drag me back to Hellfreeze?"

"Because I have a transceiver in my pants which I can use to call in my ship. No, wait, I don't."

"Yeah, you smashed it all to pieces, Mal, remember?" said Jayne. "Not one of your smarter moves."

"Okay, then you'll just have to trust me," said Mal to Weng. "We do have a ship somewhere up there, and I can't signal to her right this moment, but her crew will come looking for us sooner or later, I guarantee it. I'm not a convict. We none of us are. Well, she is." He pointed at Meadowlark. "Only, she isn't really. More like a victim of the Alliance, same as you."

"You… have landed on Atata… with the express intent of liberating me?" Weng spoke slowly, as though he was still having difficulty taking all of this on board.

"Sure have."

"And you're definitely not inmates of Hellfreeze?"

"Do we look it?"

"Somewhat." Weng gestured at Jayne with one bearpaw-swathed hand. "Him definitely."

"Hey, why's everyone keep going on like that about me?" said Jayne. "First it's Meadowlark tellin' me I could be a murderer. Now you. Is it the goatee? Can't be the face. My momma always said I've got a nice face."

"But why?" said Weng. "That's what's puzzling me. Why have you—a bunch of complete strangers—come for me? Who am I to you?"

"You, Doc," said Mal, "are the best chance we have of saving the woman I... the woman I need to save."

"I see."

"You and your targeted artificial immuno... whatsits."

"Immunomodulatory microorganisms," said Simon.

"Her name is Inara Serra and she's dying," Mal said. "Cancer. But you are going to fix her. And now, while I'm enjoyin' this moment of triumph and vindication, I am going to pause, turn to my shipmates and give them a look, like this."

Mal aimed a big, gloating grin at Zoë, Jayne and Simon.

"And I am going to dance a jig, like this."

He shuffled up and down on the spot for several moments.

"And I am going to tell them 'I told you so,' like this. *I told you so.*"

Zoë rolled her eyes. "Sir, you are never more insufferable than when you're being smug."

"Don't care. We got to Dr. Weng. Inara's gonna be okay. You can say what you like, but in spite of everything, against all the odds, we have pulled it off. We have chalked up a big, fat win!"

"Reluctant as I am to rain on your parade..." Weng began, but before he could finish the remark, Jayne let out a soft moan and sank to his knees. Next instant, he keeled over sideways into the snow.

"Jayne?" said Zoë, crouching beside him. She patted his face. "Jayne?" She shook her head. "Out cold."

"Shock. Blood loss," said Simon.

"Anything you can do?"

Simon knelt beside Jayne and grabbed a couple of handfuls of snow, which he used to scrub the wound as best he could. He packed more snow over the wound—the cold would help inhibit the blood flow—then unfurled the muffler from his face and bound it tightly around the arm as a makeshift bandage and compress.

"That should hold him for now," he said when he was finished, "but we need to get him patched up properly. I don't have any medical supplies on me."

"I may have a few useful items in my cave," said Weng. "It isn't far from here."

"You have a cave?" said Mal.

"I'm a bear," Weng said, indicating the pelt he was wearing. "Naturally I have a cave."

52

They offloaded the food cans from the travois quickly and strapped in Jayne in their place. Those wolves might return for a second try at any moment. Mal and Zoë dragged him, with Dr. Weng leading the way. Simon tramped along behind them, and Meadowlark a little behind him, each of them carrying a few food cans. Simon kept directing looks over his shoulder at her, as though trying to gauge her mood. Meadowlark steadfastly refused to meet his gaze.

It was a journey of about two miles to the cave, mostly uphill. As Weng guided them through the forest, he pointed out various animal traps he had set. Here, a snare fashioned from braided ivy stems, the loop dangling a few inches off the ground; there, a deadfall trap made out of a log balanced at an angle atop a twig that served as a trigger.

"Rabbits and squirrels is what I catch, mostly," he said. "One time, I got a marmot. Another time, this terrafreak thing that was maybe a marten or a weasel—some sort of mustelid, anyway. It wasn't pretty to look at but it was surprisingly tasty."

The forest thinned, petering out altogether as the group reached a long, low crag. They walked parallel to the crag for several hundred yards, until they arrived at the cave. Its entrance was a horizontal slit approximately three feet high. They crawled through this aperture on hands and knees, and almost immediately were able to straighten up and stand. Mal and Zoë leaned back out and hauled in the travois, with Jayne still on it.

The cave interior was roughly dome-shaped, with a fissure crossing the ceiling and a couple of small alcove-like depressions inset into its granite walls. The remnants of a wood fire smoldered in the center of the floor, giving off a faint orange glow and a strong resinous odor. A skein of smoke filtered up from the embers into the fissure, which evidently extended all the way to the surface above, forming a natural chimney. The narrowness of the entrance kept the worst of the cold out. A dense nest of pine fronds banked up against one wall clearly served as a bed. The place was homely. You might even call it cozy.

Weng shrugged his way out of the bear pelt and stuffed it in one of the alcoves.

"Phew," he said. "That thing has saved my life on more than one occasion, but good God, does it smell something awful. I can put up with it but only because it serves a purpose. While I have it on, wolves are apt to leave me alone, and so are other bears. It used to belong to the former occupant of this cave."

"You kill the grizzly yourself?" Mal asked.

"Me? Oh dear heavens, no. I'd never have been able to. No, what happened was that I stumbled across the cave on… I think it was my third night after leaving Hellfreeze. Blizzard conditions, and I was half frozen, in the early stages of hypothermia, and I knew if I didn't find shelter I would die. It didn't even occur to me there might be a bear in here. You can imagine how terrified I was when I spotted the animal at the far end, curled up asleep—or so I thought. Turned out, on closer inspection, it was stone cold dead. It had probably died while hibernating, of natural causes. Of course, I was obliged to skin it and dismember it before it began to rot. Once the pelt had dried out, I put it on for warmth. It wasn't until later that I discovered its wolf-repelling qualities, a happy by-product. I came across a lone wolf while I was out laying traps, and it took one look at me and ran. That was how I knew."

He waved a hand self-effacingly.

"But listen to me, rambling on. You can tell I haven't had company for quite some while. Let's take a look at this fellow's arm. You." Weng was addressing Simon. "You're clearly some kind of physician, judging by the way you dealt with the wound out there. More to the point, you were comfortable using the phrase immunomodulatory microorganisms."

"Yes, I am a doctor. Simon's the name." Judiciously, Simon didn't add his surname. Weng might have heard of Dr. Tam, fugitive from the Alliance, and even though Weng was surely no fan of the Feds, Simon didn't want to give the man any reason to mistrust him. "Pleased to meet you."

"What's your specialty?"

"I am... I *was* a trauma surgeon."

"'Was'? What happened?"

"Long story. My life has taken some interesting turns since."

"So it would seem," Weng remarked. "Anyway, your friend here... Jayne? Is that his name? Perhaps I can help you with him."

Weng and Simon knelt down either side of Jayne. Simon carefully peeled back the muffler from his forearm and wiped away the blood-pinkened remnants of snow, to reveal a gory mess. Glimpses of exposed bone gleaming in the daylight that seeped in through the cave entrance, through mangled muscle and shredded skin.

Together the two medics examined the injuries, dispassionately discussing them. Meadowlark looked on over Simon's shoulder with a hand to her mouth, seeming both appalled and fascinated by the blood and the ripped flesh. Meanwhile, Mal and Zoë fetched faggots of wood from a stack in a corner and got the fire going again, bringing renewed warmth to the cave.

"The hand itself is intact," Weng said, "but there's significant damage to the extensor tendons. He may never regain the use of it."

"That's the hand he does his favorite thing with," Simon said.

Weng raised an eyebrow.

"Pull a trigger," Simon explained.

"Ah. Well, absent proper surgical intervention, it'll be as good as paralyzed, or at best be left with severely impaired function. With regard to the tissue laceration, that's extensive too. No bone fracture, though, which is a blessing. I have a basic first-aid kit, containing surgical needle and thread among other things. It comes courtesy of Mr. O'Bannon. One of the few items I took with me when I left Hellfreeze. However, I reckon any attempt to suture this wound would be a mistake. Don't you agree?"

Simon nodded. "I do. The light in here is poor, and we could cause permanent damage if we don't do the job exactly right. Not to mention there's the likelihood of introducing infection."

"I don't see, then, that there's any choice but to bind the wound up again, as you did before," said Weng. "After that, we should get this man to a proper medical facility at the earliest possible opportunity. He needs operating on, under full sterile conditions, if we're to save the arm, and indeed possibly his life. I don't suppose your ship has an infirmary?"

"It does. Not a great one, but good enough."

"And how soon do you think it'll be coming to collect us?"

"Hard to say."

"Soon would be good, as far as Jayne is concerned."

"Huh? Whazzat?" Jayne stirred, coming round from unconsciousness. "Soon would be good for what?"

"Your arm, Jayne," said Simon. "We can't do anything for it at the moment but keep it bound up. It needs operating on, though."

Jayne looked at his wound and winced. "Okay. Just do what you haveta."

Weng fetched the first-aid kit and passed Simon a tube of

antiseptic gel and a roll of conforming bandage. "I have a feeling it would be better if you were to treat him, rather than me. You are friends, after all."

"I wouldn't go that far," said Jayne.

"But you're less likely to lash out at him in response to pain than at a stranger, Jayne, surely."

"You simply ain't got the measure of our relationship, Dr. Weng."

"Well, even so…"

"It's okay," said Simon to Weng. "I'll manage. I'm used to him. I warn you, though, Jayne, it isn't going to be pleasant."

"Ah, just get on with it, willya?"

The big mercenary grimaced and hissed as Simon smeared antiseptic gel over the grisly wound. He called Simon's professional qualifications into question, and also his parentage and his sexual prowess. There was at least no lashing out, though.

When Simon had finished applying the bandage, Jayne surveyed his handiwork. "Not bad. And now," he added, "if nobody minds, I think I'm gonna lay here and just… you know…"

He drifted off into unconsciousness again.

By this time, Mal had unlidded a couple of the food cans, using the opener borrowed from Simon, and was heating them on the fire. One contained baked beans, the other hotdogs. The combined smells filled the cave and set some very hungry stomachs rumbling.

They ate using their fingers and passing the cans around. They were all grateful for the sustenance but Weng, in particular, was rhapsodic.

"Fresh meat has been hard to come by these past few days," he said. "The local wildlife seems to have become wise to my traps. I've been subsisting on my supplies of jerky and the occasional edible root. This is a treat. A banquet!"

After the meal, Mal formally introduced himself to Weng, and Zoë and Meadowlark did likewise. Weng told them it was a pleasure to make their acquaintance and expressed how grateful he was that they would be taking him off-planet. Mal, in return, thanked him for coming to their aid in the woods.

"Don't mention it," said Weng. "I saw some people in trouble. The instinct to help out our fellow humans is strong in all of us— strong enough to override any natural caution I might have felt."

"Still, you needn't have, Doc, and you did. We owe you."

"You're getting me out of a very bleak situation. I'd say the debt is going to be amply repaid."

"Don't take this the wrong way, Dr. Weng," said Zoë, "but you seem to have held up pretty well out here on your own. I wouldn't have pegged somebody like you as the wilderness type."

"Somebody like me, Miss Alleyne? You mean a soft-handed lab jockey who's never done anything more strenuous than polish a test tube?" Weng chuckled. "You might be right. It's remarkable, though, what one can accomplish when one has to. I've endured the cold and the deprivation this long simply because the only alternative is dying and I have no wish to do that. Admittedly it's been hard. Thanks to my poor diet, my digestion is in ruins and two of my back teeth are loose and in danger of falling out. There have been days when I've gotten so sick I could hardly move. There have been a fair few emotional lows, as well. A fair few dark nights of the soul. More than once, I've thought about ending it all. I even considered making my way back to Hellfreeze and throwing myself on Mr. O'Bannon's mercy—that's how desperate it got."

"What stopped you?"

"The knowledge that Mr. O'Bannon doesn't *have* any mercy. If I went back, he and I would find ourselves exactly where we were before, at a complete impasse, with the threat of torture and death hanging over me. You're aware of the circumstances of my departure, I take it."

"Uh-huh."

"Then you know that Mr. O'Bannon is dying and I cannot heal him."

"Maybe you could have pretended to try."

"Hoodwinked him, you mean? Led him on until the final moment? That did occur to me, but it would have been an incredibly difficult trick to pull off. I'd already told him several times that his cancer was incurable, at least with the very limited facilities at my disposal. Do you think he'd believe me if I showed up again, promising I could treat him after all? It would never have worked. He'd have seen through it in an instant. And while we're on the subject of cancer ..."

Weng turned to Mal.

"This friend of yours. One can only infer that she has contracted one of the more virulent forms of the disease. Why else would you have gone to such lengths to seek me out?"

"It's Kiehl's myeloma," Mal said.

"Oh my. That is serious indeed. The poor thing."

"But you've got the knowhow to save her, right? Your tech'll do the trick, yeah?"

Weng looked down at his hands. "Well now..."

"Come on, Doc," Mal cajoled. "This ain't the time for modesty. You can cook up a batch of your little viruses and Inara'll be right as rain in no time. Yeah?"

Sheepishly Weng said, "This runs counter to my own interests, but I feel I must be honest. I can't promise to be able to cure her. In fact, I'd say the chances of success are close to zero."

53

Mal was silent for a moment. Then he said, "Nah. I don't believe you."

"Whether you believe me or not, Mr. Reynolds," said Weng, "it's the truth. I could claim otherwise. Perhaps I ought to. You're my ticket out of here, after all, and why would I jeopardize that? But the fact is, my artificial immunomodulatory microorganisms haven't proved to be the panacea that I thought they would. Let me explain."

"I think you'd better," said Mal tersely.

"The ambition of my research was to create a means of promoting cellular regrowth."

"We know that."

"Do you? Yes, you must do. The end product would, I hoped, be markedly improved treatments for a whole host of illnesses, not just cancers. The artificial immunomodulatory microorganisms—I call them 'AIMs' for short—could be programmed to attend to the specific ailment. A failing organ? They could rebuild it. A broken bone? They could act as both scaffold and cement, enabling it to heal at a far faster rate than nature normally allows. Infinitely variable remedial medicine that can be tailored to suit any need—that was the aim of AIMs."

"But…?"

"I had some successes with laboratory tests on live specimens. I had some failures too. Fine-tuning the AIMs proved incredibly hard. Sometimes they worked. Sometimes they didn't. And sometimes they worked far too well, overloading the test subject's innate growth and healing processes and causing egregious mutations and deformities. I would say that I was several years away from getting the process absolutely right. But that didn't prevent the Alliance from taking an interest. One day, a man came calling at my lab on Greenleaf. A man wearing blue gloves."

Simon stiffened. Mal and Zoë looked grave.

"Blue gloves?" Simon said. "A bit like surgical gloves?"

Weng registered their reactions. "I see you've met him."

"I have," Simon said, "or someone like him at any rate. Couple of them, in fact."

"And from what Simon's told us," Zoë said, "these ain't people to be messed with."

"I had that impression too," said Weng. "It was odd, because he never gave his name, this fellow, nor did he once take off those gloves. And he had this eerie politeness about him, and a voice that was flat, almost monotonous, as if normal human interaction didn't come naturally to him. He told me he was a contractor for the Union of Allied Planets and that his superiors had taken an interest in me. He didn't specify who his superiors actually were, but I could make an educated guess. Either someone high up in government or someone in the Blue Sun Corporation."

"Like there's much of a difference," said Mal.

"Well, quite. Those two entities are so inextricably linked, they might as well be the same thing. The color of his gloves, though, minds me to think it was the latter. And he offered me funding. Funding like you would not believe. Up until then I had been scraping by on charitable grants, and now, all of a sudden, these large sums of money were being waved under my nose. Remarkably large sums.

So large that I could buy all the state-of-the-art equipment I needed, hire assistants, and more."

"What would a blue-gloved man want with an advanced medical treatment?" Simon mused. "What would be the benefit to him and his bosses?"

"I asked him the very same thing," said Weng. "Obviously my thought was that Blue Sun wished to monetize my AIMs. The funding would, I assumed, have strings attached. Blue Sun would take out a lien on my patents, maybe even own them outright if I wasn't careful. But I didn't dedicate half my life to this research only to see the results become someone else's property. My intention was always that AIMs should be free to all."

"Idealistic of you," said Mal. "You tellin' us you wouldn't want to make a single credit out of your virus things?"

Weng shrugged. "Perhaps a small consideration. A nominal fee per usage. Enough to keep me comfortable, but it was never about becoming wealthy. It was always about helping people. I assumed this nameless blue-gloved man would admit that his superiors, whoever they were, wished to buy me out and profit from my work, and I was all set to tell him where to stick his money. His actual reply was worse. He talked calmly about 'applications' for AIMs. I asked what sort, half knowing the answer already. 'Military applications,' he said."

"I don't see how AIMs would work in a military context," said Zoë.

"I think I do," said Simon. "Speed up wound recovery time. Get injured troops back out onto the battlefield far sooner."

"More than that," said Weng. "The AIMs could, in theory, be adapted to enhance the skeletomuscular system, reduce fatigue, boost stamina, thicken skin—making soldiers who are tougher, hardier, and much harder to kill."

"Mr. Blue Gloves told you that?" said Mal.

"In so many words, yes. He was fairly frank about his superiors' motives. He told me he was giving me a chance to do something incredible, to change the face of warfare for all time. From the way he spoke, it was as though this was some splendid opportunity that I'd be a fool to pass up. But it seems I *am* a fool, because I flatly refused. We all remember the war. Death and destruction on an unprecedented scale. A rift in civilization. Anything that furthered the goals of warmongers and that might even make a similar conflict more likely in future, I wanted nothing to do with. I was adamant that AIMs would not be used for that purpose, not if I had my druthers."

"I bet your visitor wasn't happy about that," said Zoë.

"He was not. Oh, he tried to hide his frustration. He smiled at me—a lips-only smile, not a shred of warmth in it—and he suggested I think about his offer for a while, sit with it, mull it over. Maybe, in time, I'd come to see that what he was proposing would be for the benefit of the whole 'verse, but also, more to the point, *my* benefit."

"A threat if ever I heard one."

"Absolutely," said Weng. "And so, as soon as that he left my lab, do you know what I did?"

"Set fire to it," said Mal.

"You're damn right I did. You know about that too?"

"I know the place burned down, and it's said you were responsible."

"It seemed like the best option. I destroyed it all—my notes, my files, my lab apparatus, my AIMs samples—so that there'd be nothing anyone else could get their hands on. It wasn't an easy decision to make, believe you me. All those long years of work, gone up in smoke. But I realized that Blue Sun or the Alliance or whoever it was would never leave me alone otherwise. They'd keep hounding, harassing. This way, there was nothing left of the entire AIMs project. Not a trace except the basic concept in my head. There was no way I could re-create the viruses from memory alone. Not without access to a whole raft of data and materials that no longer existed."

"Really?" said Simon.

"It'd be like trying to retrace the steps of a very long and complicated journey without a map. You'd never stop off at all the exact same spots you did the first time. You'd likely lose your way and maybe wind up at a different destination altogether. And that's what I told the Feds when they bashed down my apartment door at three o'clock the next morning and arrested me. I said there'd be no point them trying to force me to give them AIMs, whether with bribery or beatings or whatever. They could stick me in a laboratory with everything I needed and I still wouldn't be able to get back to where I was before. Too much development had gone on, too many happy accidents, all that convoluted evolution—it couldn't be repeated. In hindsight, what I should have done is hightailed it to some far-flung Rim planet as soon as I set fire to the lab. Call me naïve, but I thought that if I stayed put and had a chance to argue my case, I'd be able to convince the authorities to drop the matter and then I could simply get on with my life."

"Yeah, that *was* kinda naïve," Zoë said.

Weng acknowledged this with a brisk chuckle. "Instead, they put me on trial. I was accused of violating medical ethics and essentially being some sort of mad scientist who was carrying out vivisection and other horrendous practices. It was abundantly clear what the Feds were up to. They thought I was bluffing and they were trying to intimidate me into capitulating. And when it became apparent that I *wouldn't* capitulate—because I couldn't—the trial became about teaching me a lesson instead. Verdict: guilty. Sentence: life, on Atata. And here I am."

Mal sighed heavily. His shoulders slumped. "So that's it, huh?" He sounded defeated, utterly despondent. "After all this, we're no better off than we were before. We've risked so much, been through so much, and we may as well not have bothered."

"I'm sorry," said Weng. "Sincerely I am."

"Ain't your fault, Doc," Mal said, but not without an edge of resentment in his voice.

"And we'll still take you with us when our ship comes," Simon chipped in, "if you were worried about that." He looked at Mal, seeking confirmation.

Mal nodded, albeit grudgingly.

"It's the least we can do," Zoë said. "You got a raw deal from the Feds. We can even up that injustice if nothing else."

"That's good of you," said Weng. "I appreciate it. And, in a spirit of full disclosure, I should tell you that, in truth, I was lying my ass off to the Alliance about AIMs."

Mal canted his head to one side. "What's that? What did you just say?"

"I didn't destroy *everything*. I did keep one sample of the virus."

"You did?"

"Don't get excited. I already told you I was years away from getting the process absolutely right. But I do have a functioning AIMs prototype. It's safely stored in a vessel that provides a perfect growth medium."

"Well, where? Where is it? Can we get to it? Maybe we can use it."

Weng pointed at himself. "It's right here."

54

"Before I burned down my lab," Weng said, "I took the step of injecting myself with an inert specimen of AIMs. The latest iteration of the virus, and the most responsive and promising version I'd yet developed. It's flowing through my bloodstream right now. It's like a passenger inside me, and my body is keeping it alive. Within me the AIMs live, die, replicate, while having no effect whatever on my physiology."

"I thought you didn't want anyone else getting their hands on the stuff," said Zoë.

"I wanted to make sure no one else could reproduce AIMs. Hence the lab fire. I couldn't let go of my dream completely, however. I felt that at some later date, after all the fuss had died down, I might be able to start anew, and this way I'd at least have something to work with. All I'd need to do is draw some of my blood, isolate the AIMs within, and perhaps, with luck, I could pick up more or less where I left off."

"So you *were* bluffing the Alliance," said Simon.

"To some extent, yes," Weng said with a twinkle in his eye. "Call it an insurance policy. Of course, I couldn't have predicted where I would end up. Really, I was sure the trial would collapse and I, an innocent man, would be allowed to walk free. I might serve time for arson, perhaps, but nothing more serious. That naïveté of mine again."

"And you didn't think of using the AIMs inside you as a bargaining chip?" Zoë asked. "To get your sentence nullified? Blue Sun could have arranged that, if they'd known."

"But then I'd have been back where I started, wouldn't I? Forced to give the corporation what they wanted, what I didn't want to give them. Besides, I was in a state of shock. My head was reeling as they whisked me out of court. Next thing I knew, I was on a transport ship and it was too late to do anything about anything."

"Does this mean that we could extract some AIMs from you," said Mal, "and maybe use them on Inara after all?" His expression was that of someone trying desperately not to get their hopes up.

Weng gave a noncommittal nod. "The version of AIMs inside me is generic. You could call it a template, a blank slate. There is just the remotest possibility that it can be programmed to counteract the effects of Kiehl's. But, to reiterate what I said not so long ago, the chances of success are close to zero."

"'Close to zero' ain't the same as zero."

"There's no faulting your grasp of math, Mr. Reynolds. With access to a high-spec med computer, I could interface with the viruses and turn them into dedicated microscopic heat-seeking missiles that would eradicate the rogue blood plasma cells in your lady friend's body and ensure that her bone marrow does not produce any more. I'm not saying with any certainty that it'd work."

"But it might."

"But it just might. Dr. Tam, does your ship's infirmary have a med computer?"

"Yes, but I don't think it's anywhere near as advanced as you need, Dr. Weng. She's a Firefly, and a pretty old one at that."

"I thought as much. Few ships carry an above-basic level of healthcare technology aboard, especially not Fireflies."

"However," Simon went on, "where Inara's being looked after right now, the equipment is top notch, as I understand it. Isn't that right, Mal?"

"And whatever other pieces of newtech you could wish for, we have a rich friend who can easily get hold of them," said Mal. "No matter what it costs."

"Then," said Weng, "that's what we'll do. But I must state once more for the record that the odds of—"

"Yeah, Doc, okay, we get it," Mal said, waving a hand. "Between slim and nothing. Thing is, me and my crew have bucked those odds before, and we can do it again."

"We have?" said Zoë. "Usually we just seem to get ourselves into trouble and get out of it again by the skin of our teeth."

"Same thing, ain't it?"

"I guess."

"All we have to do, for now," said Mal, "is sit tight and wait for *Serenity* to come looking for us."

"And how are the people on your ship going to find us?" Weng asked. "Seeing as you don't have your transceiver anymore…"

"A Firefly in low atmo makes one hell of a ruckus. We're not too far from CU #23. When they come in for a flyby, we'll hear 'em. Then we can signal 'em."

"How?"

"The old-fashioned way. Like castaways on a desert island. Set a distress fire. Plenty of smoke. They'll spot it and come to investigate."

"That would seem to be a fairly tenuous method of attracting their attention," Weng opined.

"It'll work," Mal said. "It has to."

"And they *are* coming? You know that for sure?"

"Oh yeah." Mal set his jaw firmly. "You can count on it."

"And we know who else is coming," said Zoë. "Regulators."

"My goodness!" exclaimed Weng, with a jump of fright. "You really ought to have mentioned that a bit sooner. You have Regulators on your heels?" He went to the cave entrance, bent down and peered anxiously out.

"We don't know it for certain," Mal said, shooting Zoë a look.

"But it's likely," she said. She told Weng how they had stolen a Slugger from Hellfreeze and left it in the woods after it broke down on them. "Chances are Mr. O'Bannon will be wanting it back—and wanting us dead too, I should imagine—and he'll have made moves in that direction, siccing his pet bullies on us."

"Our tracks are clear as day," said Weng. "They lead right to my front door. How far behind you do you reckon the Regulators are?"

"Not sure. A few hours maybe."

"Assuming they're comin' at all," Mal said.

"Oh, if I know Mr. O'Bannon, they're definitely coming," Weng said. "The only question is how soon."

55

The two Alliance corvettes were definitely coming. The only question was: "how soon?"

The long-range scanner screen on the control console showed River that the ships' spiraling search pattern was bringing them ever closer to *Serenity*'s current position. If they continued on the same course, at the same rate, then by her estimate it would be little more than an hour before they came within visual scan range. The wreck of the freighter was just too obvious a hiding place for them not to check it out.

Kaylee was awake and back at work on the engine. River contacted her over the ship's intercom for an update.

"How soon are we going to be space-able again?"

"Couple more hours at least," Kaylee replied.

"Two Alliance ships are honing in on us. We don't have that long. Can you make it an hour?"

"I'm an engineer, River, not a miracle worker. But okay, I'll try."

Next, River hailed the infirmary over the intercom.

"Wash? How are you feeling?"

"Just peachy," came a very strained-sounding voice.

"No, but really."

"Weak as a newborn kitten, and my eyesight's still refusing to straighten out. It's like the worst hangover in the world, but without any of the fun beforehand. I'll fly if I have to, but I can't promise we won't crash into an asteroid or something."

"You won't have to," River assured him. "I've got this."

"You sure?"

"Sure as eggs is chicken balls."

There was a pause, then Wash said, "I can't quite tell. Does that mean yes or no?"

"It means don't you worry your pretty little head about a thing, young fella. Pilot Tam has the conn and it is *on*."

River cut the intercom connection, then sat back and eyed the console. Her gaze fell on the plastic toy dinosaurs parading around the rim. Wash's little personal touch. She wondered whether, if she were ever officially *Serenity*'s pilot, she would replace them with some small customization of her own. Then she wondered why she thought that such a thing might even happen. It was a feeling, that was all. Faint and elusive. More like a hunch. A foreboding.

And speaking of forebodings, her sense that Simon was in trouble had diminished but not entirely gone away.

River and Simon had always been close. As children, they had been inseparable, and where many an older brother would not have liked his little sister constantly tagging along with him, Simon had never seemed to mind. Sure, there were times when it had been clear she was bugging him, but he had done his best not to show it. She had known his moods, and whenever it appeared that he was getting irritated with her, River would simply go away and leave him alone for a while. Her adoration of him was a constant, however, and she knew he adored her back.

Everything had changed when she was sent to the Academy. It had been a wrench, leaving home and family—leaving Simon, especially—but their parents had insisted it was a marvelous opportunity and River should not turn it down.

And then…

The things.

The things those so-called doctors at the Academy did.

The brain things that had altered her, twisted her, made her strange and clever and simple and powerful and perplexed and perplexing and a whole lot more besides.

What they had not managed to do was break her bond with her brother. Quite the opposite. After Simon rescued her, smuggling her out of the Academy and eventually onto *Serenity*, River had grown to realize that she was now even more deeply connected to him than before. The emotional bond remained just as strong, but there was another more intimate and indefinable link too. Whereas before she had been able to intuit what Simon was thinking from his facial expressions and body language, there were times now when she just *knew*. She knew his thoughts with crystal clarity, almost as though she could hear them, as though he was speaking them aloud. The same was true of most people around her, not least the ship's crew, but with her brother it was like she could read his mind. Perhaps she *was* reading his mind.

And that same connection accounted for the feelings she was experiencing at the moment. Even though Simon was several thousand klicks away, River could feel a tremor in her brain. A delicate tingle of alarm, as if some intangible, infinitely elastic thread that stretched between them was vibrating.

She could tell that a trap was closing around Simon and he remained blissfully unaware. He was about to be set upon by someone vicious. A woman. A frightening, very violent woman. River wasn't sure how soon this was going to happen, but she did know it wouldn't be long.

So apparently it was going to be her turn to rescue *him*. But to do that, she had to get to Atata as soon as possible.

Kaylee had better hurry up.

Time was running out.

For all of them.

56

Ornery Annie surveyed the scene.

Blood spatters everywhere. Scuff marks in the snow. Signs of a fight.

Not to mention two terrafreak wolves sprawled on the ground.

One of the wolves was dead, its skull bashed in. The other lay on its side, just barely alive. Its breathing was sharp and irregular. Frothy blood speckled its muzzle.

Its ribs had been stoved in, Annie could see. A lung must be punctured. The animal was not long for this world.

She knelt, unsheathed her shiv, and sped the wolf on its way to oblivion. As the light faded from the creature's eyes, she wondered which of the group of impostors had been responsible for mortally wounding it and killing the other wolf. Zoë, most likely. Annie had no way of knowing this for certain, but she could easily imagine it: Zoë in a faceoff with a pair of wolves, and the wolves coming off worst.

Otis was staring down at an untidy heap of tin cans. "They dropped alla this food they took. Now why in heck would they do that?"

"They abandoned the Slugger as well," Pops said. The Regulators had come across the vehicle a couple of miles back. "Leave a lot of things behind 'em, don't they?"

"The Slugger died on them," Annie said. "They didn't have a choice. Seems like they didn't have a choice about the food either. They'd been using a kind of stretcher thing to haul the cans along. Those drag marks in the snow leadin' away from the Slugger, right? And then they musta needed it for something else."

"My guess would be one of them's been injured," said Michael Pale Horse.

"Mine too."

The Hobhouse twins were crouching beside a patch of brown goop that was spilled on the snow. They were taking turns dipping a finger in and licking the stuff off. There was a split-open can lying nearby, and Annie hoped and prayed that the brown goop was what it looked like, chocolate pudding, and not something more disgusting. Although, with those two, there was no knowing.

"We gonna keep on after 'em, right?" said Cleavon.

"Why wouldn't we?" Annie replied. "They've not got a Slugger anymore and now one of them can't walk. They're slower than ever."

She studied the tree shadows. The sun was past its zenith. There were three, maybe four hours of daylight remaining.

The shadows themselves were dimming. Clouds were moving in, and if Annie didn't miss her guess, there was going to be a snowfall. A big one. You could sense it in the air, a kind of looming heaviness.

"They're gonna go to ground before it gets dark," she said. "They have to. They're tired. They need to rest. My feeling is we're going to find them sooner rather than later. We just have to forge on. Any objections?"

She didn't expect any, and there were none. The other six Regulators were keen to get the job done and return to CU #23. Perhaps not as keen as Annie was, but keen enough.

"This way, then," Ornery Annie said, striding away from the carnage.

57

Commander Levine stood at her station on the bridge of *Constant Vigilance*. Hands clasped behind her back, spine ramrod straight, she was a picture of determination.

She was also, despite appearances, exhausted. She hadn't left the corvette's bridge once since the search for *Tranquility* began, not to eat, not even for a bathroom break. She was known for driving her crew hard but she drove no one harder than herself. She was like a terrier. Once she had her teeth into something, she hung on and didn't let go till she was done with it.

"Sir?" said her communications officer. He and the rest of the flight crew were showing signs of tiredness, even if Levine wasn't. There had been sporadic bouts of yawning all across the bridge over the past couple of hours, one yawn setting off another in a kind of chain reaction. Glazed, bloodshot eyes stared from every face. At one point the weapons officer had even nodded off in his seat, until Levine had roused him with a sharp rebuke.

"Yes?" Levine said.

"*Freedom to Choose* is hailing us."

Levine stifled a sigh. "Put it through."

"Commander," said Marvin Ransome.

"Commander," said Levine.

Ransome looked wrung out and rough around the edges—even rougher around the edges than normal. "We've been at this for about fifteen hours. My guys are on their last legs. I'm thinking maybe we can take a pause? Just for a short while? We go on like this, without resting up, mistakes are going to happen."

"On your boat perhaps, Ransome. Not on mine. Don't forget, you volunteered to help. I never asked you to. If you haven't got a big enough pair of balls to see this through to the end…"

"Ain't nothing wrong with the size of my balls," Ransome replied hotly. "What are you trying to prove anyway, Levine? The size of yours?"

Levine did not rise to the taunt. "I'm trying to prove that you do not attempt to outwit the Alliance, and you certainly do not damage an Alliance corvette, with impunity. That gorramn Firefly is somewhere round these parts and it is not going to get away from us a second time. Furthermore, Ransome—"

"Sir?" said Levine's executive officer.

"What?" she snapped at him.

"Don't mean to cut in, but we're getting a ping from a warning buoy."

"So?"

"So it means we're approaching the wreck of the freighter. You know the one. *Angel of Enterprise*, I think it's called. Got punched all to hell by meteors a few years back."

"What of it, XO?"

"Well, I was just thinking. If you have a ship that's taken a few knocks and you need somewhere to hole up awhile in order to carry out emergency repairs, somewhere that'll give you a bit of cover…" He left the sentence unfinished, seemingly worried that he had said something ridiculous, so ridiculous it would incur his commanding officer's wrath. Levine's crew feared her as mice fear a cat.

"XO?"

"Yes, sir?" came the timid reply.

"That is an excellent suggestion."

The lieutenant commander beamed from ear to ear. "Thank you, sir."

"Navigator? Put us on a heading for *Angel of Enterprise.*"

"Aye-aye, sir."

"Ransome?" said Levine, turning back to his image on her console. "Is *Freedom to Choose* coming with? Or would you and your crew rather go beddy-byes and have a nice little nap-nap?"

"All right, we're coming with," said Ransome testily, adding, "And by the way. *Cāo nǐ ma*, Vicky."

Levine smirked at him. "I think you'll find, Ransome, that it's '*Cāo nǐ ma*, Commander Levine.'"

58

"Kaylee?" said River over *Serenity*'s intercom. "This is it. We can't wait any longer. Those two Alliance corvettes have abruptly course-corrected. They're making a beeline right for us."

Which, she thought, *is kind of funny when you think about it. Hornet-class ships. Beeline.*

"Engine's not completely ready, River," came the reply from Kaylee.

"Is it ready enough?"

A pause. Then: "I guess so."

"Okay. Good. I'm starting her up."

"You might want to cross your fingers."

"Can't fly a ship with crossed fingers," River said. "Makes pushing those buttons and levers so much trickier."

River initiated the ship's startup sequence. There wasn't time for the standard round of pre-flight checks. Either *Serenity* would go or she wouldn't.

She hit the ignition command.

For a moment there was nothing, just a pregnant silence. It was as though *Serenity* was making up her mind, deciding if she had the wherewithal to move.

Then came a low thrum that stuttered then steadied, becoming a deep, familiar vibration. River pictured *Serenity*'s bulbous stern-mounted propulsion unit starting to glow. A nimbus of rippling, golden coruscation manifesting.

On the control console screens, a host of systems status indicators lit up. A few were red, but most were green. *Serenity* was operating at near optimal capacity. Not perfect, but better than River could have hoped. Kaylee had been wrong. She *was* a miracle worker.

River eased *Serenity* away from the freighter. She felt a little sad to be leaving the larger ship's sheltering shadow. She felt intrepid, too, like a fledgling bird trying out its wings, making its first tentative moves towards independence.

Kaylee arrived on the bridge. Positioning herself beside the pilot's chair, she studied the scanner screens over River's shoulder. "We're on the corvettes' blind side for now, but you can bet they'll do a full sweep around the wreck. What's our play here? We just gonna go hell for leather? Try to outrun 'em and lose ourselves in the Black?"

"No. We have to head straight to Atata."

"What for? We ain't heard from the captain yet."

"Doesn't matter. Something's about to happen to them down there. Something bad. To Simon especially. They need us, and they need us right now."

"Okay," said Kaylee. "You sound like you know, and I don't know how you know, but if you know, then you know."

River grinned lopsidedly. "I know, right?"

"But the Feds are gonna chase us every inch of the way."

"Not if I can help it."

"You have a plan."

"I remember Zoë saying once that if you're in a jam, the best course of action is think what Mal Reynolds would do and then do the exact opposite."

"Sound advice."

"Only, on this occasion I'm not going to take it. I'm going to do something Mal-Reynolds-like."

"Now I'm worried," said Kaylee.

"Don't be. Ever heard of the Kessler syndrome?"

"Can't say as I have. Is it some kind of disease?"

"It's from back in the old times. See, there were once so many satellites and chunks of spaceflight debris in orbit around Earth-That-Was that there was the fear of something called an ablation cascade. This astrophysicist, Donald Kessler, proposed a hypothetical scenario where one of these objects would collide with another, and that in turn would cause further collisions, and so on and so on…"

"Kind of a domino effect," said Kaylee.

River nodded. "Exactly. And each impact would create all these smaller pieces of debris, until eventually there would be nothing up there in the exosphere but a swirling cloud of broken-up, whizzing-fast junk. It would make it almost impossible to send up any rockets, because there's a very good chance they'd hit something. It would also obscure the sky, so that astronomers couldn't stargaze anymore. None of that happened, but the Earth-That-Was authorities were very concerned it might. It was one of the things that spurred Madame Xiang to start organizing the mass exodus which led to all those generation starships seeking out new worlds to colonize. That and environmental degradation, of course. She wanted to get people off the planet while they still could. You could even say it's part of the reason there's a 'verse."

"All right, interesting, but how does it apply here?"

"I'm going to Kessler syndrome the debris around us," River said. "I'm going to knock one piece of wreckage against another with *Serenity*'s nose, and if I do it right, it'll set up an ablation cascade."

"Which we can use as cover to fly out of here. River, you're a gorramn genius."

"It's been said."

"You're also insane."

"It's been said too."

"Unless we're very careful, and very lucky, we could be caught up in the cascade ourselves. Get hit by something. The propulsion unit gets taken out, and we're dead in the water."

"I know," said River. "And also we could find something large and heavy ramming into the hull at a thousand miles an hour, bashing a great big hole in the ship, and then it's *adios*, nice to meetcha, seeya on the other side."

"But you can do it, yeah?"

River switched her gaze back and forth between the forward viewing ports and the console screens. In her mind's eye, she was calculating vectors within the debris field. Working out trajectories. Analyzing speeds and angles. A whole vast, inordinately complex geometrical computation was taking place inside her brain.

"Sure," she said finally. "Think of it as the ultimate pool shot, with *Serenity* as the cue."

59

The wreck of *Angel of Enterprise* was just a distant dot in *Constant Vigilance*'s main viewing port.

"Engage forward cameras," Levine ordered.

An image of the debris cluster popped up on her console.

"Increase magnification by fifty."

With a lurch, the image expanded to fill the screen. Levine squinted. She couldn't see anything anomalous amid all the freighter fragments. Not yet, at least.

"We'll circuit the wreckage slowly," she said. "Everybody, keep your eyes peeled. Bonus of a week's pay to whoever spots that gorramn Firefly."

If the Firefly was even in there. But Levine had the feeling it was. She had got the measure of *Tranquility*'s crew, she thought. Lurking among that wreckage was just the sort of sneaky stunt those people would pull.

As *Constant Vigilance* drew nearer the remains of *Angel of Enterprise*—with *Freedom to Choose* tagging along behind—Levine spied movement.

The debris, she knew, had been entirely static for years.

Now, all of a sudden, there was a peculiar disturbance within.

It started small, confined to a single spot. As Levine watched, however, the disturbance grew, spreading through the cluster. It was as though someone had poked a spoon into the debris and started stirring. Soon—astonishingly soon—the entire mass of wreckage was in motion, every bit of it twirling and spinning.

Fragment caromed off fragment. Pieces of spaceship began spiraling outward. The cluster was expanding, losing cohesion, breaking apart. Even the main bulk of the freighter was drifting from its original position. The gigantic, hollowed-out hulk heeled over to one side. The meteor strike all those years ago had practically bisected it, with just a few spars of the ship's frame left holding the two sections together. These began to snap one by one, until none remained intact and the two parts floated free from each other.

The disintegration was mesmerizing to behold. There were so many separate elements to it—thousands, perhaps even tens of thousands—it was impossible to keep track of them all. Levine at least had the presence of mind to order *Constant Vigilance* to halt. It would be unwise for them to get any closer to this bristling, growing chaos than they already were.

"This is them," she said. "This is their doing."

"But what are they up to?" her XO asked. "If they're in the thick of all that, they're as good as committing suicide."

Commander Ransome's face flickered into life on one of her screens. "Levine? You seeing what I'm seeing?"

"Yes."

"Can't be coincidence. Your Firefly's in there somewhere."

"You don't say," Levine drawled.

"We're going in for a closer look," Ransome announced.

"I don't advise that."

"Why the hell not?"

"Because this stinks of distraction technique. If the Firefly's going to break cover, now's its moment."

"Then the nearer we are to it, the better chance we have of intercepting it."

"Also, that debris is shooting off in all directions. No predicting where it's going to go. It's safer maintaining distance, as we are."

"Know what your problem is, Levine?" said Ransome. "You're too sensible."

"And you're too reckless. Hold your position for now, Ransome. That's an order."

"You don't outrank me, remember?"

"We agreed I would take lead on this mission."

"Yeah, well, I'm tired of that. I'm tired of you. I'm just overall gorramn tired. I want this thing done and dusted. We're moving in."

"Ransome..." Levine growled.

"Hey, screw you, Vicky, you *bù huǐ hèn de pō fù*. Really. Just screw you."

Ransome cut the connection.

Levine cursed under her breath.

The wreckage maelstrom was still increasing not only in size but intensity. *Freedom to Choose* appeared in the viewing port, on a course that was headed straight for it. The corvette accelerated from half speed to full.

"No," Levine said softly. Then, more loudly, "No," again. She thumped the console with both fists. "That Firefly is mine. Mine, d'you hear? Not yours, Ransome. Not anyone's."

"Sir?" said her XO. "Do you want us to go after *Freedom to Choose*?"

"Yes. Not just after them. Overtake them."

As the XO relayed the order, Levine turned to the weapons officer. "Weps? Cycle up all armaments. First sign you see of the Firefly, take it out. Don't hesitate. Don't wait for my command. Just do it."

60

River held her breath. Any second now…

Amid the myriad of mental calculations she had performed, there was one which predicted the precise moment when *Serenity* could make her escape. A gap would open up, a tunnel leading safely through the debris to empty space. This window of opportunity was due to appear imminently.

Her fingers closed around the handles of the steering yoke.

Outside, everything was a blizzard of motion. The forward viewing ports were filled with swirling spaceship debris, like screen static on a sourcebox. River could sense Kaylee beside her growing tense. Her grip on the back of River's chair was tightening. River wished she could give her some kind of reassurance, just a word or two, but she was too busy concentrating on other things. She needed every ounce of focus if she was going to get this right.

There!

Now!

Almost magically, the clouds of moving debris parted, leaving just enough room for a Firefly to pass through. Beyond lay pure, open Black.

River shoved the steering yoke forward.

Serenity lurched into life. She hurtled towards freedom.

Then faltered. Lost power. Lost speed.

"What?" said River. "No. No, no, no…"

It was as though *Serenity* had caught her toe on a rock and stumbled. She came to a shuddering halt.

"The coaxial compression coupling," Kaylee said with a heavy sigh. "The seal on the coaxial compression coupling is too loose. I was afraid of this. The original nut broke and I had to use a two-inch nut to secure it because I didn't have a spare one-and-seven-eighths. I hoped it'd be enough. Clearly it ain't."

"Come on, girl," River said to the ship. "You can do this."

The window of opportunity was closing. Closing fast.

River routed auxiliary power to the thrusters. It wasn't much but it might just give *Serenity* the boost she needed to overcome the fault with the coaxial compression coupling.

Lights dimmed all over the ship and life-support systems went into sleep mode, even as *Serenity* lumbered back up to full speed.

Debris was starting to hurtle across the channel that led to the outside.

This was going to take some fancy flying.

Deftly, if not very delicately, River steered a course, avoiding each and every scrap of ex-freighter that came her way. *Serenity* pitched. She rolled. She yawed.

To River, a trained ballerina, it was more like dancing than piloting. It was pirouette and jeté and entrechat. It was reel and hornpipe and gavotte. It was twist. It was even shimmy. One thing it was not was a cakewalk.

Her awareness was heightened to an acute degree. The moment an item of debris entered her field of vision, she instantly worked out how fast it was moving and where it was headed, and made the necessary corrections.

"River!" Kaylee yelled in warning.

A stainless steel commode came hurtling out of nowhere towards them.

River threw the ship into a tight turn. The commode bumped along *Serenity*'s swanlike neck and over her rounded topside, then went careering off upwards at a steep angle.

"*Wáng bā dàn de biǎo zi*," Kaylee said.

"Pottymouth," said River, quirking one eyebrow.

"Oh, ha ha."

One last barrel roll, a final seesawing of the wings, and suddenly *Serenity* shot clear of the tumult.

"You did it!" Kaylee cried. "I could gorramn kiss you. In fact, I will." She planted a smacker on River's cheek.

"Not quite out of the woods yet," River said. She nodded at the scanner screens.

The two Alliance corvettes were zeroing in.

"They've seen us."

Kaylee was crestfallen. "I thought, with all this stuff whirling around…"

"They'd have held back and wouldn't have seen us until too late, or even at all. That's what I was counting on. But it's okay."

"It is?"

"Kaylee, do you trust me?"

"I have a choice?"

"Not really."

"Then I'm gonna have to."

River swung *Serenity* hard about.

The Alliance ships were a matching pair, both of them sleek, state-of-the-art machines, armed to the teeth.

Yet, for all that they were so alike, they differed. The one captained by Commander Victoria Levine, *Constant Vigilance*, was precise, efficient, orderly. The other was not. River could tell this in the same way she could tell so many things that wouldn't be apparent to someone whose brain had not been tampered with like hers had. There was disorganization aboard the other corvette. A lack of restraint. It was flying straight at *Serenity*, but this wasn't just eagerness. River thought of a small child rushing across the road in pursuit of an errant ball, heedless of the traffic.

"Come get me," River whispered to whoever was in command of the second ship. "I know you want to."

She swooped in front of the corvette's nose, darting past. The corvette pulled a sharp about-turn, pivoting on its axis.

Constant Vigilance was incoming. *Serenity* was poised between both corvettes.

"Weapons," Kaylee said, jabbing a forefinger at the screens. "They've gone weapons hot. They have target lock on us. We're in their crosshairs."

"Shh," River said.

The corvettes zoomed in from fore and aft. Crackles of light from their gun ports—they had opened fire simultaneously.

Serenity jinked and dodged. Kaylee flinched reflexively, but not one of the shots found its mark. River was evading enemy fire coming from opposite directions at once. It was incredible piloting.

The corvette behind them was so close, it was practically sniffing *Serenity*'s backside. The corvette in front loomed alarmingly fast.

61

Commander Levine didn't see it coming.

    Until—too late—she did.

Freedom to Choose was hot on *Tranquility*'s tail. Commander Ransome was flushing the ship towards *Constant Vigilance*, like a gundog with a game bird. This might not have been his intention but it was the result all the same. The Firefly's pilot—Jed Race— was clearly panicking, not paying attention to where he was going, just fleeing blindly.

Levine's weapons officer began firing, as ordered. At the Firefly's rear, Ransome's weapons officer did the same.

That was when it dawned on Levine that, panicking or not, this Race fellow was phenomenally good at his job. *Tranquility* hopped, skipped and jumped around both sets of oncoming blasts. She had never seen astrobatics like it. Neither corvette scored a direct hit. They didn't even wing the Firefly.

"Hold fire!" Levine yelled, as the wildly darting *Tranquility* got ever nearer. It was possible a stray shot from *Constant Vigilance* might hit *Freedom to Choose*, and vice versa. If there had been time, Levine would have opened communications with Ransome and told him to stand his weapons down too. As it was, she just had to pray he saw sense.

He did. *Freedom to Choose*'s guns ceased blazing too.

And then it all went wrong.

Over the course of the next five seconds, events unfurled with horrifying slowness. Those five seconds, the final ones of Commander Levine's life, saw her realize that no amount of precision, discipline or adherence to protocol could make up for the waywardness and unpredictability of other people. When it came down to it, nothing was ever truly under control. This wasn't so much a revelation for Levine as a sad acknowledgement.

The Firefly abruptly veered upward, its downturned thrusters flaring.

Now *Constant Vigilance* and *Freedom to Choose* were heading straight at each other.

Standard procedure when two spacecraft were on a collision course was that, as in conventional aviation, both vessels should swerve to starboard.

"Starboard!" Levine yelled, and the response was immediate. Her flight crew were well drilled.

Constant Vigilance turned.

Freedom to Choose also turned.

But not to starboard. To port.

At the crucial moment, *Freedom to Choose* had made the wrong choice.

Everyone on the bridge of *Constant Vigilance* was agog.

Someone screamed.

As for their captain, all she said was: "Marvin Ransome, you *liú kǒu shuǐ de biǎo zi hé hóu zi de bèn ér zi.*"

These were Commander Victoria Levine's last words, and she growled the profanity with as much venom as she could muster, wishing her opposite number aboard *Freedom to Choose* could have heard.

Then she closed her eyes.

IAV *Freedom to Choose* plunged headlong into IAV *Constant Vigilance*.

There were no survivors.

62

Wash staggered up from the infirmary and onto the bridge. River had turned *Serenity* around to give them a clear view of the fireball consuming both *Constant Vigilance* and *Freedom to Choose*. Wash arrived just in time to see the roiling mass of flame begin to disperse. Nothing burned for long in hard vacuum, and soon all that remained of the corvettes was a collection of charred, incinerated ship parts pinwheeling off in a hundred different directions. Some of the fragments joined the still-expanding debris field from the freighter, merging with it. Others went hurtling away into the eternal blackness. A few bumped harmlessly off *Serenity*'s hull.

"What'd I miss?" Wash asked, as if he couldn't guess the answer.

"Nothing much," said Kaylee, grinning. "Just River being a total gorramn badass."

"That was an Alliance corvette, right?"

"Two."

"*Zhè zhēn shi gè kuài lè de jìn zhǎn.* And you outflew them, River? Made them crash into each other?" Wash shook his head wonderingly.

"Wasn't so difficult," River said. "Somebody zagged when they should have zigged."

"And did you know that was gonna happen?" Kaylee asked her. "As in, y'know, *know* know?"

River shrugged. "I didn't *not* know, if that makes any sense."

It didn't, not to Wash at least, but obviously a lot had transpired while he'd been lying in a pain-wracked stupor on the med couch. Most notably, it seemed River was a competent pilot. More than competent. Downright skillful.

But then, wasn't that always the way with River Tam? More and more it was becoming clear that the girl could turn her hand to just about anything and do it exceptionally well. Wash had a feeling there was no limit to her talents. This amazed and scared him in equal measure.

"We're safe, for now," River said.

"That's good to hear," Wash said.

"How're you doin', by the way, Wash?" said Kaylee.

"Head still hurts but not as bad. It's gone from 'agonizing' to 'just a little bit less than agonizing.'"

"Feel up to pilotin' again?"

"Why? Where are we going? Did Mal send a signal?"

"No, but River says we've got to get back to Atata anyway. The crew's in trouble."

"Really?"

"Really," said River, her face solemn.

Wash didn't inquire how River could be so certain about this. He didn't dare. Among those many talents of hers were a few that were uncanny, not to say supernatural. Those were the ones that amazed and scared him most of all.

"Okay then, let's go," he said. "But," he added, "I don't know as I'm up to flying just yet. My eyesight still hasn't sorted itself out. Unless, that is, each of you has an identical twin I didn't know about."

"You are definitely *not* sitting in that chair," Kaylee said. "River?"

"On it," said River.

"And I'll see if I can jury rig that coaxial compression coupling so it holds together. If I have to use sticking plasters, then sticking plasters it is."

So saying, Kaylee quit the bridge.

River pushed the steering yoke forward, and *Serenity* gained speed.

Wash stayed beside her. He had exaggerated about his condition. His head definitely still ached but he wasn't seeing double. His eyesight was fine now, pretty much. A little blurry, but he could have managed at the helm.

And it was hard for him to let someone else fly this boat. He felt as solicitous about *Serenity* as a parent does about their child. Nobody really should be in charge of her except him.

That said, he was curious to see River in action. As far as he was aware, River had no flying experience. Yet she was currently displaying a sure, deft touch at the controls, and of course there was the small matter of her getting the better of those corvettes.

Maybe, he thought, *I can take her under my wing. Train her up. She could spell me when I need to take a break. I'd rather have someone human flying* Serenity *when I'm not than put her on autopilot.*

River Tam. Prodigy protégée. Future *Serenity* pilot.

Amazing.

Scary.

63

They conducted an inventory of their weapons.

It didn't take long.

There were Dr. Weng's homemade hunting spears. He had three of those in total. There was also a tiny pair of scissors in the first-aid kit.

And that was it.

"Don't forget my can opener," Simon said. He waggled it in the air in a jokey fashion.

Nobody was amused. Not even Meadowlark, who looked at the can opener with a little knot forming between her eyebrows.

"Okay." Simon stowed the implement away in his pocket again. "Just trying to lighten the mood. But if you're going to be like that…"

"Rocks," said Mal. "Gotta be plenty of those lyin' around. We can gather a stack of 'em."

"I can perhaps make a shiv out of one of those cans," said Zoë.

"Get to it," Mal said, "and if you've time, make one for me as well." He studied the layout of the cave. "This is a fairly good position, defensibility-wise. Access is restricted. You can't get in except on hands and knees."

"You can also only get out the same way. If the Regulators lay siege to us, we're here for the duration. Any attempt to leave, and they could pick us off easily."

"That's assuming they've a hankerin' to draw this thing out. Look out there."

Through the cavemouth everyone could see that snow had started to fall. A few wind-blown flakes wisped inside, melting in the relative warmth of the cave's interior.

"Nobody wants to be hangin' around in that for hours on end," Mal said.

"The snow may also bury our tracks and the Regulators won't be able to follow them anymore," Weng said hopefully.

"Depends how far behind us they are," said Zoë. "I wouldn't count on it, my own self."

"And you really didn't bring any guns with you to Atata?"

"Couldn't. Not if we were going to pass ourselves off as prisoners."

"Shame. It just seems crazy, using rocks and spears and knives to fend off an enemy."

"Maybe, but if that's what it comes down to, that's what we're gonna have to do."

"I realize that, but still. How primitive."

Zoë cast a glance around Weng's cave home. "And this isn't?"

"A good point, well made," Weng conceded.

As Mal began scouting around the cave for loose rocks, Zoë set to work fashioning shivs. She stomped one of the empty food cans underfoot, then flexed the flattened piece of steel back and forth down the middle until it snapped in two, generating a pair of narrow but strong metal rectangles. After that it was a case of taking one of these rectangles, binding up one end of it in a strip of material torn from her shirt so as to create a handle, then scraping the other end against the cave wall until it developed a sharp edge.

The result was far from pretty but looked crudely effective nonetheless. Zoë tested the "blade" on the ball of her thumb and drew blood.

Then she set about repeating the whole process with the remaining half of the can so that Mal might have a shiv too.

All the while, Dr. Weng squatted at the cave entrance, keeping lookout. The snow was coming down thicker and faster. Small flurries of it whipped in around his feet.

Meadowlark sidled up to Simon, who was examining the sleeping Jayne.

"Why're you looking him over like that?" she asked.

Simon felt Jayne's pulse. "I'm checking for early signs of infection and fever. He was savaged by a wolf. Those things have a ton of bacteria lurking in their mouths."

"Oh. Okay. So, do you people often find yourselves in situations like this?"

Simon nodded wearily. "More often than I care to think."

"And you come out of them unscathed?"

"Mostly."

"That's reassuring," Meadowlark said, sounding far from reassured. "Simon, I just want to say something. This Kaylee girl. I need to know what she means to you. It makes all the difference."

"Now's not the time, Meadowlark."

"I think it is. There's a chance, maybe a good one, that we're not going to make it through this."

"Don't say that."

"And I could really do with knowing the truth."

"Listen, Meadowlark, seriously, let's table this conversation for later."

"That's what I'm saying. What if there *is* no later?"

He laid a hand on her arm. "There will be. I'm sure of it."

Meadowlark looked at the hand, then at Simon, and slowly nodded.

"Everyone," said Weng in a soft, urgent hiss. "I think I see movement outside."

64

Mal joined Weng at the cavemouth and peered out.

"You sure, Doc?" he said. "All's I see moving is the snow."

"No. Over yonder. Just inside the treeline."

Mal followed the direction of Weng's pointing finger. "Nope, I don't... Wait." He peered harder through the screen of fat, tumbling snowflakes. "Yup. That's movement all right. *People* kind of movement."

Zoë crouched down beside him. "How many, you reckon?"

Mal eyed the figures flitting furtively between the tree trunks, some thirty yards distant. "Hard to say. Five at least. Could be six. Could be more."

"They know we're here?"

"Way they're skulking around, I'd say definitely. Must've gotten here before the snow started buryin' our tracks. From the looks of it, they're dividing into two groups. Suggests they're gonna attack from two sides at once."

"This is it, then." Zoë passed him the second shiv she had fashioned. "Ain't had time to hone it as sharp as I'd like, but it'll do in a pinch."

"Thanks. How's this gonna go down, Zoë? We just gonna leave 'em to come at us?"

"Only way I can see it working. We charge out to fight them, we lose our one advantage. Let *them* make the running. They want us, they'll have to winkle us out of here. No more'n two of them can get through this hole at a time. It's a pinch point, and we can use it to whittle their numbers down."

"Us against superior forces," Mal said. "Just like old times."

"Not everything is a rerun of Serenity Valley, Mal."

"Not to you, maybe. Doc?"

"Yes?" said Weng.

"No, the other Doc."

"Yes?" said Simon.

"What's the status with Jayne?"

"Still out cold."

"Any chance you can bring him round? We could do with an extra pair of hands right now."

"I'm reluctant to try. And even if I do, he won't be a *pair* of hands. His right arm's pretty much useless."

Mal worked his jaw from side to side, weighing things up. "Okay. He can stay as he is for now. If things start to get hairy, though, I want him up on his feet and swinging. Even a one-armed Jayne Cobb is worth havin' on your side in a scrap. Doc?"

"Yes?" said Simon.

"No, the other Doc."

"Yes?" said Weng.

"My advice is you step back from the entrance. We're in shadow, with firelight behind us. Chances are the Regulators haven't spotted that you're *you*, but it won't be good if they do. Far as they know, there's no one in this cave but us folks who caused ructions at Hellfreeze and stole their Slugger. They realize none other'n the fugitive Dr. Weng is hiding out here too, that'll change everything. They'll be more desperate than ever to get in, 'cause Mr. O'Bannon wants you bad."

Nodding, Weng retreated into the cave.

Zoë was still beside Mal. He lowered his voice confidentially.

"Zoë, we're gettin' Weng to Inara, come what may. After all we've gone through findin' him, I don't aim to let him slip through my fingers now."

"You mean whatever it takes, we do."

"I mean exactly that. Are we on the same page?"

"We are."

"Glad to hear it."

Tense minutes passed, with no further activity visible outside. The Regulators were entrenched, in position. The next move was theirs.

Then a voice sounded from the forest, somewhat muffled by the falling snow.

"You in there!"

"That's Ornery Annie," Zoë said to Mal. "Bet you anything Mr. O'Bannon's put her in charge of the Regulator posse. I would have. Out of all of them I've met, she's the smartest by a country mile."

"I know you're all hunkered down in that there cave," Annie called. "I'm gonna give you one chance. Come on out now, hands in the air, and we'll see if we can settle this without resortin' to violence."

"And how do you propose doin' that?" Mal called back. "If you're after the Slugger we took, I'm guessin' you've already found it back in the woods. If you're after the food we took, mosta that's in the same place. Way I see it, there's only one reason you've kept on following us, and that's to kill us."

There was a brief silence from Annie, and then she said, "Okay, you got me there, pal. It was worth a shot."

"Yeah. So really there's only one thing I can say to you, and don't take this the wrong way, but screw you."

"Well now," said Annie, "that's plain uncivil."

"Ain't it just. Now, are you gonna stand around jawing, or are you gonna attack? I'm gettin' bored already."

"You tryin' to irk me? Get me to do something rash and stupid?"

"Maybe. It working?"

"Not as such."

"Thing is, Annie, at the moment it's pretty clear we have a standoff," Mal said. "We can't come out, you people can't come in. It'd be suicide for whichever of us tried to. So unless something happens to break the standoff, we're all gonna be stuck like this for the rest of the day and long into the night. Now, for us that's not a problem. We're sittin' pretty. We have shelter. We have a fire. We're toasty warm. For you guys in the cold and the snow, though, it's a very different story. How much longer do you reckon you can last? I'm talking to *all* of you out there. Your hands have got to be starting to seize up, haven't they? Fingers won't be able to hold a weapon soon. And your feet—you're startin' to lose the feeling in your toes, right? And dark's comin', meaning it's only gonna get worse. I were you, right now I'd be askin' myself if this is worth it."

He paused, waiting for a response. From Ornery Annie. From any of the Regulators.

None came, so he continued, "Maybe your best tactic is to say enough's enough, go back to Hellfreeze and tell Mr. O'Bannon you couldn't find us. You can retrieve the Slugger later, providing you can rustle up some fresh sparkplugs for it. That way, you'll have achieved pretty much everything you set out to achieve. Wouldn't be so bad, would it? If I were in your position, that's what I'd do."

More silence.

Then there was a sudden disturbance.

Feet shuffling.

A scuffle.

A cry.

But the commotion wasn't coming from among the trees.

It was coming from behind Mal, in the cave.

65

Ornery Annie knew that she was speaking with the man she and Otis had turned away outside the Regulators' private quarters in CU #23, the same man she'd later beaten up in the refectory.

She also knew that he had a point. She'd studied the lie of the land. There was no approach to the cave except from the front, and a frontal assault would be pretty much futile. As soon as any Regulators poked their heads through the cave's restricted entrance, the people inside could just pick them off. Zoë and her pals were holding all the aces, dammit.

But Annie couldn't simply leave them alone. Her life depended on capturing them—some of them, at least—and killing the rest.

The only solution was an all-out attack. She and the other Regulators would have to rush the cavemouth in unison, force their way through, and hope they didn't take too many casualties in the process. Once inside, the playing field would be leveled.

Moreover, to judge by the bloodstained snow back in the forest, one of their opponents was injured. Maybe quite badly. If it came to a straight fight, that tipped the odds a little further in the Regulators' favor.

In short, it was all or nothing. Do or die.

For the Regulators to have the best chance of success, however, they would have to wait until nightfall. Darkness and the falling snow would afford some cover as they crossed the open terrain between the forest and the cave. The people in the cave wouldn't see them coming until the last moment.

The daylight was now a grim, gloomy gray, and the grayness was deepening with every passing minute. Sundown would be arriving in a little under an hour's time. Annie and the other Regulators could wait until then, easy.

Annie was standing with Otis, Michael Pale Horse and Cleavon. The remaining Regulators—Pops and the Hobhouse twins—were positioned a couple of dozen yards away in a second group. She whispered her plan to the three beside her. The guy in the cave was still addressing her, going on about how cold it was and other stuff, but she ignored him. Pale Horse then crept across the gap to relay Annie's plan to the rest.

Just as Pale Horse was sneaking back, there was a ruckus from the cave. A female voice could be heard. She was calling Annie's name.

"Annie? Can you hear me, Annie? It's Meadowlark Deane."

"Huh?" said Otis. "Meadowlark Deane? What's *she* doing with them?"

"No idea," said Annie. "Didn't even know she wasn't in Hellfreeze anymore."

"Must've been her had the fifth thermal suit."

"Must've."

"I've got ahold of one of them," Meadowlark said. "He's my hostage, and I'm going to kill him if they don't let you guys in."

Annie scowled. She couldn't believe it. Was it possible? Meadowlark Deane, of all people, was presenting them with a way out of the deadlock?

"And get this, Annie," Meadowlark went on. "Dr. Weng is here."

Now Annie was sure her ears were playing tricks on her.

"No word of a lie," said Meadowlark. "He's right here. Dr. Esau

Weng, in the flesh. And he's all yours. Come get him."

A ruse. Some kind of trap. Had to be. And if it was, then there could be no juicier bait than Esau Weng. No name was guaranteed to provoke a reaction from Annie, or most any Hellfreezer, quite like that one.

Weng was dead. Annie was sure of it. He couldn't still be alive, not after all this time.

Could he?

"Come on, Annie," Meadowlark said. "You're never going to get a better chance than this."

66

Ninety seconds earlier

"Simon," Meadowlark said, "mind if I take a look-see at that can opener?"

Mal, in the meantime, was still conducting his shouted dialog with Ornery Annie.

"What for?" said Simon. "You don't seriously think it'll make a viable weapon?"

"Just give it to me."

With a shrug, Simon took the opener from his pocket and passed it to her.

Meadowlark studied the implement for several seconds. She parted the hinged arms fully to expose the serrated wheel.

"Oh yeah, I think you could easily hurt someone with this," she said at last. "Kill them, even."

"How?" Simon asked.

"Like so."

Suddenly the serrated wheel was pressed against Simon's throat. Meadowlark was pinching the key between thumb and forefinger so that the wheel could not revolve.

"Stand up, Simon," she said.

Simon gaped at her. "Meadowlark, what is this? What are you doing?"

"What I do to all liars. What I've always done." Her voice was no longer bright and breezy. It was in deadly earnest, and her face was twisted into a sneer. "Now do as I say and stand up, or I'll open a vein."

Simon was incredulous. This was some kind of bizarre aberration, that was all. The pressure of the situation had got to Meadowlark, and she had snapped. She surely couldn't be serious about her threat to kill him. Not her.

Meadowlark dug the serrated wheel into his skin, hard enough to break it. Simon felt a tiny trickle of warm wet liquid run down his neck.

She *was* serious.

"Okay, okay," he said. "I'm standing."

Simon got to his feet, Meadowlark rising with him. He knew he had to act fast, before things went any further. The months he'd spent with the crew of *Serenity* had taught him that in a tight spot, it was better to be unpredictable. Meadowlark would be expecting him to talk, to try and negotiate his way out of the situation. She wouldn't be expecting sudden, violent resistance.

He tensed, shifted his weight onto one foot, then rammed himself against her, shoulder first.

He had been hoping to knock her off-balance, but apparently Meadowlark had foreseen this. She stepped smartly aside. Simon stumbled. Next thing he knew, Meadowlark was chastising him—"Nuh-uh-uh!"—and holding the can opener firmly at his throat once more.

Mal, Zoë and Dr. Weng all turned round, startled.

"What in hell—?" Mal said.

Meadowlark took up a position behind Simon, placing him between her and everyone else. She had one hand on his arm, gripping tight. The can opener quivered, poised over his Adam's apple.

"I will kill him," she said, with eerie calmness. "Any of you try anything, I will slit his throat."

"Meadowlark," Zoë said, "put the… Is that the can opener?"

Meadowlark nodded.

"Well, girl, put it down."

"No, I don't think so. It may be just a can opener, but it's drawn blood, as you can see. It can do a whole lot worse, too, if I so wish. And I do wish."

"Okay," said Zoë. "I don't understand what you want with Simon, what you're hoping to achieve by all this. But trust me when I say, you harm my friend, and you'll have me to answer to."

"Oh, I know that, Zoë," Meadowlark said. "I'm not an idiot. It's just, I've been meaning to do this for a while. I've been waiting for the right moment, and it's come along. This way, I also make sure the Regulators don't kill *me* for associating with you guys. They'll know I'm on their side, not yours. Speaking of which…"

Meadowlark raised her voice.

"Annie? Can you hear me, Annie? It's Meadowlark Deane. I've got ahold of one of them. He's my hostage, and I'm going to kill him if they don't let you guys in."

"Meadowlark, don't," Zoë said. "You think you can strike a bargain with her? You think that'll work?"

"And get this, Annie," Meadowlark continued, oblivious. "Dr. Weng is here."

"*Gū yang zhōng de gū yang,*" Mal hissed.

"No word of a lie," said Meadowlark to Annie. "He's right here. Dr. Esau Weng, in the flesh. And he's all yours. Come get him."

"Meadowlark…" Simon pleaded.

"Come on, Annie," Meadowlark said. "You're never going to get a better chance than this."

67

Zoë rose into a crouch, with her tin-can shiv held forward. Her weight was on her back foot. She was ready to pounce. .

"Uh-uh, Zoë," said Meadowlark, shaking her head. She pushed the can opener harder against Simon's neck. "Don't. Don't move. Don't so much as blink."

Simon fixed Zoë with an imploring look: *Get me out of this.*

"Why, Meadowlark?" Zoë said. She was doing her best to keep her voice calm, unmenacing. "You say you've been meaning to do this for a while. What has Simon done to you that's so bad, he has to die?"

"Hmm. Let's see. Lied." From the sound of it, it was the most obvious thing ever. "Simon is a liar. You all are, with your whole fake-convicts thing. But Simon's the worst because he played nice with me, tried to make out he wanted to be friends. Friends and more."

"I never—" Simon began, but Meadowlark pushed the can opener up under his jaw, closing his mouth.

"First of all, Simon, shut up. And second of all, really, shut up. *I'm* talking. Don't know if Simon told you this, Zoë, but I have a thing about honesty. I prize it above all else. And by the same token, I hate liars. Hate 'em with a vengeance. Always have. I've spent years searching for an honest person, one truly honest person in this whole damn lousy 'verse. Know how many I've found in all that time? None. Not a one."

"Is this about men, Meadowlark?" Zoë risked a small, careful step forward. "Have you been cheated on?"

"No! It's nothing like that."

"Because some men just are two-timers. They see the chance of a bit of tail on the side, they take it."

"Yeah? And what would you know about that? Smoking-hot warrior queen like you? Nobody'd ever cheat on *you*. And yeah, maybe I've killed a man because he played around on a woman. Not me, some other woman. Maybe I've done it a couple of times, in point of fact. Maybe I've killed a woman, too, for doing the same thing to a man. But that's not the only reason I've killed people."

"Come on," Zoë chided. "That's never happened, Meadowlark. You? I don't believe it."

"Oh, you think just because I look like this sweet, harmless little thing, I couldn't possibly have it in me to commit murder?" Meadowlark's speech patterns had changed. The lilting, girlish cadence was gone. Now, her voice was dark, smooth and deep, like a serene sea under a moonless sky. "Lotta folk have made that mistake. It's why I've been able to get away with it for so long. Nobody'd even dream I'm capable of it. I learned that the first time out, back on Salisbury. I told Simon all about that. Didn't I, Simon?"

Simon did not reply. He was, Zoë thought, obeying Meadowlark's command about shutting up. Sensible man.

"I told him how there was this Shepherd in our town who was making whoopee with this married woman," Meadowlark continued, "and how he got himself killed by some bum who broke into his chapel. Only, that wasn't the whole story. Far from it. The bum got blamed for killing him, for sure, and the sheriff arrested the guy and there was a hanging. But the bum went to the gallows protesting his innocence, and know what? He *was* innocent."

"And you know this because…" said Zoë.

"I'd sit there in the congregation on Sundays," said Meadowlark, "and I'd watch the Shepherd stand in front of us with this big, smug smile on his face. I'd listen to him, the Lord's representative, telling us what the Bible says we should and shouldn't do, and all the while I knew full well—'most everyone did—that he was practicing the opposite of what he preached. I'd sit there and I'd think to myself, 'How gorramn dare you!' Until one day, I couldn't take it anymore. So I went to him for confession. I was sixteen years old. I knelt beside him at the altar rail, and I asked him to ask God to forgive me for my sins, and then… And then I cut his throat. Just like I'm going to cut yours, Simon. I had a kitchen knife up my sleeve, and I took it and I slashed the Shepherd's windpipe wide open, and I watched him choke to death on his own blood on the chapel floor. It was easy. So easy."

"Zoë…" Mal hissed from the cavemouth.

"I have a situation here, sir," Zoë said, not taking her eyes off Meadowlark and Simon.

"I know. Fix it."

"Doin' my best. Meadowlark…" Zoë took another almost imperceptibly tiny step forward. If she could just keep the girl talking…

"You stay right there, Zoë," Meadowlark said. "I see you creeping towards me. Don't think I don't. I told you not to move, remember?"

"All right, all right." Zoë made a pacifying gesture. She was now almost within springing distance. Almost, but, to her frustration, not quite. "I'm not moving."

"Good, because you come an inch closer, and Simon gets it."

To illustrate her point, Meadowlark thrust the can opener hard up under Simon's chin, so that he had to tilt his head right back.

"That Shepherd," she said, picking up her thread from earlier, "he was just the first. I made it look as though someone had broken into the chapel, and he'd disturbed them and gotten himself killed for his pains. That's how suspicion fell on the bum. I went along to the hanging. Everyone in town turned out for it. It was kind of like a celebration. Someone played a fiddle. Folks drank and cheered and danced. Not a one of them suspected who the real culprit was. And as they put the noose around that bum's neck, and he blubbered and gibbered, insisting they had the wrong man… Well, it was all I could do not laugh my ass off."

She paused, lost in recollection for a moment.

"After that, I realized I had a mission. I'd seek out liars, the worst of them, and I would punish them. I left Salisbury and went traveling, moving from world to world. Deadwood, Whitefall, Jiangyin, Aberdeen… I kept on the go, never staying any one place for long. And wherever I went, I'd always find someone. Someone in a position of power who was supposed to be squeaky clean but wasn't. Someone who lacked integrity. Someone who deserved to die. I'd get close to them, I'd test them, I'd give them every chance to prove they were honest. Every time—*every* time—they'd disappoint me."

"But that's just people, Meadowlark," said Zoë. "Everybody'll let you down in the end, somehow or other. It's a fact of life. You were simply setting your victims up to fail. You would hold them to an impossible standard, and they'd never meet it, and that gave you your excuse."

"No."

"Mission, my ass. Jayne was right about you, wasn't he? He said, for all we know, you could be a gorramn serial killer. He was just joshing, but it's the literal truth."

"I don't like that description," said Meadowlark airily. "Serial killer. Makes me sound sorta, I dunno, indiscriminate. I've never killed just *anybody*. Only people who have it coming."

"And that stuff about graffitiing public buildings. That was a lie."

"Wrong, smartass," Meadowlark retorted. "I did do that. Another way of making my point, just more publicly. And it's the reason I ended up on Atata. That's all one hundred percent true."

Zoë nodded slowly, the penny dropping. "But you've never been convicted of your real crimes."

"I know! How's that for irony? I was busted on a misdemeanor, when I've actually left a trail of bodies behind me."

"How many?"

"Gotta be fourteen, fifteen now."

"And Simon's next."

"He's typical. This smart, well-spoken guy who lies and lies and lies, and thinks no one'll call him on it just because he looks and sounds so trustworthy."

"He *is* trustworthy," Zoë said. "I promise you that. Simon is one of the most honest human beings I have ever met."

"Then how come he's hooked up with you lot? Answer me that."

"Bad luck, I'd say, mostly. His, not ours."

"Well, I only have your word on that," said Meadowlark. "And seeing as you all came to Atata on false pretenses, and you've not been straight about anything up till now, I'm of the opinion that your word, Zoë, ain't worth a gnat's toot."

"But, Meadowlark, have you considered this?" Zoë said. "Everything you've done on this so-called mission of yours has involved *you* lying. If you yourself were honest, you wouldn't go around secretly killing people and covering it up. You'd be up-front about it. You even let an innocent man take the rap for your first murder. Did that bum deserve to die? How d'you square that with this cockeyed morality of yours?"

"It was just necessary."

"Maybe you should take a long, hard look at yourself, Meadowlark. Maybe you're no better than anyone else. Maybe you're even worse."

Meadowlark blinked. "No, that's... I ain't. That's bullcrap."

"In fact, this could be the first time you've ever told the truth about who you are. *What* you are."

"No." Meadowlark was becoming agitated. Losing her cool.

That was good. That was what Zoë was after. It was something she could use.

"No," Meadowlark repeated. "I have to hide it from people so that… so that I can keep doing what I do. And that's okay. That's allowed."

"Is it?" Zoë said. "Or are you finding it hard to accept that, when it comes down to it, you are the biggest gorramn hypocrite of them all?"

The girl clenched her teeth. Zoë sensed she was about do something impulsive, something drastic.

Simon sensed it too. Zoë saw him close his eyes, as if accepting the inevitable.

She knew she had seconds in which to act. Seconds before Simon was dead. Meadowlark Deane did not seem to care that killing her hostage would lose her any leverage she had. Her insane "mission" seemed more important to her, at this moment, than any other consideration. Or at least, so she wanted Zoë to think, and Zoë was prepared to give her the benefit of the doubt on that. In her view, the girl was crazy enough to put satisfying her bloodlust before self-preservation.

"Zoë," said Mal.

Zoë did not take her eyes of Meadowlark. "Mal," she said, tight-lipped. "Not now. Really."

"Yeah, yeah. I know. Trouble is, we got Regulators on the move. They've made up their minds. They're coming for us, and fast."

Meadowlark's gaze strayed towards the cave entrance. Just for a fraction of a second, but Zoë spotted her chance and took it. She lunged.

Meadowlark, however, had anticipated this.

She dug the can opener into Simon's throat.

68

The Hobhouse twins took point. Ornery Annie sent them in first because, well, she didn't like them much and regarded them as expendable.

Side by side, Belinda and Matilda darted through the snow like a pair of mad sprites. They were unarmed, but then they had never needed weapons. They could do more than enough damage just with their teeth and their sharpened, clawlike fingernails, and indeed they preferred it that way. A kill was all the more delightful for being intimate. The feel of flesh tearing in their hands. The taste of blood in their mouths.

Pops followed a few yards behind. Otis and Cleavon came next, leaving Michael Pale Horse and Annie to take up the rear.

All seven Regulators crossed the gap between the forest and the cavemouth in a matter of seconds. They were more determined than ever to fight their way into the cave, if only so that they could discover whether Dr. Weng really was inside. Weng was hope. Weng was the possibility that Mr. O'Bannon might live.

A rock came hurtling out from the cave. It flew through the air, arrow-straight, and struck Matilda Hobhouse on the left temple. There was an audible *crunch* of bone breaking, and Matilda went down as though she had run headlong into an invisible brick wall.

Belinda let out a squeal of horror and flung herself down by her sister's side. She patted Matilda's cheek and called her name.

Her twin did not stir. There was a large and ugly dent in the side of her head. She lay still.

Very still.

Lifeless, indeed.

Belinda rose, her face reddened and contorted with grief-born rage. She screeched an obscenity and sprinted towards the cave again, even faster than before.

Another rock flew out, catching her on the shoulder. Belinda was hurt but shrugged it off. Ducking down and uttering a high-pitched, wordless war cry, she dived into the cavemouth.

Her ululation was cut short. Belinda staggered backwards. She straightened up. She put a hand to her chest, just below the breastbone.

A dark stain appeared, spreading around her hand.

Belinda turned and looked at the other Regulators. Her expression was both baffled and indignant.

She took her hand away to reveal a stab wound. It was deep and bleeding profusely. She tottered back across the snow towards Matilda. She sank to the ground beside her twin. She lay her head on Matilda's breast and closed her eyes. Life left her body with an audible sigh. In death, the Hobhouse twins were once more united.

Pops was now at the cavemouth. He entered with a great deal more circumspection than Belinda had. He was holding a crowbar, which he started swinging as soon as he was halfway in.

There was a brief struggle, then Pops was propelled from the cave by a kick from a booted foot. He rolled over in the snow, cursing. He was now minus his crowbar and plus a nasty gash in his hand.

Otis, Cleavon, Pale Horse and Annie reached him. Annie helped him to his feet.

"He's one tough hombre, the fella who's guarding the way in," Pops said. "Just let me get my wind back and we'll give it another try."

"Yeah, about that," said the aforementioned tough hombre from inside the cave. "It's been fun showin' you guys who you're dealin' with. Only problem is, it's been brought to my attention that I need to let you in now. That's on account of there's a nutjob in here called Meadowlark who's been threatening to kill one of my people, and she says if we don't surrender, she's really, truly, honest-to-gosh going to do it."

"Yeah, right," Annie drawled. "You've taken two of us down, and suddenly you're layin' out the welcome mat and expecting us to just come moseyin' on in. Forgive me if I'm a mite skeptical."

"You must've heard me earlier, Annie," said Meadowlark Deane from within, "telling you this was your chance. Zoë thought I was bluffing. She's seen the error of her ways. Mal didn't believe me, either. That's why he resisted you even after I warned him not to. He's had to change his thinking too."

"All right," said Annie. "I hear you, Meadowlark, and knowing the type of person you are, I'm minded to believe you. What'll sway me once and for all is if I hear Dr. Weng. Dr. Weng? Esau Weng? You in there?"

After a brief pause, a voice replied, "Yes, Annie." It sounded resigned, and it was recognizably Dr. Weng's.

"And is everything like Meadowlark says?"

"She does have us at somewhat of a disadvantage," Weng said.

That decided it as far as Annie was concerned. Weng was a prize worth any risk.

She went down on all fours and scrambled through the cave entrance.

69

A few moments earlier

Zoë looked on, appalled, as Meadowlark roweled the can opener wheel across Simon's neck, like a rider spurring their horse's flank hard.

Skin split. Blood flooded out.

The can opener halted just below Simon's ear, and Meadowlark gave Zoë a look as if to say, *See? I meant what I said.*

Zoë saw, to her relief, that the wheel had not cut deep. The blood flowed freely but slowly. It wasn't the jetting spray of a severed artery. Simon's eyes registered considerable pain but she could tell he knew, as well as she did, that he wasn't fatally injured. Not yet, at any rate. Meadowlark hadn't gone as far as Zoë had feared she would, but she had shown she wasn't bluffing. Next time it could—would—be that artery.

In the interim, Mal was engaged with repelling three of the Regulators—a pair of identical twins and a gray-headed fellow, one after another.

"Tell him to knock it off," Meadowlark said to Zoë, nodding at Mal. "You know as well as I do there's a big fat blood vessel below Simon's ear. You can see it standing proud, just here. I don't have to cut too deep into his skin to get to it. Once the blood starts coming out, it won't stop.

I've watched it happen, plenty of times. It's a bad way to go."

"Mal," Zoë said.

Mal looked round.

Zoë shook her head at him. She indicated Simon, his neck covered in a slick cravat of gore.

Mal was momentarily wracked with indecision. Zoë could tell he was balancing one person's life against another's on his set of mental scales. If he conceded to Meadowlark's demands, he stood to lose Inara. Was he willing to sacrifice Simon in order to keep Dr. Weng safe and out of the Regulators' clutches? Could he live with himself if he did?

Then Mal's shoulders sagged. With every sign of reluctance, he turned to the cavemouth and invited the Regulators in.

Meadowlark's and Dr. Weng's input into the conversation clinched the deal, and now Ornery Annie was straightening up from her bent position, brushing snow off her hands and knees, while another four Regulators crawled in through the entrance behind her.

"Well, well, well," Annie said, as her comrades fanned out to block the exit. "Lookee here. Dr. Weng. You didn't get too far, did you?"

"Far enough that the likes of you couldn't find me," Weng retorted.

"Not for want of trying. It cost Otis, searching for you."

Otis, with feeling, tapped his absent ear.

"Beau as well," Annie went on. "And it cost us all, in another way. 'Cause you ain't been around to cure Mr. O'Bannon. We've had to watch him get sicker and sicker. Of course, all that's changed now."

"I told Mr. O'Bannon several times, Annie, and I'm telling you now," said Weng. "There's nothing I can do for him. Not on Atata."

"And that's fine, seeing as these people you're with appear to have the means to get *off* Atata. They must have. Otherwise there'd be little damn point them coming here to fetch you."

"They do," said Meadowlark. "They have a ship. It's up in orbit and it's coming for them."

"And I'm thinking there'll be room aboard for Mr. O'Bannon," said Annie. "Dr. Weng can keep him alive in transit, until they get to somewhere where Mr. O'Bannon can receive proper treatment."

"I don't think that's how it's gonna go at all," Mal said. "Dr. Weng's leaving Atata with us, and you folks are staying put."

"You say that like it's a done deal," said Annie. "But who's holdin' the aces 'round this particular table? Sure as hell ain't you, pal. We got Meadowlark over there. She seems to be on our side now, and she has your buddy at her mercy. Girl's got a lot more spunk than I gave her credit for."

"That's because you don't know the half about her," said Zoë. "Turns out, she's a gorramn psychopath, with a long list of kills to her name."

Annie did a double-take. "That a fact? I thought she was just some rebel with a spray can of paint and a big beef with the Alliance."

"She's just confessed. Sung like her namesake. Haven't you, Meadowlark?"

"And I *am* going to kill Simon," Meadowlark said, "but I want you to promise me something, Annie. That I don't get in trouble with you guys for it. I've helped you out, haven't I? If not for me, you wouldn't have gotten into this cave and you wouldn't be taking Dr. Weng back to Mr. O'Bannon. I figure I'm owed a favor."

"Said favor bein' that boy's death."

"And no comebacks, for this or anything else, when we all return to Hellfreeze."

Annie gave a phlegmatic little shrug. "Don't bother me none. I figure we can make you an honorary Regulator in this one instance. Meanin' you get a free pass. The boy's yours to do with as you please."

The leader of the Regulators rubbed her palms briskly together.

"So then," she said. "I see you have a neat little homemade knife,

Zoë. And you've got one as well—Mal, is that your name? Along with Pops's crowbar. I'd advise you to lay 'em all down on the floor, nice and slow. You know what's comin'. It's comin' for both of you, and also for that big fella lyin' asleep on the floor." She jerked a thumb at Jayne. "No more resistin'. Make it easy on yourselves."

"That is just not going to happen," Zoë said, firming her grip on her shiv.

"'Less it does, Simon there is going to suffer the consequences, courtesy of honorary Regulator Meadowlark."

"He's going to die, we're *all* going to die, if you people have your way. Don't know about you, but I prefer to go down fighting."

"Spoken like a true Dust Devil," said Annie. "Never say die. Until, y'know, you actually die."

Zoë and Mal exchanged glances.

"Serenity Valley," she said to him. "Sir."

Mal acknowledged the remark with a half-grin. "That's the spirit, corporal."

Both of them went into fighting stances.

Then, abruptly, Simon said, "Disappearances."

70

"What's that?" said Ornery Annie.

Simon could hear how strained his own voice sounded, how quavery from the pain. He fought to keep it under control. He was taking a hell of a gamble here, and at stake was his life.

Yet if he could give Mal and Zoë an opening, an opportunity…

"Meadowlark," he said. "She's been lying to you, Annie. She's killed since she came to Atata."

"No," Meadowlark said. "No, I haven't."

"Zoë said you told her there had been a couple of disappearances at Hellfreeze. People leaving unexpectedly."

"Sure there have."

"They never left," Simon said.

"Simon…" said Meadowlark. A warning.

Simon talked fast. "They never left because Meadowlark killed them. And I know where she did it, too. The same place she stashed the bodies. She's got this little lair. A crawlspace behind the dryers in the laundry."

"*Simon.*" Now Meadowlark waved the can opener in front of his face. "Remember this? You hush up, y'hear."

"Go on, Meadowlark. Kill me before I can say any more. It'll only prove I'm right."

"I will. I will do it, Simon, I swear to God."

"That crawlspace—there's a very bad smell in there, Annie. I'm a doctor. I know the smell of rotting flesh. I should have recognized it at the time. Somewhere deeper into the crawlspace, I expect you'll find some very decayed corpses."

"That's it," Meadowlark said. "You're dead."

The can opener was back touching Simon's neck. Simon braced himself.

"No!" Annie barked.

Meadowlark froze.

"Let him finish, Meadowlark."

"He's talking horseshit, Annie. You know it. You know I'd never do something like that. I'd be crazy to. If anyone found out, Mr. O'Bannon would—"

"Would order us to kill you, without even thinkin' twice about it. Look me in the eye, girl. Tell me it's not true."

"Of course it's not true," Meadowlark said. "Simon's a liar. You can't believe a single word that comes out of his mouth."

Simon himself had been far from sure of his theory about Meadowlark, but from the way she was protesting, the tremor of desperation in her voice, he was beginning to think he was right on the money.

"Two more murders, carried out by Meadowlark on Atata," he said to Ornery Annie. "The victims must have disappointed her in some way. Didn't meet her criteria for honesty. Shouldn't have thought people like that would be too hard to find in a prison."

"No," Meadowlark insisted. "Don't listen to him. He'd say anything right now to save his own skin."

"She's broken the Hellfreeze rules," Simon said. "Twice. Are you going to let her get away with it?"

"Meadowlark," Annie said. "As I recall rightly, both the inmates who we thought left Hellfreeze left in the past few months. Since, in fact, you came."

"So?" said Meadowlark. "Coincidence."

"What were they on Atata for?" Simon asked Annie.

"One of 'em was a port authority official caught taking bribes from people traffickers. Can't remember what the other did."

"College lecturer," said Otis. "Had a sideline selling hard drugs to his students."

"Just the type Meadowlark hates," said Simon. "They betrayed public trust. Deceivers in high places."

He could see Annie weighing things up in her head. In one pan of the scales: it seemed very possible that Meadowlark had violated the code that everyone lived by at CU #23 and which Annie herself helped to enforce. In the other pan: Meadowlark had provided the Regulators with valuable assistance at the cave, and Annie *had* promised her an amnesty, of sorts.

What this meant, apart from anything else, was that Annie's guard was down. Her focus was on Meadowlark. So, to a lesser extent, was the focus of each of the other Regulators.

Simon had done his bit. Now it was all down to Mal and Zoë.

And Mal and Zoë obliged.

71

The two of them moved as one, with an instinctive synchrony, like the experienced combat veterans they were.

Mal lashed out at the Regulator nearest him, the one with the widow's peak and ponytail. He cracked the crowbar across the man's kneecap, shattering it. The Regulator collapsed with a howl of sheer, unbridled agony.

At the same time Zoë's shiv flashed through the air, in, out, and the old-timer Regulator gasped. Clutching his ribs, he slumped against the cave wall. His legs buckled and he slid down the wall, breathing wetly and wheezily, blood frothing at his lips. A lung had been punctured. Already his eyes were dimming.

All of this took no more than three seconds.

Ornery Annie spun on her heel. As she realized what was happening, her face fell, becoming a mask of dismay.

Zoë moved towards another of the Regulators at speed, shiv to the fore. This was Cleavon, with the rounded, babyish features and the somewhat dim expression, not to mention the pair of rough-looking steel teeth replacing his top two incisors.

Mal, meanwhile, was turning on the largest of the Regulators, Otis, the one with the missing ear. He swung the crowbar.

Otis batted the crowbar aside with one hand, aiming a punch with the other. Mal ducked under the blow, and his shiv darted upwards in a low thrust, piercing Otis's inner thigh. Otis reared back violently, which tugged the shiv out of Mal's grasp.

The big Regulator looked down at the sliver of flattened steel protruding from his thigh. He seemed to think that he had just been handed a tremendous gift. He yanked the shiv free.

This was a mistake.

A fatal one.

Blood started gushing from his leg, vast quantities of it.

Otis clearly understood he had been badly injured but perhaps not *how* badly. His femoral artery had been sliced open, and the blood was pumping out unchecked. His remaining lifespan could be measured in minutes.

Regardless, he came at Mal with the bloodied shiv. Mal clouted his hand with the crowbar, forcing him to drop the blade. Otis returned the favor by whacking Mal's wrist so hard with one fist that Mal lost all feeling in his fingers. The crowbar fell to the cave floor with a clang.

Now both men were weaponless. That did not deter Otis, though. He grabbed Mal around the neck with both hands and started strangling him.

Mal tried to punch him. Otis's reach, however, was so much greater than Mal's that he was able to keep out of range of the blows. As he tightened his grip on Mal's neck, crushing his windpipe, Mal turned his efforts to prizing Otis's hands away.

The Regulator, as if to demonstrate just how strong he was, hoisted Mal bodily off the floor. Mal's legs dangled in the air. He thumped and clawed at Otis's ham-sized hands in vain. His legs pedaled and his face turned puce as he fought for breath.

Zoë and Cleavon clashed. She feinted at him once, twice, three times with the shiv. His response was to say, "I thought you wuz a nice lady," sounding tragically disappointed.

"I am, Cleavon," Zoë replied, "unless my back's against the wall. Then I'm the meanest sonofabitch you ever met."

The Regulator made a grab for the shiv. The two of them grappled, hand to hand, shoving each other to and fro, wrestling for control of the blade.

As for Simon, Meadowlark's grip on his arm slackened, only a little but enough to tell him that she was taken aback by the sudden reversal of the Regulators' fortunes. He exploited her distractedness by kicking backwards at her with one heel, catching her hard on the shin. Meadowlark reeled away from him, bumping into the supine form of Jayne and almost falling over.

Regaining her balance, she threw herself at Simon with a shrill cry of anguish and defiance.

Only to stop before she could reach him.

She looked down.

A hand had grasped her ankle, halting her.

The hand belonged to Jayne, whose eyes were now wide open.

Yanking hard, Jayne flipped Meadowlark face first onto the floor. Then, before she could get up, he crawled onto her, planting a knee in the small of her back and bearing down. Meadowlark snarled and writhed, flailing backwards at Jayne with the can opener, but Jayne just raised his good arm and started whaling on her. After a half-dozen blows, she was unconscious. Jayne then sagged back down onto his butt.

Simon nodded thanks to him.

Jayne returned the nod blearily.

Ornery Annie made towards Zoë with quick, purposeful steps. She seemed to have decided that out of the two other Regulators still in the fight, Cleavon needed help more than Otis.

That was when Dr. Weng got involved.

To his cost.

72

Dr. Weng snatched up one of his spears and leapt at Annie, clearly intending to impale her before she got to Zoë.

Annie reacted with reflexive speed. Her own shiv was already out, and there was a foe suddenly coming at her from one side, brandishing a spear. She didn't pause to check who it was. She deflected the spear with her forearm, at the same time swinging the blade around in an arc, backhand, and slashing Weng's belly open.

Weng staggered away, dropping the spear.

Annie looked aghast at what she had done.

"No," she breathed. "I didn't... I shouldn't have..."

Weng's face, as he crumpled to the floor, had a distraught, almost plaintive expression.

Simon dashed over to him. He examined the wound. He kept his face professionally dispassionate even as he surveyed the long, jagged gash and the section of Weng's lower intestine bulging out through it.

Ornery Annie leaned over him. "Is he...?" she began.

"I've got this," Simon said. "I'm a doctor."

"So you can fix him, right?"

"I can do my best."

"Do it. Save him. You gotta." Annie turned away and moved off.

Simon's gaze met Weng's. Weng was breathing hard, irregularly. His complexion was turning pale. In his eyes there was a look of sad knowledge.

Simon stripped off his parka and began rolling it up.

Weng laid a hand on his arm. "No. There's no point."

"But I can use this to apply pressure to the wound and staunch the bleeding."

"And then what?" Weng gasped. "I'm perfectly well aware… what's been done to me. There's no coming back… from this. Unless, that is, you… happen to have a full trauma unit… on standby."

"I could attempt battlefield suturing. That ought to hold it until we can get you aboard our ship."

"Doctor, really, we both know it's futile. Funny, isn't it? To think that I survived this long… got this close to freedom… only to fall at the last hurdle. And by funny… I mean terrible."

"Please, Dr. Weng, let me try *something*."

"No, Dr. Tam. Listen to me. This… is what you're going to do. There is a hypodermic syringe… in the first aid kit. Draw a… sample of my blood. Cryo-freeze it… as soon as you can. However little you take… there are bound to be… AIMs in it. You can use them… on your friend. The dying one."

"What? But I have no idea how to program the viruses."

Weng's breathing was slowing. His life was ebbing fast.

"You seem… a very intelligent young man," he said. "I'm sure you'll… figure it out."

Simon wavered.

"Go on," Weng insisted with what little vigor that remained to him. "Hurry."

Simon scrambled over to the first aid kit. He returned with the hypodermic.

Weng gave a calm, contented nod of the head. "I was hoping…

to cure everyone. But if I can cure… just one person… that'll have to be good enough."

Simon slid the needle into the median cubital vein in the crook of Weng's elbow and siphoned off thirty milliliters of blood.

As he extracted the needle, he looked up at Weng's face. The oncologist's mouth hung slack. His eyes had a fixed, faraway stare.

Simon reached out and gently closed Esau Weng's eyelids with thumb and forefinger.

73

Annie had never felt ornerier.

Everything had turned to *gŏu shĭ*. Dr. Weng was hurt bad, and it was pretty much all her fault, and unless the young doctor guy had magic powers, she was fairly certain Weng was a goner.

This was on top of the fact that only two of her fellow Regulators were still in the fight, and neither of them for much longer. Otis was bleeding out from his leg wound. So much of the stuff was coming out, in fact, that it was amazing he was still standing. He was throttling Mal, but it was like some kind of grim race. Which of them would die first, Mal from asphyxiation or Otis from blood loss?

Even as Annie watched, Otis's grip on Mal's throat loosened. Mal slid from his grasp, tumbling to the cave floor, coughing and wheezing. Otis himself sank down too, his knees landing in the large, spreading pool of his own blood. He swayed for a moment, then toppled backwards. His body convulsed, twitched, lay still.

As for Cleavon, Zoë had got the better of him. She was behind him, with her arms locked around his neck. She still had her shiv in her hand, but instead of using it on him, she was forcing him into submission with a chokehold. Cleavon's eyes rolled up in their sockets, showing white. His limbs went limp. Zoë let go of him and he fell face down into the dirt.

Zoë could have killed Cleavon but had opted for rendering him insensible. Annie could only assume she had shown leniency because Cleavon was such a simple soul.

Nevertheless, Annie saw red.

Head down, blade out, she charged at Zoë.

Zoë saw her coming and, in the nick of time, dived out of her way.

Annie spun round and lunged again. This time Zoë wasn't able to evade. All she could do was block the swing of Annie's knife arm. Annie rammed into her like a linebacker sacking a quarterback. Both women crashed to the ground and, tangled together, went rolling out through the cavemouth into the snow.

Outside the cave they fought tooth and nail, trading kicks, punches and headbutts with an almost animal ferocity. At some point Annie realized she had lost her shiv and Zoë had lost hers. They must have both dropped them when she had tackled Zoë. This bothered Annie less than it might have. Battling Zoë barehanded seemed somehow more satisfying and more appropriate. Annie wanted to rip her apart. Zoë was largely to blame for this whole disaster, she felt, and a quick, clean death by knife blade was too good for her. Annie was out for payback, and Zoë needed to suffer.

But the former Browncoat and Dust Devil was no pushover. For every solid body blow Annie landed, Zoë landed one back. She knew how to take a hit, too. She was as skilled and as resilient a brawler as ever Annie had come across, and rapidly the fight became a war of attrition. It wasn't about who could deliver the decisive, knockout punch, it was about which of them could last longer, could soak up more punishment, had the greater stamina and endurance.

Soon both women were covered in snow and blood, and both were heaving for breath. They fought on, and gradually Annie felt she was gaining the upper hand. Zoë was tiring faster than she was. A little bit more pummeling, and she would surely be left too weak to resist anymore. Then Annie would continue beating her until there was no life left in her, and she would feel not one ounce of remorse as she did so.

All at once: a roar like thunder, and a blaze of light filled Annie's vision, so bright it was as though she was staring into a miniature sun.

The trees nearby thrashed. Snow whipped in all directions.

A voice resounded from on high.

"We have you targeted. Step away from Zoë or we'll blast you to smithereens."

Annie squinted against the light, half shading her eyes with one hand.

"I repeat," said the voice, female, commanding, "step away from Zoë. You have three seconds to comply."

Annie grunted in fury and chagrin. There was some kind of ship hovering above, the downdraught from its thrusters creating a localized cyclone. Its searchlight glared down on the scene like the eye of some vengeful god, and the voice that boomed from its external loudspeaker brooked no compromise.

"One," said that voice.

Annie was faced with a stark choice. Fight on and die, or surrender.

She was sorely tempted by the first option. If she could kill Zoë before whoever was in the ship killed *her*, she would consider that a fair trade.

"Two."

But Ornery Annie had a strong sense of self-preservation. And, moreover, she had kids. Stevie and Billie. She hoped to see them again one day, after she'd done her stretch. She yearned for that prospect. Lived for it. Maybe she could repair her relationship with them, beg their forgiveness for what she'd done to their other mother, make up for the time she had lost with them...

"Three."

In an agony of reluctance, Annie did as bidden and stepped away from Zoë.

Zoë rose to her feet unsteadily. She spat a wad of blood into the snow. Then, with a pitying shake of the head, she said, "That's a Firefly." She had to shout to be heard above the tumult of noise generated by the ship overhead.

Too late, Annie understood.

"Fireflies don't carry weapons, dumbass," Zoë said, and she swung a fist at Annie, and a firework went off in Annie's head, and then there was only darkness and silence.

74

Darkness and silence still reigned when Annie came round, untold minutes later.

Then, amid the darkness, her eyes perceived the tiniest glimmer of light. It came from the embers of the fire in Dr. Weng's cave. Outside, night had fallen. There was no sign of the Firefly, nor of Zoë or any of her colleagues.

Annie stood. Her head was ringing. Her body was a throbbing mass of aches and bruises. She felt like throwing up.

As her eyes adapted to the near-absolute absence of light, she took stock. There was Cleavon, lying on his back, breathing shallowly, unconscious. There was Michael Pale Horse, also unconscious. His busted leg had been immobilized with a crude splint. The bodies of Pops and Otis lay where they had fallen. Likewise the body of Dr. Weng.

As for Meadowlark Deane, she was out cold too, same as Cleavon and Pale Horse. However, unlike them, her wrists and ankles were secured using strips of torn cloth. There was a gag around her mouth as well.

Annie spied a note pinned to Meadowlark's chest. She plucked it off and scanned it. The signature at the bottom caught her attention first. It said "Zoë."

Forehead creasing into a frown, she read the rest of the note.

Annie,

Bet you're asking yourself, "Why am I still alive? Why did those folks drag me out of the snowstorm into the cave? I was helpless. Why didn't they kill me when they had the chance?"

Answer is, all said and done, I don't reckon you're a bad person anymore. You may have made mistakes in the past, big ones, but the Annie I've seen at Hellfreeze is a good lieutenant who does her job and follows orders. In that way, speaking as a (mostly) good lieutenant myself, you and I have more in common than separates us.

Like it or not, CU #23 needs you. Mr. O'Bannon isn't going to last much longer, and without him keeping control, maybe Hellfreeze will go all to hell. The regime he's created sure isn't perfect but it's better than nothing, and someone has to carry it on, and that someone could be you.

That's why you're getting this second chance.

The Deane girl, you can do with her as you see fit. If it were down to me, I wouldn't show a whole heap of mercy.

Good luck.

Zoë

Annie reread the note, and her frown slowly eased. Her lips, swollen from the fight with Zoë, turned up at the corners.

Damn, woman, she thought, admiringly.

As dawn broke the next day, three people set out from the cave, heading back to Correctional Unit #23. Michael Pale Horse lay on the travois that had been used to transport Jayne. Cleavon and Annie took turns dragging it.

They left behind the bodies of the other Regulators and Esau Weng in the cave for the wolves and carrion birds to scavenge.

They also left behind the body of Meadowlark Deane.

As Zoë had advised, Annie had shown the girl no mercy.

Late that night, the group arrived back at CU #23, exhausted, bedraggled, half-frozen.

Annie went straight up to Mr. O'Bannon's cell to report.

He did not take the news well. His yellowed eyes burned. With as much wrath as his enfeebled body could muster, he cursed Annie for her failure and threatened her with dire repercussions.

Annie took the chastisement calmly.

Then, just as calmly, she drew her shiv and drove it up through the underside of Mr. O'Bannon's jaw. Its blade penetrated his tongue and his soft palate, all the way up into his brain. He was dead in an instant.

Annie straightened up from the body in the bunk, wiping the shiv on her pants leg. There were tears in her eyes.

There was also resolve.

She had put Mr. O'Bannon out of his misery. She regretted it, but it was a mercy killing.

How would Hellfreeze fare now without his stabilizing influence? Would it descend into anarchy? Would violence and chaos be the order of the day, as they were at most of the correctional units on Atata?

That was down to her. Annie had to be the replacement for Mr. O'Bannon. She had to stamp her authority on the inmates. She had to recruit new Regulators and keep the peace.

It would not be easy. It would take effort and willpower. She might not succeed.

Zoë had robbed her of the opportunity to get off Atata early. Annie had to face that fact. The prospect of seeing her kids sooner rather than later had been dangled tauntingly in front of her and then snatched away. No less cruelly, Mr. O'Bannon had lost his last hope of a cure, thanks to Zoë and her pals.

All said and done, though, the woman *had* given her a second chance.

And Ornery Annie was not going to waste it.

75

Simon looked up from the microscope eyepiece.

He was dog-tired. Since *Serenity* landed at Stanislaw L'Amour's house on Bellerophon six days ago, he had been working flat out, surviving on barely a couple of hours' sleep per night. Even when he'd been doing his medical residency, pulling back-to-back shifts as part of the process of earning his license, he'd never driven himself this hard.

The cut on his neck, put there by the unhinged Meadowlark Deane, still hurt. It was itchy, too. A dermal mender had knitted the skin together, and his body's natural healing processes were busy doing the rest of the work.

Now, Simon was coming to the end of his latest stint in the laboratory that L'Amour had set up for him. He had been going for over twenty-four hours with scarcely a break.

He craved food. He craved caffeine. Above all, he craved the refuge of a soft, warm bed.

Yet, for all the exhaustion and the physical discomfort, he felt good.

Around him was a host of high-spec equipment which the billionaire had acquired in accordance with instructions Simon sent him while en route from Atata. Every item was gleaming new, and altogether it must have set L'Amour back a small fortune.

River was there, too. Throughout Simon's labors, she had accompanied him every step of the way, advising, suggesting, prompting. Together, brother and sister had isolated the AIMs from the sample of Dr. Weng's blood. They had linked them via a wireless biotech interface to a top-of-the-range med computer. They had figured out how to manipulate the viruses so that their generalized curative properties became specialized. The AIMs were little blank slates waiting to be written on. Worker ants awaiting their queen's command. They just needed direction and organization.

The insights and leaps of deductive logic River had provided were ones that Simon, on his own, would never have managed. In many ways she had done the bulk of the work, fathoming the structure and operation of the AIMs far faster than he himself ever could have. Dr. Weng's genius had found its match in River's, and without her Simon would not be where he was now.

Which is to say, ninety-nine percent certain he had made a breakthrough.

Currently River was curled up in an armchair, fast asleep. She had more than earned the respite, and Simon was reluctant to wake her, but he wanted her to double-check his results.

Her nudged her gently. "River? River?"

She stirred. Opened her big brown eyes. Yawned deeply. Grinned.

"They work," she said, as if she knew what he was thinking.

"I'm not sure. I want a second opinion."

"They work," she reiterated firmly. "I know it. Just put them in an injectable solution and give them to Inara."

"But if we've got it wrong…"

"*If* so, then we go back to the drawing board."

"We can't. We only had a limited quantity of AIMs to work with, and we've used the lot up. If this dose doesn't do the trick, we don't get a second shot."

River took the information on board, before saying, "Then you just have to have faith, Simon. In yourself. In me."

"In you, *mèi mèi*, always," Simon said. "In myself…?"

"Hey, big brother. I found you on Atata, which was pretty incredible of me even if I say so myself, and flew you off of there, which wasn't so incredible but still worth mentioning. I didn't do that only to have you get all 'wiffle-waffle, where's my head at?' on me now. Come on. Inara's down the corridor, waiting. She's not got long. It's now or never, Simon."

Simon steeled himself. River was right. Now or never.

Shortly afterwards, Simon strode through L'Amour's sprawling mansion towards the room that had been turned into a single-occupancy hospital ward for Inara. River trotted alongside him. In his hand was a hypodermic syringe, and in that syringe was a clear liquid containing a swarm of microorganisms, invisible to the naked eye.

And containing, also, hope.

Mal, Zoë, Jayne, Wash, Kaylee and L'Amour were all stationed outside the door to Inara's room, either slumped on chairs or leaning against a wall. None of them looked to have slept much more than Simon had since their return to Bellerophon. Mal's and Zoë's faces were patchworked with bruises in all the colors of sunset. Jayne's injured arm was enveloped from wrist to elbow in a rehabilitation sheath and supported by a sling.

Mal stepped forward. "Is that…?" he said, gesturing at the hypodermic.

"I think so," Simon said.

"And will it…?"

"I'm not making any promises."

"It will," River said.

L'Amour held the door open for Simon. "In you go, young man."

"Want some moral support in there?" Zoë offered.

Simon shook his head. Then, looking round at everyone, he said, "I've no idea how long it'll take the AIMs to work. It won't be instant, that's for certain. You should go get some rest, all of you. I'll let you know as soon as there's any improvement. *If* there's any improvement."

Kaylee took his hand. "You've cracked it, Simon. I know you have."

Simon looked at her. Briefly he recalled Meadowlark Deane, whose smiling outward innocuousness had belied a dark, twisted soul. He had been lured in by her, lulled into a false sense of security, largely because she'd reminded him so much of Kaylee. Yet the two women could not be more different. Kaywinnet Lee Frye was pure at heart, not an ounce of malice in her. Unlike with Meadowlark, with Kaylee what you saw was what you got.

Her belief in him was like a jolt of electricity, galvanizing. Almost without thinking about it—and if fatigue hadn't lowered his inhibitions quite so much, he might never have done it—Simon grabbed her by the waist, pulled her to him, and planted a huge kiss on her lips.

Kaylee, though startled, quickly got over it and kissed him back. Warmly. Passionately.

Simon broke the clinch, turned, and went into Inara's room, leaving a flush-faced Kaylee looking embarrassedly around at her crewmates. L'Amour pulled the door to behind him.

Inara lay on her floating bed, sallow, skeletal. As Simon approached, she craned her head round to look at him. The effort this small movement required was enormous.

"Simon," she said. "Always a pleasure."

"Don't talk, Inara," he said. "Save your strength."

"Just remember, it doesn't matter."

"I'm sorry?"

"If this treatment of yours fails. I won't mind."

"It's not going to fail. I'm pretty sure it isn't."

"Promise me, Simon, you won't blame yourself if it does. *I'm* not going to hold it against you, that's for certain. I'm just grateful that you've tried. You and the rest of the crew. I know the lengths you've gone to, the ordeal you've been through. I love you all for it."

"Please, Inara, like I said, save your strength."

"Very well, Dr. Tam. Let's get on with it, then."

Simon rolled up one sleeve of her kimono and held the hypodermic ready.

Hours later, he found the others. They were gathered in L'Amour's vast, gleaming kitchen. Dishes heaped with muffins, cookies and neatly sliced fresh fruit sat on the table, largely untouched. Jayne, alone, was eating.

Without saying a word, Simon staggered over to the coffee machine, helped himself to a mugful and drank it down at a single gulp.

Expectant gazes surrounded him.

Simon wiped his mouth.

Then, slowly, guardedly, he began to smile.

Epilogue

"You know your face is on upside down?" said Inara to Mal.

"Are you denigrating my good looks?" Mal replied. "Because I'll have you know, in certain quarters I am considered quite the hunk."

They were at the belvedere overlooking the lake. Mal had pushed Inara out there in an antigrav med chair, which now hovered stationary beside the bench he was sitting on. It was a week since Simon had administered the AIMs, and there was already a marked improvement in Inara's health. The pallor was gone from her complexion, her hair was regaining its luster, and she had put some weight back on. Above all else, her eyes were bright again. Bright and wonderful.

"No," she said. "It's just, you're frowning so much, and your mouth's downturned, but if I could flip your head over, you'd look as happy as can be. What's making you sad?"

"I ain't sad," Mal said.

"Good, because how can anyone be sad on a day like this? In a spot like this?"

She waved a hand—a hand whose fingers had lately been so skeletal that they couldn't bear rings, but now did again. The gesture took in the landscaped grounds; the trees, still in their autumnal pomp, if now shedding the odd leaf; the lake with its myriad of flickering golden fish. The sunlight was just the right temperature, warm but not oppressively hot. A few white clouds lazed against the blue firmament.

"A wealth of beauty," she said.

"Beauty created by wealth."

"Don't be such a miseryguts. You don't envy Stanislaw his money."

"Maybe, but I wouldn't mind havin' a little bit of it. Listen, Inara…"

"Uh-oh," she said playfully. "What's coming?"

"What do you mean?"

"You say you're not sad, so this must be your sincere face instead, and when Mal Reynolds gets sincere, then things must be serious."

I am serious, Mal thought. *I don't think I've ever been so serious.*

"It's just… On Atata, it was a struggle," he said. "For all of us. There were times when I was convinced we weren't gonna make it. But we kept going. *I* kept going. Because I had to. Because I didn't have a choice."

"I know," Inara said. "You never gave up. You have no idea how much that means to me."

"I knew if we failed, you'd die. I couldn't have that. I didn't want it. I wanted you to live, more'n anything."

"Believe me, Mal, I am thankful beyond words. I owe you everything."

Mal was poised on the edge of the bench. He hadn't rehearsed this moment, hadn't prepared for it. But he'd decided it was going to happen, the moment he'd parked Inara's chair at the belvedere. In these surroundings, it felt right. It felt like there would never be a better time or place.

He just wished he had had the foresight to buy a ring first. A ring he could safely lodge on Inara's finger, now that she was able to wear rings again.

Saying the words would have to do. The ring could come later.

And then, before Mal could make his move—propel himself down onto one knee in front of her, adopting a posture he hoped would be winningly old-fashioned—Inara said, "I won't forget everything you did. The whole crew, but you most of all. I'll cherish the memory."

Mal froze. *Cherish the memory*. He did not like the sound of this. He did not like where it seemed to be headed.

"And," Inara said, "that makes what I'm about to say a lot harder to say."

Mal had to force the words out. "Which is?"

"I've had a brush with death, Mal. I got nearer to it than I ever have. I felt it inside me. Like this tide of ice-cold water slowly rising, slowly engulfing me. It was frightening but it also wasn't completely unpleasant. It felt… natural. Inevitable."

She laid her hand on his.

"It's the kind of experience that changes a person," she said, "and I need time to absorb it, make sense of it. Time… and space. Stanislaw's told me I can remain his houseguest for as long as I like. So I won't be rejoining you on *Serenity*. I'm going to stay here. Stay and recuperate and process what I've been through."

"Okay."

"After that, maybe I'll return to House Madrassa, I don't know. For all the problems they have with me there, it's the only place I've known that's felt like home."

"Okay."

"You understand why, don't you, Mal? I've thought long and hard about this, and it seems like the right thing to do. The only thing to do."

"Okay."

"Are you going to say something other than 'okay'?"

"Okay."

"Go ahead then."

Mal paused, then said, "How long for?"

"How long for…?"

"How long d'you plan on staying at House Madrassa for, if you go?"

"I really don't know," Inara said.

"Not indefinitely, though."

"Definitely not indefinitely."

"So you can see a day when you might come back to *Serenity*?"

"I'm not ruling it out. And in the meantime, there's no reason you can't come and visit me on Sihnon. Also, there is, y'know, this newfangled thing people do called 'sending a wave'."

"Yeah, I've heard of that. It's all the rage with the kids."

Inara looked him in the eye. "Are we good, Mal? You and me?"

He looked back at her, filled with both disappointment and hope, unsure which was the more painful of the two emotions.

"I think," he said with deliberation, "we are."

They sat side by side for a time, taking in the view, neither feeling the need to speak any further, Inara's hand still on Mal's. It was a perfect fall day—perhaps the last fall day before winter's chill began to make itself felt—and both of them chose to enjoy it. If colder times lay in the future, so be it. Summer would come round again soon enough. It always did.

ABOUT THE AUTHOR

James Lovegrove is the *New York Times* bestselling author of *The Age of Odin*. He was short-listed for the Arthur C. Clarke Award in 1998 and for the John W. Campbell Memorial Award in 2004, and also reviews fiction for the *Financial Times*. He is the author of the Dragon-Award winning *Firefly: The Ghost Machine*, *Firefly: The Magnificent Nine*, and *Firefly: Big Damn Hero* with Nancy Holder, along with several Sherlock Holmes novels for Titan Books.

firefly

BIG DAMN HERO

JAMES LOVEGROVE
(ORIGINAL STORY CONCEPT BY
NANCY HOLDER)

Captain Malcolm Reynolds has been kidnapped by a
bunch of embittered veteran Browncoats who suspect
him of sabotaging the Independents during the war.
He's placed on trial for his life, fighting compelling
evidence that someone did indeed betray them to
the Alliance all those years ago. Mal must prove his
innocence, but his captors are desperate and destitute,
and will settle for nothing less than the culprit's blood.

firefly

GENERATIONS

TIM LEBBON

Mal wins an old map in a card game. Ancient and
written in impenetrable symbols, the former owner
insists it's worthless. Yet River Tam can read it, and
says it leads to one of the Arks, legendary ships that
brought humans from Earth-That-W
as to the 'Verse. The salvage potential alone is
staggering. But the closer they get to the ancient ship,
the more agitated River becomes. She says something
is waiting inside, something powerful, and very
angry…